# COUNTER BET

## COUNTER BET

### HARLEIGH BECK

Cover design by Jay Aheer

Editing: Chris Williams

Proofreading: Paula Hevia Riveiro

*Not suitable for readers under 18

*For my best friend, Paula.*

And so I was scared. I was scared of my own sexual hunger, which felt so secretive and uncharted.

- CAROLINE KNAPP

# TRIGGER WARNING

# CHAPTER

*one*

## EMILY

I LINE my lips with my favorite red lipstick before glancing at my latest painting on the easel. I stayed up until the early hours, mixing colors to get the right shade, but I'm still not entirely happy.

Placing the lid back on the lipstick, I eye the result in the mirror. My makeup is flawless as always.

"Are you ready, Emily? Rick is waiting," my mom calls from downstairs.

I breathe a tired sigh as I run my fingers through my blonde hair. Here's to another year of pretending to be so goddamn perfect all of the time.

Today is the first day of my senior year, and while the thought of putting high school behind me should excite me, it doesn't. It terrifies me. I play my role perfectly at Hedgewood High. I'm the head cheerleader with the perfect grades and the clean-cut boyfriend who also happens to be the star quarterback.

Cliché, you say? That's because it is.

I'm not ready for everything to change next year. I don't even know why it fills me with so much dread. I'm already unhappy, so a new start should be a positive thing, but I'm comfortable behind my mask. I'm at the top of the hierarchy.

People see what I let them see, and the anxiety beneath the

surface is kept behind lock and key where no one can see it except for me. Mostly though, I think I'm bored. Life is predictable in every sense of the word.

I grab my bag off the bed and leave my room. As I skip down the stairs, I find my boyfriend ruffling my little sister's hair. She's three years old and cute as a button.

Rick is dressed in a pair of light blue jeans paired with a white Henley. His letterman jacket lies on the kitchen table.

He looks at me, then smirks as he crouches down to whisper in my sister's ear. Her adorable giggles fill the room.

"What are you two whispering about?"

My little sister pokes her tongue out and runs off.

I watch her little piggy tails bounce. "I sometimes think you like her more than me."

Rick's hazel eyes dance with mischief while he wraps me up in his big arms and leans down to nuzzle my neck. "Are you jealous, baby?"

He smells delicious with his freshly washed hair and the new cologne I bought for his birthday.

"Hands off my daughter, Rick," Dad booms in a loud voice as he walks into the kitchen.

Rick jumps back in surprise. "Yes, sir. Sorry, sir."

Dad rolls his eyes. "How many times have I told you to stop calling me 'sir?' It makes me feel old."

"Sorry, sir," Rick says, a wide grin on his lips. My dad chucks him on the back of the head, earning a disapproving look from my mom.

She puts my freshly pressed cheer uniform in my bag. "Try not to ruin this one, sweetie."

I bite back my retort. Technically, Rick ruined my last one, but she doesn't need to know that.

"Are you ready?" I ask Rick, gesturing to the door and pushing his broad back to get him moving when he snatches a freshly cooked waffle.

———

Rick parks in his reserved spot next to the front steps of the main building. It's one of the many perks of being the star quarterback and having a father who's one of the most successful lawyers in town.

Our dads are close colleagues and work for the same firm. Needless to say, they were over the moon when Rick asked me out after school two years ago, and I said yes, not because he sets my soul on fire but because it's the most logical decision.

"Are you okay?" Rick asks with a sidelong look in my direction as he cuts the engine. "You're quiet."

I unfasten my seatbelt and plaster on my most convincing smile. "I'm great."

Rick looks unconvinced but doesn't comment. We exit the vehicle, and he puts his arm over my shoulder as we make our way over to our friends. As always, Rick is oblivious to the longing looks girls throw his way. Or he simply doesn't care.

"Hey, man," he says to his best friend, Jamie. They do some weird handshake and shoulder thump while Hailey pulls me into a bone-crushing hug like we didn't see each other yesterday.

I laugh through a mouthful of her hair.

"He fucks like an animal. I can hardly walk," she whispers, looking pointedly at Jamie.

I follow her line of sight. Jamie, the school's star receiver, looks pleased with himself as Rick and the other guys laugh at one of his rare jokes. He reaches up and sweeps his unruly blonde hair off his forehead. I can see the appeal, but he's a notorious player.

"I called it, didn't I?" My smile is boastful. They flirted with each other for the better part of last year, but they both refused to act on it until this summer. I now know more about Jamie's cock than I care to admit, thanks to Hailey.

We make our way into school. The hallway is bustling with students and bleary-eyed teachers who look anything but happy to be back after their summer vacation. Rick keeps close to my side with a possessive hand on my hip while Jamie talks about the upcoming football season.

I tune out, lost in my own thoughts. My workload this year will be even more challenging with cheer practice and art classes. I need to keep my head level.

————

I move the pasta around on my plate as Hailey launches into the latest gossip. I couldn't care less about who sucked whose dick and pulled what girl's hair. Sometimes, I feel like an outsider looking in. Still, I appreciate the normality of my friends laughing and gossiping in the lunch hall.

A football flies over my head. Rick catches it, then passes it on to Jamie. I push my tray back, leaving my food untouched. Unease twists my stomach for reasons I can't pinpoint. It's been happening a lot lately.

Rick pulls me onto his lap and kisses me until I'm lightheaded. I don't pull away. He angles my head to the side and trails kisses over my jaw, his cock hardening in his jeans.

I scan my eyes across the bustling lunch hall. My mask is still intact. But only just.

Students laugh with their friends, and teachers look fed up at being back at work even though it's only lunchtime. An empty coke can flies across the room.

Rick grabs my ass, nipping my skin with his teeth.

Am I the only one who's empty inside?

I feel eyes on me. Not the everyday envious glances from other girls or appreciative looks from boys. Someone is observing me.

I shake off my self-deprecating thoughts and sweep my gaze across the room until they collide with a set of kohl-rimmed blue eyes.

*Dallas Garcia.*

She's new to the school. I don't know much about her. Only that she hangs out with the emo kids and is a regular in detention.

I swallow past the thick lump in my throat while she continues studying me as if she can see right through me. It makes my skin itch.

"Let's get out of here," Rick whispers in my ear, then steals another kiss.

Averting my gaze from Dallas's penetrating eyes, I kiss him back, ignoring the unease knotting my stomach.

There's a crack in my façade.

———

Mr. Greenwood stands at the front, pointing to his barely legible handwriting on the whiteboard. There's a dried coffee stain on his wrinkled shirt, which is also missing a button.

My eyes drift over my shoulder.

Dallas pops gum and taps her foot to the beat playing in her earphones while typing on her phone. I count at least three piercings, one in her nose and two in her eyebrow. Both of her arms are covered in tattoos.

"Dallas!" Mr. Greenwood sighs, pinching the bridge of his nose.

Steph, Dallas's best friend, nudges her shoulder. My eyes drop to Dallas's legs beneath the desk. Creamy skin peeks out through the holes in her ripped black jeans.

She pulls out her earplugs and frowns at Steph, who nudges her head to the teacher.

Mr. Greenwood holds out a detention slip. "I'm running out of detention slips, Dallas."

Sliding out from behind the desk, she grabs her bag off the back of the chair. Her scuffed black Chucks are so unlike my expensive heels.

Placing the detention slip in her bra, she grins at Mr. Greenwood. "Better get some more then."

I stare after her. She's everything I'm not, and it's intriguing me. What's it's like to simply not care? I've lived my whole life under the spotlight. Always had expectations of me.

Hailey nudges me. "Are you okay? You seem distracted."

"I'm fine." But she's right. I *am* distracted. When the bell rings, the notebook in front of me remains blank.

# CHAPTER
## *two*

## EMILY

EXHAUSTED, I strip out of my uniform. Today's practice was brutal, and my muscles ache in the best way possible.

"I'm hoping Nate will be at the party this weekend." Naomi grins, brushing her dark curls.

Buttoning up her jeans, Hailey rolls her eyes. "Girl, he's been with half the school. You can do so much better than him."

Naomi's lips curve in a sly smile. She puts her hair up in a messy bun. "I'm not looking to tame the beast, Hailey. According to rumors, he's got an eight-inch dick." She mimics a blow job with her fist.

We all burst out laughing.

"You're crazy," Hailey replies, still chuckling. "But I get it. I wouldn't mind a little fun with Nate myself if I wasn't fucking Jamie. He's an animal in bed, but he hasn't got an eight-inch dick."

Naomi turns her attention on me. "Rick is fine too. I'm not trying to break girl code, but if you hadn't strapped him down, half the female population at this school would be on their knees for him."

"Like that stops them from trying," Hailey scoffs, sitting down on the bench to tie her shoelaces.

I zip up my bag. "I'm lucky."

"They can try, but Rick is oblivious. Girls could literally kneel in front of him, naked and willing, and he wouldn't notice." Naomi laughs.

My smile falters. I busy myself by putting on my shoes, so they don't notice my unease. Where are these feelings coming from? I've always been happy with Rick. He doesn't spark a fire in me, but he is safe. Our relationship is comfortable, and he makes me smile, so why do I feel like I'm lying to myself?

———

That night I lie in bed, tired from a long day at school and cheer practice. I look up Dallas's profile on Instagram. I don't know where this curiosity is coming from, but I've started to notice her more and more at school lately. It's like I can't unsee her.

Her profile picture is of her and a taller guy at the beach. They both smile at the camera. Dallas scowls a lot at school as if she carries the world's weight on her shoulders, so to see her look happy tugs at something inside me.

As I scroll through the rest of her posts, I don't ask myself why I'm so curious, but the thought is there in the back of my mind.

Before last year there were plenty of photographs of her with the guy in the profile picture. I take a closer look. They have remarkably similar features. The same black hair and almond-shaped eyes. It must be her brother? There are other pictures of them too with an older couple who I guess are their parents. The family resemblance is there. She hasn't uploaded any more family pictures in the last year.

Not since she moved here.

I scroll back up and look at the latest post she uploaded a couple of days ago. It was taken at the local lake late at night. Dallas sits next to a bonfire, looking out over the water. Her skin looks impossibly smooth, and her plump lips…

I almost drop my phone when a text message pops up on the screen.

Rick: Parents in bed?

I hurry over to the window and slide it open. The warm evening breeze feels nice on my skin as I look outside.

"Good evening, fair maiden." Rick grins, climbing the trellis below. It's a miracle how it holds his weight after all these years.

His dark head pops up. He palms the frame, hoists himself up, and throws a leg over. His heavy feet land on the floor with a thud.

I hush him. My parents are asleep. I don't dare to think what my dad would do if he caught him in my bedroom this late.

Rick's hazel eyes gleam with mischief. He stalks me deeper into my room, sweeping his gaze down my body, lingering on my bare legs in his football jersey.

My back hits the wall.

He trails the backs of his fingers down my cheek and the column of my neck. My skin erupts in goosebumps, and I inhale sharply when he pinches my hardened nipple through the thin fabric.

"I like you in my jersey." He skims his hand over to my other breast and palms it. "But you already know that." His lips descend on my neck, kissing and nibbling. He smells of Rick, a heady mix of citrusy cologne, soap, and something uniquely him.

My eyes flutter shut. I grip his broad shoulders and arch my neck to give him better access. His lips capture mine, more demanding this time.

"Rick," I breathe, fisting his letterman jacket. He spins me around, kicks my legs apart, and works his belt. My phone taunts me on my bedside table. The screen is still lit up with Dallas's profile.

Rick shifts behind me, and I feel him at my entrance just as he grabs my hair and sinks into me on a grunt.

The phone screen finally goes dark, but Dallas's carefree smile still burns the back of my retinas.

Rick starts thrusting. I can't shake the image of Dallas's

slender hands and the glimpse of her creamy thighs peeking through the rips in her jeans. Or the expanse of her neck as she tucks her hair behind her ear. The way she sucks her plump lip between her teeth when she concentrates…

My cheek is squished against the wall, and Rick fondles my breasts beneath the jersey with one hand. His other hand is on the wall next to my face. It's almost as big as my head. I've watched him throw countless perfect footballs with that hand, making scouts froth at the mouth.

He finally comes with a deep groan, breathing heavily in my ear.

Tears prick my eyes as I stare at the phone.

I feel nothing.

———

Dallas grins, pointing her fork at Ben—a boy with green-dyed hair —just as another girl throws her head back on a laugh.

I sweep my eyes over their table across the lunch hall. My mom would suffer a conniption if I tried to leave the house with purple lipstick and black eyeshadow like Dallas and her friends. I have an image to uphold.

I roll my eyes and take a sip of my orange juice.

*I should try it for fun one day. See how she reacts.*

My treacherous eyes soon flick back up. Ben holds out his tattooed arm and smirks while the others inspect a new tattoo of his. He's got a reputation as one of the bad boys in town. Another troubled kid from the wrong side of the tracks.

I compare him to Rick, who's currently in the process of choking on his sports drink after one of the guys on the team made him laugh. They're like day and night. Rick is your typical footballer. Big and bulky, and is rarely seen without his letterman jacket. The weight of it on my shoulders right now proves my point.

Ben is slim and tall with enough definition in his arms to make you look twice.

Rick laughs a lot. Even now, his raucous laughter rings out in the crowded lunch hall, and his body shakes from the force of it next to me. As if he can feel my eyes on him, he glances at me and wraps his arm around my shoulder.

Ben rarely smiles, but he smirks a lot, just this slight, dirty tug to the left side of his mouth. It makes you want to linger there with your eyes. There's something unpredictable about him.

Something untamed.

A sudden laugh to my left tears me from my thoughts.

Jamie punches Rick in the arm, then ducks as Rick launches out of his chair. They fight to get each other in a headlock, laughing like scrapping kids while the other guys at the lunch table holler in encouragement.

I move my food around on the plate, half-listening to Hailey's conversation about the latest clothing shop opening up in town.

Rick sits back down, grinning. He runs a hand through his tousled hair, then steals a kiss. "Are you staying to watch the practice later?"

My eyes flick up and land on Dallas as I reach for my glass.

She straddles Ben's lap.

"Maybe," I reply distractedly. They must be fucking, right? Why else would she be nipping his jaw with her teeth in the cafeteria of all places?

She brazenly shoves her hand down his jeans and begins stroking him in plain sight. My eyes widen. I place my drink down on the table and scan the nearby tables. No one pays them attention. Not even the others at their table.

Dallas is like that. She doesn't care about anything.

———

"Stop there, young lady!"

I come to a halt, barely managing to suppress a groan.

"Hall pass?" Mr. Emerson holds his hand out, his mustache twitching.

I hand him my hall pass, rolling my eyes. It's like he's taken it upon himself to personally guard these corridors on his quest to find unruly students. Unlucky for him, I have a hall pass and a reason for being out here.

"Alright then," he says, after studying my hall pass for too long. "It looks genuine."

I raise my eyebrows.

He holds it out for me. "You may carry on."

My smile melts butter. "Thank you, Mr. Emerson."

I'm about to pee myself. I tug on the hall pass, but he won't let go. "Mr. Emerson?"

This can be cataloged as one of the weirdest encounters of the year. Possibly ever. I finally manage to free it from his clasp.

I hold it up between us. "Can I go pee now?"

He sniffs. "Very well."

I'm bouncing on the spot as he turns on his heel. "Have a great weekend, Mr. Emerson."

Shaking his head, he mutters, "Youngsters!"

He's too easy to rile up. I clutch the slip in my hand and hurry to the bathroom. My heels click on the floor in the empty hallway. Thank god it's only around the corner.

As soon as I burst through the door, I stop short. Breathy moans echo in the small room. My bursting bladder is momentarily forgotten as I creep along the short cubicle wall. I peek around the corner and suck in a breath.

Lauren, the mayor's daughter, a sophomore with curly brown hair, leans against the back wall. My eyes travel past her torn open shirt and exposed breast to the girl kneeling in front of her.

I know that mass of raven hair and those scuffed Chucks.

"Aahh!" Lauren moans, fisting her hand in Dallas's silky strands. "Don't stop!"

I can't believe what I'm seeing. Since when is Lauren into

girls? Not that I've ever seen her with anyone, but she is the mayor's daughter. And Dallas? I thought she was with Ben?

Dallas bites the inside of Lauren's creamy thigh, marking her perfect skin.

Jealousy twists my insides when Lauren rolls her hips. I've never been into girls before, but watching Dallas eat out the mayor's daughter makes my pussy clench.

Dallas hums low in her throat and moves her head in time with Lauren's rolling hips, holding her in place against the wall. I can't believe that I'm watching this like a creeper. My clit throbs. I should leave, but I can't look away.

"You like that, don't you?" Dallas purrs in between long strokes of her tongue. She slides her hand down Lauren's thigh and lifts it up, spreading her open. "Your pussy is so tight."

*Oh god…*

I press my lips together to suppress a whimper of my own. I want to hear her talk like that again.

Lauren cries out in pleasure, her lips smeared with Dallas's purple lipstick. "Yes! Yes! Oh god!"

Leaning back, Dallas sinks her fingers inside Lauren's pussy. Her smile is filthy. "What would your Daddy say? Good little Lauren, having her pussy fingered at school."

I cover my mouth with both hands, so I don't squeak out loud in surprise, and stare wide-eyed as Dallas leans back in.

"Do you want to come?"

Lauren doesn't hesitate. "Please!"

Right now, she looks nothing like my main rival for valedictorian with her tousled hair, flushed cheeks, and torn shirt. I can't believe that Dallas could so easily ruin Lauren's perfect reputation. If others got wind of this…

Lauren's knees buckle when she comes. She presses her hands flat to the wall, and her lips part on a soundless cry as Dallas licks up every last drop of her arousal.

My own heartbeat is loud in my ears.

Dallas removes her fingers. Her face glistens in the fluorescent bathroom light as she smirks cruelly and says in a bored voice, "You can fuck off now."

I bristle, and so does Lauren.

Standing back up, Dallas smooths down her hair in the mirror and roots through her backpack for her lipstick.

Lauren is motionless.

After sucking her fingers clean, Dallas turns on the faucet to wash her hands. The sound of running water breaks Lauren out of her stupor. She tugs her skirt back down and runs from the room, clutching her shirt.

I stare after her, wondering if she's aware of the smeared lipstick and smudged mascara on her face? I've never seen the mayor's daughter look anything less than perfectly polished. We're alike in that way.

"Did you enjoy the show?"

My heart jolts in my chest. I slowly peek around the corner. Dallas is staring back at me in the mirror with a knowing smirk on her lips.

My hackles rise.

"If I didn't know better, I'd think you're into me with the way you're watching me." She switches off the tap, dries her hands with a paper towel, and throws it down on the sink. Not in the trash can. Her steps are slow and measured as she turns and walks toward me.

I feel like prey, a fly in her web.

She cages me in, placing her hands on each side of my head. Her hot breath falls across my lips, and I breathe her in. She smells of flowery perfume and sex. Images of her face between Lauren's spread thighs flash through my mind.

Heat pools low in my stomach. I'm shamefully aroused.

Leaning in, she brushes her plump lips against my ear. "Did you enjoy the show, princess?"

The problem is that I liked it a little bit too much. I grip the hem of her black T-shirt and arch my back, pressing myself against her.

*What am I doing?*

She's like a matchstick to the raging inferno burning inside of me right now.

She chuckles in my ear. "I wonder what Rick would say if I bent you over the sink and fucked you until you screamed my name?"

*Jesus…*

Swallowing thickly, I meet her hooded eyes. Would I stop her if she tried? I think we both know the answer to that question.

She pushes off the wall, sweeping her eyes down my body. My toes curl in my shoes.

She snaps her teeth at me like a vicious animal, then walks out, leaving me to stare after her as the door clicks shut.

What just happened?

I'm panting with desire now. Closing my eyes, I bang my head against the cubicle wall.

I'm in such deep shit!

———

"Oh fuck!" I throw my head back, riding Rick harder, digging my freshly manicured nails into his chest. Images of Dallas on her knees flash through my mind. Leaning back, I change angle until Rick's cock hits the right spot. I use his thighs for balance as I roll my hips in time with my pants, my eyes squeezed shut.

Rick's fingers dig into my hips. He's right at the edge. "Fuck, Em."

I tune him out.

*Dallas's full breasts sway beneath her as she crawls between my spread legs. Grabbing my thighs and leaning down, she smiles against my throbbing sex. "I've waited a long time for this." She flattens her tongue and takes one long, slow lick.*

"Fuck," I whimper, picking up speed. My long hair tickles my lower back.

*Reaching down, I fist her hair, loving the sight of the black strands between my fingers. She latches onto my clit and proceeds to eat me out until her face glistens and her damp hair lies plastered to her cheek. "You taste so fucking good, princess."*

I explode, clamping around Rick's cock.

He hisses, then flips us over and begins drilling into me, pounding his hips. "Fuck, fuck, fuck!" he growls, burying his face in the crook of my neck.

There's a stain on my ceiling. Hailey threw slime on it once when we were eight years old. It stuck for a while before falling to the ground with a splat. We thought it was hilarious at the time. Now it seems to be the only thing stopping these tears in my eyes from falling.

# CHAPTER
## three

## DALLAS

MY UNCLE IS A NO-SHOW AGAIN. I drop the backpack on the bed, breathing a deep sigh of relief. I've felt on edge ever since my family perished in a fire a little over a year ago, and I was sent to live with my estranged uncle. He makes no secret of the fact that he doesn't want me here, as evidenced by my bruised ribs. The latest bruise on my jaw has finally faded. It's not obvious unless you look closely.

I take a seat on the threadbare mattress and rest my elbows on my knees, running my hands through my hair.

*"Dallas, wake up." Melissa nudges me.*

*I open one eye. My mouth tastes like shit, kudos to too many drinks last night. "Come back to bed, Mel. It's too early."*

*Melissa worries her lip. "The police are here to see you."*

*I stare at her for what feels like an eternity before sitting up and scooting back on the bed, clutching the sheet around my naked breasts. "What do you mean? The police?"*

*"I don't know the details. They want to speak with you."*

*She's dressed already. I clear my throat and glance at the door. Reaching down for my clothes on the floor, I get dressed in silence. If the police are here at eight in the morning, it's bad news.*

*There's nothing to be done about the rat nest on my head, so I pat it down as best as possible and step out in the hallway. The stairs creak beneath my bare feet, fear rising inside of me at the sight of the two offi-cers on the couch. They both clutch their hats in their hands.*

*The middle-aged police officer with the receding hairline stands up, his shoulders hunched. "Please, have a seat, miss."*

I close my eyes, blowing out a breath. The sadness creeps in whenever I'm alone. I can still hear the deep sound of my brother Aaron's carefree laughter. When he laughed, others joined in. He had that effect on people.

It makes me wince to think what he would say if he saw me cower beneath my uncle's fists and make a complete mess of my life. I miss my parents too. Mom with her kind, blue eyes that crinkled at the corners when she smiled, and Dad, who used to ruffle my hair and call me "kid."

"Fuck," I whisper shakily, tearing at my roots until my scalp screams in pain. I curse again, louder this time, before screaming at the top of my lungs. Why did this happen to me?

Jumping up, I kick over the bedside table next to my sorry excuse of a bed. The sound of crashing furniture clears the fog of anger. I'm panting, staring at the splintered wood. Every day is a struggle. A part of me wishes I hadn't spent the night at Melissa's.

What do I have left to fight for? I know what my brother would say. He would tell me to smile again—not to let their deaths be in vain. But my dreams died with my family.

My phone chimes with a new text.

Steph: It's Friday. Are you up for some fun?"

I type out a reply and hit send. Fuck if I'm staying in with my memories all night.

———

*"Sis, Aaron shouts, waves lapping at his waist. His surfboard bobs on the water. "See that? It's a big one. You ready?"*

*"I was born ready, Aaron."*

*"Hell yeah!" He whoops, lying down on his board in preparation.*

*My raven hair lies plastered to my face despite the ponytail. "I'm gonna beat you this time, brother!"*

*With a quick glance at the approaching wave, he flicks his head, sending water droplets flying. "The day you beat me will be a rainy day in hell."*

A knock on the window startles me from my thoughts.

Steph leans an elbow on the car roof and eyes me with a crease between her dark brows. "Are you planning on sitting out here all night?"

I don't miss the note of concern in her voice. There's a weight on my chest, and my lungs feel clogged. I slide my hands down the steering wheel before unfastening my seatbelt. She slaps the car roof and walks back to the house

I stare at the rundown property for a moment. The paint is flaking, and the screendoor hangs loose, slamming in the wind. The small front yard is overgrown with weeds, and an old, over-weight Doberman lies asleep on the porch. At least no one beats on her at home or tells her she's a waste of space.

I step out of the car and follow her inside, mindful not to step on the rotten wooden planks marked with red spray paint.

Steph shuts the fridge door as I step into the kitchen. She hands me a cold beer, eyeing me over the rim of hers. I can't help but feel like I'm under a magnifying glass.

She quirks an eyebrow. "I hear you gave Lauren the time of her life today?"

I smirk, taking a swig. "Guilty as charged. You know I don't back down from a bet. Besides, corrupting virgins is fun. You should try it."

Steph scoffs, but a smile plays on her lips.

"How did you find out about it anyway? Ben and I kept this bet under the radar."

Lauren doesn't want her perfect reputation tarnished, so she won't have said anything. The only other person besides Ben who knows is Emily, the head cheerleader.

As I recall the look in her eyes, my core tightens. I could've slid her panties down and had her right there in the school bathroom. She wouldn't have stopped me. Despite being the head cheerleader and the future homecoming queen, she's not as clean-cut as she wants everyone to think she is.

Steph throws her head back, laughing. "You're not subtle. You know that, right?" She takes another swig of her beer.

I shrug. "Doesn't matter anyway. I'm not going back for seconds. Besides, it was just a bet which I won." I wink.

Amused, Steph shakes her head. The movement makes her curls bounce. "Whatever. Let's get this show on the road. I've got a treat for us tonight." She grabs the car keys off the counter. "Can you get the bag on the chair over there."

"What am I? You personal slave?" I joke, grabbing the bag and hooking it over my shoulder. I follow her outside, past the sleeping dog to her rusty old car parked at the end of the drive. It's a death trap, but it still runs. Tossing the duffel bag in the back, I steal a sucker from the glove compartment.

"Where are we going?" I ask.

Steph straps on her seatbelt and cranks the engine. The car coughs to life, filling the air outside with a cloud of gray exhaust fumes. She looks over her shoulder as she reverses out of the driveway. "You know Jamie Parker? The receiver?"

I narrow my eyes.

She completes the maneuver. "Jamie is throwing a party tonight. The whole football team is gonna be there."

I pull the sucker out of my mouth. "And?"

We never go to their parties.

She taps her fingers on the steering wheel in time to the music playing on the radio. "We're gonna play a little prank on Jamie."

"Okay?" I reply, dragging the word out.

Steph nudges her head toward the backseat. "Look in the bag."

Unfastening my seatbelt, I stretch my body between the seats to grab the bag. Whatever she has planned is going to get us into trouble.

I place my sucker on the dash and unzip the bag, peeking inside. It's too dark in the car. The passing street lights are not enough to see by. Reaching up, I switch on the overhead light.

Steph sings along to the chorus while I dig through the bag, chuckling darkly. I lift out a can of spray paint and reach for my sucker, placing it back in my mouth. "What's the target? His house?"

Steph starts laughing. "You're unhinged, Dallas."

"Hey!" I point my sucker at her. "I'm not the one who's bringing my best friend and a bag of spray paint to a party I'm not invited to."

Steph glances at me. "Smartass!" She steals my sucker off me, putting it in her own mouth. I try to grab it back, but she bats me off. The car sways on the road, and she rights it.

"We won't arrive there in one piece if you keep that shit up."

"Don't steal my candy."

She smiles around the sucker. "I believe it was in *my* glove compartment."

"Semantics."

We fall silent as we turn down Jamie's opulent street. The houses here look like small mansions, and the cars in the driveways cost more than I dare to think about. It's such a contrast to the rundown streets we call home, where hookers fight over street corners, and the walls are so thin you can hear your neighbor beat up his wife.

"I don't know about you," Steph whispers, pulling up at the curb, "but I can't wait to see the golden boy lose his temper."

I drag my eyes away from the sprawling driveway, my lips curving in a Cheshire smile. "It'll be fun to ruffle his feathers a bit."

———

Music and laughter filter from the backyard as we walk up the winding drive filled with parked sports cars. It looks like a page out of a car magazine.

My eyes dance over the white pillars, the wrap-around balcony, and the award-winning rose bushes that line the house. I think we even saw statues on the gate pillars earlier.

Emily and Rick run in the same circles too. All the kids at this party are bored, overprivileged rich kids with too much money to spend.

"Over here!" Steph whispers, motioning to Jamie's canary yellow McLaren. It's a beauty. No wonder he likes to lean against it in the parking lot with one foot crossed over the other, blue eyes hidden beneath his Ray-Bans while girls flock around him.

He's not my type, but I can see the appeal if you're into popular jocks. The car certainly adds a little extra. How many girls has he fucked on the hood?

*Urgh!* I hate my own thoughts sometimes.

I drag my eyes away from his defiled hood. The gravel crunches loudly beneath my Chucks as I make my way over to Steph. She hands me a green can before grabbing one for herself, and we get to work.

Laughter filters from the backyard, keeping me on edge. The spray paint hisses with every stroke. I paint the leaves and stalks first before rooting through the bag for a purple spray can. I set to work on the petals.

"Psst!"

I pause, listening.

"Dallas!"

Kneeling down, I press my cheek to the gravel. Steph grins at me from the underside of the car. "How's it going?"

"Splendid!" I reply in my best British accent.

"What are you painting?"

"A flower. You?"

Steph blows a strand of hair away from her face. "Little alien people."

"Little alien people?" I repeat, sucking my lips between my teeth to suppress a laugh.

"My imagination failed me. It was the first thing that popped into my head."

"I don't know," I whisper. "Some would argue it's very imaginative."

She grins.

"The gravel hurts my cheeks."

"I know, right? Maybe we can make gravel indentations a new fashion trend?"

I laugh, inadvertently digging my cheek further into the gravel.

"I just like the craziness of us kneeling on the ground and talking to each other through the clearance of Jamie's McLaren. We should do this more often."

"You think?"

She nods. "Definitely. Let's make this a regular thing."

I laugh, then wince, picking a piece of gravel from my lipgloss. "Which part? The one where we kneel and talk to each other through the undercarriage of a car? Or the spray painting?"

"Why do you always ask such hard questions? That's like being forced to pick between chocolate or sex."

I grimace. "Shit. Yeah, that's an impossible choice."

"Right!" she says, pushing up on her hands. "My little alien people need a baby and possibly even an alien dog if I have time."

Her head disappears from view.

Chuckling, I sit back up and reach for the pink spray can.

When Steph has finished her little alien family, she joins me on my side. "Oh my god." She laughs behind her hand. "That looks like it was drawn by my baby cousin."

Tilting my head, I purse my lips. It *does* look like it was painted by a three-year-old. Standing up, I round the car to inspect Steph's work. The laughter that bubbles up inside me reminds me of easier times. "Wow, Steph. What a masterpiece!"

She rests her forearm on my shoulder. "I know, right? I bet Van Gogh is turning in his grave with jealousy."

"Oh, yes. Definitely." I reply, holding back a laugh. "And not just him. Mozart too."

Steph snorts a laugh. "Mozart? Really? He was a composer, Dallas?"

"Even so," I reply, looking at her pointedly as I pack away our discarded cans. "I bet he's turning in his grave with jealousy. The dude could compose music, but could he paint?"

Amused, she hands me the last can. "Good point."

As I look at the car, a thought occurs to me. "You do realize his dad will take the car for a new paint job, and it'll be like nothing happened."

Brushing her curls away from her face, she takes the bag off me. "But not before his friends see it."

We share a smile.

Just then, I spot something out of the corner of my eye. I look to the end of the drive, where Ben swaggers along between two parked cars. There is no other way to describe his cocky walk.

His friends trail behind him.

Ben is dressed in his usual skinny black jeans with rips at the knees, and his favorite black and white Vans. A black band T-shirt with a tear in the collar hugs his chest. He makes everything look effortless.

"What do you think?" Steph beams, holding her hands out like she's presenting the car to a potential buyer.

Ben whistles, and Matt and Josh laugh behind him. "Wow…"

"Wow?" Steph puts her hands on her hips. "Is that all you have to say?"

Ben scratches the stubble on his jaw, glancing over at Matt and Josh for help. "It looks…" He blows a raspberry, at a loss for words, and lifts his hand before dropping it back down by his side. "I dig the flower theme."

I grin, turning to Steph. "He digs the flower theme."

Pursing her lips, she gives me a look that says, *'You think you won this round?'*

My smile grows wider. *'I know I won this round.'*

"Well," she says, taking Ben's elbow. She steers him past Nina and April. "What about my side?"

He squints. "Are those green blobs?"

Steph squeaks.

I double over laughing, stifling the sound with my hand.

"It's an alien family, Ben! Do they look like blobs to you?"

He peers at me over the car roof before meeting her glare. "Is that a trick question?"

"What are you guys doing here?" I ask when I finally get my laughter under control.

Ben saunters my way with his hands in his pockets. His trademark smirk makes an appearance as he comes to a stop in front of me. Swiping his tongue over his bottom lip, he drags his eyes down my body. "Steph messaged us."

"I'm just bummed I'm too late for the spray painting party," April groans, picking up a piece of gravel and throwing it at Josh. It hits him square in the back.

"You're not too late." Steph hands her a can, grinning like the evil devil on April's shoulder. "Have at it."

Ben scans his eyes over the big house, rubbing his bottom lip with his thumb. "Looks like a big party. Want to crash it?"

The spray can hisses behind us.

"They will know this was our doing if we crash their party."

"Babe," he twirls a strand of my hair between his tattooed fingers, "look around you. How many cameras do you think are facing us right now?"

I freeze, my eyes bouncing between his. "Shit!"

Of course someone this rich has top-notch security installed.

Steph, the traitor, laughs. At least she has the decency to try and cover it with her hand. "You should see the look on your face."

"What the fuck?!" I blurt loudly before I can stop myself.

Glancing at the path leading to the backyard, I breathe a sigh of relief when it becomes evident that no jocks are going to rush us with pitchforks. I could strangle Steph right now.

She pats my cheek. "You really are cute."

Smiling, I swat her hand away. "Go ahead and laugh all you want."

"How about we crash the party?" Ben asks.

My eyes scan the parked cars in the driveway. The entire football team is here. Rick's white Porsche is parked between two other sports cars. If he's here, Emily is here too. She's probably seated on his lap like some royal queen overseeing her court.

*I push my tits against hers, my eyes sliding down to her lips. "Does Rick not fuck you hard enough?"*

*Gripping hold of the hem of my black T-shirt, she arches her back, pressing herself against me. Her tits strain in the confines of her expensive designer dress as a whimper slips past her lips.*

*Lips I long to taste.*

*"I wonder what Rick would say if I bent you over the sink and fucked you until you screamed my name?"*

"I know that look," Ben drawls. He grips my waist and pulls me flush to his body.

I look toward the top floor where the bedrooms are located. An idea is forming in my head. I do enjoy a good challenge, but to simply fuck the princess isn't enough of a challenge. She would bend over willingly at the first chance. I need something a little bit more out there.

I admit that I'm curious about her. She took me by surprise in the bathroom when she gripped my T-shirt and pressed herself against me instead of slapping my face in outrage, as most girls would do. What kind of darkness is hiding under her mask? She never stumbles, and the façade never slips. It'll be fun to see just how far we can push her. It's the perfect challenge to spice up the weekend.

"How about we play a little game?" I whisper, running my

hands over his hard chest, his heat warming my palms through the fabric.

He takes his sweet time answering, watching my hands before gripping hold of my wrists with his calloused hands. His touch is firm, bordering on uncomfortable—a hint of the alpha male I know he is, especially between the sheets.

With my hands trapped between us, I lean forward to trace my lips along his stubbled jaw. He likes to act indifferent, but the shiver running through him gives him away.

"Emily is here," I whisper, nipping his jaw.

His grip on my wrists tightens. "Emily? The cheerleader?"

I try to pull free to no avail, smiling against his scratchy beard. "I'm gonna fuck her boyfriend Rick."

Leaning back, Ben stares at me incredulously.

Steph's mouth falls open and a peal of laughter bubbles up from her chest. "You're out of your mind if you think—"

The veins in my wrists throb as I cut her off with a pointed look. "Not only that, but Emily is gonna watch me fuck him and love every minute of it."

The others burst out laughing. Everyone but Ben. His eyebrows shoot up in surprise and he eyes me appreciatively. The cogs are turning in his head. He looks over at the house. Ben is bored with life too and loves a good challenge, hence why we make these outrageous bets.

"You wanna make a bet?" he asks, training his eyes on me. It's impossible to miss the challenge in his voice.

"I do. You wanna play?"

April groans. "Come on, another bet? Wasn't the last one enough?"

Ben smirks, maneuvering my hands behind my back. His eyes drop to my parted lips and linger.

"I want to play," he whispers, "but I want to make a bet of my own too."

I raise an eyebrow. My shoulders ache from being pushed up

against him with my wrists restrained behind me. "What's your counter bet?"

Pressing a thigh to my core, he darts his tongue out, toying with his lip barbell. "If you fuck her boyfriend and make her watch, I'll get her to agree to a threesome with us."

My core throbs. He smirks knowingly, shifting his thigh between my legs. The jerk is toying with me.

"You're both fucking crazy," Steph says, placing her hands on her hips. "Miss Perfect hasn't got it in her to risk her reputation like that. Don't get me started on Rick. No offense, Ben. You can't be any more different to him."

Ben shrugs, unperturbed. His dirty smirk is still intact. "You're right. It's why Emily won't be able to resist choking on my dick. I'll be the perfect escape from her boring little life. The rebellious golden girl can ride my dick, give the middle finger to her rich daddy and leave me used and spent when she's done. I won't complain. Besides," he pulls me closer, sliding his thigh along my core, "I quite like Dallas's twisted little mind."

"Are you warming me up, big boy?" I goad, trying to break free. His strength only turns me on more.

"Is it working?" Glancing at the parked cars, he grins. "Ever been fucked on the hood of a $200,000 sports car?"

"Oh, yeah," I purr, ignoring the others laughing behind us. I trap his bottom lip between my teeth, biting down on the soft flesh. "I fuck on expensive cars all of the time."

He herds me over to Jamie's car and forces my chest down on the spray-painted heart that April left behind on the hood. Pushing my leather skirt up around my waist, he yanks my panties down. The warm evening air hits my bare skin while he massages my ass before dipping his fingers between my wet folds.

I press my forehead to the hood with a groan, whimpering when he sinks his fingers inside me.

"Anyone else wants to fuck on cars?" Josh asks behind me.

"Fuck off, Josh. Here, take this. You can carry the bag."

Their footsteps retreat.

Ben rips a condom with his teeth, sheats his cock, and leans over me. He plants his hand beside my head on the hood, tightening his grip on my wrists behind my back. "Do you know what I like about you, Dell?"

I'm panting now. His hard cock crowns my entrance. "You like many things about me, Ben. My snarky humor. Shitty attitude. My terrible cooking. Pick your poison."

He chuckles, the deep sound vibrating in his chest as he grips my jaw and bends my head back. His lips hover over mine. "I like that you're insatiable." He slams his hips home and covers my mouth with his big hand.

―――――

Students stare when we enter through the front door. I can't blame them. We stand out like a sore thumb in this crowd of footballers and cheerleaders.

"Do you think they wouldn't notice us if we came dressed in cheer uniforms?" Nina shouts over the music, earning a laugh from Ben.

"They're not the brightest, so I wouldn't put it past them."

Steph leans in. "We put in our bets while you were busy being fucked on Jamie's hood. Unfortunately, it's not looking good for you. I'm the only one who put a bet in your favor, so don't disappoint me. I need the cash."

I snort a laugh as we enter the crowded living room. "It's in the bag, Steph. I never lose."

"Don't be so sure of that," Ben says, nudging his head toward the couch where Rick is seated with Princess on his lap.

How predictable.

I roll my eyes.

If not for the loud, thumping music, you could hear a pin drop as, one by one, they start noticing us. Rick leans over to speak to Jamie, who sits spread out on the recliner chair with his own cheerleader on his lap. It's Emily's best friend, Hailey. The four of them remind me of a royal court.

Jamie's eyes drift over to us. The bored expression on his face doesn't shift, and he soon dismisses us, his hand disappearing beneath Hailey's skirt.

Emily is staring daggers at me. A fire burns in her eyes as if she somehow knows that I'm up to no good. It would be a very accurate assumption.

I run my eyes down the skimpy, golden dress she has on. It shows ample cleavage and has a slit that comes up high on her thigh. It's far more revealing than anything she wears at school. I can see why she turns heads with her pouty lips and blue eyes.

Ben is checking her out, too. He's not even remotely subtle. He eyes her up like she's a meal, most likely imagining himself pounding her pussy while she does the splits in the air.

Narrowing my eyes, I punch him in the shoulder. "Dickhead!"

He laughs.

People are still staring. It's so cliché. I feel like I've stepped onto the movie set of a cheesy 90's flick. The only thing I need now is for one of these cheerleaders to take me under their wing, teach me all things cheer, and give me a makeover and voila, I'll win homecoming queen.

"Whatever," I huff, shouldering my way through to the kitchen and grabbing myself a plastic cup from the stack. I pour myself what I can only assume is very expensive vodka. Either that or paint stripper. I don't bother mixing it before throwing it back, relishing in the burn.

"What's the plan?" April asks, shimmying up next to me. She pours her own drink.

I look back inside the living room. Rick is stroking Emily's thigh as he talks to his friends. Emily, on the other hand, is glaring daggers at me.

Pouring myself another shot, I take a swig, wincing. "Rick will get more handsy. It won't be long until he takes her upstairs, and then I'll join them."

Ben snorts as he joins us in the kitchen, stealing my drink off me. He drinks the last of it and pours a refill. "Oh, yeah? Your plan is to walk right in and hope they welcome you with open arms? Great plan."

Unbothered by his sarcasm, I smile. "You underestimate me, my friend."

I was in that bathroom with Emily. I know there's more to her than she lets the world see. She won't object. It's Rick I need to convince.

"We need video evidence," Matt cuts in from across the marble island.

Josh nods in agreement. "Yeah, we do."

"You're such perverts," I laugh, knocking back another shot. I can handle my drink.

"They're right." Ben rakes a hand through his green hair.

I look over at him and shrug casually. "Alright. It doesn't bother me. If the two horndogs require material for their spank bank, they can have it."

Josh grabs a baby plant from the window and puts it in the front pocket of his hoodie.

"What exactly are you doing?" Matt asks, staring as Josh picks up a much bigger plant and attempts to conceal it in his jumper.

"Souvenirs, dude. Houses like these are like a grand tour in a royal palace in England."

"Why plants, though?"

Josh hands Matt the plant before crouching down and rooting through the cupboard beneath the sink. "Why not plants?"

Matt stares incredulously at the green thing in his hands as if it holds the answers.

Josh pops back up with a grocery bag in his hands. He takes the plant, puts it in the bag, and gestures to the doorway. "Unless you want souvenirs too, let's go."

———

Emily is dancing, hips swaying to the sultry beat. I'm getting antsy. It's a matter of time until someone walks outside and discovers what we did to Jamie's car. I don't want to be here when that happens.

Emily's eyes are locked on mine as she gyrates her hips in time to the beat. There's something very intimate about it, as if she's dancing solely for me.

What's going on inside that pretty head of hers? She's toying with me; that much is obvious. To throw her off her game, I place two spread fingers over my lips and flick my tongue between them, mimicking oral sex.

The dim lighting can't hide her blushing cheeks as they flame red. She throws me a venomous glare.

Laughter bubbles up inside of me, and my shoulders shake against Ben's hard chest behind me.

He wraps his arms around my midriff. "Rick hasn't been able to tear his eyes off her for the last half hour." His hot breath wafts over my neck. "He's readjusted his hard-on at least three times. It's showtime soon."

I look over to where Rick sits perched on the couch. He palms the visible bulge in his jeans, and heat sinks to my clit.

"Well, well," Ben drawls against the sensitive skin below my ear, running his fingers up my arms. My skin erupts in goose-bumps. "Looks like the alcohol has loosened his ambitions. Maybe he's not quite the good boy everyone thinks he is."

I turn in his arms and palm his hard dick through the fabric of his jeans. I'm not the only one affected by our games. "Who's insatiable now?" I smile, squeezing his hard length.

He grunts, grabbing my ass possessively.

"Does the idea of Rick ramming his dick down my throat turn you on?" My voice drips like honey. Leaning in, I sink my teeth in his neck hard enough to make him hiss through his clenched teeth. He fists my hair, slamming his mouth to mine. He's not gentle, and neither am I. Our tongues duel for dominance.

Emily is watching us. I know because her intense eyes burn my back.

When her tied-down angel wings finally erupt from her back, they'll be black as night.

Ben breaks away, lifting his chin. "It's showtime. Are you ready to dethrone the royals?" Flashing a devilish grin, he gives my ass one last squeeze.

"Watch this space." I follow Rick and Emily upstairs.

Rick pulls her along behind him, adjusting the front of his jeans. Emily's blonde hair falls down her back in soft curls, and her hips sway seductively.

Trailing my eyes over her ass, I suppress a tortured groan.

As I reach the stairs, I grip the banister and peer over my shoulder. My friends are watching me with matching grins and dollar signs in their eyes. I flip them the bird before ascending the stairs. Rick and Emily enter one of the bedrooms further down the hallway. They haven't noticed me yet.

Sneaking down the hallway with my back pressed up against the wall like I'm in a spy movie, I find a bathroom and lock myself inside. It's a spacious room with a twin sink, a claw tub, and a walk-in shower.

You're considered lucky in my part of town if you have a shower, never mind a shower *and* a separate bathtub.

I inspect my make-up and hair in the mirror. Luckily, Ben didn't do too much damage outside on Jamie's hood.

After reapplying my purple lipstick, I push my boobs up and run my fingers through my black hair.

I look nothing like Emily—the golden girl—dressed in my favorite leather skirt, combat boots, and fishnet hold-up stockings.

Inhaling a deep, steadying breath, I open the bathroom door.

# CHAPTER
*four*

## DALLAS

I STOP OUTSIDE THE BEDROOM, my heart hammering wildly in my chest. Pressing my ear to the door, I listen. The music downstairs is too loud for me to hear anything, so before my nerves get the best of me, I turn the handle and step inside.

Rick and Emily break apart, staring wide-eyed as I turn the lock.

"It was unlocked." I hook a thumb over my shoulder. "You should lock it if you don't want someone to walk in here." It's dark in the room, but enough light filters through from beneath the gap in the door.

Rick's mouth is smeared with Emily's red lipstick, and Emily's hair is in disarray. The strap of her golden dress has been pulled down off her shoulder, revealing the pale curve of her naked breast.

When she notices me looking, she hurriedly pulls it back into place.

Rick snaps out of his stupor, pointing to the door. "Get out!"

I tut, shaking my head as I walk over to the bedside table and switch on the lamp, bathing the room in light. I'm not letting him fuck me in the dark. "I can't do that."

Anger contorts his handsome face, and he fists his hands by his sides. I saunter over. Rick towers over me and I have to crane my neck to look up at him. Ben is tall, but Rick is both tall and bulky, thanks to hours of football practice.

Let's see who the bigger alpha is.

I sweep my eyes down his body, appreciating the way his muscles fill out his white Henley. His sleeves are pulled up over his elbows, offering a nice view of his muscular forearms.

I cock my head. His jaw is like concrete, and his hands flex by his sides. He is holding himself back from punching something.

Probably me.

My gaze trails back up his tense body until my eyes clash with his stormy grays. I nudge my head toward Emily by my side. "Your girlfriend here approached me at school the other day."

His eyes flick over to Emily.

I can't believe I'm trying to seduce the quarterback in front of his girlfriend. Emily stares at me in horror as I continue, "Your girlfriend likes to watch people fuck."

Blushing fiercely, she averts her gaze.

*"Did you enjoy the show, princess?"*

Rick frowns. "Em, what is she talking about?"

His attention snaps back to me when I take a step closer and brazenly place my palms over his muscular chest. His nostrils flare, and his turbulent eyes clash with mine.

I swipe my tongue over my bottom lip. "She fantasizes about watching you with someone else." I wait for the shoe to drop.

A deep crease forms between his brows.

Looks like I will have to spell it out for him. "Your girlfriend wants to watch us fuck."

He recoils, taking a step back while Emily stares at me like a deer trapped in headlights. She shakes her head infinitesimally and I smirk, raising an eyebrow.

Her eyes narrows. *"You didn't go there."*

My smile widens. *"Oh, but I did, princess. Are you gonna call me out?"*

She tears her blazing eyes away, flashing Rick a sugary smile.

"Yes, babe. I didn't know how to tell you. I wanted it to be a surprise." Her voice doesn't waver.

My mouth drops open. I don't know what I expected here tonight, but certainly not the challenge in Emily's blue eyes when she turns to me with a quirked brow and her hand on her cocked hip. She's playing me at my own game.

*Fine. I'll play along.* Walking over to the dresser, I place my bag down. When they're not looking, I surreptitiously angle my phone toward the bed and press record. Emily and Rick stand with their heads bent together, talking in heated voices as I begin undressing. When my clothes are in a neat little pile on the floor, I pick up Emily's phone on the dresser and send myself a text message. I save down her number and clear my voice.

Rick's head snaps up. He swallows thickly, his hazel eyes sliding down my body, lingering on my hardened nipples visible through the black lace. I glance over at Emily. There's a part of me that wants her to like what she sees too.

Her brilliant, blue eyes are glued to my thighs as I saunter over to her with extra sway in my hips. I like that I have her attention.

I come to a stop, running my fingers over her bare shoulder and the column of her neck before grabbing a fistful of her silky blonde hair. I tug sharply, mesmerized by her reaction to my touch. Her breasts strain against the confines of her dress. Placing a kiss on the pulsing hollow at the base of her throat, I linger before skimming my lips over her jaw. Her body smells of summer evenings, feminine and floral, and her long hair smells of coconut shampoo.

She makes a sound in her throat when I finally taste her soft, warm lips. Her hands land on my hips tentatively, but her hungry kiss tells a different story. I'm left breathless by her drugging kisses as she tightens her grip on my waist. My lungs scream for air. I don't want to stop, but I'm not here to seduce *her*.

I smile into the kiss before reluctantly breaking away and pointing to the bed. "Sit down, princess."

Rick squeezes the hard outline of his cock while Emily takes her sweet time walking over to the bed. She makes a show of climbing on and crawling forward on her hands and knees, flashing us the globes of her creamy ass and silk panties.

*Such a tease.*

Leaning back against the headboard, she smiles tauntingly, confirming my suspicion. Her little show was deliberate.

I look over at my phone propped up on the dresser, recording this scene. "Spread your legs and touch yourself. I want your boyfriend to see that pussy glisten when I suck his dick."

Emily blinks, her mouth opening and closing in stunned surprise. The town's beloved princess is not used to dirty talk, it seems. She hesitates for a brief moment, then spreads her tanned legs and slides her hand down the front of her golden dress.

The bed dips under my weight when I place my knee on it, my hand trailing up her smooth leg. Her skin erupts in goosebumps and she whimpers softly as I reach the apex of her thighs.

Tracing my thumb over her silk panties, I apply just a hint of pressure.

"Eyes on me, princess," I whisper so only she can hear. My fingers hook her silk panties and slide them slowly down her legs, tossing them on the floor. I lower my gaze to her pussy. It glistens in the ambient lamplight, begging for a lick. "Wet already," I tease, leaning in and brushing my lips over her arched neck.

She fists the sheets.

"Watch me fuck your boyfriend, princess," I whisper. "If you're a good girl, I might reward you in the bathroom next week. We both know how much you'd like that."

Her eyes follow me as I make my way over to Rick. I drop to my knees and make quick work of his belt, pulling it through the loops before unzipping his jeans.

He looms over me like a dark shadow.

I look up and meet his hungry gaze. Something tells me Emily is the only girl who's been on her knees for him.

*Until now.*

The intensity in his dark eyes takes my breath away as I slowly inch the zipper down.

He looks nothing like the golden boy everyone loves and reveres, who makes magic happen on the pitch. With his hazel eyes, parted lips, and brown, unruly hair, he looks like a delicious snack.

I wince as he grabs my chin in a punishing grip, forcing my head backward. He bares my neck, digging his fingers into my skin. Eyes resembling two black orbs, he looks over at Emily. It's intoxicating, as if someone flipped a switch, and out came this demon.

*Fuck, I love it.*

"Is this what you want, baby? You want to watch me fuck her mouth?"

Emily's responding moan is all the encouragement he needs. He lets go of my jaw and grabs a handful of my hair. It hurts. I love how rough he is. Does he touch Emily this way? I dismiss the idea.

My knees ache on the hardwood floor as I stare up at him in anticipation. I hope he chokes me on his cock.

*Fuck, I want to taste him so bad…*

His his grip on my hair tightens and he thrusts his hips in my face, forcing me to lean back or topple over.

My scalp burns.

"Take me out and make it worth my time."

Not one to dawdle, I reach forward with eager hands and pull down his jeans and boxers past his thick thighs. His cock springs free, bouncing against the white henley covering his tight abs. My mouth waters at the sight of him towering over me like an avenging angel.

Leaning forward, I swipe my tongue over the bead of precum on the thick head. The taste explodes on my tongue, salty and delicious.

"Fuck," he groans, fisting his dick and slapping it on my tongue and cheeks repeatedly. It's dirty and demeaning. I love every minute of it.

"Open up!" He jostles my head, eyes glued to my mouth as he pushes forward.

My lips stretch around his thick length, smearing purple lipstick on his shaft. I gag when he hits the back of my throat. My instinct is to pull back, but he holds me to him with a firm grip on my hair, forcing me to take him deeper. I'm left with no choice but to hold on to his thighs as he begins fucking my mouth hard and fast.

Rick shifts on his feet so he can watch his cock slide in and out, and I stare up at him, my vision blurred by tears.

His dark hair falls in his eyes, sweat beads on his brow, and his lips are curled back. He's magnificent like this.

"Is this what you want? My cock choking you?" His eyes burn with fire. "Well, you got your wish. Now take it!" He forces me down on his length with a firm hold on the back of my head until his balls slap my chin. I'm dripping, I'm that wet. Who knew the golden boy had such a devil hiding underneath the perfect façade he puts on.

My nails dig into his thighs. I'm growing lightheaded from the lack of oxygen. It's a fucking good thing that I mastered deep throating years ago because fuck, Rick is going for it.

Just when I think he's about to come, he pushes me off him, and I fall to the ground, staring up at him in pleasant surprise.

He points to the bed. "On all fours. I want Em to see your face when I fuck your tight little pussy."

My, my, he's a bossy one. I grin as I climb on, winking at Emily.

She watches me through lowered eyelids, biting her bottom lip as she works her fingers in and out of her dripping pussy. I never thought she had it in her to do something like this. She's usually so prim and proper.

Rick shifts behind me. He tears the condom wrapper open with his teeth and sheathes his thick cock before smacking my ass with such force I nearly topple over.

*Fuck, that was a hard slap.*

Soothing the sting with his palm, he lands another punishing slap. When I cry out, he growls and slaps me again. "Shut the fuck up!"

*Oh god…*

Rick twists my hair around his wrist with one hand, grabs hold of my hip with the other, and slams into me in one thrust.

I cry out, squirming against the intrusion of his hard length as he buries himself balls deep. Emily's eyes widen, heavy and dark with lust.

Pulling out, Rick slams back in, groaning. "Fuck, so tight!"

*Thrust!*

I fist the sheet, grinding back against him. I'm pretty sure I'm mewling like a fucking cat, but shit, his cock feels so good.

Emily picks up speed with her slender fingers, fucking her pussy faster and harder while she watches us.

Unclipping my bra with skillful fingers, Rick snakes an arm around my front, palming my tit. His slick chest sticks to my back as he tweaks my nipple until it hurts.

"Fuck, Rick," I moan, arching my ass higher. He slaps my tit, wrapping his hand around my throat. His stubble scratches my cheek.

"Does it turn you on to watch me fuck someone else?" he whispers to Emily, and I groan when he treats me to a deep thrust.

"*Fuck!* Give it to me, Rick!"

Biting my shoulder, he draws blood, his hips pumping.

Everything he does, from how he fucks, to throwing a ball on the field, is so intense.

Emily cries out, working her fingers faster as a violent orgasm crashes through her. Rick picks up the pace, slamming into me and chasing his own release. My arms tremble with exertion. I'll be bruised and sore in the morning.

"Wait!" I push up on my knees. "Emily has been a very good girl, don't you think? She deserves a treat."

Rick doesn't need guidance this time. He pulls out and

removes the condom before walking over to Emily, who gets up on her knees and takes him in her mouth, moaning loudly.

She's fucking beautiful with her mouth stuffed with cock, her plump lips stretched thin, and her eyes at half-mast.

Watching her bob on his length, Rick buries his hand in her blonde locks. He's gentler with her than he was with me, but I can tell that he's holding himself back. He reminds me of a caged tiger, trembling with the restrained need to ram his cock down her throat and force her to take it like he did to me. But he won't let himself lose control.

Not with her.

Pulling her back by her hair, he fists his cock and begins stroking himself.

It's an alpha move.

Emily enjoys every moment of it, judging by the look in her eyes and the goading grin on her lips. She tweaks her own nipples and sticks her tongue out as Rick continues pumping his cock.

He comes with a guttural groan, coating her face in white strings of cum that drip from her tongue.

I can't look away.

Leaning in, I suck his cum off her bottom lip before claiming her mouth in a hungry kiss.

"Oh fuck, that's hot," Rick groans behind us, stroking his already stiffening dick. The man is a goddamn machine, ready for a second round. I got what I came for. Rick played his part perfectly, and I have the evidence I need for the bet.

I break away, leaving Emily to catch her breath on the bed as I get up to retrieve my belongings off the dresser. "Well, this was fun." I wink at them both. "Let's do it again sometime."

They stare after me as I turn and leave the room.

———

I'm grinning from ear to ear as I walk downstairs after putting my clothes back on in the bathroom. My friends are still where I left them, and when I approach, they look up from their phones.

Steph jumps up from the couch, laughing in disbelief. "No fucking way!"

"Way!" I reply, grinning.

Matt and Josh stare longingly at the phone in my hand, vying for the recording.

My eyes roll. "Not here, you assholes. Besides, we need to leave before Jamie or anyone else spots what we did to his car."

"You mean what you and Steph did." Matt grins. "Don't involve us in your antics."

We all laugh, drawing looks our way as Ben chucks Matt on the back of the head.

Steph links her arm through mine. "Let's go. I wanna watch Rick fuck."

————

Back at Steph's place, we make ourselves comfortable in her small living room as Nina raids the fridge for alcohol. Steph's parents are rarely home, but they always keep the fridge well-stocked with beer.

Ben tugs me down on his lap, and I go willingly, grinding my ass on his dick with a mischievous smile.

He cocks an eyebrow. "Did Rick not hit the spot?"

I roll my eyes, chuckling as Steph gets the TV set up. Rick definitely hit the spot.

"Last chance, Dallas. Are you sure you want the two horn dogs over here to watch your sex tape?" Steph gestures to Matt and Josh. They're stuffing their faces on popcorn as if we are at the cinema and the chosen movie is a blockbuster.

Josh scoffs in mock offense, leaning back in the armchair and spreading his legs wide. "It's not like I haven't watched Dallas fuck a ton of times before." Throwing a single popcorn up in the air, he catches it in his mouth and winks at me.

I cross my arms. "Thanks, Josh. You sure know how to make a girl feel special."

Josh pops another popcorn in his mouth. "Oh, I can make you feel really fucking special if you ditch the green-haired boy."

Ben's shoulders shake behind me as he tries to contain his laughter.

"What the fuck, Ben? It's not that funny." I poke the laugh dimple in the side of his cheek. It only makes him laugh harder.

He wraps his strong arms around me and rests his chin on my shoulder. His hot breath wafts over my cheek as he smiles. "Come on, Dallas. It is. We always fuck in front of them."

"Whatever," I grumble.

Steph hushes us just as the screen flicks to life.

Ben leans forward, his warm chest heating my back. "Insatiable," he whispers in my ear.

My lips brush his cheeks. "Jealous?"

His grin widens.

Matt and Josh both groan while the video continues playing, and April and Nina whisper about the size of Rick's cock.

Steph takes a sip of beer. "Fuck, bitch. I'm jealous. Who knew Rick is such a beast between the sheets?"

I laugh. Rick is a surprisingly good lay despite his golden boy persona. I wriggle on Ben's lap, my clit throbbing from watching myself fuck on TV.

He grips my bruised hips to hold me still, pressing his forehead to my shoulder. "Fuck, baby, be still unless you want me to take you right here for everyone to see."

Sinking my teeth into my bottom lip, I turn to look at him with a glint of mischief in my eyes before slowly scooting off his lap and sliding down on my knees between his spread legs.

Ben groans, his head falling back on the chair. He drags his hands down his face. "Fuck, Dallas. You drive me insane!"

I undo his belt and free his dick, pumping the hot, silky length. "Your dick is always gonna be my favorite." Leaning down, I lick his cock from base to tip.

He groans, gripping the armrests so fiercely, his knuckles turn white as I wrap my lips around the head.

"Oh, for fuck's sake!" Matt whines. "Why do you always get lucky, Ben? I'm fucking horny too."

Gathering my hair in a ponytail, Ben smirks. "I've got game, man. You don't," he shoots back in a lazy drawl, thrusting his hips. "April, why don't you help a guy out? Matt is needy."

"Fuck you, Ben. I'm not going anywhere near his disease-ridden dick."

Steph chuckles from her spot on the floor. "That's not what you told me on Halloween."

April lets out a frustrated screech. "Fucking girl code, Steph. That was a secret."

With a scoff Steph, gestures to Ben and me. "Do you see that? Does it look like we keep secrets here? I've seen you all fuck."

I release Ben's dick with a pop and wipe my mouth just as Steph walks over to Josh and Matt.

"Dallas's homemade little movie has got me riled up. Think you guys can help a girl out?"

Matt pulls her down on top of him, and Josh grabs her face, stealing a kiss before Matt has a chance to object.

Exchanging a look, April and Nina stand up and walk out, shouting a bored goodbye over their shoulder.

As the door shuts, Ben grabs the back of my head and guides me back down on his cock.

"Who's insatiable now?" I taunt, brushing my lips over the engorged head.

Applying more pressure, he smirks and I gag as I swallow him down, taking him as deep as I can. His cock twitches in my throat while tears spring to my eyes.

He turns up the volume on the TV and leans back in the recliner. Brushing my hair off my face, he swipes his thumb through the mascara streaks on my cheek. "Dell, you're choking on my dick. If anyone is insatiable, it's you."

# CHAPTER

*five*

## EMILY

JAMIE'S TIRES screech as he comes speeding into the school's parking lot. The spray-painted flower on the passenger door and the pink heart on the hood stand out even more in the daylight.

It doesn't take a genius to figure out who the culprits are. Jamie fumed when one of the linebackers burst into the living room to tell him about his precious car, but Dallas and her friends were long gone by then.

Rick and I haven't discussed what happened that night with Dallas. In fact, we haven't talked much at all. We got dressed in awkward silence after she left the room, both deep in our own thoughts.

I can't wrap my head around what came over me, and it's not for lack of trying. The only thing I can put it down to is my own stubbornness. For some reason, Dallas brings out a darker side of me, one I'm not entirely comfortable with. I didn't want to appear weak in front of her. The damn challenge in her eye when she told my boyfriend that I wanted to watch him fuck someone else. I had to play her at her own game.

I worry more about my own reaction. I can't stop thinking about her and what we did.

My thoughts are interrupted when Jamie slams his car door shut. By the looks of it, he's still pissed.

Rick goes to greet him.

I've never seen that side of Rick either. He fucked Dallas with so much aggression, and I wish he would touch me that way too.

*When he fisted my hair and stroked himself until he came on my face...*

I can still taste his cum on my tongue and feel it running down my face. Maybe I shouldn't have liked it as much as I did, but I can't deny that my clit throbs when I think about it.

Hailey sidles up next to me. "Jamie is pissed because his parents refuse to pay for a new paint job. I'm surprised too. Apparently, he needs to learn to take more responsibility."

I press my lips together to stop myself from laughing. This is the kind of thing we'll laugh about thirty years from now, but today is not the day.

"He's gonna to murder Dallas when he finds her."

That sobers me up, and I scan my eyes across the parking lot in search of Dallas's car. If she's smart, she'll know not to show her face today. Pictures of Jamie's car are already on social media for everyone to see.

Rick puts his hand on Jamie's shoulder while they talk in hushed tones. Jamie is tense. He fists his hands by his sides and nods once before putting his ray-bans back on and stalking off.

I have the feeling that Rick worries Dallas will run her mouth if Jamie confronts her. He likes my pure reputation, or the thought of it, at least. After last night we both know there is nothing pure about me.

My core tightens as I recall the look on Dallas's face. The way her breasts bobbed with every slam of my boyfriend's hips.

I know we can't let it happen again.

Besides, do I really want to be the kind of girl who watches her boyfriend fuck other women? Or even worse, do I want others to find out how much I enjoyed it?

I'm pulled from my thoughts when Ben walks past with his blonde-haired friend, Matt.

I share an art class with Matt on Wednesdays. He's insanely talented, but unlike me, he prefers to sketch rather than paint. I'm the opposite. Abstract art is my strong side. I like colors and chaos. It's not uncommon to find a splatter of paint on my arm or cheek.

Matt is the kind of guy with charcoal-smudged fingers who'll ask you to pose naked on a fur rug. Well, I don't know about the naked part…

Ben winks as he walks past.

Winks…

The blood drains from my face.

*He knows…*

I stare after him with my heart in my throat.

Dallas told him. She fucking told him what we did. How dare she tell her friends about that night?! Maybe it's not a big deal to her, but it is to me.

I say goodbye to Hailey and take chase.

Ben is dressed in black jeans with ripped knees, a dark gray T-shirt with cut-out sleeves, and black and white Vans. He's lean but not as big as Rick.

My eyes trail over the broad width of his shoulders, lingering on the definition of his upper arms. His bicep pops enticingly when he reaches up to scratch the back of his neck.

I nearly trip over on the front steps.

*And his ass…* The way his black jeans mold to it perfectly.

Sucking my bottom lip between my teeth, I groan inwardly as I step through the front door to the school building.

Why does he dye his hair green of all colors, and why am I so curious about him? I could have chased him down and confronted him already. Instead, I'm following behind like some creep.

As they come to a stop at Ben's locker, Matt clasps Ben's shoulder too hard the way boys do, and then he's gone.

Intent on chewing him out, I march up behind Ben, but before I have a chance to open my mouth, he speaks.

"Did you follow me over here to suck my dick, princess? I'm sure we can find a quiet nook somewhere."

I come to an abrupt halt.

*The nerve of this guy!*

My blue eyes burn his back as he opens his locker and begins to unload his bag.

He hasn't even looked at me yet.

Why does he have to have such broad shoulders anyway? It's impossible not to look.

*Urgh!*

Closing my eyes, I count to ten in my head. I refuse to let him rile me up like this. Not today.

When I blink my eyes open, Ben is watching me. I lift my chin defiantly.

He rubs the corner of his mouth to hide his amused chuckle, and the movement draws my gaze to his lip piercing. My physical reaction to him angers me even more.

Invading his space, I take a step forward, not realizing my mistake until it's too late.

He smells delicious.

"Stop looking so fucking smug," I hiss, poking him in the chest.

Forearm on the locker, he crosses his feet. "Wow, the princess curses."

Why is he so infuriating?

I glare at him until I remember where we are, and he chuckles as I scan the hallway for listening ears.

"What, princess?" he taunts, following a passerby with his eyes before leaning in close. "Afraid everyone will find out you fingered that tight pussy of yours while your boyfriend was balls deep in Dallas?"

My blood turns to ice. "What did you say?"

He rakes a hand through his green hair, leaning in close. I catch a whiff of his cologne again, a mix of cinnamon and leather with a hint of citrus.

"I know that cologne," I whisper just as he opens his mouth to speak.

Ben frowns.

I blush fiercely. Apparently, my brain malfunctions in extreme situations. I shake my head to clear it, narrowing my eyes back on Ben. I poke him in the chest with my manicured nail. *A ridiculously hard chest.*

I squash that thought like a bug. "I don't know what Dallas told you, but I'll kill you if you so much as breathe a word to anyone."

Ben chuckles heartily, riling me up even more.

"Don't you dare laugh!" I poke him again. We stand close—too close.

Pushing off the locker, he curls a strand of my hair around his finger as he whispers, "I get hard when you're angry."

I freeze, held captive by his brown eyes. I know I should stop him, but I don't.

"Breathe," he whispers knowingly, then lets go of my hair and trails his fingers down the column of my neck in an intimate touch that sets my skin on fire.

My lungs burn from lack of oxygen.

He looks over my shoulder. "What would Rick say if the recording ended up in the wrong hands?"

"Wha…?" I search his eyes. My heart is pounding, chest thumping as my mind races.

*Dallas recorded us?*

Rick's heavy arm lands on my shoulder, and I startle, catching a whiff of his woodsy cologne.

"Is everything okay, Em?" Rick asks, not taking his eyes off Ben.

I struggle to form a response, my mind scrambling to make sense of Ben's bombshell. *Dallas filmed us? But why?*

"Everything is peachy," Ben says when I fail to respond.

Next to me, Rick stiffens. "You better watch your back. We know what you did to Jamie's car."

Ben raises both hands placatingly and smirks. "I had nothing to do with it. But you have to admit, it looks hell of a lot better."

Rick charges, throwing Ben up against the locker. I grab his arm, trying to pull him away, but he's too strong. Fear courses through me like a steam train with malfunctioning breaks. Dallas recorded us that night, and Ben has a copy of it. Nothing stops him from sharing it with the whole school if Rick and Jamie go after him.

I need to stop this.

"Rick, he's not worth it! The coach will bench you. Let's just go," I plead, pulling on his arm.

Rick fists Ben's collar, growling in his face. "You better watch your back! And stay the fuck away from my girlfriend. If I see you anywhere near her again, I'll kill you!" He steps back and lets go of Ben's creased collar, but not before smoothing it down. "Do we understand each other?"

I want the ground to swallow me up.

Smirking, Ben pats Rick on the cheek. "Sure thing, golden boy. I'll stay away from your girlfriend, but I can't guarantee she'll stay away from me." His brown eyes collide with mine. "After all, *she* chased me here."

My throat jumps.

*"I get hard when you're angry."*

His lips curve knowingly.

Rick goes to charge again, but Luke, one of the guys on the football team, steps in to help me haul him away. Rick can't afford to get into a fight. He'll get benched by coach and could lose his chance at college football.

"You better watch out!" he threatens for the third time as Luke drags him away. I follow behind with my head down, painfully aware that we've attracted an audience.

"See you later, princess," Ben chuckles behind me.

I don't look back, his eyes burning through me the whole way.

———

Dallas finally makes an appearance at lunchtime, weaving between cramped tables. She makes a beeline for her friends. Her black hair is up in a messy bun and her lips are lined with purple lipstick. She's dressed in ripped skinny jeans and a tank top, but there's something different about her.

Ben looks up from his plate when she plops into the chair next to him. His smile falls away and he narrows his eyes, dropping his fork down on the lunch tray.

Blowing a strand of hair away from her mouth, she pops the lid on her drink.

He grabs her soda, places it down on the table and lifts her chin to inspect her face. She tries to pull away, but his grip is too strong. He says something to her, and she shakes her head, trying again to pull her chin away.

I frown when he lets her go, catching a glimpse of her split lip and bruised cheek.

*Who did that to her?*

Did she get into another fight over the weekend? Why do I care? I shouldn't be curious about Dallas Garcia. She's bad news.

———

As I'm heading to my locker at the end of the school day, I spot Dallas turning down a side corridor.

After checking that the coast is clear, I run after her, my heels clicking loudly on the floor. She's got her earplugs in and is too absorbed in her phone to notice me.

"Dallas!" I shout, hitching my bag up higher on my shoulder.

She turns in surprise and removes her earplugs. I'm the last person she expects to see right now, judging by the look on her face.

Grabbing her elbow, I steer her into an empty classroom. Sunlight streams in through the drawn blinds, and the faint sound of students on their way home filters through an open window. We're in the chemistry lab. The whiteboard still has the notes from today's lesson. Rick is waiting to take me home, so I don't have long.

I lock the door. Up close, the bruising on Dallas's face looks far worse. Her entire left cheek is swollen, and her bottom lip has a jagged cut going through it. It looks sore.

"Who did that to you?" I ask, reaching out to touch her face.

I stop myself.

We're not friends.

Dallas narrows her eyes. "It's none of your business, princess."

She reminds me of a venomous snake, coiled and poised to strike.

I rub at the sudden ache in my chest. It pains me to see the shame she tries so hard to disguise. My eyes land on my red heels. I picked them this morning because I like how they contrast with my gray summer dress. I'm not so sure I do now. Our class difference is glaringly obvious.

I stare at my expensive red heels next to her scuffed and dirty Chucks. My shoes cost more than her entire wardrobe. It doesn't make me feel proud. Quite the opposite. We're from different worlds entirely.

"Why did you do it?" I whisper shakily.

There's something about Dallas. She makes me feel emotions that I'm not ready to acknowledge yet. My hands are clammy, and my heart is racing.

Her shoes brush up against mine. "Did what?" She frowns. "Look, if this is about the other night, I wanted to challenge you. I saw the way you looked at me in the bathroom. I figured—"

I shake my head. "No, not that."

"Then what?"

I hug myself and step back to create space between us. I feel oddly vulnerable as tears blur my vision. The silence in the room is deafening despite the sounds coming from outside.

Inhaling a shuddering breath, I blink rapidly to stop the tears from falling. "You filmed us, Dallas…."

There it is—the hurt. Despite everything, I'm not angry about what happened between us. I don't regret it. I'm hurt that she filmed us without my knowledge and consent.

She doesn't respond, which is all the confirmation I need.

Something inside me shifts. I drop my hands down by my sides. "Why did you do it?" I'm surprised by the acidic tone in my voice.

She stays quiet, eyes trained on the floor. I laugh incredulously. *Doesn't she have anything to say for herself? Not even an apology?*

I wait for her to say something. Anything. What did I expect? She doesn't care about anyone but herself, so why would this be any different? This is what she does, she ruins people. What the fuck happened to make her so heartless and cruel?

"Nothing to say?" I seethe, my nails digging into my palms. I'm boiling over with emotion, and she won't even look at me or admit out loud what she did.

When she doesn't respond, I shake my head, laughing bitterly. "Unbelievable." I turn on my heels. Done with this—with her. "Fuck you, Dallas!"

"I won't show it to anyone if that's what you're worried about," she calls out as I reach for the door handle.

Pivoting on the spot, I walk up to her and slap her uninjured cheek.

Her face snaps to the side.

Outside, an engine revs.

She hisses through her teeth but stays silent, cradling her reddening cheek. Strands of black hair shield her eyes from me.

"You mean like how you showed it to Ben and your friends?"

Her blue eyes collide with mine, shining with a range of emotions I can't place. Surprise? Remorse?

I taste tears on my lips. "You're despicable, Dallas. Stay away from Rick, and stay away from me!"

I leave her to stare after me as I storm out. The door slams shut behind me, startling the poor cleaner in the process of mopping the floor. Her eyes follow me as I turn the corner.

Bursting through the front door, I squint against the sunlight.

I'm grateful Rick parks right at the front, so I don't have to maneuver my way through students and cars. Especially now. My hands still tremble.

Rick's hazel eyes connect with mine across the car park. I descend the steps, hitching my heavy bag higher on my shoulder. I never got around to emptying out the unnecessary books.

Rick looks at me questioningly but makes no comment as I open the door with too much force. When he's back in the driver's seat, he starts the engine. I put my seatbelt on with shaky hands and look over at the classroom window where I left Dallas.

*Is she still in there?*

I deserve an explanation and an apology. We're not friends, but my gut still twists with betrayal.

Rick grabs my headrest, looking over his shoulder as he reverses out of the parking spot. Catching me staring, he winks before straightening in his seat and revving the engine for my benefit. He knows I love the vibrations beneath my bare thighs.

I lean my head on the window as we leave the school grounds. The traffic is heavy at this time, so it's a slower-than-usual journey home. I don't mind. It gives me time to think.

Switching on the radio station, Rick rolls down his window. "Are you okay?" he asks, tapping his fingers on the steering wheel and squeezing my bare thigh with his other hand.

I look down at his tanned skin. His palm engulfs my thigh. "I'm just tired, I guess."

I feel his eyes on me before he nods and focuses back on the road. We drive in silence. There's a new tension between us. I don't know how to bring up Friday, and he doesn't bring it up, either.

We pull up next to my house, a two-story colonial style home with a gray shingle exterior, black window shutters, and a raised, wrap-around porch.

Rick leaves the car running, which is the first sign that something is wrong.

I turn to face him fully. "Are you not coming in?"

He rests his arm out the window, staring at something in the distance. "I can't. I've got things to do," he says, glancing at me.

The silence in the car is heavy.

"Okay… Will I see you later?"

Something is definitely wrong.

Rick smiles, but it doesn't reach his eyes. "Look, Em. I'm…" He falls silent, looking over my shoulder. Mom is watching us in the doorway, probably wondering why we haven't left the car.

Rick leans in to undo my seatbelt, and I catch a whiff of his cologne before he leans back in his seat. "I'll see you tomorrow, okay? I'll be busy with the boys tonight."

I stare at him for a long moment, searching his face. "Okay, sure. No problem," I whisper before gathering my bag and opening the door.

I don't look back.

My stomach twists uncomfortably, and there's a thick lump in my throat as I walk up the drive.

Mom is standing by the stove, stirring the pan as I walk in and drop my bag on one of the kitchen chairs.

"Is Rick not staying for dinner?" she asks, placing the lid back on the pan.

I busy myself by grabbing plates and cutlery. Rick is probably just spooked by what happened between Dallas and us. He'll be fine in a couple of days.

I put the plates down on the table. "No, not today. He's busy."

My dad ruffles my hair on the way to the fridge. "Hi, pumpkin. Good day at school?"

"Yes, Dad." I grab my bag and escape to my room before they ask more questions.

———

I'm highlighting a passage in my book when my phone vibrates next to me on the bed. I'm ahead in my subjects, but I can't shift the unease inside me. I need the distraction. Rick hasn't messaged me tonight.

Reaching for the phone and swiping the screen, I frown as I read the text from an unknown number.

Unknown number: I'm sorry.

Me: Who's this?

I nibble on my thumbnail while I wait for a reply.

Unknown number: Dallas.

My heart jolts in my chest.

Me: How did you get my number?

Dallas: You should set up a pin code on your phone, princess.

When did she get access to my phone?
Another text comes through.

Dallas: What are you doing?

My eyebrows shoot up. Is she making small talk? I reread her message, debating whether to reply or not, but I'm too intrigued not to.

Me: Homework. How about you?

Dallas: Why doesn't that surprise me? I'm watching a movie.

Me: Where's Shrek and the others?

It's unnerving how curious I am about her. I try to picture

her on the bed, hair fanning the soft pillow, or sitting in the living room with her legs curled up and a bowl of popcorn in her lap. I like that I'm on her mind. I'm angry, but the intrigue wins out.

Dallas: Ha! Shrek! I'll let him know you have the hots for him ;)

I snort a laugh and type out a reply before she decides to follow through on her threat.

Me: Don't you dare! I don't have the hots for Ben!

Dallas: My lips are sealed.

I'm typing out a reply when another message pops up on my screen.

Dallas: Tell me something about you. Something no one else knows.

I scoff. What game is she playing now?

Me: Do you expect me to trust you with my secrets?

I chew on my bottom lip, watching the dots on the screen. She's typing.

Dallas: I'll go first. I'm scared to lose myself completely.

*What?*
My fingers fly over the screen.

Me: What do you mean?

Dallas: I lost my family in a fire a little over a year ago and got sent to live here with my uncle. I'm fucking numb and feel like I'm slowly fading. I don't know who I am anymore.

Dallas: That's my secret…

Wow…

This conversation got dark fast.

I rub my chest to ease the sudden ache, unsure how to respond.

*Her family died in a fire…*

Me: Is that why you get into trouble at school? Because you're numb?

Dallas: You should pay less attention to gossip, Emily.

Me: You're always in detention and covered in bruises. Tell me that's not just gossip?

She doesn't reply.

Maybe I overstepped? Throwing caution to the wind, I type out another message.

Me: I worry about what others think of me. I feel like I have an impossible image to live up to, and it's slowly drowning me.

Me: What happened between us was so out of character for me. I should probably feel embarrassed about Friday night, but I don't. I don't regret a single thing! It's the most free I've ever felt.

I lay back on my bed, staring up at the slime stain on my ceiling. I can't believe I shared my truth with Dallas of all people. Rick doesn't even know. Neither does Hailey.

I feel lighter.

I shouldn't trust Dallas, but she shared something of herself with me.

The phone pings in my hand, and I bolt upright in my rush to unlock the screen.

Dallas: Thank you for trusting me, princess.

I suppress a smile. My heart feels too big for my chest and my stomach flutters with a new feeling I haven't felt before.

# CHAPTER

## EMILY

"CAN I COME OVER TONIGHT?" Rick asks, stroking his fingers through my hair.

I tear my gaze away from Dallas and her friends. I've spent the last half an hour of my lunch break imagining what it would be like to sit at their table.

Rick looks apologetic. It's been over a week since he climbed my trellis. I'm pent up with sexual frustration and fed up with him avoiding me.

"Sure," I reply, picking up my discarded fork and stabbing a fry.

I want to see him. Of course, I do…

Threading his fingers through mine below the table, he leans in, stealing a kiss before I have a chance to eat the fry. His attention is reassuring, but I still can't shift the unease inside me when I catch Dallas watching us.

My phone vibrates next to my plate on the table.

Dallas: Tell me another secret.

I look up from my phone. Dallas is engaged in conversation with Steph while Matt twirls a strand of Steph's curly hair around his finger.

Debating what to reply, I tap my nail on my phone. My friends are too busy talking to pay attention to me as I type out a quick response.

Me: I hide behind a mask.

I hit send, fidgeting with the hem of my skirt while I wait for her to reply.

She doesn't.

The bell rings, but still nothing.

"Em?" Rick holds out his letterman jacket for me. I push my chair back and stand up.

"Thanks," I say when it's on, and he wraps his arm around my shoulder.

I don't look back as we walk out.

———

Hailey drops down in her seat next to me with a heavy sigh as we wait for the teacher to enter the classroom. "I just want this day to be over," she whines. "Practice is gonna be a bitch later, no offense. I don't know how you came up with this new routine, Em. It's good. Really good. I just hope we're ready for Friday's away game."

"We will be. We've practiced hard."

Dallas walks past to sit in the back next to Steph. I follow her with my eyes.

"What's up with that?"

I tear my gaze away from her ass.

Hailey nudges her head at Dallas.

"What's up with what?" I frown.

Hailey rolls her eyes. "Em, you're staring at her. Is something going on?"

Reaching for my bag, I get my books out. "How are things with you and Jamie?" I'm deflecting. Hailey loves to talk about herself. Ask her a question, and she can gladly talk your ear off.

Leaning in conspiratorially, she grins. "His parents invited me along to stay with them at their estate in the Hamptons this summer. I think we're getting serious."

My eyebrows hit my hairline. Jamie is a player, so it must be serious if he's okay with his parents inviting her over for the summer. "Hailey, that's great news!"

She beams. "I know, right? You need to come with me to shop for new bikinis and dresses. I need to look fantastic."

The teacher chooses that moment to start the lesson.

I can't help but feel a sense of guilt for not telling her what's going on in my life but at the same time, she's happy. I don't want her to worry.

My phone vibrates halfway through class with a text from Dallas. I glance at Hailey, but she's too busy taking notes to notice the smile on my face.

Dallas: Everyone hides behind a mask, Em.

I narrow my eyes at the nickname. Only my friends call me Em.

Me: Are we on a nickname basis now?

Dallas: We can be.

I draw in a shaky breath, unsure if I'm ready to go there with her just yet.

Me: A secret for a secret, remember? Tell me yours.

I look over my shoulder.

Balancing on the chair's back legs, she types out a reply. Her hair shields her face like a curtain, and I itch to tuck it behind her ear. Unlike me, she doesn't hide her phone beneath the table. She doesn't care if she gets caught texting.

The phone vibrates in my lap.

Dallas: I feel alone.

I do as well, despite being surrounded by friends and family.

Me: Tell me a happy memory.

Hailey turns a page in her book, removes the highlighter from between her teeth and marks a passage.

Dallas: My mom's pancakes. She used to make them every Sunday. Aaron and I would fight over the last one like a pack of hounds.

Me: Who won?

Dallas: Me, of course. Aaron had the build, but I had the speed.

I chance another look over my shoulder, and we share a smile before she ducks her head, typing on her phone.

Dallas: You're beautiful when you smile.

My core clenches and I drop my phone on the desk like it's on fire, squeezing my thighs together. What is she doing to me? I've even got flutters in my stomach.

"What's up?" Hailey asks, capping her highlighter.

I shake my head. "Nothing."

The urge to look over my shoulder is an uncomfortable itch. I don't remember having such a physical reaction to someone before. Especially not a girl. What would my friends say if they found out? And my family?

———

Rick strokes his fingers over my back while laughing at a funny part in the movie. Tonight is the first time he's been here in over a week.

I listen to his steady heartbeat beneath my ear.

*"You're beautiful when you smile."*

I can't stop thinking about her. Every time my phone pings, my heart does a somersault.

Lifting my head off Rick's chest, I reach for my phone on the nightstand. I take a selfie of us and upload it to Instagram. When I check my notifications, I notice Dallas has started following me.

The annoying butterflies return.

My hands tremble slightly as I follow her back. I go to Ben's page and follow him too. It's probably not the smartest move I've made, but curiosity killed the cat, as they say.

After checking to make sure Rick is engrossed in the movie, I scoot up in bed and reach for a pillow to use behind my back.

Ben's page is filled with photographs of him and his friends. I scroll through and spot several of Dallas too. In one, she sits on Ben's broad shoulders with her tongue out. I also find one of her asleep on Ben's lap.

Curious, I stop scrolling.

Ben is looking down on her sleeping form with a soft smile.

It's said a picture speaks more than a thousand words. In this case, it's true. Ben cares about Dallas. I can see it in his smile.

My eyebrows shoot up in surprise when I read the caption: *Though she be but little she is fierce.*

Shakespeare. Ben pays attention in class, after all.

I look at Rick. He's scratching his jaw and chuckling at a funny part in the movie. His dark hair is still damp from showering after football practice.

*Does he look at me like that?*

I turn my attention back to the phone in my hand.

I've gone to the same school as Ben my whole life, but I never paid much attention to him until now. He was never on my radar before, but there's something about him that I can't unsee. My body lights up like a fucking firecracker whenever he enters the room.

"Are you okay?" Rick asks, shifting on the bed.

My heart jolts and I angle my phone away. "I'm fine." I may look calm on the outside but on the inside…

Satisfied with my reply, Rick turns his attention back to the movie.

I slump in relief. It's silly. I haven't technically done anything wrong. I'm just looking at photographs, right? Never mind that this particular person happens to make my clit throb with its own heartbeat.

My fingers tremble while I browse through Ben's page, pausing to look at a photo dump of him and his friend Josh. They sit shirtless at the edge of a jetty with their feet in the water, looking over their shoulder at the camera.

Sucking my bottom lip between my teeth, I trail my eyes over Ben's broad back, lost in the intricate details of his tattoos. There's a skull with a tilted crown on its head, a script tattoo on his left rib, and a steampunk clockwork tattoo. On his left wrist, a set of leather wristbands bring attention to his sexy forearms.

As I swipe to the next photograph, I'm rewarded with a frontal shot of his bare chest. He's got a nice six-pack and a smatter of dark hairs that lead down to a mouthwatering 'V.'

He's stood next to Matt with a fishing rod in his hand, his head thrown back mid-laugh.

Rick shifts on the bed as the credits start rolling. I hurry to lock the screen, placing the phone on the nightstand before straddling his lap. My clit throbs and my nipples ache.

Lip trapped between my teeth, I roll my hips, whimpering with need. "I missed you, baby."

His cock hardens beneath me as I brush my fingers through his dark hair. Is Ben's just as soft? "Did you miss me?" I tug on the dark strands, imagining what they would look like between my fingers if they were green.

Pressing a swift kiss to my lips, Rick strokes his big hands down my sides. Before I have a chance to move in for another kiss, he pulls back. "I should get going. It's a busy day tomorrow with school and the away game."

My brows shoot up. This is not how these things usually go.

Rick lifts me off him and climbs off the bed, grabbing his letterman jacket off my desk chair.

"Are we okay?" I blurt when he's at the door. My clit is still throbbing painfully, and I can't hide the slight shake in my voice.

Frowning, he looks over his shoulder. "Yeah, why wouldn't we be?"

*Maybe because you haven't fucked me since the night with Dallas.*

I hesitate.

Am I paranoid?

Flashing a weak smile, I run my fingers through my hair. "Ignore me. It's nothing. See you tomorrow?"

Rick nods once, then leaves the room.

The door clicks shut behind him, and I stare at it, swallowing past the thick lump in my throat. There's a weight on my chest. I feel I can't breathe.

I think we're okay one minute, and then he turns me down the next when I make it clear that I want him.

I shake off the unease. Rick is right—tomorrow *is* an important day. We're performing our new cheerleading routine at the pep rally in the morning. Then the boys are going up against our main rivals in the away game after school.

Breathing a heavy sigh, I lie back down on the bed and reach for my phone on the nightstand. I send a quick message to Hailey.

Laughter filters through my open window. My parents have friends over for a late meal in the backyard.

As I open Instagram, I shoot upright in bed when I see a message from Ben in my inbox. It's embarrassing how fast I click on it.

Ben: Are u stalking me, princess?

I scoff.

It's not like I scrolled through his pictures and then tried to seduce my boyfriend. *Nope, not at all.*

My tongue swipes over my bottom lip as I try to think of what to write. I contemplate not responding, but I'm too curious.

Me: I thought I did a better job of hiding my obsession with you? I need to improve my game. What gave me away? Was it the creepy binoculars or the collage of pictures taped to the inside of my locker?

It doesn't take long before my response gets marked as read and the dots appear. I wonder if he's smiling too or if it's just me?

Ben: The binoculars, babe. They just don't make them that big anymore. I can get you a smaller replacement with night vision if you want. I sleep naked ;)

I burst out laughing, shoulders shaking.

Me: I'll pass, thank you. I like big binoculars. It makes them easier to grip, less likely to get lost in the shrubbery, and most importantly, they're all the better to see you with ;)

Am I flirting?

Shit, I *am* flirting. And with Shrek…

I nibble on my thumbnail while the dots disappear and reappear.

Ben: Admit it, princess. You love my red cloak.

Ha! He got my Little Red Riding Hood reference.

Me: I didn't take you for a fan of Charles Perrault?

Ben: Don't make me google shit.

I laugh again, surprised by how easy conversation flows between us.

Me: Don't strain yourself.

Ben is silent for a while before a selfie pops up on the screen.
I slap a palm to my mouth to stifle the loud laughter bubbling up inside of me. He's wearing a red blanket tied around his neck like a cape—or a cloak.

Ben: You can eat me anytime, she-wolf. I won't fight if you decide to gobble me up.

My cheeks heat at the sexual innuendo.

Me: Careful with what you wish for, little piggy.

Ben: I said to gobble me up, not blow my house down.

My cheeks ache from smiling.

Me: I'm off to bed now. I have the pep rally in the morning and an away game after school.

Ben: You in a cheerleader uniform. Say no more, princess. ;)

Me: Good night, Ben.

I exit the chat, ignoring my warm insides. Ben is trouble, and I should stay away if I know what's good for me.

# CHAPTER

*seven*

## BEN

I LEAN AGAINST MY LOCKER, scrolling through my conversation with Princess last night. Who knew she could be funny and easy-going? I assumed she was stuck up like the rest of the rich kids at this school, but she made me laugh last night.

It surprised me when I received a notification that she had started following me on Instagram. It makes it easier for me as my part of the double dare is up, and I refuse to lose to Dallas on this one.

"How's the bet coming along, lover boy? Ready to admit defeat yet?" Dallas grins, coming to a stop at my locker.

I scoff, wiggling my phone in the air. "Dream on! I'm doing prep work. Don't you worry, I'll soon have our Princess on her knees with her pouty lips stretched around my dick."

"You're full of shit," she replies with a laugh.

Amused, I shrug. "She's just another girl, Dell. She won't be that hard to seduce."

The football team walk past in their jerseys, hollering and jostling each other. One guy at the back throws a football over the heads of the others.

Dallas scowls. "I hate game day."

"Yeah? Muscular guys in jerseys don't do it for you?"

She shoots me a death glare. "Very funny, you dick."

We both know Dallas will never be a jersey chaser, but she's not immune to muscles.

"You love my dick," I tease, palming myself.

Dallas cracks a smile. "Can't argue with you there."

We pause when Rick and Jamie walk past with a handful of giggling girls trailing in their wake.

There's no sign of Princess yet.

Rick fills out his jersey thanks to hours of football practice; it's not difficult to see why Princess likes him. With muscles like that, girls are bound to fall to their knees for him. Thanks to Dallas's recording, I've seen Princess on hers. Just the thought makes my dick harden in my pants even as a weird sensation, not so unlike jealousy, twists my insides.

Rich and preppy girls are not my type, but Emily is one of the hottest girls at this school. Rick is a lucky fucker to get to pound her tight pussy every night. If I was fucking her, she wouldn't be able to walk at school.

"Did you see Jamie's car? It looks brand new again. I might spray paint a Disney princess next time," Dallas says, interrupting my train of thought.

Pushing off the lockers, I chuckle as we join the stream of students.

"I'm sure Jamie would love that."

"What are we doing this weekend?"

A couple of cheerleaders walk past in their tiny uniforms, and I stare after them longingly. Rich girls aren't my type, but their legs in those skirts…

"Pig!" Dallas huffs next to me.

Nudging her with my elbow, I flash my pearly whites. "Jealous?"

She scoffs like the thought offends her. "You fucking wish, Ben."

I place my hand over my heart. "You wound me, baby. You truly do. But to answer your question, we're heading to McKenzie's to get buzzed. Are you in?"

"Benny-boy, do you not know me at all? Of course, I'm fucking in."

Throwing my arm over her shoulder, I grin widely as we enter the classroom. "That's my girl."

———

Football is a huge thing here in our small town, and the entire school is buzzing about today's away game. It's sacrilege if you're not into it.

We find seats toward the back of the bleachers while the principal taps on the microphone, causing it to make a high-pitched screech that nearly deafens us all.

"We need face paint next time," Josh says, taking a seat next to me.

Matt unscrews the lid on his soda, then throws it at an unsuspecting student a couple of rows down. "I told you. I'll paint my face black and blue when you fuck Miss. Betty."

Josh pales. "Can you not suggest someone more attractive than the receptionist? She's ancient. As if that's not bad enough, she wears those pleated checkered skirts that go below the knees. Not the sexy kind that British girls wear to school. No! The grandma kind."

Matt tips his head back and downs the soda. His throat bobs before he lowers the bottle and replies, "Like I said, when you fuck Miss. Betty, then we'll talk."

"She has a spot on her nose, Matt. It's huge."

April grabs Matt's drink from him, ignoring his incredulous stare. "It's a wart, Josh." After drinking the rest of the soda, she throws the empty bottle behind her carelessly.

Josh drops his head back with a groan. "Why is this my life? I just want us to show some school spirit."

Dallas looks up from the game on her phone. "You need locking up, Josh. Probably even the old shock treatment."

Squashed between Matt and Josh, I search the room for Princess. She's seated at the front with the rest of the cheer squad.

Dressed in her blue and black cheer uniform, she looks like a damn snack with her blonde hair tied up in a high ponytail and her long creamy legs on full display. If she's nervous, she doesn't show it.

I play games on my phone while the principal drones on and on about the football team's achievements and the importance of school spirit—all the things I don't give a shit about.

Up next is the school band, and their music is crap, as always. A group of five-year-olds could play better music with pans and cutlery.

Groaning with boredom, Dallas rests her head on Steph's shoulder. Nina entertains herself in typical Nina fashion. Using a pair of stolen scissors, she leans forward and cuts ringlets off the girl in front. April pops her gum, chewing loudly.

Matt and Josh play Rock, Paper, Scissors. Much to my annoyance, since I'm squashed in the middle.

I glare at Josh, who shrugs.

"One more time. Best of three wins."

And they're off again, waving their fucking hands in my face.

"Rock, paper, scissors, shoot!"

Matts wraps his hand around Josh's closed fist and whoops. "Paper beats rock."

"Yeah, but my rock is too heavy for your paper. Look at that, your paper is tearing down the middle. Oh, what a shame."

I lean back as they jostle each other.

"My paper owns your fucking puny rock."

"The only thing your paper is good for is to shoot spitballs. I can crack coconut shells with my rock."

I roll my eyes.

*Snip!* There goes another lock of hair. Nina winks at me.

The cheerleaders take to the floor, and Matt and Josh abandon their game of 'Fuck with Ben.'

I breathe a sigh of relief.

'Play with Fire' by Sam Tinnesz starts playing through the speakers. Emily leads the group through a choreography consisting of complicated dance moves combined with traditional cheer stunts.

The girls throw her up high, and she does a perfect spin mid-air before landing in the arms of the only two guys on the team.

Those boys are obviously on to something if their choice of sport involves catching girls in short skirts. It sounds more tempting than getting sacked by huge guys in sweaty jockstraps.

Princess is a damn sight to behold when she cheers. Her moves are sharp and precise, her passion clear as day on her face. She's at home out there, shaking her hips as well as those damn pom-poms.

She finishes the routine with a series of back handsprings while the girls in the back do some other fancy shit that I can't name.

The room explodes in cheers and hollers. Emily, out of breath and with sweat beading on her brow, smiles big as she takes a seat.

Hailey leans in close to be heard over the noise when the principal walks back to the podium and continues his mission to bore us all to death.

I ignore the football team when they take to the floor, my eyes staying glued on Princess. She scans the crowd and smiles when she spots me but then seems to catch herself. Cheeks blazing, she looks away.

I wait patiently, and it doesn't take long before her curious eyes are back on me. My smile fades the longer we stare at each other. Some unknown emotion flickers in her eyes, and my hardening cock twitches in my jeans.

She takes me by complete surprise when she brings her hands up and pretends to look at me through a pair of binoculars.

Throwing my head back, I laugh, startling Josh and Matt next to me.

Dallas lowers her phone, and I flash her a grin, nudging my

head toward Princess. She follows my line of sight, her gaze sweeping over the room. I can tell the minute their eyes collide by the slow smirk forming on Dallas's lips.

Something is brewing between the three of us. Something deliciously dark.

My phone vibrates in my pocket, and I fish it out, unlocking the screen.

Dell: I bet you that I can make her come before you do when we get her in bed.

I scoff, glancing at Princess, who quirks one of her perfect eyebrows. Her feistiness is a turn-on.

Leaning forward and resting my elbows on my thighs, I type out a reply to Dallas.

Me: It's on!

As Dallas meets my gaze, we share a Cheshire smile.
Emily is playing a dangerous game.

——————

*Dallas.*

I knew it was the wrong choice to return home when I opened the front door and heard people laughing in the kitchen. My uncle has friends over.

Music and cigarette smoke filter through the gap in the kitchen door. I sneak down the hallway, careful to step over the empty beer cans on the floor.

After closing the bedroom door behind me, I grab clean clothes and stuff them into my bag. I'm almost finished packing when the door opens, and one of my uncle's guests steps inside. I recognize him as Greg Clifford, one of the regulars down at the local bar. It's not the first time Greg has been to visit, and he's always overly handsy.

I'm instantly on high alert, backing up against the edge of the bed.

He's dressed in loose jeans, and the buttons on his creased shirt are done up wrong. Scratching his unshaven beard, he locks the door.

The very door I forgot to lock in my rush to pack a bag and make my escape.

My heart thuds heavily in my chest as he stops in front of me, flashing his yellowed teeth.

"If it isn't my favorite girl."

I'm trapped against the bed with nowhere to escape while he palms my breast through the fabric of my tank top.

"I wondered when I would see you next." His sour breath turns my stomach.

I slap his hand away. "My uncle will kill you if you touch me!" It's a lie, my uncle won't give a shit. Greg knows it too.

He calls me out on it. "Your uncle doesn't care about you. You're an inconvenience to him." His fingers brush the fading bruise on my jaw. "He does like to take his anger out on you, doesn't he?"

I rip my jaw away from his touch.

"Now, sweetness, this will be over so much quicker if you don't fight," he says, taking hold of my wrist and pressing my palm over his hard length.

Panic seizes me. Pushing past him, I sprint for the door. I don't get far before he grabs my hair.

I cry out in pain as he pulls me back.

"You ungrateful little bitch!" he growls, throwing me down on the bed. His fists rain down on me, punching me repeatedly in the ribs and stomach until I lie sobbing on the rumpled sheets.

Everything hurts.

I draw my legs up in the fetal position while he leers down at me, unbuttoning his jeans.

"I told you not to fucking fight. Now, look what you made me do." He kicks the bed, and a startled scream escapes my lips. "I didn't want to have to hurt you, but you gave me no choice."

Kneeling down on the bed, he wraps his big hand around my throat. It hurts. I struggle to take a breath.

"Now, are you going to be a good girl, or will I have to discipline you some more?"

I claw his wrist, drawing blood in my fight to pry his fingers off. He's too strong, stealing my breath.

"Maybe you enjoy a heavy hand?" His smile is cruel and the evil glint in his gaze turns my stomach. He releases me, freeing his dick. Then he begins stroking the long length, watching me with his beady eyes. "Come here and wrap your hand around my cock."

When I don't make a move to comply, he grabs my hand in such a fierce grip, I feel as if the bone might snap. Wrapping my fingers around his length, he guides my movements up and down his veiny dick.

"That's it. Good girl."

He fucks my hand, grunting deep in his throat.

I feel sick.

His fingers tangle in my hair, and he fists the strands tightly. I'm in so much pain already that my stinging scalp barely registers.

"I'm going let go of your hand now, sweetness, and you're going to make me feel real fucking good, understood? If you don't, then I'll have no choice but to bend you over and fuck your tight little ass."

I whimper in fear. Greg's voice tells me he would like it very much if I resisted him.

"Good girl," he breathes when his hand falls away, and I'm still stroking him. Tears pool in my eyes, threatening to fall. The pain in my body has nothing on the emotional agony.

I pick up my speed to get him off faster, so this hell will be over sooner.

His grip on my hair tightens until I'm sure he'll come away with chunks of hair. Stroking him faster and harder, I squeeze my eyes shut. If I don't look, I can pretend it isn't happening.

"Stick your tongue out."

I shake my head, my eyes still squeezed shut. Anything but that. "Please, no."

Greg lets go of my hair and slaps my cheek hard. Then he does it again before I've had a chance to recover from the first blow.

"Stick your fucking tongue out!"

I do. I just do.

My cheek burns and throbs.

"That's it, sweetness. See how much easier it is when you listen." His hand is back in my hair, and he takes charge with his other hand, guiding my strokes with his sweaty palm until his warm seed squirts on my tongue and cheeks. It's all I can do not to puke.

Greg pushes me back on the bed like a used rag. He tucks himself in before walking over to the door and grinning over his shoulder. "See you again real soon, sweetness."

The door clicks shut as I break down sobbing. My tears mix with his cum and I shuffle on the bed, gasping in pain. My ribs are on fire. The pain is so severe, I struggle to breathe. Grabbing a discarded T-shirt off the floor, I use it to rub him off me until my skin hurts. I can still taste him on my tongue, though. I need to rinse my mouth out and wash him off me, but I don't dare to leave my room.

Besides, I can't possibly walk with the amount of agony I'm in. My cheek throbs, and pain sears through my ribs with my every inhale. I probably need medical attention.

Just then, the phone lights up on the nightstand, and I crawl over. Swiping the screen and pressing it to my ear, I hiss in pain as I curl up in the fetal position. "Ben?"

"Dell?"

I press my face into the pillow to silence my wheezing breaths. It frightens me that I'm struggling to breathe.

"Dell, are you okay?" There's urgency in his voice now.

I can't lie to him.

"No," I whisper on a sob.

I'm not okay. I've been sexually assaulted, and there's nothing I can do to stop it from happening again. Greg will take it further next time.

"I'm coming to get you." The line goes dead.

Whimpering in fear, I clutch the phone when I hear voices and footsteps outside my bedroom. The sound drifts away, and silence descends on the house when the front door shuts.

I breathe a wheezy breath of relief. Ben wouldn't hesitate to kill Greg for laying a hand on me, and I don't want him to get into trouble because of me.

As the minutes go by, I drift in and out of consciousness. The bed shifts and a warm hand brushes strands of hair from my face.

I startle, releasing a scream as I scramble back on the bed.

"Shhh," Ben soothes, scooping me up in his arms. "It's me, Dell. I won't hurt you."

"Greg made me touch him." I cling to his T-shirt, soaking the fabric with my tears.

"You're okay." Ben strokes my back soothingly. "He can't hurt you now."

"I had no choice."

He rocks us on the bed until the shaking subsides, and I drift off to sleep.

"I've got her," I hear him say as he shifts us off the bed. "Get her backpack. Josh, grab a couple of bags from the trunk and pack as much of her stuff as you can."

———

*Ben.*

.  .  .

Steph runs out of the house, sidestepping the snoring dog on the porch. She fusses over Dell in my arms.

"Did you run the bath?" I ask as we enter through the front door and make our way down the hallway.

Steph holds the bathroom door open. "Of course. It's ready."

Stepping through, I place Dallas down on the toilet seat, being careful with her injuries. She stirs, slowly blinking her eyes open.

I crouch down, brushing her hair off her brow. "Baby, you're gonna have a bath, okay. We'll get you cleaned up."

"Please… I need him off me."

Rage courses through me, and I grind my teeth before pressing a soft kiss to her temple. "I know, baby. I know."

Steph wipes tears off her cheeks but says nothing. Dallas is usually the strong one in our little group, and I know it hurts Steph to see her best friend reduced to this.

Helping Dallas out of her clothes, I curse under my breath when I lift her T-shirt. Angry bruises cover her ribs and stomach.

Behind me, Steph gasps, her palms flying up to her mouth.

I inspect Dallas's injuries with shaky hands. There are more bruises on her neck.

*The fucker choked her.*

When she's fully undressed, I scoop her up and carry her over to the bath. She doesn't make a sound, and her eyes barely open as I lower her carefully down in the warm water.

Steph clears her throat. "I know you care for her, but she's already had one man touch her today. I'll wash her." She begs me with her eyes to understand.

Rising to my feet, I nod reluctantly.

I do understand. Dallas is vulnerable and needs a friend who can sympathize with what she's gone through tonight.

I squeeze Steph's shoulder on my way out, and she meets my gaze before crouching down in front of Dallas. Lathering up the bath sponge, she speaks to her in a soothing voice.

I leave them to it and join Matt and Josh in the living room. They're engrossed in the Xbox game.

Dropping down on the couch, I rub my tired face.

I'm exhausted.

Matt pauses the game, drops the controller on the coffee table and looks at me expectantly.

Leaning back, I prop a foot on the coffee table. "Steph is looking after her now."

They exchange looks.

"What's the plan?" Josh asks.

We can't go to the authorities. Nothing good will come of it. Greg will get off lightly, and Dallas's uncle will punish her. It won't be pretty.

"She's staying with me. Dad is never home, and Mom is too spaced out on her meds to care or notice. Dallas will be safe here."

"What if her uncle reports her missing?"

I give Matt a pointed look. "He hits her. She's not going back there. Besides, Dallas is nearly eighteen. Her uncle won't care, trust me." I look at Josh, then Matt. "We're gonna pay Greg a little visit. Make sure he never lays another finger on our girl."

Josh rubs his hands together in anticipation. "Hell yeah, that's what I'm talking about!"

"We want in on that too," Nina announces from the doorway, patting down her windswept, black bob.

I look over in surprise. "Didn't hear you come in."

The door opens behind her, and April walks through, carrying a heavy-looking duffel bag. She drops it on the coffee table. "I'll overlook the fact that you fuckers didn't send out an SOS in the group chat. We had to receive a message directly from Steph."

Matt groans, but April cuts in before he has a chance to reply. "No fucking excuses, Matt. The chat is there. Use it!"

"You women use the group chat as a fucking gossip central. We can't get a word in otherwise. An SOS would get lost amongst all the talk of shoes and manicures," Josh points out.

April glares at him, then unzips the duffel bag.

With a scoff, Nina walks up behind Josh and smacks the back of his head.

I chuckle. Nina has a lot of fire in her.

"When do we ever talk about shoes and manicures?"

"Anyway," April says, dragging the word out and smiling mischievously, "you're stealing my thunder with your whining. I brought toys to the party."

I whoop and holler along with the boys when she pulls out baseball bats and hands us one each.

April grins while we inspect the clubs, clearly pleased with herself.

"I love how fucking vicious you are, baby. It makes me hard," Matt says, pointing the bat at her.

She shoots him a look of distaste. "Not happening." Their sexually charged banter is highly amusing, and it's a mystery why they skirt around each other.

Nina makes herself comfortable on Josh's lap. Placing his bat down on the floor, she says in a sugary tone, "While you boys were too busy sucking each other's dicks, we did some digging. We know where Greg is tonight."

"Isn't he down at the local pub where he always is?" Josh asks before grimacing in pain when Nina pulls his ear.

"Did you say something?"

"No?"

Matt jumps up, interrupting their banter. He grabs April's hand and drags her along behind him.

She tries and fails to dislodge her hand from his. "Matt, you shit, let go of me!"

"Nope," he says, popping the 'P' as they walk out. Their voices carry up the driveway. "No time to waste. I'm about to risk my life, baby, and you're gonna reward me on your knees afterward for my bravery. But not before I make you scream my name. Ladies come first."

"How chivalrous," April hisses, sounding like an angry alley cat.

"At least he's generous," Nina jests, making us chuckle.

"I bet you twenty that she fucks him tonight." Josh slaps

Nina's ass as she rises to her feet.

Picking up the bat off the floor, Nina peers over her shoulder. "I highly doubt that. They've done this dance for-fucking-ever. I can't see tonight being the straw that breaks the camel's back."

"You never know," I cut in as I make my way over to the door. "Blood and adrenaline are the best kinds of aphrodisiacs."

# CHAPTER
*eight*

## EMILY

RICK'S white Porsche sits parked when I pull up in his driveway. It's been weeks since the night with Dallas, and he's still distant. I don't know what to do anymore, so here I am.

After flicking the visor back up, I exit the car and walk up to the front door. The doorbell used to be a standard chime. It has since been replaced with one that plays a tune when you press it —a tune that never seems to end.

Footsteps sound on the other side before the door opens. Rick's mother, Mrs. Taylor, smiles at me. She's a beautiful woman with dark hair and the same color eyes as her son.

"Hi, Emily. What a lovely surprise. Rick is upstairs in his bedroom." She holds the door open for me. "We haven't seen you in a while. Your mom tells me that you and the girls have a new cheer routine?"

I smile politely as I step through the door. "Yes, we performed it for the first time at the pep rally on Friday and then again at the away game."

Mrs. Taylor sighs tiredly. "I wish I could have been there, but I'm swamped with another big case. I'll make sure to come to see you soon. I don't want to miss your new routine. You girls work so hard."

If anyone knows, it's Mrs. Taylor. She used to be a cheerleader herself in high school.

"Up you go. I'm sure Rick will be excited to see you."

*I'm not so sure about that.*

I offer her a parting smile before making my way up the sweeping staircase.

Rick is on the bed, watching TV when I step inside and close the door behind me. He looks over in surprise as I lean back against the door.

I smile, but it's a sad, tired smile. "We need to talk."

He sits up, his feet on the floor, his elbows on his knees. Rubbing his big hands through his dark hair and dragging them down his face, he blows out a heavy breath. He meets my gaze with tired eyes of his own. "I'm sorry."

I push off the door and join him on the bed. It dips under my weight when I sit down. The silence in the room is heavy, despite the TV. Rick picks at his cuticles. He doesn't look at me as he says, "I don't know what came over me, Em. I never wanted you to see that."

He's referring to that night.

"It's okay, Rick. I liked it," I reply quietly, fidgeting with the hem of my dress. "I liked it a lot, and I don't want you to think otherwise. You didn't do anything wrong."

His head lifts and he searches my eyes for the truth.

I let him see it as I compose myself for what needs to be said next. My heart aches, but I know it's the right decision. "We aren't together for the right reasons, Rick."

My heart is breaking, but it's also stitching itself together.

A deep sigh whooshes out of him, and he drops his head, staring down at the floor between his bare feet.

We sit in silence.

"You're right," he replies, looking at me. "It doesn't undermine what we had, Em. I need you to know that."

*Had.* Past tense.

Tears pool in my eyes, blurring my vision. Even though I know he's right, it still hurts.

"I know." I attempt a weak smile. "You're the best, first boyfriend I could've ever asked for, Rick."

He's been there for me since childhood. My rock for as long as I can remember. Maybe we got together because it was easy and pleased our parents, but things have changed lately. The night with Dallas was the catalyst. I want Rick to fall head over heels in love one day, but we both know it won't be with me.

Taking my hand and threading his fingers through mine, he smiles sadly. "I'll always be here for you. You know that, right?"

I rest my head on his shoulder. "I know. And I will always be your number one supporter. Don't forget it when you're swamped with jersey chasers."

We chuckle, but it's bittersweet. My heart hurts. Deep down, I know we're doing the right thing.

Rivers sometimes meet and flow together, heading downstream before splitting apart again. Rick and I have reached the fork in our road.

———

I'm in good spirits on Monday morning. I did a lot of soul-searching the night before. It would have frightened me a month ago not to have Rick by my side, but something is changing inside me.

Little by little.

It doesn't send me into a tailspin anymore to think about the future. It's still scary but not overwhelming. I'm not tossing and turning at night with anxiety. The emptiness in my chest is slowly filling up with genuine smiles and moments of happiness.

Like right now, I'm feeling reckless and mischievous. We're painting a fruit bowl in art class which is so cliché.

Dipping the paintbrush in the cup of water to make it nice and wet, I glance over at the teacher. She's not looking, so I swirl the brush in the purple paint before turning and flicking it at Matt.

It hits him right on the cheek.

"What the...?" He wipes it, smearing the paint, and I press a palm over my lips to suppress my laughter. His eyes flit up and he looks directly at me.

"Oops!"

Inspecting the paint on his hand, he chuckles. He picks up his paintbrush, dips it in the red paint and holds it up threateningly in the air. "Oops, you say?"

I look over at the teacher.

"Oh, she can't help you now." He abandons his canvas and walks toward me.

I hold my hands up, giggling. "It was an accident."

"Sure," he grins, taking another step closer. His blonde hair falls in his eyes. "You just happened to flick paint at me from two rows over."

"I have involuntary reflexes."

His eyes sparkle. "Like this?" he pretends to flick the brush.

I squeak and duck. "Look," I lift my hands placatingly, "it was definitely an accident. I wouldn't dare flick paint at you."

It would sound more believable if I wasn't smiling.

He comes to a stop in front of me and grabs me by my chin, painting a line down my nose. This time I really do laugh, batting him away.

"Oh, look at that," he says, staring at the hand holding the brush like he can't believe what just happened. "Involuntary reflexes."

"Mr. Young!" our teacher snaps. "Back to your canvas now!"

He winks at me, walking backward. "Word of advice, don't rub it, or you'll look like Rudolph."

———

"What on earth happened to you?" Hailey asks when I pull out my chair at lunchtime.

I plop down, looking at her questioningly, and she points at my nose. "Oh, that." I peel back the yogurt lid and lick it, shrugging. "Art lesson happened."

"It's red."

"I know."

"Like very red!"

Reaching for the spoon, I laugh. "I got red paint on my nose and I tried to wipe it off."

Jamie does a double-take when he sees me. "You got a nasty cold or something?"

Hailey laughs. "Art lesson."

The chair scrapes on the floor as Jamie pulls it out and takes a seat. "I didn't know you do face painting in art?"

"Ha! Ha!" I roll my eyes. "I had an accident."

"What kind of accident involves painting your own face?" Jamie takes a bite of his sandwich while Rick sits down next to me. "I'm genuinely curious."

I scoop up yogurt with my spoon. "I don't know. One minute I was painting the canvas, and the next—oops."

Hailey sniggers next to me.

Jamie lowers his sandwich, chewing slowly before swallowing. "Oops?"

Rick frowns and grabs hold of my chin. "Did you try washing it off with soap and water?"

"That thought never entered my mind."

Pushing my face back, he chuckles. "Smartass."

"Seriously, though. I went to every toilet in the school and couldn't find soap anywhere. What's up with that?"

Hailey scrunches up her nose. "That's so unsanitary."

"Tell me about it." I scoop up another spoonful of yogurt.

When I glance across the cafeteria, Matt winks at me.

I grin around the spoon, but my smile only lasts a fleeting second when I notice that Dallas is missing.

The chair next to Ben is empty.

*Where is she?*

————

It's Wednesday, and we're in the locker room after cheer practice when my phone finally pings with a notification from Dallas. I nearly drop it in my haste to unlock it.

Hailey looks at me questioningly but doesn't comment. She bends down to tie her shoelaces.

Dallas: Tell me a happy memory.

My belly flutters, and I bite my lip to suppress my smile, surprised at how relieved I am to hear from her.

Me: The first time Rick decided to climb my trellis, he lost his grip and fell off just as my dad came around the corner, looking for the dog. Rick landed right at his feet. My dad had steam coming out of his ears for weeks.

Rick had to master the art of sneaking in undetected like a stealthy ninja. He never fell off the trellis again.

Dallas: *laughing emoji* That made me laugh :)

Me: Trust me, it made me laugh too! Your turn.

"Are you coming?" Hailey asks, tightening her ponytail.
I hurry to read Dallas's response.

Dallas: Sunsets at the beach. I grew up on the coast.

I smile, my fingers flying over the screen.

Me: When are you coming back to school?

Dallas: Soon.

———

Dallas keeps messaging me random texts here and there asking for happy memories or secrets, but she's still not at school.

I don't dare ask her why. It feels intrusive somehow.

I'm walking back from the library on Thursday after lunch when I spot Ben and the others hiding behind the bleachers. I pause in my step.

I can smell the weed from all the way over here.

I should walk away and leave them to it, but before I know it, my heels sink into the grass. My treacherous feet carry me over to where they stand.

Matt spots me first, raising his eyebrows in surprise. He nudges April next to him and lifts his chin.

She sneers at me. "Should you fraternize with poor kids like us? What would your rich football friends say?"

Her words sting, but I don't let it show. I won't let her intimidate me with her prickly personality. I understand her animosity toward me, even if it isn't warranted.

Ben is sitting on a boulder, watching me while he smokes. I make my way over to him and heave myself up. It takes a few attempts.

He sucks on the joint, pinching it between two tattooed fingers. "Want some?" he asks, holding it out to me.

I wrinkle my nose. "No, thanks."

Shrugging, he offers it to Josh. "Your loss, princess."

I pull my skirt down to cover more of my bare thighs. I look so out of place in my yellow sundress with its thin spaghetti straps. The boys wear their usual ripped, black jeans and T-shirt combo.

Everything is black.

Ben sports scuffed black and white Vans, and April is dressed in a black knit dress with fishnet stockings and Chucks.

Steph, with her brown and unruly curls, wears leather pants and a black crop top with a print of Kurt Cobain on the front. Nina is similarly dressed in skinny, black jeans and a hooded, dark gray jumper with the arms cut out. Her combat boots have neon green laces. It's the only dash of color in a sea of black.

Matt breaks the silence when he winks and says, "Your fruit bowl turned out good."

I feel a blush creep up my neck. I don't know what made me flick paint on him.

April rolls her eyes as he accepts the joint from Steph. "Thanks."

She looks at me, and the tip glows orange when she takes a deep drag. "Why are you really here?"

*Good question.*

My eyes dance over their little group while I ask myself what possessed me to come over. I'm very different from them. They probably don't want me here, but I feel drawn to them for reasons I can't explain.

"I don't know," I answer truthfully.

April lifts her chin, blowing smoke in the air.

"Lay off her, April," Steph warns before offering me a reassuring smile. "Ignore April. She needs to get laid."

Returning her smile, I hold my hand out for the joint. "I changed my mind."

April's eyebrows shoot up.

"Let her have some," Ben says, drawing his leg up and resting his elbow on the knee. I like his deep, baritone voice. That, and his tanned arms. Even his hands are sexy.

I reach out and touch his leather wristbands, tracing my fingers along his wrist. My eyes are drawn to the smatter of dark hairs on his arm.

He looks up in surprise, and I blush fiercely, drawing my hand back. Sometimes, I don't think before I do stupid shit.

"Sorry," I mumble.

"It's okay, princess." He passes me the joint, and I take it gingerly. My palms are clammy with nerves as I bring it to my lips. I mimic April and take a deep drag, inhaling the smoke into my lungs. I've never done this before, but some deep part of me wants to fit in with these people.

They all laugh when I start coughing violently. My throat burns, and my eyes water as I hack up a lung.

Ben takes the joint from me and places it between his lips, his eyes crinkling with mirth. The tip sparks orange, crackling in the silence while we gaze at each other.

Steph interrupts our moment. "Where's lover boy?"

I reluctantly look away from Ben's brown eyes, shrugging. "We broke up."

Ben's gaze warms my skin.

They all exchange glances, communicating silently. I try not to feel uncomfortable, but it's difficult. I don't know these people.

I worry my lip as Ben removes a piece of weed from his tongue and flicks it off his finger. "Is Dallas okay? I haven't seen her around this week."

A shadow crosses his eyes. Heaving his big body off the boulder, he throws the joint down on the grass and crushes it beneath his heel. "She's unwell. She'll be back next week if she's feeling better."

They leave.

Steph smiles at me as she walks past, and Matt puts his warm hand on my shoulder, squeezing gently.

"See you around."

I stare after them, feeling lonely and confused.

# CHAPTER
## nine

## EMILY

I USUALLY LOVE Fridays during football season because I get to wear my cheer uniform to school to raise the school spirit ahead of the upcoming game.

That's not the case today. I feel out of place as I take my seat at the lunch table, reaching for my bottle of orange juice. I unscrew the lid as Jack, one of the cornerbacks, sits down next to me.

He turns his body to face me fully and grins. Taking a sip, I eye him as I swallow. Jack is dressed in his football jersey, and his brown hair is overdue for a haircut.

"I want to take you out," he says straight to the point, flashing a dimpled smile.

It's impossible not to smile back. Jack has a certain charm about him.

"Wow, you sure come on strong."

Leaning in close, he brushes my hair off my neck. His touch lingers and his eyes drop to my lips. The way he looks at me makes it difficult to breathe, and the hitch in my breath doesn't go unnoticed. He smiles. "Can't fault a guy for trying."

I feel eyes on me, and I search the room for the source. Ben's jaw is like concrete while he stares at me with furrowed brows.

I look away and bring my attention back to Jack. His hot breath fans my lips as I whisper, "I'm not dating right now."

It's too soon. I'm not sure how I feel about Jack's attention.

He's attractive with his jade eyes and dimpled smile. My parents would approve of him. Still, I'm drawn to the brooding boy with green hair and tattoos.

Undeterred, Jack grins and puts his heavy arm over my shoulder.

Jamie drops down in the seat opposite, eyeing Jack's arm around me with a frown but makes no comment. He's Rick's best friend. The breakup is still fresh, so Jamie's not impressed that his teammate is moving in on his best friend's girl so soon. Even if I'm not technically Rick's girl anymore.

My eyes soon stray, and I find myself locked in Ben's gaze. He leans in, whispering something to Steph before pushing his chair back. Striding out without a backward glance, he throws his entire dinner tray in the trash.

My eyes trail over his tense, broad shoulders, and his ass in those black denim jeans that leave very little to the imagination. *God, he's fucking delicious.*

I excuse myself, ignoring Jack's puppy eyes, and follow Ben outside to his car.

Where is he off to in the middle of the day?

Before I can talk myself out of it or even question what I'm doing, I rush forward, opening the car door.

Ben looks up in surprise as I drop down in the passenger seat, pulling the door shut. I fasten my seatbelt with trembling hands, my heart racing in my chest.

He stares at me in wide-eyed disbelief, one hand on the steering wheel, his body half-turned. "What are you doing, princess?"

*Thud. Thud.*

My heart beats heavily against my chest like it wants to escape its confines. "I don't know. Take me somewhere."

Ben watches me for a moment, then cranks his car. His tattooed hand engulfs the gearstick as he puts it in drive and pulls away, spinning the wheel with his palm. Everything about him is so untamed and unpolished.

He drives a red, rusty old mustang, far different from my Range Rover. My eyes dance over the cracked leather interior. Ben keeps it tidy. It smells of him—cinnamon, citrus, and leather mixed with something uniquely him.

I studiously ignore the pulse in my ear while I watch him drive. He drums his fingers on the steering wheel and drags his free hand through his green hair, mussing it up. He glances at me. "Not quite the horse and carriage you're used to, huh?"

"I like your car," I reply honestly. It may not be a sports car, but that's the charm. It has character.

Ben shoots me a dubious look. I don't miss the brief flash of vulnerability in his eyes before he slams his mask back in place. "It works and it gets me where I need to go."

We fall silent, but it's a comfortable silence.

I gesture to his stereo. "May I?"

He keeps his eyes on the road as he nods. "Sure. CDs are in the glovebox."

Looking through his collection of rock albums, I settle for Closer by Kings of Leon. I press play and turn up the volume, then lean my head on the window.

Ben keeps glancing at me and I pretend I don't notice. I secretly love how his attention makes me feel. I like that he's intrigued by me.

We pull up at a lookout spot about half an hour's drive from home. Ben parks the car and cuts the engine but makes no move to exit the car. He leans back against the driver's door, puts his foot on the seat, and rests his elbow on his knee.

Shifting in my seat, I mirror his body language.

Ben searches my face before dragging his eyes down my body and then back up again. His gaze sweeps over every inch of me. My eyes and lips. The soft curve of my breasts. My bare legs. Then back up to my eyes.

My panties are damp as I squeeze my thighs together to relieve the ache.

Ben is drinking me up, undressing me with his eyes. The

tension-filled silence stretches on. We are entirely alone out here in his car, and there are no sounds except for the occasional bird caw in the distance.

Biting my lip, I decide to take something for myself for once.

*I want Ben.*

I hold his gaze as I slowly crawl to him and straddle his lap on the bench seat. Ben doesn't object. The rough fabric of his denim jeans feels delicious against my bare thighs beneath my cheer skirt. My heart beats loudly in my ears, pounding in time with the throbbing between my legs.

Leaning his head back, he looks up at me through lowered eyelids, and the intensity in his dark eyes makes my nipples harden.

Taking charge, I grab his tattooed hands and place them on my hips. I grind down on him. The heat of his palms burns all the way down to my core, and his fingers dig into my flesh as I roll my hips again.

I whimper with need when his hard cock in his jeans rubs against my throbbing clit. My head falls back on a moan. I grip his shoulders and begin to ride him through our layers of clothing. "God, Ben…"

He lets go of my waist and his tattooed hands disappear beneath my skirt. Dragging his fingers up my thighs, he hooks my damp panties, teasing my wet slit.

I make a needy noise in the back of my throat. It never felt like this with Rick.

"What do you want, princess?" His voice is thick with lust, but he won't take things further until I ask him to.

I want him to destroy me with his touch. Burn me to ashes with his hot lips.

"I want you," I whisper into his ear, my lips curving in a smile.

His cock twitches in his jeans.

*I might die if he doesn't touch me soon.*

Searching my eyes for any signs of uncertainty, he fists my blonde hair.

He won't find any.

His eyes fall to my lips and linger. "Take me out."

I shiver, my clit throbbing painfully. I make quick work of his leather belt and zipper, freeing his hard length. It's silky and heavy in my hand. I don't recognize this side of myself that's so eager to please.

I stroke him once, then twice. Tightening his grip on my hair, he groans deep in his chest. I want him to make that sound again, so I stroke him a third time.

He wets his lips. "Suck me, baby."

Shifting off his lap and holding his heavy gaze, I lean down. My lips brush over his bulbous head. I want to taste him so badly. His big cock is throbbing in my hand, and Ben's thumb is brushing over my bottom lip.

"I can't wait to see these sexy lips wrapped around my dick." He dips his thumb into my mouth, and I give him a preview as I suck it deeper, batting my eyelashes. He groans, pushing down on my lip. I stick my tongue out and flatten it, looking up at Ben with my best doe-eyes.

Fisting his thick shaft with his tattooed hand, he rubs the head over my tongue. "Fuck baby, keep looking at me like that!"

My core clenches while he repeatedly slaps his dick on my tongue before guiding me down on his cock with a firm hand in my hair. Ben shows me exactly what he wants and how he wants it.

He makes a choked sound when I take him deeper, my lips stretched thin around his thick length.

"*Fuck,*" he groans, brushing my hair away from my face so he can watch me fist his shaft. I suck hard, hollowing my cheeks and moaning around his length. I bob on his cock, pausing every so often to slap it on my tongue because I love the reaction I get from him when I do.

My panties are soaked as I reach down to rub my throbbing clit. I need to ease the ache.

"You're so fucking hot," he growls, brushing his thumb over

my stretched thin lips. "I've fantasized about this so many fucking times."

Releasing him with a pop, I look up at him through my long lashes. "Don't hold back on me, Ben. I want it all."

I dive back down before he has a chance to reply, sucking greedily and moaning around his length every time he hits the back of my throat. I don't recognize this side of myself, but I like it a fucking lot.

"Fuck, baby…" His fingers are in my hair, and he fists the blonde strands with both hands as he takes control, thrusting into my mouth. "That's it!"

Drool slips past my stretched lips while I gag. I'm close to coming already, I'm that turned on. This is how roughly Rick handled Dallas, and I wished then that Rick would touch me like that too.

I moan even as the tears stream down my cheeks, and I'm left with no choice but to swallow around his thick head. I feel him down my throat. My fingers pick up the pace, rubbing my clit so fiercely it tethers on pain. Fuck, I'm so close. *So fucking close.*

Releasing my hair, Ben smacks my hand away. "I'm getting you off!" Then his hand is back in my hair, forcing me down on his cock once again. "Fuck, yes, princess. Suck me just like that. Good girl!"

It turns out I quite like being called a good girl while my mouth is stuffed with cock.

I suck him harder and faster until he comes down my throat. My scalp screams in pain from his tight grip on my hair while I greedily swallow down his salty cum.

Catching his breath, he watches me lick his shaft in long strokes and suck on the head like it's my favorite lollypop.

Right now, it is.

"Good girl," he whispers huskily, stroking his fingers down my face to cup my jaw. It's a tender touch, so unlike a minute ago.

Brushing the pad of his thumb over my swollen bottom lip, he mutters, "What are you doing to me?" His eyes search my face before he straightens and tucks himself in. When he's done, he turns his brown eyes on me, and I feel it down to my soaking, wet core.

"Lay down on your back, princess. Knees up high."

Heat sinks to my clit at the command in his voice and I slowly scoot down on the bench seat. I lie back, holding my breath as Ben crawls on top of me. Resting his elbows on either side of my head, he takes me in beneath him as if I'm a vision worth memorizing.

I squirm under his weight, seeking more pressure. More of everything.

"Be still, baby. I'll take good care of you." His lips connect with mine and he wastes no time deepening the kiss, swallowing my soft gasps. I feel the press of his soft lips, warm tongue, and hot breath down to my toes. They curl in my shoes.

It's a kiss that starts out slow but soon becomes frenzied as the chains on his control snap. He kisses me harder and his touch turns rougher when I dig my nails into his biceps. My clit pulsates. Sparks of desire shoot down to my pussy. Ben groans into my mouth and bites my lip. Tasting blood, I pull him to me with such force our teeth clash.

"Fuck," he breathes into my mouth, running his hands all over my body. Exploring my every curve. I'm too lost in him to care that we're out in the open.

I tear my lips from his, throwing my head back with a moan when he yanks up my cheer top and sports bra. The cool air slaps my naked tits before the heat of his mouth envelopes my nipple, and he tugs the rosy bud between his teeth. It's not gentle. I cry out in surprise, and Ben soothes the sting with his warm tongue, lapping at the hardened peak. I love how he touches me. He's rough, grabbing me a little too hard.

Squeezing my breast in his big palm to the point of pain, he sucks on my hard nipple. It's primal and possessive. I never want gentle hands on me again.

"Please, Ben." I'm moaning and rocking against him, seeking

pressure. One of his calloused hands is wrapped around my throat while the other is squeezing my tit. "Please…"

"Shhh." He crawls down my body and settles between my legs. I lean up on my elbows, so I can watch him.

Inching my cheer skirt up until it pools around my waist, he looks down at the briefs I have on. They're a far cry from the usual silk and lace I like to wear, but I can't do tumbles and back-flips in a thong.

With my bottom lip trapped between my teeth, I take in the sight of him palming my mound. His green hair flops in his eyes. I long to run my fingers through the strands and tug sharply until he growls.

It turns me the fuck on to see his tattooed hand cup my pussy possessively over the fabric of my underwear like he owns me.

God knows, at this moment, he does.

Whimpering with need, I rock against him while palming my breasts and tweaking my sore nipples. Ben watches me play with my tits. He slowly begins to inch my briefs down my legs before throwing them on the steering wheel behind him. Lowering his eyes to my wet slit, he wets his lips in anticipation.

I open my legs and bring my knees up high like he asked. I can't believe I'm fully bared to him like this with my soaking wet pussy and ass on full display. I was never this brazen with Rick.

Ben screws his face up like he's in actual pain. *"Fuck!"* he groans, still staring at my wet cunt. It's a tortured sound, filled with desire and longing. "Prettiest fucking pussy I've ever seen."

I bury my fingers in his green hair, unable to resist the urge to touch it. It's as smooth as I imagined. I tug on the strands until I hear him hiss. "Stop playing with me, Ben."

Chuckling deeply, a look of mischief flashes across his eyes. "Maybe I won't let you come. I'll just keep you on edge, princess."

*Jackass.*

Tightening my grip on his hair, I buck up, rocking my pussy against his chin. The scratchy stubble on his jaw feels incredible against the inside of my thighs.

Ben's devilish smile spells trouble. He dips his chin, eyes on me, and laps at my center. His pierced tongue buries in my wet slit. I cry out in pleasure as my body comes alive with sensation. My hips roll and I grip his hair in a vice, chasing the release I've been denied for too long.

"Ben!" I moan, falling back on the seat and breathing hard. He spreads my thighs even wider until I'm lying with one foot on the dash and the other rests on the back of the seat.

"Oh god!" I cry out when he plunges his tongue inside me, fucking me with it like it's his cock and rubbing my clit with his fingers until I see stars. He then swaps and dips his thick fingers inside me and sucks my clit into his mouth.

"Oh god, oh god, oh god!" I chant, delirious with pleasure. The windows are steamed up from my panting breaths. Ben knows exactly what he's doing with his skillful tongue.

"You're such a good girl," he praises, watching his fingers move in and out of me. I'm dripping on his leather seat. "Tell me how much you love it when I fuck you with my fingers, princess."

*God, his dirty words...* I moan so loudly it shocks me. "Ben, please. Please!"

Removing his fingers, he sucks them clean, groaning deep in his throat. My body rocks back on the seat when he plunges three fingers back inside my tight pussy.

It hurts in the best way possible.

I buck against him, crying out in a heady mix of pain and pleasure. I love that he doesn't touch me like a porcelain doll.

"I didn't hear you, princess," he mocks, slapping my nipple. The sharp sting makes me gasp and squeeze around his fingers. He's so filthy. Rick never touched me like this.

"You like that, huh?" Ben chuckles knowingly, slapping my nipple again. Much harder this time. He pinches it painfully before doing the same to my other nipple.

It's too much. There's a chance I won't survive Ben.

"I love it!" I barely recognize my own voice.

*Smack!*

"You love what?"

I clench around him. "Jesus! I love it when you finger fuck me. Please, I need to come."

Ben smirks. "My name is not Jesus, but since you asked so nicely, Your Highness." He lowers his head back down and laps at me, faster and faster until I don't know my own name anymore. My body rocks on the cracked leather with every powerful thrust of his fingers.

Grabbing the top of the seat with one hand, I push against the glovebox with my other to keep myself from falling off. My eyes roll back. Fuck, I've never experienced anything close to the insane pleasure I'm lost in now.

Ben shifts, rubbing his finger over my puckered hole, and I tense. Rick never ventured near that area, and the new sensation is almost too much.

Sucking my clit between his teeth, Ben pushes his finger inside until it's knuckle-deep. It takes me over the edge. The feel of his finger in my ass is so forbidden that I explode around him. My back arches off the seat as the orgasm crashes over me violently like a burst dam. I shudder, moaning his name.

I'm lost in sensation.

*Lost in him.*

I lie spent, catching my breath. I've never come so hard in my life.

Ben sits back up, wiping his mouth. He looks smug in the way only a man can when he's ruined his woman.

*His woman.*

What am I thinking? I'm not his. We're not an item.

With that thought in mind, I sit back up and readjust my clothing.

I'm about to ask him to take me back when he opens the door. He steps outside and ducks his head back in. "Come on. Let's go for a walk."

———

Ben walks with determined steps while I struggle to keep up behind him. I can tell he knows the area well. We step off the path and walk through thick foliage, dodging and stepping over fallen branches. I do my best to keep up, grateful to be wearing my sneakers and not heels for once.

We reach a clearing, and a gasp slips from my lips as I come to a stop. We're standing at the edge of a cliff. Stretching out below is a carpet of fir trees. The sun sits low in the sky, not a cloud in sight.

"It's beautiful!" I whisper in awe.

Ben lowers his body down, legs dangling off the edge. I join him, and we sit in comfortable silence. It's quiet up here except for the breeze blowing through the trees and the occasional bird call.

"Dallas got attacked by one of her uncle's friends. He beat her up real bad. She's staying with me."

I look at him in surprise, unsure what to reply. He's placing his trust in me. I don't want to say or do the wrong thing in case I break this bubble we're in.

"I'm not letting her go back there," he growls, his jaw tense.

"We've been texting," I admit quietly.

"I know."

So they talk about me? I'm even more curious now.

"Do you miss him?" he asks after a beat of silence.

I furrow my brow. "Rick?"

He nods, searching my eyes.

I clear my throat. "We've known each other our whole lives. Our families are close. I have photographs of us when we were three years old in the paddling pool." I smile and pick up a small stick, throwing it over the cliff edge. "We used to live next door to each other, but Rick moved when his parents bought a bigger house."

Sighing, I meet his brown eyes. "It was easy with Rick. Comfortable. The answer to your question is yes. I miss our close friendship, but we were never in love. Not really. For the longest time, I was okay with that. Rick was too. But things have been different lately."

Scanning the horizon and watching an eagle swoop down, I shrug. "I want more. I don't want comfortable. I want passion. Pain even, if it means I feel alive."

I chance a look at Ben.

"You're different than I first thought."

I don't think I'll ever get used to the intensity in his dark eyes. When he looks at me, it's as if he sees all of me. Even the parts I try to hide from the world.

"How?" I ask quietly. It's strange to feel seen.

He looks sheepish as he scratches his chin.

"Oh no," I laugh. "I know the look in your eyes."

He chuckles. "Sorry."

"I can't believe that you, out of all people, buy into clichés." I scoff. But in truth, I'm amused and I can't stop smiling.

"Hey," he says, raising both hands placatingly, a wide smile spreading across his lips, "we're both cliches. You're the head cheerleader with the quarterback boyfriend." He points to himself. "Me? I'm the poor and angry emo kid with attitude issues."

We laugh together, then settle into a comfortable silence once more. I enjoy Ben's company, and I think he likes spending time with me too. At least, I hope he does. I feel more like myself sitting here on this cliff with him than I've ever done. For the first time, I like who I am.

# CHAPTER
## *ten*

## EMILY

DEAFENING cheers rise from the bleachers as the final whistle blows.

We're still on a winning streak.

Jack stalks over to me, rips his helmet off, and plants one on me. He's sweaty, but fuck it. His lips are soft and I'm on a high.

"That's what I'm fucking talking about, baby!" he whoops when he pulls back.

Rick lifts me up on his shoulders, parading me around on the football pitch. "We're on fire, Em. We're going all the way this year!"

I laugh, waving to Hailey on Jamie's shoulders. "You better! I'm not cheering for no losers."

Chuckling, he squeezes my bare thighs. "Do you doubt me, woman?"

"Are you gonna let me down anytime soon?" I laugh.

He high-fives a teammate. "I'm on a winning high. Let me enjoy it with my favorite girl on my shoulders."

"You stink. You realize that, right?"

After lowering me down, he wraps his arms around me and rubs himself on me. "It's the odor of success!"

I manage to free myself, squealing with laughter as I run and hide behind Jamie. "Save me. Rick is determined to smoke me out with his stink."

Hailey laughs from her spot on Jamie's shoulders. She's still waving her pom-poms. "You're on your own. I'm taking my sweaty man home for a roll in the sheets."

I wrinkle my nose. "Gross. Don't you want him to at least shower first?"

Jamie winks. "She loves being fucked by a sweaty star receiver."

I pretend to bork. "I'm out of here."

"Are you coming to the party tonight?" Hailey asks.

Grabbing my bag, I shake my head. "Not this time."

She pokes Jamie in the ear. "Let me down, babe." Her feet hit the grass and she eyes me as she tugs down her cheer skirt. "You never miss a party. "

I shrug, unscrewing the cap on my bottle of water. "I'm just not up for it this time."

"Fine, but I'm coming over tomorrow."

I grin, taking a sip. "It's a date."

———

Empty popcorn bowls lie discarded on the floor, and the movie credits rolled over an hour ago. Hailey has now made it her personal mission to fill me in on the latest gossip from last night's party.

She paints my pinky nail, her perfect brows furrowed in concentration. "There, done. Blow on your nails." She screws the lid back on.

"My nails look great. Why do I get them professionally done when I have you in my life?"

Hailey watches me, hesitating. "Em?"

I look up, still blowing on my nails.

"Amber was all over Rick at the party. They even went upstairs for a while."

"Huh." My heart squeezes. I'm happy for him—I truly am—

but I'm not stone-cold. We were together for two years. Of course, I feel a mixture of emotions.

"I didn't want you to find out at school tomorrow."

I continue blowing on my nails. "It's okay."

"Is it? Are you?" she whispers, placing her hand on my knee. I haven't told her about Ben and Dallas because I don't want her to make a big thing of it.

I smile reassuringly. My heart is feeling lighter already. "Trust me, I'm definitely okay. I want Rick to be happy."

Her eyes shine with sympathy as she presses her lips together. "I'm here if you need to talk."

There are a lot of things I need to tell her about, and my breakup with Rick doesn't fall into that category. The more I think about it, the lighter I feel. Worrying about Rick has been a heavy weight on my shoulders. He's moving on, and that can only be a good thing.

———

Dallas drops down in the seat next to me, opens her notebook and begins to copy the notes on the whiteboard. I stare at her in surprise before scanning the classroom for Hailey. She hasn't arrived yet.

Dallas digs in her pocket, pulling out a hair tie. She puts her hair up in a high ponytail while I stare at her creamy neck. She is yet to talk to me or look at me, most likely thinking I don't want to be seen with her in public. Am I really that shallow?

Sliding a piece of paper to me, she flashes a quick smile.

I pick it up and turn it over in my lap. It's not a piece of paper, after all. It's a photograph of Ben, seated on a stool in the bathroom with a towel over his bare shoulders, and his hair covered in green hair dye.

I lift my gaze and look at Dallas questioningly. "Why are you giving me a picture of Shrek?"

"Ha! Shrek! Good one," she sniggers. "It's a gift from Ben. He said it's an addition to the stalker collage you keep of him in your locker. This way, he gets to control the narrative." Her lips twitch.

I stare incredulously at the photograph in my lap for a long minute, then burst out laughing, startling a couple of students nearby

"Do you want to do something tonight?"

My laughter dies in my throat and I search her blue eyes. "I have cheer practice, but I'm free after that."

"Good." She smiles, pushing her chair back. "The abandoned warehouse at seven. Be there." Standing up, she walks over to her usual seat. I stare after her, missing her blue eyes on me already. I'm about to call her back when the chair next to me scrapes against the floor, and Hailey drops down.

"Sorry, I'm late. Jamie dragged me into the supply closet for a quicky. That boy doesn't know the meaning of the word."

"Most women consider that a good thing, Hailey."

She nudges me playfully with her shoulder. "Do I look like I'm complaining?"

"No, you don't, but you should probably cover up those two hickeys on your neck," I reply, pointing them out.

She clamps a hand over her long throat. "You're kidding, right?"

"Nope," I say, popping the P.

She lets out a shriek so loud, the whole class looks over. She's oblivious, of course. "I'm gonna kill him!"

I rub her back soothingly. "Now, now, babe. Let's take a deep breath. There's no need for violence."

"Em, you're a genius." She grins and I feel bad for Jamie when she chuckles darkly like a villain in a movie. "I just won't cover them up and let Daddy see them. Jamie will be dead before sundown."

Poor Jamie. Hailey's father will go straight for the shotgun and ask questions later.

I laugh along with her, loving these rare moments when it's just the two of us.

———

At seven in the evening, I stand waiting outside the abandoned warehouse, fidgeting nervously with my dress. I wasn't sure what to put on, so I picked a midnight blue skater dress and paired it with black flats. I don't own the kind of clothes they do, so I stand out regardless of what I wear.

Everyone knows where the warehouse is, but I've never been before. It's notorious for attracting rough crowds, which should make me nervous, but I'm strangely excited.

I eventually see them turn a corner, walking toward me. They're all here, which makes me even more nervous. April doesn't like me and has made no secret of the fact. Nina has never spoken a word to me, and the others don't seem to care either way.

"You showed up." Dallas's smile is big.

"Here I am." I blush, cursing myself for being so awkward. It's strange to feel unsure of myself. I'm at the top of the food chain at school, but now I'm an outsider trying to fit in.

Ben leans in as he walks past. "Relax, princess."

I stare after him, ignoring Steph's knowing smirk. God, I can still feel his hands on my body and his tongue inside me.

"You skate?" I ask, quirking an eyebrow when I notice that they all carry skateboards.

Dallas nods. "I first started when I moved here. The others have skated since childhood. This is where they all met and became friends."

My eyebrows shoot up in surprise. "Here?" I take in the derelict building in front of us. It has seen better days. The paint is peeling off, there's graffiti on the walls everywhere I look, and the windows are broken or missing entirely. I struggle to imagine young kids playing here.

She laughs at my incredulity. "There's a skatepark inside the warehouse. It's been here for years. Come, you'll see."

I take it all in as I trail closely behind. The evening sunlight streams in through missing parts of the roof, reflecting off the wet puddles on the floor. I can hear music and people up ahead.

We enter a big open space. I turn in a circle, sweeping my eyes over the many different launch ramps, half pipes, and rails.

Ben hands me a skateboard and smirks when he sees the look on my face.

"You expect me to ride a skateboard?" I splutter, staring at it like it's a foreign object from an unknown planet. The idea is absurd.

Nina drops a duffel bag on the floor next to me. I take in her short black bob and purple lipstick as she pulls out a helmet and hands it to me. Next up are shin and elbow pads. I stare at them too. I must look confused because Matt chuckles.

He walks up to me with his hands in the front pockets of his black jeans. Eyes shining with amusement, he rocks back on his heels. I probably look foolish with my arms laden with stuff. "Do you need help with those?"

"Err?" I look to Dallas for help. She invited me here, after all.

Strapping on her helmet, she winks.

Much help she is.

Ben stops in front of me and takes the helmet from my hands, holding it up for me. "See this, princess? It's called a helmet, and it goes on your pretty head," he quips, placing it unceremoniously on my head.

I give him my best 'no shit' look, but on the inside, I'm engaged in full-on warfare with the butterflies in my stomach. Especially when I get a whiff of his cologne. Oblivious to my inner turmoil, he adjusts the strap, his brows furrowed in concentration. He's got a smatter of freckles on his nose that I didn't notice until now.

His eyes collide with mine for a brief second before he taps the helmet with his knuckles and winks. "You're good to go, Your Highness. You just need the shin and elbow pads."

I look at the offending items in my arms. My mother would die of shock if she saw me out here.

I follow their lead and strap on the protective gear. I'm clumsy and awkward, but I get there in the end. "Okay, what now?" I ask when we make our way over to the ramps.

It's a busy night, and plenty of young people are skating or practicing tricks on their BMX bikes. I recognize a couple of kids from school, who shoot me funny looks at first, wondering why I'm showing my face in this part of town.

Dallas makes the introductions. It's easy to be welcomed here. I know I stand out in this crowd, but no one cares. The same can't be said about my own friends. In the world of popular jocks, you're either in or out. You're either a somebody or a nobody. Here, none of it matters. No one cares who your parents are, what car your drive, or what shoes you wear.

It's an eye-opener.

The only thing that matters to these kids is to have a good time. And that's what I do. In fact, it's the most fun I've ever had.

"Ouch!" I'm groaning and laughing at the same time. My skirt lies pooled around my waist, flashing my panties to everyone. "Oh, great. I'm giving you all an eyeful." I sit back up and pull it down.

Matt grins. "I dig the little heart."

"Oh, shut up!" I laugh, picking dirt from the bleeding scrape on my knee.

Ben rolls to a stop and kicks the board up into his hand. "Looks sore. I saw you fall a couple of times."

"She's doing great!" Dallas says. "She's learned how to step on, balance, and push off."

Amused, I scoff. "I still need to work on the balance part."

Unscrewing the cap on the water bottle, Ben takes a sip before crouching down and pouring some over the scrape.

I hiss. "Fuck, Ben!"

"Maybe later." He winks, placing the lid back on and tossing the empty bottle into a nearby trash can.

Dallas helps me up. "Let's go again."

Groaning, I let her pull me along.

"Right, step on."

"Fine." I hold on to her shoulders, squealing and flapping my arms like a chicken when she steps out of reach.

"Now, push off."

"You're a tyrant, Dallas." I laugh, placing my foot down on the ground and pushing off. It doesn't take long until I'm rolling along the flat ground, still flapping my arms like a bird learning how to fly. "Dallas? How do I stop this thing?"

She's laughing behind me.

My eyes widen. I'm heading straight for April. "Oh, shit!" I flap my arms some more like that's going to slow me down. All it does is make a couple of kids laugh over by the rails. "April, lookout!"

Too late.

We crash to the ground.

"What the fuck, princess?" She laughs, shoving me off.

I stare up at the tall ceiling. "Where are the pearly gates?"

"You're not dead." Chuckling, she pushes up on her elbows. Her blonde hair sticks out from under the helmet.

"How do you make it look so easy?"

"What? Skating?" She brushes a strand of hair off her brow.

I nod, pushing up on my elbow. At least my panties aren't on full display this time.

She sits up on her knees and offers me a helping hand up. "Practice. Lots of fucking practice."

Grabbing the board, I point to a nearby bench. "I'm taking a breather."

"Em!" she calls after me.

I half turn, looking over my shoulder.

"You'll catch on in no time." She drops the board to the ground and skates off.

I take a seat and remove the helmet, shaking out my hair. Who thought I would ever do something like this?

Dallas sits down next to me and removes her own helmet.

She's silent, watching a guy perform a loop in the air. "Are you enjoying yourself?"

Her raven hair is pulled over one shoulder, drawing my gaze to her long neck and dewy skin.

"I am. Thank you for inviting me."

She shifts on the bench to face me. Reaching out, she caresses my cheek. Her touch is hesitant and soft, just a brush of fingers. I feel it everywhere as my skin erupts in goosebumps.

Her blue eyes search mine, and my heart beats wildly in my ribcage when I lean into her touch. I want her to kiss me. I long for it so much that my body aches with need.

Dallas traces her fingers down my cheek until I feel her touch on my tingly lips. Brushing her thumb over my bottom lip, she pulls it away from my teeth before pressing down, causing a spark of desire to shoot down my core. "You're so beautiful."

I doubt that. My hair is a sweaty, matted mess and my make-up is smudged. I'm covered in dirt and I'm bleeding on my knees and elbows, but she still looks at me as if I'm the most beautiful thing she's ever seen.

Leaning in slowly, she gives me the option to pull away.

I don't.

I want her to kiss me more than I need the air I breathe.

She's so close.

Her hot breath hits my skin a brief second before she presses her plump, soft lips to mine.

I gasp and Dallas takes it as an invitation to deepen the kiss, caressing my tongue with hers. My body comes alive, and I moan into her mouth. She smiles against my lips, plunging her tongue back inside. I need to touch her. Feel her. Make her mine. My hands bury in her raven hair, fisting the silky strands. She smells of coconut shampoo and watermelon lip balm.

Cupping my jaw, she guides the kiss, tasting me like the finest wine. So many emotions fight for space inside of me. It's my first time kissing a girl. It feels right, but I worry about Ben. What will he think? Does Dallas know what happened between us in the car? I suspect that she does, which confuses me more. I want them both, and I don't care how greedy that makes me.

I run my hand down her neck, past her collarbone, and brush my fingers over her smooth cleavage. I moan with need. God, we have to find somewhere more private, so I can touch her.

*Feel her.*

She breaks the kiss, breathing hard while I sit with my hand suspended mid-air, pulsating painfully between my legs. Her face is flushed, and mine is too. The air around us crackles with sexual tension.

She breaks eye contact first, nudging her head toward the ramp. "Come on. We're not leaving until you have a go at the ramp."

I stare after her in surprise as she makes her way over to the boys. Ben pushes off, rolling down the ramp with skilled ease.

I throw my head back on a groan and grab my helmet. Putting it back on, I grumble to myself. Dallas Garcia is going to be the death of me if the ramp doesn't kill me first.

# CHAPTER
## *eleven*

## DALLAS

"HERE," Ben says, handing me the controller, "you and Matt are up."

We're playing Halo in his living room, sprawled out on the couches.

"Just one second, let me get some snacks first." Leaning over the coffee table littered with chip bowls and empty candy wrappers, I grab a bowl of Jalapeno cheddar balls.

"They're for everyone, you know?" Steph laughs, quirking an eyebrow.

"I'm not sharing these. You know I'm like a mama bear around Jalapeno flavored cheddar balls." I gesture to the bowls on the coffee table. "There are five other bowls there. Don't be greedy." I lean back and pop a cheddar ball in my mouth.

I've healed from my physical injuries, but there's no cure for the shame. I'm grateful it only happened one time. If Ben hadn't got me out and offered me a place to stay…

I shudder.

It's been two weeks since that night. Ben offered to sleep on the couch in his bedroom, but it sags in the middle and is too small for his tall frame, so we share his bed. It's cramped, but I don't mind. Anything is better than my uncle's place.

"Are you okay?" Ben asks, watching me closely.

I swallow the cheese ball, avoiding eye contact. "I'm fine."

Ben hasn't touched me sexually since that night, and I know it's because of a certain blonde.

Picking my character on the screen, I smile as I recall how sketchy he was when he returned from taking her to the lookout spot the other day. It's not like him to protect the women he fucks, but he's been surprisingly tight-lipped about what happened between them, which tells me two things: something did happen, and he likes her.

*He may have even fallen for her.*

I don't know what it is about Emily, but she's slowly digging her claws deeper into us both.

"When are you bringing Princess around for the threesome? We added more money to the pot the other day," Josh says, interrupting my thoughts.

Oh, yes, the bet.

Nina, slouching on the couch, rolls her head. "I told you, she'll never go for it. She's too fucking prissy."

Josh chuckles, running a hand through his tousled, black hair. "More money for me when she spreads those fine legs."

"It's in the bag," Ben cuts in, surprising me. He's lying on the floor next to my feet.

"Yeah? When? You've not grown soft on us and changed your mind, have you?"

"Yeah? When Ben?" April taunts from her spot on the floor between Matt's legs. The two of them finally hooked up.

Ben scoffs and sits up, pulling his T-shirt down and reaching for the rolled joint on the coffee table. He lights it up, speaking with the joint hanging off his bottom lip. "I'm just warming her up a little." He smirks, then takes a deep drag and motions for me to lean down.

I do.

Gripping the back of my neck and bringing me close, he blows smoke into my mouth. I inhale, holding it in my lungs before blowing it out in his smirking face. When he grins, I push his face back with my hand.

Ben falls back on the floor and chuckles to himself. The tip of his joint glows orange as he takes another drag.

"I heard you took her out for a romantic trip to the lookout," Steph teases, wagging her eyebrows. In her hands is a bottle of tequila.

Ben blows out a cloud of smoke and shrugs. "She was bored."

"Bored? Uh-huh." Steph looks at me, eyes sparkling. "What about you then, Dallas? What's your excuse for kissing her at the skatepark?"

I glare at her. Why does she have to drop me in it?

She smirks knowingly, pouring us all shots. I accept mine and throw it back, wincing. "What Ben said." I nod to him on the floor. "Groundwork."

Ben's lips quirk while Steph necks her own drink.

"Whatever, you're both full of shit!"

Nina and Josh laugh. Well, fuck them.

"Dell, you're not even trying. Fuck, I've killed you five times now!" Matt groans in exasperation.

He's right. My character is lying in a pool of blood.

"Here," April says, reaching for the controller in my hand, "I'll kick his ass."

I hand it to her as Steph joins me on the couch and drops her phone in my lap with a mischievous smile. I raise my brow.

*Emily Brooks joined the group chat*

Steph: Hey, girl!

Emily: Hi, how's it going?

Steph replied to her question with the photograph she took of Ben blowing smoke into my mouth earlier.

Steph: Why don't you join us?

My head snaps up, and Steph taps the phone in my hand with a smirk. "Keep reading."

Emily: Are you sure?

Steph: Fuck, we can do with your crazy. Ben looks like a sad puppy. Dallas has hearty eyes and stares at her phone every five minutes. Don't tell me you haven't got anything to do with that...

I laugh. "Fuck you, Steph. I don't have hearty eyes, and I don't stare at my phone every five minutes!"

She suppresses a smile. "Maybe not in the last half hour."

Ben shoots upright, scrolling through his own phone. He glares at Steph. "A sad puppy, Steph? Really?"

Amused, Matt grins. "You do kind of look like a sad puppy."

"Shit!" Ben gets to his feet. "She's on her fucking way." He walks to his bedroom and shuts the door behind him.

"What was that about?" I ask.

Matt leans forward in his seat. I'm surprised the controller in his hand doesn't break with how aggressively he presses those buttons. "He's probably rubbing one out before she gets here, so he doesn't shoot his load too soon."

Steph groans. "Urgh! Gross, Matt."

Chuckling, I bring my attention back to the group chat.

Emily: Okay, sure. I'll be there soon. What's the address?

My eyes skate up to Ben's closed bedroom door. This thing between us is about more than a dare. We can't deny it anymore. Why else does the thought of her spending the evening with us make my hands clammy? What if she doesn't have a good time? What if she wishes she could spend the evening with her rich football friends instead of our little group of misfits.

It feels like forever while we sit and wait for Emily to arrive.

April beats Matt in the game twice. He curses loudly and throws the controller to Josh, who catches it one-handed.

"Beat her ass! Don't fucking disappoint me, man."

"You've got it, chief." Josh grins.

Ben rejoins us in the living room, freshly showered and changed.

I quirk an eyebrow at him, which he studiously ignores as he goes about picking up the empty plastic cups and pizza boxes off the floor.

"Dude, why the fuck are you cleaning?" Matt asks, looking at him like he's grown three heads.

April doesn't stop shooting as she replies, "His girl is coming over, and he wants to make a good impression, Matt. You could take a page out of his book, you know? You would get laid more often."

"Fuck!" Josh shouts, startling Nina next to him. "Sorry, dude," he says to Matt, passing the controller to Steph, who holds her hand out for a go. "April is fucking brutal!"

April sticks her tongue out to Josh. "I thought this was a boys' game?"

Standing up, he flips her off and walks over to the coffee table. He pours himself another shot, ignoring her gleeful smile.

"You've got it wrong, though," Nina says to April, popping her gum. "She's not just Ben's girl. She's Dallas's girl too."

"Will you all shut the fuck up!" Ben growls, picking up an empty beer bottle. "She's not anyone's girl, alright! It's a fucking bet!"

The others exchange glances, communicating silently.

It's time to lighten the mood, so I joke, "You're just worried I'll make her come first and ruin your reputation when we get her in bed. I'm a woman, after all. I know the female anatomy better than you."

He shoots me an incredulous look. "I never heard you complain."

Well, I can't argue with that. Ben is good in bed, and he knows it.

He walks around the back of the couch and leans in, whispering in my ear, "You stand no chance. So just admit defeat."

I gasp in mock outrage. "Not a fucking chance!"

The doorbell rings, and we both freeze, staring at each other. Ben jogs over to let her in, leaning his shoulder on the doorway. He lays it on thick with his trademark smirk. Ben has game when he wants to and doesn't struggle to get laid. When I first met him, his bedroom was a revolving door of girls. Things have calmed down since Emily stepped on the scene, and I can see why as she walks inside, looking around nervously. Ben's eyes follow her as if she's the most important person in the room. If he ever falls for a girl, it will be her.

Worst of all? The same emotions are reflected in my own eyes.

Emily wrings her hands and sweeps her doe-eyes over the room, lingering on Ben's broad form as he walks past. She looks nervous and unsure.

April waves the Xbox controller in the air. "We're playing Halo. Do you know how to play?"

Her eyebrows shoot up. "Rick taught me."

Weirdly, a twinge of jealousy knots my stomach at the mention of his name. I look over at Ben. Sure enough, his jaw ticks too.

*Interesting.*

"Awesome," April replies, holding the controller out for Emily to take. "Why don't you have a go? Show us what you're made of."

Josh tries to grab the controller in Steph's hands. "Give me that."

Steph scoffs. "Fuck off, Josh. I invited her, so I'm playing."

They bicker back and forth as Princess takes the offered controller from April.

I scoot over and pat the seat next to me.

She sits down, glancing at me briefly before selecting her character on the screen. Her perfume is soft and floral, and her bare thigh presses against mine.

I push back.

"Are we doing this then?" she asks, her long hair teasing my arm when she leans over me to speak to Steph.

Ben hands her a shot. "A little something to warm you up first."

He winks and I roll my eyes. He *is* laying it on thick tonight.

Emily breathes out a soft thank you as she gets herself comfortable on the floor in front of our feet. Her eyes don't stray far from Ben when he lies down next to her. I don't have to look to know that she's discreetly eyeing the sliver of tanned skin and the dark happy trail on his stomach where his gray T-shirt has ridden up.

I smile. This is going to be fun.

Emily necks the shot, grimacing. "Shit, you guys don't mess around with your alcohol, do you?"

Ben smirks. "Can't handle it, princess? What do the footballers make you drink? Cocktails?" His baritone voice is smooth and laced with honey.

April laughs before reaching up behind her and pulling Matt down for a kiss, moaning into his mouth.

Emily ignores them, staring at Ben with fire in her eyes. "Oh, I can handle it!"

My throat goes dry at the dark promise in her voice.

"If you're gonna fuck, do it someplace else!" Ben yells at Matt and April as he gets to his feet. He looks outraged.

April breaks away from Matt, a taunting smile on her face. "When has that ever stopped you? Or are you changing your tune because of tonight's fine company?"

Ben stares her down before striding off to the kitchen in a huff, his shoulders stiff.

Rising to her feet, Emily walks over to the coffee table and pours herself another shot. She swigs it, then refills the shot glass. "What are we waiting for? Let's play, Steph."

The girl in question throws me a smug look, leaning back against the couch. "Let's do this."

The game starts up, and we settle in to watch. Fifteen minutes later, we're staring in disbelief. Emily knows how to play.

"You make me hard, princess," Josh groans, palming himself before gesturing to Steph impatiently. "Give me that. You've hogged her long enough. It's the boys' turn to play."

Ben smacks him on the back of the head as he walks past. Handing Josh the remote, Steph shakes with laughter. The game starts up. Emily and Josh play in intense silence, both focused on the game.

Josh fares no better against Emily.

Always the troublemaker, Steph puts her arm around my shoulder. "Hey, Em," she calls out, winking at me.

I glare at her. I know that look in her eyes, and it's never good.

"Hmm?" Emily jumps up, frantically pushing the buttons on the controller. "Ha!" she shouts, grinning at Josh.

"Shit!" he curses, throwing the controller down on the floor.

Matt laughs. "Told you, man, these fucking women!"

"Sorry, did you say something?" Princess asks Steph, then looks at Josh and adds, "I was too busy whooping the baby's ass."

Josh shrugs while the rest of us laugh. "I should be offended, but you're too fucking hot, baby."

Clearing her throat, Steph smiles sweetly at Emily.

My hackles instantly rise and I sit up straighter.

"Are you up for a game of truth or dare?"

Ben's head shoots up off the floor and he stares at Steph, shaking his head subtly. He's suspicious too. I can see it when we exchange a loaded glance.

"Aren't we a bit old for that kind of game?" Emily asks carefully. I don't blame her. Whatever Steph is up to is not good news. She reeks of mischief.

Steph cocks her head and sweeps her tongue over her bottom lip. "Let's just say it's a more grown-up version of the game."

"Steph!" I hiss, glancing nervously at Emily. She'll never trust us if we come on too strong. It's not like she knows how crazy things can get around here and how far we tend to take things. Or that we don't have any inhibitions with each other.

"It's okay," Emily cuts in, interrupting what I was about to say. She squares her shoulders. "I'll play."

Ben meets my eyes, and I swallow thickly.

"It's okay, princess. We don't have to pla—"

"I want to."

I gulp. She never ceases to surprise me. My assumptions about her were wrong. She's not reserved and uptight. She's adventurous, playful, and curious.

"I'm warning you, it can get graphic," Steph smiles, looking like the cat who got the cream. Or, in this case, caught the helpless and unsuspecting canary.

Emily stares at her for a long minute before she nods. "I want to go first."

My heart picks up speed, beating painfully against my ribcage.

Are we really doing this?

Steph shrugs. "Whatever you want, princess." With a devilish smile, she looks at April. "Pour us shots. It's about to get interesting."

April rolls her eyes but gets up off the floor and proceeds to pour the shots.

I neck mine, watching Emily drink hers.

Our eyes collide and she looks away, pointing at Josh. "I want you to go down on Matt."

I choke on air, and Nina and Steph double over with laughter while Ben has the misfortune of spraying his tequila shot everywhere. He shakes his wet hands, staring down at his soaked T-shirt.

Josh's mouth hangs open; the surprise on his face is comical.

A smirk draws across Matt's face as he lifts an eyebrow. "Well, Josh, are you gonna look after me or not? Make me feel good."

Breaking out of his stupor and chuckling, Josh throws Princess an appreciative glance. "Wow. Just wow."

Emily's smile is smug.

"You want me to suck off Matt?" he points to himself, then Matt as if he's sure he misheard her and needs clarification.

I'm not the only one staring at Princess. She has us all in the palm of her hand, playing to her tune. I'm not sure what Steph had in mind when she challenged her, but I don't think she ever expected to see this dark side of Emily.

"Well," Josh drawls, adjusting the front of his jeans before continuing in a husky voice, "what the princess wants, she gets." To Matt he says seductively, "Are you ready to have your world rocked, lover boy?"

Nudging April to move, Matt leans back and spreads his legs wide, fingers interlaced behind his head. "Have at me, Josh. I'm all yours."

Emily looks on while Josh walks over and drops to his knees in front of Matt. For a split second, a look of uncertainty flicks across her face before she squeezes her thighs together, and then it's gone.

Ben is watching her too, and we exchange a look. *Princess is aroused.*

"Josh," Emily calls out.

He looks over at her questioningly.

"You have ten minutes to get him off. If you fail, you have to run naked down the hallway at school tomorrow."

I slap a palm over my mouth. *Fuck, this girl!*

Beside me, Steph is laughing too. It's too funny not to. Shaking his head, Josh mumbles about how girls like Emily are apex predators. His fingers expertly undo Matt's belt and he pulls down the zipper, heightening the anticipation in the room.

Matt smirks, his ass lifting off the chair to make it easier for Josh to pull down his jeans and boxers. His cock springs free—big and proud—and Josh wastes no time palming it.

I peer over at Emily. The look in her eyes is something else entirely as she watches the scene unfold with her bottom lip trapped between her teeth.

The puppeteer and her puppets.

Leaning forward, Josh takes Matt's cock in his mouth, groaning deeply.

*"Fuck,"* Matt grunts, dropping his hands from behind his head and gripping the armrest at his sides. Josh is no stranger to dick. He came out as bisexual before I moved here, but Princess doesn't know that. Matt, on the other hand, just likes to have his dick sucked. He doesn't care who does the sucking as long as he gets off.

There's no teasing on Josh's part. No pausing to suck leisurely on the head. It's a race to climax. His head bobs while he works the length with his big hand.

Meanwhile, Ben doesn't take his eyes off Princess.

I watch her too. She enjoys this game, like she did the time I fucked Rick in front of her. Her eyes sparkle as the scene unfolds. She reminds me of something caged in the dark for a long time that's been let out to play.

Matt grabs hold of Josh's short hair and starts to thrust into his mouth, a deep groan rumbling in his throat. "Oh, fuck!"

It's not long before his eyes roll back as he comes. Shoving Josh down on his dick, he stiffens, grunting with pleasure. It's hot as hell to watch.

When Matt finally loosens his grip, Josh stands back up and wipes his mouth. "Happy, princess?"

"Very." She curls a finger at him in a 'come here' gesture while Matt tucks himself away. Josh's eyebrows shoot up, but he doesn't say anything as he walks over to her. With a grin, she pulls him down by the back of his neck and kisses him. Josh grunts in surprise, hands held up by his sides. His initial shock doesn't last long before he kisses her back with equal fervor. As we watch, she sucks on his tongue, fingers tangled in his short hair. Diving back in, she devours his mouth.

A muscle ticks in Ben's jaw while his hands fist rhythmically on his thighs. He's jealous. I keep quiet, willing Ben to do the same. I was there that night with Emily and Rick. This new side of her is one she needs to explore. Ben knows it too, since he lets it go without comment.

Princess pulls back, humming in satisfaction before looking over at Matt and purring in a sugary voice, "You taste good."

For a brief second, no one makes a noise, and then the room erupts with laughter. This girl never ceases to surprise us.

Josh drops down in his seat and rubs his chin in thought, flashing a devilish smile. "Okay, princess. You challenged me, so it's my turn. You didn't technically give me the option to choose between truth or dare, but I forgive you." He winks. "I'm feeling kind tonight, so I'll let you choose. Truth or dare?"

"Dare." The awkward girl who wrung her hands when she first arrived is nowhere to be seen, and the girl that sits in front of us now holds her chin high. I try hard not to stare at her peaked nipples, visible through the thin fabric of her light blue dress.

Josh settles his eyes on me, grinning like the devil. "Fuck Dallas."

My heart stops and I glare at Josh. Emily has never been with a girl before. Somehow, I doubt she wants her first time to be in a room full of people for a stupid dare.

"Here, on the couch?" Princess asks.

I gulp. *She wouldn't, would she?*

"Sure." Josh shrugs. He doesn't think she'll go through with it.

Steph gestures for Nina to move, and I stare after them as they sit down on the floor.

Emily walks over to me, and for the first time tonight, I feel uncertain. I don't want her to be uncomfortable. It matters to me that she likes my friends and feels welcome here. I'm painfully aware that most normal people don't do this.

"To clarify, Princess is gonna fuck you, Dallas. Not the other way around, so keep your hands to yourself. If I see you touch her, it'll be you streaking naked down the hallway tomorrow." Josh says, looking smug.

I turn to Emily. "You don't have to do th—"

"Shhh!" She silences me with a finger pressed to my lips, causing my heart to hammer as I stare at her.

Slowly sliding down the shoulder straps, she holds my gaze, and the room draws in a collective gasp when her dress falls around her feet. Emily is a vision in white lace.

Eyes darkening, she trails a manicured nail over her supple breasts, circling her nipple through the lace of her bra.

If she wants my attention, she has it.

She places her knee between my legs and leans over me. As she grabs hold of the back of the couch, her tits strain against the lacy bra. My mouth waters and I dig my nails into the couch to stop myself from pulling down the cups and sucking on her nipples.

Emily runs her nails over my collarbone and dips a finger inside my cleavage. "Remember the time I spied on you with Lauren in the bathroom?"

*How can I forget?*

She leans in closer, and her lips brush my ear as she whispers, "I think about it when I fuck myself at night."

Chest heaving, I dig my nails in further.

"Take your clothes off," she orders, walking over to the coffee table and pouring two shots.

I don't take my eyes off her while I remove my clothes, shivering with nerves.

Emily downs the first shot before arching her back and pouring the second shot down her front. It soaks through the lace of her bra, revealing her rosy nipples. She chucks the shot glass on the floor, and the sudden sound of smashing glass startles us all. Leaning over me again, she pushes her ample tits in my face. "Lick the tequila off my skin."

*Jesus…*

The boys groan.

I grip her tightly by the hips, run my tongue over her perfect tits and suck on her peaked nipple through the fabric before teasing it with my teeth.

Her smooth skin erupts in goosebumps. The room is deadly silent except for her needy whimpers.

Pushing off the couch, she circles a finger in the air. "Turn around. Hands in front of you at all times."

Turning and placing my hands on the back of the couch as instructed, I feel her move behind me. My clit pulsates with its own heartbeat and my nipples ache as I arch my back, pressing my tits against the rough fabric on the couch.

A sharp sting makes me hiss. *She bit my ass...*

Hushing me, she begins massaging the tender bite mark, soothing it with firm squeezes. I moan in stunned surprise. Emily slides her fingers down the creamy globe until she's dangerously close to my soaking center.

I need to feel her, so I push back against her hand, pleading without words.

"So eager," she mocks, squeezing my ass cheek one more time before smacking it hard. I cry out at the delicious sting, and she smacks me twice more with such force that I rock against the seat.

Matt groans, telling the others how hot it is, but I'm too lost to care that we have an audience.

I shiver in anticipation when Emily shifts behind me. My body is alive in a way it's never been before.

She pulls me back by my hips and runs her palm over my arched back before fisting my hair in a ponytail and wrapping the length around her wrist. With a sharp tug, she forces my head back.

*Jesus Christ!* I'm shaking.

Her fingers slide up the back of my thigh and skim my pussy lips.

"Please, touch me!" I beg, rocking back against her hand.

Kissing a path along my spine and over my shoulder, she bites down on the sensitive skin. I'm beyond caring at this point. I'll beg her all night if I have to.

———

*EMILY.*

"Please touch me," she begs again as I soothe the bite with my tongue. I've never been with a woman before, but wow, it's such a rush. She's so responsive.

When Steph challenged me to play, I felt intimidated. I wasn't sure if they were all mocking me or not, but then Josh played along. I think, if anything, I surprised them tonight.

I bury my nose in her neck, inhaling her sweet scent. She's making these pleading sounds in her throat, and I'm throbbing with need. Drunk on the power I have over her right now.

Her body jerks when I trail a finger over her slit, smearing her wetness around.

"Is this for me?" I stroke her clit in firm circles, loving my name on her lips. This new side of me terrifies and excites me in equal measure. I want to make her fall apart at my touch, but I also yearn to hurt her. Mark her perfect skin. Bite it until blood rushes to the surface and spoils her perfection while she moans my name in pleasure.

Brushing my nose along her neck, I breathe her in once more. "Are you gonna be a good girl for me, Dallas?"

She rocks against my fingers. "Yes, Em. God, yes! I promise."

"I didn't hear you." I pinch her clit between my fingers.

She cries out. "I'll be good! Fuck, Em. Please…" Gripping onto the couch for dear life, she fights the urge to reach for me and take control.

I hush her, smoothing my palm over her back. "Touch me, and I stop."

She whimpers like she's in pain.

I drop to my knees behind her, massaging her round ass cheeks, pulling them apart. Her swollen, wet pussy begs to be licked and sucked on. I wet my lips and lean in, circling her tight entrance with my tongue.

When I slap her ass cheeks, she rocks forward, gasping in surprise.

"I've wanted to taste you for so long," I whisper, grabbing her creamy globes again and squeezing the flesh. Dallas bites down on the couch to stifle her cries of pleasure, and I sink my tongue deep inside of her throbbing pussy until my nose butts up against her.

"Oh fuck!" she moans as I begin taking her with my tongue. "Oh god!

*Fuck, indeed!* Slapping her ass cheeks again and grabbing the flesh, I dig my nails in. She won't be able to sit comfortably tomorrow. Her juices are smeared over my nose and cheeks, and the damp strands of my long hair stick to my skin.

I work three fingers inside of her. She's tight, but I don't allow her time to adjust as I set a punishing pace, fucking her into the couch. The sudden intrusion stings, but she takes my fingers like a good girl.

Whimpering, she bites down on the couch and rocks back against me while I shift my position behind her. I add a fourth finger, fucking her until she's half lying, half sitting on my face. The floor is hard and uncomfortable, but I'm too lost in her to care.

Biting the inside of her thigh, I dive back in between her pussy lips, flicking her clit with my tongue. Faster and harder until she's clawing at the couch. She falls apart with a wordless cry, writhing and tightening every muscle in her body. Her thighs quiver as I hold her to me, keeping up the relentless sweeps of my tongue until she's fighting to get away from my touch.

"That was fun!" I sit back up, putting my dress back on. It's only when I'm fully clothed that I notice the silence in the room. "What?" I ask, wiping my wet mouth with the back of my hand.

"Holy shit!" Josh breathes, staring at me like he's never seen me before.

I smile innocently, turning to Step. "Truth or dare?" She's the one who initiated this game. Let's see what she's made of.

# CHAPTER
## *twelve*

**EMILY**

I GRIN as I walk up the front steps to the school the following day.

April: I can't walk, Matt. You're in deep fucking trouble!

Matty: Don't blame me, sugar. I simply followed Emily's instructions. Beat her up! She's the devil cast from hell to corrupt our innocent souls.

April: *eye roll* You're still dead, Matt. Just you wait!

Steph: Thank me, I invited her ;) Where are you, princess?

Me: *devil emoji*

Josh: *drool emoji*

Ben: Fuck off, Josh!

Josh: *laughing emoji*

I think I made friends with them all last night. Even April seems to accept me now. Last night, I discovered a new side to myself that I didn't know existed, and it's both scary and exciting to trust that part of myself with them. Something seems to shift and change inside of me every day, evolving into something more resilient.

I spent hours last night researching colleges and art programs until the early morning hours, thinking about my future and what I want to do. I'll see the career counselor later, but I know I don't want to study law like my parents want me to do.

I've spent my entire childhood trying to be the perfect daughter, friend, and student. It's time to do what I want for a change. Besides cheerleading, I genuinely enjoy art, so it makes sense to pursue it.

I enter the school building and make my way down the hallway. There's a pep in my step and a lightness in my chest. When I open my locker, something flutters to the floor and I bend down to pick it up. It's a photograph.

*"Did you see that?"* I squeal. *"I rolled down the funbox and didn't fall!"*

*Dallas gives me the thumbs up as she skates by. "You're getting better!"*

*Ben pulls me into his side and holds up the camera. "Smile."*

*"Wait," I laugh, removing my helmet and patting down my wild hair. Ben rolls his eyes, but a smile is playing on his lips.*

*Wrapping my arms around his waist, I smile up at him. "Now I'm ready."*

*"Are you sure?"*

*I bite my bottom lip to suppress my own smile. "I'm very sure."*

*He ducks down so fast that I squeak in surprise. Stealing a kiss, he clicks the shutter. "Still sure?" he whispers.*

*I nip his bottom lip. "Try me."*

*His fingers dig into my waist and he begins to tickle me, then clicks the shutter again.*

Smiling from ear to ear, I scan the corridor, but there's no sign of Ben and Dallas amongst the students milling around.

When did they put it in my locker? I look back down at the

photograph in my hand and turn it over to read the handwriting on the back.

*For your stalker collage.*
*-Ben.*

Ben did this? My cheeks hurt from smiling as I go to put my books in my locker. I pause when I notice something else—a small pair of binoculars with another handwritten note on top. I pick up the folded piece of paper.

*All the better to see me with.*
*- Little Red Riding Hood.*

Laughing softly, I reach in for the binoculars. I'm falling for Ben. It's the only reasonable explanation for my racing heart and this happy giddiness inside me. He will break my heart if I'm not careful.

I use some spare sticky tack to stick the photograph next to the one I have of Ben dyeing his hair. Why is he doing this? Sneaking photographs and binoculars into my locker. Why go through all of this trouble?

Deep in thought, I close my locker. I don't notice the presence next to me until I turn to leave, coming face to face with Jack.

Leaning on the locker next to mine, he flashes a disarming smile.

I hitch my bag up higher on my shoulder. "God, Jack... You startled me!"

He pushes off the locker and cages me in with his big hands either side of my head.

I catch a whiff of his cologne. "What are you doing?" I'd lie if I said I'm not affected by his nearness.

I am.

Jack ignores my question. "There's a get-together at mine on

Friday after the game. You should come." His jade eyes have specks of hazel in them. I never noticed before.

"I'll have to let you know, Jack."

Stepping closer, he presses his hard body against mine. "Come on, Em. Don't do this to me. Let me take you out."

He's gone before I have a chance to reply. Ben pushed him hard with his shoulder when he walked past. He turns, and his brown eyes find me briefly before they're back on Jack.

My heart somersaults as I take him in. His ripped jeans fit him to perfection, and the definition in his arms is on full display in a band T-shirt with its sleeves cut out.

Ben holds his hands up placatingly. "Sorry, dude. My bad. Didn't see you there." He doesn't look apologetic at all as he turns on his heel and continues down the corridor.

"Fucking prick!" Jack mutters, but I don't wait around for him to corner me again.

———

"That was very good," I praise. "I think we should practice the basket toss a couple more times. I want the timing to be sharper between Jen and Amy. Take five. Have a drink of water."

"Looks like you have an audience," Hailey comments next to me as she unscrews the lid on her water bottle.

I take a sip of mine, glancing at Dallas and Steph on the bleachers. It means a lot to me that they're here after last night. Shrugging, I place the bottle back on the floor next to my bag. "We've been hanging out."

Hailey chokes on her water. She wipes her chin. "You've been hanging out with the emo kids?"

I throw her a sharp look. "You don't need to be rude, Hailey."

With a scoff, she folds her arms over her chest. "But why, Em?"

I can't believe I have to justify myself. "They're nice, Hailey."

"Nice?" she huffs. "They do drugs and get into fights. They're trouble, Em."

She won't even give them a chance. I'm not sure what reaction I expected from her, but it hurts that she straight out dismisses my new friends.

"You haven't given them a chance. You don't even know them, and you already judge them."

She laughs incredulously. "Do you hear yourself, Em? I'm not judging them. I'm just stating facts. "And you," she gestures to me, "you're a good girl. You come from a good family. You're head cheerleader, for fuck's sake. You can have your pick of guys." She gestures to the other cheerleaders. "Fuck, all of these girls are jealous of you. They'd chop off an arm to be your friend, but instead, you hang out with those misfits. They're losers, Em. They have no future."

I pause, shocked by the venom in her voice. She truly believes her own words. "What are you saying, Hailey?" I take a step back.

Regret flashes across her face, and she tries to reach for me, but I step out of the way. "Look, I'm not trying to hurt you, Em. I'm just asking you to be smart about this. It could ruin your reputation if everyone finds out that you hang out with those kids. Fuck, Em, listen to me!"

My jaw grinds as tears prick my eyes, blurring my vision. I can't believe this from the one girl I thought had my back. Is she only friends with me to have a slice of the cake? Is our friendship genuine, or am I a step on the popularity ladder for her? I've never questioned her loyalty before now.

I square my shoulders. "You're either my friend, or you're not, Hailey. I don't care about some fucking high school reputation."

She deflates. "I'm your friend, Em."

With a glance over at the girls on the bleachers, I decide to be honest. "I'm falling in love with her."

Hailey bristles, her mouth opening and closing before she blurts, "What are you talking about, Em?"

The first tear trails a path down my cheek. I can't stop it.

"Hey, hey," she soothes, wrapping me up in her arms. "It's okay, Em. I'm here."

Burying my nose in her neck, I hold her tight, afraid I'll fall apart if I let her go.

"Go home, everyone. We'll have an early finish today," she tells the others. To me, she says, "Come on, let's get out of here. I've got a freezer stocked full of ice cream for emergencies."

—————

"Let me check that I've got this right," Hailey says, licking the spoon before pointing it at me. "Rick fucked Dallas in front of you. Then you played truth or dare at Ben's house and ended up fucking Dallas, but you also had oral sex with Ben in his car?"

We sit cross-legged, facing each other on the couch in her grand living room.

I cringe, reaching for one of the half-eaten tubs of ice cream between us. When she puts it like that, it sounds so bad. "That just about sums it up."

Hailey shakes her head regretfully. "How did I not notice something was up with you? You've been acting differently lately, but I thought it was because of your breakup with Rick. I've been a terrible friend. The things I said at practice earlier…" She wipes away tears. "Fuck, Em. I'm so sorry!"

Abandoning my ice cream, I take her hand in mine. I squeeze it reassuringly. "No, Hailey, I should apologize to you. You couldn't have known. I should have told you all of this from the beginning, but my feelings were so new. I worried you wouldn't want to be my friend anymore."

She sighs, squeezing back. "That's the thing, Em. It shouldn't have been a thought in your head in the first place. You can tell me anything. I reacted badly earlier because I care about you. I was worried.

You're falling for Ben and Dallas, and by the sounds of it, they care about you too." She chuckles. "This thing is crazy."

I smile. "Tell me about it."

It feels good to trust my best friend with my feelings. She struggles to understand how this came to be, but she supports me, and she'll be there even if I fall from my reign at school. I don't even care about an eventual fallout anymore. I'm a senior. None of it will matter this time next year.

Leaning over the ice cream tubs, I pull her in for a bone-crunching hug.

She squeezes me back, burying her nose in my hair. "What are you gonna do?"

That's the million-dollar question. "I don't know, but we'll be gone this time next year, Hailey. None of this will matter when we're at college, so I refuse to overthink it anymore. I'll just take it one day at a time and see where the road leads me. I don't want to be afraid anymore. I have you, my family, and Rick."

She leans back, wiping her wet cheeks. "Rick told me he's taking you to the fair on Sunday."

"Only as friends. It was his idea, actually. I miss spending time with him."

"I think it's a great idea, Em. You care about each other—as friends, of course." She winks.

Laughing softly, I gesture to the empty ice cream tubs between us. "We've eaten our body weight in ice cream. What do you want to do next?"

Hailey wiggles her fingers between us. "I need infills. What do you say? Girl's spa day?"

"Deal!"

———

Steph: Are you okay, princess? We're worried. Your phone is switched off.

Ben: Explain.

Steph: Cool your marbles, lover boy. We went to watch Em's cheer practice, and something happened. She was upset.

Me: I'm fine, guys. Don't worry about me :)

Nina: Who are we beating up?

Josh: *cracks knuckles*

Matty: Ooh, yes, baby! Let's break some bones!!

April: Wow, look at that. The boys do know how to use the group chat, after all!

Matty: Why don't you use that smart mouth for better things ;)

Josh: You cheating on me now, babe? It hurts, man!

Matty: You're my favorite, Josh ;)

Emily: Let me watch again next time ;)

April: *laughing emoji* *fire emoji*

Josh: I would rather lick you, princess *tongue emoji* We'll let Matt watch ;)

Ben: I'm gonna beat u up so fucking bad!

Nina: Rawr!

Dallas: *laughing emoji* meow!

Dallas phones me as I'm lying on my bed, scrolling through the group chat. It's the first time she's called me directly.

My heart begins to pound and I swipe the screen before pressing the phone to my ear.

"Hello?"

"Em, I sent a video request."

I click accept, quickly running my hands through my hair to tame the worst flyaways.

"Hey," she smiles when it connects, her raven hair splayed across the pillow. "I was worried."

"I'm okay." Tucking my hair behind my ear, I ignore the flutters in my belly as I make myself comfortable against the headboard.

"What happened?"

I drop my gaze. It's not like I want her to find out the real reason for the argument. How do you tell someone you care about that your best friend thinks they're bad for your image?

When I fail to respond, she nods knowingly. "Hailey knew we were there for you. I'm sorry."

"No!" I rush to reply, shaking my head. "She worries about me. I told her everything. *Everything*, Dallas. She's just concerned."

Eyes shining with unshed tears, Dallas sighs. "I should stay away from you. We all should."

My chest tightens. "What are you saying?"

Dallas sits up, brings her knees up to her chest and wraps her arm around them. "I didn't always use to be like this." She wipes the tears from her lashes. "Before my family died…"

I hate that I made her cry. "It's okay. You don't have to explain."

With a faraway look in her eyes, Dallas stares at something to the side. "I used to be a lot like you. Well, I was never a cheerleader…" She chuckles. "…But I was popular. My brother was the captain of the basketball team. It had its perks being his little sister." She rests her chin on her knees. "You wouldn't have had to worry about being seen with me back then."

Her words break my heart. I hate seeing her so unsure and

broken. "I'm not ashamed of you, Dallas." I need her to believe me. "We're months away from graduating. All this superficial stuff will be behind us then. No one will care who my dad is or that I used to be a cheerleader in high school. I hate this prison I'm in. I never asked to be put on this pedestal. I don't even understand how it happened."

Dallas smiles. "I do, Em. You're beautiful and kind to everyone. You come from one of the wealthiest families in town. You have the world at your feet. Everyone knows that. You know what it's like—the higher up you are, the harder you fall. Fuck, look at me."

She pauses, wiping her nose. "I had fucking everything. I have so many memories of my brother and me doing silly shit that used to drive my mom up the wall." She smiles to herself. "We had this thing where we would wake each other up in the morning in the craziest of ways possible. One morning, Aaron woke me up by playing a bongo dressed as the school team's mascot." She laughs at the memory, and I do too.

"Then the fire happened, and I was sent to live with my estranged uncle. We know how that went." She picks at the bedspread. "And now I live with Ben. I have nothing, Em. No future. I'm not going places like you."

"Stop!" I whisper. "Can't you see how loved you are? I started watching you after that night at the party. I was curious. Do you know what I saw? True friendships! The dynamics are unconventional to the outside world, but who cares? Your friends would do anything for you. That's more than I can say about my own friends. Hailey is on my side, and I know Rick would support me too through thick and thin, but Jamie and the others? They would drop me like that." I click my fingers for effect.

"You've lost a lot, Dallas, but you're surrounded by good people. What I saw when I looked at you guys made me jealous. I used to sit at my lunch table and fantasize about being a part of your group."

I shuffle down on the bed and lie back on my soft pillow. "I'm more myself with you guys than I've ever allowed myself to be. I like who I am when I'm with you." I meet her blue eyes. "I like *you*."

Dallas remains silent for a while and I hold my breath, worried I said too much.

"I like you too, Emily," she whispers.

I blush. "I like you a lot."

"You like Ben too."

It's not a question.

"I do…" I swallow past the lump in my throat. "Is that bad? Are you upset?"

She waves me off. "No, girl, I'm not upset. Ben's one of my best friends. We'll make it work."

"Really?" I stare at her in disbelief. I don't want to have to choose between them. Maybe I'm greedy, but I haven't felt this way before.

Her smile is soft. We fall silent, both deep in our own thoughts.

"Where is he tonight anyway?" I ask.

"He's out with the guys. I wanted to talk to you, so I stayed behind."

I don't hide my smile.

"Touch yourself. Let me watch."

My eyebrows shoot up in surprise. I like where this is going. "Tell me what you want, Dallas."

Sucking her lips between her teeth, she smirks. "Trail your hand down slowly and squeeze your breast."

I do as she asks, running my fingers past my racing heartbeat and over my nipple. I palm my tit and squeeze the soft flesh.

She hums low in her throat. "Pull the dress down. I want to see you."

Unzipping it at my side, I push down the top half until my front is exposed, before removing my bra. It's not easy to do one-handed while holding the phone, but I manage.

My dusky nipples harden as she takes me in. In a husky voice, she orders me to touch them. Tweaking and pulling the hard peaks between my thumb and finger, I moan at the sharp sensation.

"You're so beautiful!" Her hand dips below the waistband of her jeans, and she bites down on her plump bottom lip. "Touch yourself, Em."

Inching up my skirt, I remove my panties. My pussy is slick with arousal as I brush my fingers through my wet slit, drawing in a sharp breath.

Dallas is breathing hard too, her hand moving between her trembling legs. She's beautiful like this, with her bottom lip trapped between her teeth, and flushed cheeks.

We pant in unison while I sink two fingers inside my tight heat. I begin to fuck myself slowly, head thrown back on the pillow, a moan dancing on my parted lips.

"Imagine it's me touching you, Em," she purrs through heavy breaths. "Imagine it's my fingers inside you, stretching that tight pussy."

A whimper slips past my lips and I pull my fingers out to stroke my clit in firm, fast circles. I'm close. "Please, talk dirty to me." I push three fingers back inside my heat, moaning at the slight burn. My back arches off the bed.

Dallas is moaning, too, edging closer to her own orgasm. "Slap your pussy, baby."

"Oh god!" I moan, smacking my clit hard with my wet hand. It feels dirty but fuck, it turns me on.

"Slap it again, baby but harder this time. Make it hurt."

I watch her through the screen as I slap my clit hard enough to cause a sharp sting. I hiss through my teeth, my clit throbbing deliciously.

With a moan slipping from her soft lips, she throws her head back. "Fuck, Em, you're so hot. Tell me how tight you are."

I buck against my hand. "I'm so close!"

"Come for me, baby."

I do. *God, I do...* As my body convulses on the bed, I bite down on my lip to stop myself from screaming in pleasure and waking my sleeping parents.

Dallas cries out my name. She follows me over the edge, riding her hand until the last of her orgasm ebbs away.

"Fuck, that was..." I trail off, my fingers still buried inside me.

Dallas sucks on hers and grins. "Good? Amazing? Fantastic? Mind-blowing? Life-altering? Pick your choice."

Laughing lightly, I suck my fingers clean like she did.

"Baby," she groans. "Fuck, I want to taste you so bad."

"Soon!" I wink, sitting up and adjusting my clothing. "I have to go. I need to finish the history essay that's due tomorrow."

"I suppose I should finish mine too. How else am I gonna stand a chance at chasing you across the planet after you leave this forsaken town?" There's an edge of vulnerability in her voice.

"Hey..." I urge her to look at me. "...you're going places. You have so much to offer. It'll be me chasing you around the globe."

She smiles softly. "Good night, Em. I'll see you tomorrow, okay?"

I smile back. "Good night, Dallas."

# CHAPTER
## *Thirteen*

## EMILY

THE FOLLOWING day Ben drags me into a supply closet after the first lesson. I'm bewildered and full of butterflies as he locks the door. There's only really room for the two of us in here, and even that's a stretch. Light streams in through the gap at the bottom of the door, but it's too dark for me to see him properly.

I breathe in sharply when he cages me in with his elbows on either side of my head, pressing his body to mine. All I can hear is the sound of my own heartbeat, our shaky breaths, and the students on the other side of the door.

Ben leans down close to my face, his hot breath on my lips. "What happened yesterday, Princess?" His deep and husky voice shoots liquid fire straight to my core. I hold my breath, acutely aware of his intoxicating smell and proximity.

He slaps the door beside my head, and the sudden noise makes me flinch.

"Talk!"

What's this about? And then it dawns on me. "Nothing happened, Ben. Hailey and I had an argument. I got upset, but it's okay. We talked it through, and we're good again. I'm okay, Ben." I place a palm on his hard chest, feeling his racing heartbeat beneath his T-shirt.

"I was worried," he whispers in a pained voice, pressing his hard cock against my stomach.

"I know. I'm sorry."

His warm hand wraps around my throat. "You drive me crazy, princess. I can't stop thinking about you."

I fist his T-shirt, creasing the soft fabric. "You think about me?"

Wrenching my skirt up around my waist, he lifts me off the floor, pushing me back against the door with his hips.

*Oh god, yes…*

"Ben?" I wrap my legs around his waist and flex my chest outward. I want his hands on me so badly.

With his forehead pressed to mine, he whispers, "I need you, princess. I need you so fucking bad!" His chest heaves, and his hot breath fans my face. "Fuck, I want you so much!"

I can hardly breathe, trapped in his heated gaze.

He dips down, and our lips collide in a scorching kiss that leaves me boneless and breathless. Ben kisses me like a man possessed. All I can do is to hold onto his broad shoulders and kiss him back just as hard. Our teeth clash and our tongues duel for dominance. I climb his frame, clawing at him in need. He steals my breath as well as my soul. *I need to feel him.*

"Let me have you, princess," he growls into my mouth, grinding his hard cock against me while gripping my ass possessively.

I'm too aroused to think, let alone speak. I roll my hips, seeking release. "Ben, please…"

Pinning me to the door with his hips, he leans back to undo his belt and zipper. The clinking sound of his belt buckle makes me whimper in anticipation. I need him inside me.

"Please, fuck me, Ben," I moan as I bury my fingers in the green curls at the nape of his neck. It's smooth and the perfect length to tug.

"Jesus fucking Christ," he breathes between kisses. I hear the tell-tale sound of plastic ripping. He sheathes himself and moves back in for another toe-curling kiss before trailing kisses down my neck, biting and teasing the sensitive skin. His stubble burns deliciously.

"Ben, please…"

"I know, baby. I've got you." He moves my panties aside, impatient with need, rubbing the head of his hard cock through my wet slit.

My clit throbs as I cling to him.

"Holy fuck!" His head falls to my shoulder, and he breathes heavily as if stealing himself. His muscles quiver beneath my hands. He's holding himself back.

Ben takes me in one hard thrust and I cry out, digging my nails into his broad shoulders. He's big, and it burns.

He stills, allowing me a moment to adjust to his size. His breath is hot on my neck, and delicious shivers run down my spine when he whispers through heaving breaths. "I need to move, baby. Fuck, you're so tight!"

Fisting his green hair, I bring his lips to mine. "Fuck me!"

Ben doesn't need to be asked twice. He sets a punishing rhythm, fucking me so hard against the door, the hinges rattle. I don't care if someone hears us on the other side. The thought only turns me on more.

With my legs spread wide, I hold on for dear life. I want to hurt him just as deliciously as he's hurting me. I want to get under his skin. Biting his neck and drawing blood, I whimper. "Harder!"

His lips and teeth are everywhere, sucking, licking, and biting. I'm being consumed by him. His big cock feels like fucking heaven.

My pussy squeezes around him as I edge closer, my insides melting and warming.

Groaning, he pins me to the door by my throat. His palm is warm, and his touch is rough. "You're mine," he growls, his lips hovering over mine.

It's so possessive, I come hard, clawing my nails down his biceps while moaning his name. My pussy pulsates around his cock when he picks up speed, chasing his own release. His grip on my throat tightens until I can't breathe, and then he stills, groaning as he spills into the condom.

Laughter filters in from the hallway, but we're too lost in each other to care. His cock twitches inside me and he shudders, whispering my name. I love how it sounds on his lips.

He pulls out, chuckling to himself as he discards the condom and tucks himself in. "Fuck, baby. That was insane."

My smile is hidden in the darkness while I adjust my clothing as best as I can.

Ben pulls me to him and kisses my lips sweetly. "Here, I want you to have this." He places something in my hand. "You go first. I'll wait another five minutes." I feel his soft lips on my forehead before he unlocks the door and ushers me outside.

Squinting against the light, I make my way down the now empty corridors. I'm late for class again.

In my hand is another photograph. This one is of Ben and Dallas wearing matching skeleton outfits on Halloween. They're both smiling, and Dallas is holding a shot glass in her hand.

I smile as I turn the picture over in my hand. My heart feels too big for my chest.

*How's that collage looking, princess? Here's another one for your collection.*

*- Ben*

---

"Holy shit!" Hailey breathes behind me, and something in the tone of her voice makes me look up from my plate of food.

"What?" I scan the cafeteria.

She leans in, whispering in my ear. "Look at Ben. Please tell me that's your doing?"

My brows knit together. "Huh?"

Her voice is conspiratorial. "He's over by the cash register."

I glance over my shoulder at Ben, who is digging through his pockets for change. His arms are covered in scratches, and there are more on his left cheek. He's got a bite mark on his neck too.

I slap a hand over my mouth. He looks like he's been in a fight with an alley cat and lost.

Nudging me, Hailey quirks an eyebrow. "He's that good, huh?"

I nod, and we giggle.

"He's walking this way," Hailey whispers, laughing under her breath.

"Hey, Joker!" Jack shouts tauntingly, and my head whips up. *What is he doing?* He's never bothered Ben before, so why start now?

He points to the scratch marks on Ben's arms. "Can't get chicks to fuck you willingly? Looks like she put up a real good fight."

Hailey drops her spoon on her plate. It clinks loudly. "Leave him alone, Jack."

Jamie looks at her questioningly, and I can literally see the cogs turn in his head before he pins me to my seat with his inquisitive blue eyes.

I swallow thickly.

He narrows his eyes.

Leaning back in his chair, Jack puts his heavy arm over my shoulder. He does it so casually, I bet we look like a happy couple.

Ignoring Hailey's outburst, he flashes his whitened teeth at Ben. My stomach twists uncomfortably and I try to dislodge Jack's arm.

Ben grinds his jaw, glancing at me. His brown eyes are devoid of emotion as he says, "Trust me, Jack, she begged for it."

My mouth drops open. *Is he trying to hurt me?*

Now bored with Ben and oblivious to his anger, Jack puts his other hand on my thigh and leans in to whisper into my ear.

Meanwhile, Hailey watches the unfolding train wreck with wide eyes.

I'm frozen to my seat, unable to look away from the resignation in Ben's eyes.

Without another word, he stalks off to sit with his friends, his shoulders hunched.

I stare after him. Jack was a dick to him, but Ben hurt me in front of everyone with his dig. What happened between us in the closet meant a lot to me.

I feel sick.

"You're a fucking jerk!" Hailey shouts at Jack, glaring daggers.

He looks over at her in surprise. "What crawled up your ass?"

He really is clueless, isn't he? I can't stomach this anymore.

Jumping to Hailey's defense, Jamie growls, "Back off, or you and I will have a problem!"

Jamie is one of the most perceptive people I know, and the way he narrows his eyes on Hailey tells me he's suspicious. She doesn't usually care about anyone outside of our little circle, so what's changed? That's what he's trying to figure out.

Before he has a chance to pin those blue eyes on me, I push off the table. I'm fed up with Jack's flirting and tired with all of this drama in general.

Walking off, I don't get far before Rick grabs my arm and pulls me back. I lose balance and collide with his hard chest.

He grips my arms to steady me and leans down, searching my eyes. "I know something is up, Em. You might as well tell me now."

"Nothing is wrong." My eyes sting with unshed tears. Why does he have to know me so well? I can never hide my emotions from him, and this time is no different.

Cupping my jaw, he sweeps his eyes over my face and neck. I know the minute he spots the hickeys because his body grows tense, and his grip on me tightens. Brushing my hair off my neck, he inspects the marks. His eyes flick back up to mine, searching.

My cheeks heat. "Not here, Rick," I whisper.

He grinds his teeth as he looks over my shoulder. Ben has been watching us this whole time. I know because his eyes burn like liquid fire down my back.

Rick grabs my hand and pulls me along behind him. I go willingly, too tired and fed up to argue. Students watch us weave between tables. I know what this looks like. Us, holding hands.

The doors to the cafeteria close behind us. Rick blows out a breath and puts his hands on his hips as I lean against the wall.

I wait for him to speak.

He rubs a hand down his face before glancing over his shoulder to ensure no one is listening. We're alone. "Is he treating you well?"

My mouth opens and closes, but no words come out. That's not what I thought he was going to say.

"If not, I'll go back in there right now and teach him a fucking lesson."

I'm shocked by the vehemence in his voice. "Rick, you don't have to worry about me. I can handle myself."

He searches my face. We stand close. Close enough that I can feel the warmth coming off his skin. His smell is familiar and comforting.

I lean in closer.

"He's covered in scratches… I had to make sure he didn't force himself on you."

I stare in disbelief. "No, Rick. No! He would never hurt me like that!" I'm shocked that the thought entered his mind. I'm also grateful that he cares enough to worry about me.

Rubbing his neck, he looks uncertain and sheepish. "It's just…." He averts his gaze. "You never scratched me like that."

I blush. He's right. Our sex was always good, but it was never mind-blowingly passionate. He didn't set my soul on fire the way Ben and Dallas do.

I'm saved from responding when the doors to the cafeteria open and Ben and the others step through.

Rick leans in close, whispering, "You come to me if he hurts you, okay?"

I smile. "He won't, but yes, I promise."

Satisfied, he nods and shoves his hands in his pockets.

As he approaches, Ben bounces his eyes between us. He looks

ready to murder someone, and I like that he's jealous and posses-sive over me. I like it more than I should want to admit.

Rick offers me a soft smile, then takes a step back. "Hey, Ben. I need a word!"

*What is he doing?*

Ben looks at him questioningly before lifting his chin to the others, telling them without words to give us privacy.

I smile reassuringly at Dallas as she walks past.

"What's up?" Ben asks, straight to the point.

Rick grabs his shoulder. "Look after her. She's got a heart of gold, unlike the other girls here, so don't fucking hurt her, or I'll have to beat you up."

I cringe. Oh, how I cringe! "Rick!"

He drops his hand from Ben's shoulder and turns to face me with a serious expression on his handsome face. "No, Em. I'm fucking serious about this! Just because you're not my girl anymore doesn't mean I don't care about you. It doesn't matter if it's this punk or someone on the football team. I'm still gonna threaten them." He turns to Ben again. "I don't know you, and you have a shit reputation, but she tells me you're good to her, so I'll give you the benefit of the doubt."

Ben looks at me and chuckles at the expression on my face. Now would be a good time for the ground to swallow me up.

"I like her," he says to Rick. "I'm falling for her. She's fierce and sweet. She keeps surprising me at every turn. And her smile…." He looks at Rick. "I have a fucking terrible reputation, and I know I've made bad choices in the past, but I'm trying. I want to be good for her. To be someone she deserves."

My heart stopped beating at the beginning of his speech.

Rick clasps Ben's shoulder. "I like you, man."

I stare at Ben with my mouth hanging open while Rick presses a kiss to my cheek before walking off without a backward glance. "What are you doing?" I whisper shakily when Rick is out of earshot.

Ben takes my hand in his, threading his fingers through mine.

His touch is warm and comforting. "Come on. Let's find Dallas and get out of here."

The bell rings, and students stream through the cafeteria doors, bathing the hallway in noise and activity.

My heart hammers in my chest and I squeeze his hand as I smile. This moment feels so right. "I'd like that very much."

———

"Em, we're taking your car. It's the only one with a functioning AC," Dallas shouts over her shoulder, skipping down the steps to the school.

Ben holds my hand, unbothered by the stares and whispers. He's no stranger to this kind of attention. Let them talk. I won't let the gossip worry me anymore. For the first time, I don't care what others think of me. They're going to talk regardless, so we might as well give them something to talk about.

Dallas cries shotgun, grinning as Ben squeezes his big frame into the back. My car is big, but he makes it look like a bumper car.

It's strange to have them both in my car. My heart feels too big for my chest, and gone is the emptiness I felt at the beginning of the year.

Dallas fiddles with the radio. "Where are we going?"

Strapping on my seatbelt, I reach for her hand. "I have an idea, but it's a long drive."

"Just drive, princess. We've got all day," Ben says, leaning back against the headrest.

I want to see Dallas carefree and smiling, if only for a day, so I start the engine and drive us down the highway to the one place I know means the most to her. The car eats up the miles as we talk, laugh, and sing along to the radio at the top of our lungs. Ben uses his phone to film Dallas dancing and bouncing in her seat to the beat.

We share a grin in the rearview mirror.

With our troubles behind us and freedom on the horizon, we roll down the windows and enjoy the warm breeze.

Two hours later, I finally pull to a stop and put the car in park. Seagulls screech overhead, and the sun warms my face as I open the door and step outside.

Dallas stares at the sandy beach for a long moment, tears pooling in her eyes. Ben pulls her in for a hug. We both know what the beach means to her and the memories it evokes.

"I haven't been to a beach since the fire," she whispers in a trembling voice.

Ben rests his cheek on her head. "We know. You're okay, Dell."

"I always wanted to go." Her voice is quiet. "But it's so far away, you know?"

I reach up and wipe away a stray tear from her cheek. "We're here with you, Dallas. You're not alone." I take her hand in mine. "Let's go have some fun."

She's a vision, walking barefoot in the sand with her face tilted to the sun. Memories of happier days play across her features. There's no doubt she belongs in the water because as soon as we find a good spot, she sheds her clothes in record time.

Ben winks at me before lifting her up and sprinting toward the water with her bobbing on his shoulder.

Dallas squeals with laughter. "Let me down!"

When they're waist-deep in water, he drops her, and she falls back with a huge splash. Popping back up, she spits water. The smile on her face is contagious.

I can't stop looking. It does something to my heart to see them play like this. Dallas's wet hair lies plastered to her face when she jumps on Ben's broad back and tries to topple him, but he's too tall and big for her.

I drop down on the sand, not wishing to intrude on this moment between them. Something tells me they don't often get to have fun like this. Scooping up a handful of sand, I watch it pour through my fingers. Where is life taking me, and where will we be this time next year?

The dwindling sand in my hand reminds me that time is running out. I look out over the water just as Dallas splashes Ben. Laughing, he wipes a hand down his face.

Where will they be next year? What will happen to us? It's too soon to think about a future between us, but I can't help it. We're months away from everything changing, and I'm scared. I'm falling for Ben and Dallas.

"Princess, your chariot has arrived," Ben says, tearing me from my thoughts. He bends over with his wet back to me. "Hop on."

Shaking off my gloomy thoughts, I climb on, squeezing his waist with my thighs.

Dallas is floating on her back up ahead.

"She's happy," Ben observes, entering the water. The waves crash against his feet and calves as he walks us further out.

I press a kiss on his cheek, and his scratchy stubble tingles my lips. "I know."

"Thank you." His voice is thick with emotion.

I smile into his neck. "Ben?"

"Hmm?"

"I want this for us. You, me, and Dallas. One day we'll live near a beach just like this one. We'll have our own place and a dog."

Ben chuckles, pausing in his step when a beach ball lands in front of us, and a mom retrieves it with an apologetic smile.

"What are we gonna call the dog?" He starts walking again.

I tap my chin. "Oh, I know! Catherine Zeta-Bones."

A surprised laugh bubbles out of him. "Catherina Zeta-Bones? Really?"

I grin. "Don't you like it? Well, how about Ellen Degeneruff?"

"Do you think these names up on the fly?"

"Maybe. Maybe not." I kiss his cheek again, then shout to Dallas over his head, "Dallas, we're deciding on a name for our future dog. What do you think of Jane Pawsten?"

"Pawsten?" Her lips twitch.

Ben drops me suddenly and I fall back with a shriek. I soon emerge, shivering and spitting water. "Oh my god, it's freezing!"

They laugh while I scan the beach, trying to think of another name. "Virginia Woof?"

Ben groans. "No way! It has to be something cool like Bullseye or Burger."

Dallas snorts a laugh. "You think Burger is a cool name?"

"What's wrong with Burger? It has 'oomph!' Imagine when we take it for walks." He cups his mouth, shouting, "Burger! Come here, boy!" Looking pleased with himself, he grins.

Dallas sinks down in the water until it's up to her chin. "And I guess if we get a second dog, you'll want to name it Fries so that you get to shout Burger and Fries when we're out."

They bicker back and forth.

I snigger to myself. "We need something more original."

Dallas rolls her eyes. "What are you gonna suggest next? Woofie Goldberg?"

I click my fingers. "Yes, I like that! What do you think, Ben?"

Mirroring Dallas, he lowers himself in the water until it's up to his chin. His green hair lies plastered to his forehead. "I think it's probably best if we settle for a Hamster, Em."

"I used to own a hamster called 'Madam Ham.'"

Ben stares at me in disbelief. "Madam Ham?"

"Yep," I reply. "She was a feisty little thing."

Dallas laughs. She wades over to me and wraps her arms around my midriff, resting her chin on my shoulder. "I like your crazy."

Sighing contentedly, I smile at her over my shoulder.

She pecks my lips. "So we buy a dog and name it something ridiculous. What else do you envision in our future?"

"We'll live in a house on the beach and have breakfast on the porch every morning. We'll be the crazy neighbors who set the alarm early to watch the sunrise together because life is short. We don't want to miss out on those seemingly insignificant but beautiful things in life. Oh, and I'll co-own an art gallery with Matt."

Dallas presses her lips to my shoulder. Ben joins us, stroking his palms down my arms. My words hang in the air as a toddler squeals with laughter at the water's edge.

Ben buries his nose in my wet hair. "I don't talk about my personal life much because there's not much to say. My parents are alive. They don't beat me, so I don't like to complain. I've got it better than many kids where I'm from, but my parents are absent. My mom struggles with severe depression and is so strung out on medication, it's like she's not even here. My dad is no better. He drinks and struggles to hold down jobs, and is hardly ever home.

We never had much. I've gone without meals plenty of times because my dad drinks the money away, and my mom won't leave her bedroom." He shakes his head, deep in thought. "What I'm trying to say is that we come from different worlds, Em. You and I—we've gone to the same school our whole lives. You were always this unattainable, larger-than-life girl who had everything."

I shake my head. "That's not true, Ben."

"I know that now, Em, but we didn't talk. You never struggled for a meal, and you never had to go to school in clothes that didn't fit you because your parents couldn't be bothered to buy you new ones. You wear designer clothes, drive a top market car, and your family is one of the wealthiest families in town. You can have any guy you want. Girls fall over themselves to be your friend. You never struggled for anything, or so I thought.

It never dawned on me that maybe your struggle is on the inside. I shouldn't have judged you. You're one of the humblest people I've met. You're never mean. You care about others, and when you talk about a future for us, even a hypothetical one, it makes me want to believe in more.

In my world, you learn early that there is no point in dreaming. We're stuck children who become stuck parents. We never leave the town we grew up in, and thirty years down the line, we're washed-up carbon copies of our parents. I meant what I said to Rick earlier. I want to be better for you. I want to be someone deserving of you."

My cheeks are wet with tears. Swallowing thickly, I hold Ben's gaze.

"Nothing can touch us as long as we stick together," Dallas whispers against my shoulder.

I'm too emotional to answer.

Ben strokes his thumb over my bottom lip. "You're turning blue. Let's get out of the water for a bit."

————

We lie on the sand, swapping childhood stories. I soon find out that Dallas and her brother learned how to surf when she was eight. Ben tells me Nina taught him how to tie his shoelaces when they first met in the skatepark. She'd seen him struggle and crouched down beside him.

I tell them about last year, when Hailey and I decided to prank the football team by putting laxatives in their sports drinks before practice. The footballers still don't know who the culprits are. In fact, they falsely accused the basketball team. Haily and I still laugh about it. We plan to sprinkle itching powder in their football uniforms, but gaining access to their gear has proven difficult, especially after our last stunt.

I lie with my head on Ben's stomach, enjoying the afternoon sun on my face.

Dallas is on a mission to bury my legs and feet in the sand. "Apart from Rick and now Ben, of course." She winks. "Did you ever crush on any other boys at school?"

I wiggle my toes, disturbing the sand. My big toe, with its pink nail polish, peeks out. "Well, don't tell Rick, but I crushed on Sam for a while last year before he graduated."

"Sam?" Ben blurts out, amused. "Rick's older brother?"

I laugh, poking him in the side. "What? He's hot! I don't have to justify myself to you, Ben."

"At least he's not a footballer," he comments drily.

"New to town, remember. Tell me about this Sam guy," Dallas says, scooping more sand over my feet until my big toe no longer peeks out.

Ben shifts behind me, scratching the side of his jaw. "Sam plays drums in a local band that sounds like an unsupervised group of toddlers with pans and cutlery."

I sit forward and slap his chest, laughing. "Shut up! They're good."

He ignores me as he says to Dallas, "You know the type. Fucks everything with two legs. Thinks he's the bomb. Tattoos. Smokes cigarettes"

I giggle. "Trust me, his parents disapprove. Rick is the golden boy."

Leaning up on his elbows, he wiggles his eyebrows. "I should have guessed you have a thing for rebellious bad boys."

I shrug. "Not denying it. It's my turn to ask a question. Dallas, tell me something about Ben that he wouldn't tell me himself."

Dallas scoops another handful of sand over my feet, patting it down. "Well," she says with a mischievous glint in her eyes, and Ben grows tense behind me, "he slept with your Madison a couple of months back."

I shoot upright, disturbing the sand in the process. "You slept with Madison?"

He cringes. "Technically—"

Dallas holds up a hand, laughing. "Ben, you can't talk yourself out of this one."

My eyes resemble saucers. "You slept with one of my cheerleaders? You do realize I'll have to kill her now, right? Goddamn you, Ben! I need her on my team," I joke, trying my best to look serious but failing miserably.

Groaning, he rakes a hand through his green hair. "I didn't sleep with her. She sucked my dick. Big difference! Okay, my turn," he says before I can ask any more questions. "What's your favorite movie, princess?"

"That's easy," I reply. "Pulp Fiction."

Dallas's eyebrows hit her hairline. "Really? I took you more for a romantic comedy kind of girl."

I grin. "There's a lot you don't know about me."

She snorts a laugh as she grabs her bag. Rooting through it, she throws me a look. "Trust me, princess, I know."

"I suppose it's my turn again." I shift on the sand until I'm seated between Ben's legs, leaning back against his warm and muscular chest. "Why Lauren?" I've always wondered what made Dallas seduce the mayor's daughter in the girls' bathroom.

Dallas smirks as she hands us a granola bar each. "She was a challenge—a dare."

"A dare?" I ask, confused.

Dallas takes a bite of her granola bar, talking around a mouthful. "We do these dares. If I challenge Ben to a bet, he then makes a counter bet. It's just a silly game."

I chew on my lip in thought. "So, Ben challenged you to go down on Lauren. What was the counter bet?"

They exchange a glance over my head, and something passes between them, causing a feeling of unease to creep through me.

"I dared him to get video evidence of Mr. Roberts fucking Mrs. Flores," she admits, crinkling up the wrapper and putting it back in her bag.

My eyes bug out. "No fucking way! Are you serious? They're fucking?"

I can't believe it. Mr. Roberts is the *very* married IT teacher, and Mrs. Flores is my American lit teacher. I'll never be able to look at her the same way again.

Ben laughs behind me. "Don't sound so excited."

"I can't help it. This is crazy news. I have to give her desk a wide berth from now on." I shudder.

"You should probably avoid the desks on the front row, too," Dallas quips in an airy tone, smiling widely when she sees the look of horror on my face. She knows damn well I sit in the front row in that class. Well, never again!

———

"This is it, Em," I whisper to myself, pressing submit on my college application. It's done. It's out there now.

Picking up my phone, I collapse on my bed. I had such a great time at the beach today and haven't been able to stop smiling since I returned home.

I browse through the photos, debating if I should upload one to my Instagram. It makes me nervous. And not for the reasons you would think. It's not because I worry about my reputation or something equally ridiculous, but because it feels significant, in a way, to make it so public.

I pick a photograph of all of us lying on our backs in the sand, head-to-head, and caption it *'New Beginnings.'*

It feels good to put us out there for the world to see. I need them both to know that I'm not ashamed of them, and I'm not keeping them a secret. I'm done hiding. Whatever it is that we started, I want to see it through.

A notification pops up on my screen. Ben has posted a picture of me on his social media, but it's not a group photo like mine. It's of me snoozing on the beach in the late afternoon sun, shortly before we decided to head back home. The caption simply reads *'Princess.'*

I nearly jump out of my skin when my phone pings with a new text message.

Dallas: Good night, beautiful.

I type out a quick response. If this is what happiness feels like, I never want it to end.

# CHAPTER

## *fourteen*

## BEN

"I'M HAPPY ABOUT THIS, BEN." Mrs. Ackland beams at me behind her black-rimmed glasses. It's hard to say what possessed me to come to see the guidance counselor for advice, but alas, here I am.

"I have to say, young man, I never thought I would see the day you set foot in my office. I've chased you long enough."

I cringe. She's not lying. I always bolt when she tries to chase me down in the hallways, but one thing can be said for Mrs. Ackland—she doesn't give up on her students.

I fidget on the edge of my seat, my leg bouncing restlessly.

Noticing, she smiles softly. "Let's have a look at your grades, shall we?" She adjusts the glasses on her nose and taps away on the laptop in front of her. "Have you given any thought to what subjects you might want to study at college?"

Leaning my elbow on the armrest, I rub my lips. "Honestly? No. To tell you the truth, I just want to get out of here. Make something of myself. I'm not picky, as long as it gives me a chance at a better future."

She looks up from her screen and studies me for a moment before smiling that big smile of hers that shows too many teeth. "I'm not going to ask what's happened lately to bring about this change in you, Ben, but I like it. Now let's see what we're working with."

I sit in silence, listening to the obnoxiously loud clock on the wall above the door.

She hums thoughtfully, then picks up her coffee cup and takes a large gulp. The front reads in large bold letters, *'I became a school counselor because your life is worth my time.'*

I roll my eyes before I can stop myself.

She points at it. Her smile is too big for her face to be proportionate. "What, don't you like it?" She puts the cup back down, still beaming. "Do you know what I like about you, Ben? I like that you want everyone to think you don't care. The bright green hair. The tattoos, piercings, and black clothing with God only knows how many holes and rips. You wear it as a shield. It screams, "Stay the fuck away!"

My eyebrows shoot up in surprise.

She smiles knowingly. "But you do care, Ben. In fact, I would venture as far as to say you care more than you would ever admit even to yourself."

"Yeah? What makes you come to that conclusion?"

She takes another sip of her coffee, then looks at me over the bridge of her glasses. I wait, uneasy and intrigued by her scrutiny.

"Well," she starts, placing her mug back on the desk, twisting it until the writing faces me, "your grades tell me as much, Ben. You want the world to think you're trouble, so you don't have to live up to anyone's expectations because then you can't disappoint others. You also won't run the risk of being made to feel like a failure if things fall through. That way, you can't even disappoint yourself. But one look at your grades," she looks at me pointedly, "and I know you care more than a lot of the students at this school. So, I'm asking you, are you ready to believe in yourself?"

I stare at her. "The fuck are you talking about?"

"I'm talking about your GPA, Ben. You'll easily qualify for a scholarship if you keep this up. It's your shot at a better future, as you so adequately put it. And don't worry, your secret is safe with me."

With a wink, she removes her glasses to rub her left eye, flashing another toothy smile before placing them back on. "If you let me help you with this, I promise I won't breathe a word of it to your friends. We wouldn't want to ruin your street cred."

My mind is working overtime as I lean back in my chair. I've always done well in class, and I never neglect my schoolwork despite what other people think. But I didn't realize my effort was enough to amount to a scholarship. I never had anyone believe in me, which made it impossible to believe in myself.

*Wow…* this is precisely the kind of opportunity I need to finally escape this town, because my parents certainly can't afford to pay for college.

Leaning forward in my seat, I look Mrs. Ackland in the eyes. "Thank you!"

She smiles that big smile of hers and picks up the mug, pointing to it. "Your life is worth my time, Ben. Now, let's get this process started, shall we?"

———

"What the fuck is up with that?" Josh growls when we walk past the football field on our way to the library.

"What's up with what?" I ask, scanning the field.

He points. "Over there."

Princess and her friends sunbathe on the grass while they watch the boys' football practice. Jack, who should be out there doing ball pushups with his peers, crouches in front of Em. He brushes her hair away from her face, and I suck on my teeth as a twinge of annoyance flares up inside of me.

"He's been all over your girl for weeks," Josh spits.

"She's not my girl."

Why would she settle for someone like me when she has guys like Jack vying after her? He's rich, popular, and annoyingly good at football—everything I'm not. He can offer her things I can't.

Josh huffs next to me. "Fuck that, Ben. You need to claim her!

Trust me, if you don't, guys like Jack will be in there before you have a chance to blink."

"He's right," Matt chimes in on my other side. "You like her, don't you?"

"I do, and she knows that, but—"

Matt cuts me off. "She likes you, and you deserve something fucking good in your life for once." He turns, walking backward. "She's preppy, but she fits in with us. The girls like her too. Even April went on earlier about inviting her out this weekend. She wants another round of truth or dare."

His wink makes me laugh.

Groaning, Josh drags his hands down his face. "I get horny just thinking about it."

"You're always fucking horny!" Matt says, punching his arm. "Want to suck my dick again?"

I shake my head and smile. "You're as bad as each other."

We look over at the football field again, and I watch Princess laugh at something that Jack said. Why the fuck isn't he out there doing conditioning training with the rest of the team? Fucking annoying dick!

"He's not subtle, is he?" Matt grumbles when Jack whispers in Emily's ear.

Josh looks at me pointedly. "Jack thinks he's halfway in her panties."

I spread my arms wide. "What do you want me to do, man? Walk over there and hulk out?"

"That's exactly what you should do!"

Matt shakes his head. "I doubt that'll go over well."

I agree with him.

"Oh shit, too late anyway. Emily spotted us," Josh hisses under his breath, eyes widening in alarm.

Hiding my amused chuckle behind my closed fist, I look up in time to see a blinding smile spread across Emily's face. She waves as she gets to her feet and jogs over to us.

The confusion on Jack's face is comical.

"Hey!" Placing her hands on her hips, she smiles. She's dressed in her cheer uniform, and her blue eyes sparkle in the afternoon sun. "Has the stalked become the stalker? I can lend you my binoculars if you want. I'm sure there's a bush somewhere around here for you to hide behind." She pretends to look for one.

I really fucking like her witty humor.

"We're meeting up at Ben's later. You in?" Josh asks.

Emily taps her bottom lip with a manicured finger. "Are there gonna be games involved?" Her mischievous smile causes blood to rush to my dick.

Josh grins. "If you want there to be, then fuck yes! We'll play games."

Punching him a little too hard in the arm, I grin when he rubs the sore spot. That'll teach him.

"I'm counting on games," Princess purrs, walking up to me with purpose, swaying her hips.

I feel like a fly trapped in her web as she walks her manicured nails down my chest and stomach until she's dangerously close to my fly. She reminds me of a cat with a mouse—a hunter with its prey. Emily can switch from innocent to deadly in the space of a millisecond. It's what makes her so alluring.

I gulp.

Walking her fingers further down, she grazes my hardening dick. "Remember the time you took me out to the lookout spot?"

How can I ever forget? The image of her spread out like a buffet on my seat is imprinted on my mind.

Biting her plump bottom lip, she palms my cock through my jeans.

It twitches.

"I want you to come in my mouth again."

*Fuck!* My throat feels like sandpaper. It's that dry.

She winks, her ponytail swaying as she walks off. I stare after her like a lovesick puppy or a cartoon character with heart-eyes.

"What a cocktease!" chuckles Josh, patting me on the shoulder in solidarity. We both know I have no other choice but to rub one out in the only stall in the boys' bathroom or sit through class with a fucking hard-on.

I adjust my erection as discreetly as possible out here in the fucking open and make my way over to the main building, ignoring Matt and Josh's laughter behind me.

———

I'm rummaging through the fridge when the front door slams.

"Did you jizz all over the stall?" Steph calls out, smirking knowingly when she walks into the kitchen with April close on her heels.

"Fucking funny," I grumble. You know you're a whipped motherfucker when you jerk off in a dirty toilet stall instead of calling up one of your regulars. I might just as well cut off my balls and gift wrap them for Princess.

Steph puts several grocery bags on the table and asks April to fetch glasses. "A little bird told me Greg is finally home from the hospital."

I close the fridge a little too hard. "Is that so?"

"Well, shattered kneecaps require a very long and painful recovery time."

April reaches up in the cupboard. The cabinet door is only partly attached. "Rumor has it he's too frightened to talk."

"He better fucking be," I spit. "He's dead if he goes near Dallas again, and he knows it."

April hums in agreement as she passes glasses to Steph. "I think we taught him a lesson that he won't forget anytime soon."

"What's that?" Matt asks as he walks into the kitchen, grabbing an overripe apple from the fruit bowl and squeezing April's ass.

She slaps him on the chest, batting her eyelashes. "Remember, babe, when we played with Greg?"

Matt moves in, nipping her jaw with his teeth. "How can I

forget? Violence makes you horny. You let me ride your ass all night if I remember correctly."

"Charming," Steph says, rolling her eyes as she pours vodka into the glasses.

Matt winks at me over April's head and bites into his apple.

After handing me a drink, Steph says to Matt, "You and April won me a lot of money. I put money on you finally getting down and dirty after we taught Greg a lesson, so I should thank you." She pins me with her brown eyes. "Now, it would be great if you and Dallas could hurry up and have that threesome with Princess. I have a lot of money riding on you fucking her before the twelfth of this month."

My brows furrow. "Why the twelfth?"

Matt, who's in the process of dry humping April from behind while she giggles, explains in an amused voice, "Well, at first it was a case of 'will they or won't they?' But now it's a matter of when so we changed the stakes to make it more exciting. Josh has already lost out. He bet you would fuck before the ninth, which was yesterday. Steph is up next."

I roll my eyes, catching the half-eaten apple he chucks at me. "This has got out of hand. I like her, guys. Dallas likes her too. The bet is off."

Steph scoffs. "Fuck you! The money is already in the pot. Your flowery feelings are not coming in between me and easy money. It's just a bit of fun."

Laughing, I chuck her on the chin. "You're cute when you get all feisty. I expect a big part of the takings when you win."

She slaps my hand away, then takes a large sip of alcohol, glaring at me over the rim of the glass.

April drops down on her knees in front of Matt, who plants his feet and grips hold of the table's edge. I shake my head exasperatedly and throw the apple in the garbage as his belt clinks and April giggles. "I'm starting to think we should establish some boundaries. Our friendship is weird as fuck."

Steph laughs. "It never bothered you before, lover boy. Is Miss Prissy turning you into a prude?"

My eyes narrow while I take a swig of the drink she handed me earlier. I wince. It tastes like shit. The vodka and sprite ratio is way off, and all I can taste is vodka burning its way down my throat. "Don't you have anything better to do? You're getting on my fucking nerves."

Steph shrugs, unperturbed, when the front door slams.

"I'm here!" Josh shouts in an obnoxiously loud voice as he joins us in the kitchen, carrying trays of beer with Nina in tow.

*Thank fuck!*

Walking over to the sink, I pour the sad excuse of a drink down the drain.

"Who've you got down there, Matty?" Josh grins. "April, are you getting the party started early?"

I smack Josh on the back of the head. "Put the beer on the coffee table. Let's play some fucking Halo and leave Matt to get his dick sucked in peace."

Matt grunts in acknowledgment.

"Where's Dallas?" Josh asks as we enter the living room. Dropping down on the couch, he reaches for the controller on the coffee table.

"She's been in the bath for the last hour. She'll be a fucking prune when she gets out."

Josh smirks. "I'm sure she wouldn't mind it if you joined her."

I smirk back but don't tell him that things have changed between us after Emily stepped into our lives.

Since then, we haven't touched each other sexually. It no longer feels right to use each other for release when we care about the same girl.

I'm not sure when things changed for me. I'm not even sure how I feel about it. Everything was easier before Princess came along and turned everything on its head. Dallas used me for her needs, and I got my dick wet with random girls. It worked, but now I can't get Emily out of my head. I'm whipped by a fucking cheerleader—a princess from the wealthy parts of town. It's almost comical.

"Where's Princess? Shouldn't she be here soon?" Josh asks, bringing me back to the present.

I check my phone. "She messaged me fifteen minutes ago to say she's on her way."

We start up another game while Nina and Steph move the coffee table forward. They can settle by our feet on the floor, rolling a joint.

Steph licks the edge and says to Nina, "Did the guy from chess club finally grow a pair of balls and talk to you yet? He's had googly eyes for you for months."

Nina looks intrigued. "Who?"

"You know? The brown-haired guy with really curly hair who wears chinos and tucked-in-shirts."

Nina lights up. "You mean the guy who fainted when we dissected frogs last year?"

We all chuckle. The poor guy didn't handle it well.

"The one and only," Steph replies, placing the joint between her lips. She digs in her front pocket for a lighter and lights it up.

Grinning, Nina sinks her teeth into her bottom lip. "Thanks for the heads-up. I always wanted to train a virgin. He's kind of cute if you look past the preppy clothes and the fact that all he seems to talk about are math equations and global warming." She squeals, making us all cringe. "I'll suck him off. It will make his day at school on Monday. I can't wait to see his reaction. He'll probably blow his load the minute I take him in my mouth, but trust me, he'll be my personal sex slave in no time."

There's a timid knock on the door, and Princess steps inside.

"Ah!" Steph grins, holding her joint up in the air for Emily to see. "Just in time for the ganja."

Emily puts her bag down on the floor. "Where's Dallas?"

"Good fucking question," Steph replies before hollering at the top of her lungs, "Dallas, get the fuck down here!" She smiles at us. "That should do it. Why don't you take a seat on Ben's cock in the meantime? He's been broody as shit today."

Rubbing my hands over my face, I scowl at her. "Thanks, Steph."

She has no fucking filter.

"You're very welcome, Benny-boy. Just being helpful."

Princess walks over to me and makes herself comfortable on my lap as if she's always belonged there. I like it a lot. Especially when she puts her hands behind my neck, toying absentmindedly with my hair.

She frowns. "Where's Matt and April?"

"Well," Josh replies without taking his eyes off the screen, "Matt was busy getting his dick sucked when we left the kitchen. He probably has April spread out on Ben's rickety kitchen table like a five-course meal by now. My advice? Stay in here."

Dallas enters the room, her hair still wet from the bath. "I would listen to Josh. April can get very vocal when she wants."

Emily shifts on my lap. "Trust me, I remember from last time." She turns her attention to Josh. "Are you ready to have your pretty little ass spanked again?"

Chuckling, I twirl a strand of her blond hair around my index finger. She wiped the floor with him last time they played on the Xbox.

"The day I play you again is a cold day in hell, princess."

"Afraid to lose?" Emily taunts with a grin, waving her controller in the air.

Josh throws her a bemused look before he smirks and says, "Ben should play. He likes to have his ass spanked."

I narrow my eyes at him just as Dallas joins us on the couch.

Studying the three of us, Steph blows smoke rings. We take turns with the joint, talking about random shit. Emily wriggles and squirms so much that I soon sport a hard-on.

April and Matt look flushed as they rejoin us in the living room. Matt rests his elbows on the back of the couch. "Your girl is brutal," he says with a grin, referring to the game.

His lips are far too fucking close to my ear. "Fuck off, Matt. You reek of pussy," I growl before taking a deep drag on the joint and passing it to him.

"Jealousy looks bad on you." The joint sparks as he sucks on it, squinting at Emily. "Looking hot today, babe. I dig the dress."

"Oh, this little number?" she grins, glancing down at her black mini-dress. "It goes with the theme, don't you think?"

She's referring to our black clothes.

"Sure does." He offers the joint to Dallas, then leans forward with a grin that tells me he's up to no good. "I hear there's a party at Jack's tonight."

Definitely suspicious. I narrow my eyes on him. "What are you doing?"

Matt flashes his teeth, and his dimples pop. He could easily pass for a golden boy with his blonde hair and smile dimples if it weren't for the ripped black clothing.

Shifting on my lap and grinding her ass on my hard cock, Emily places the controller down on the table. I grit my teeth. If she's not careful, I'll bend her over the coffee table and fuck her right here.

"Unless you're ashamed of us, of course?" Matt asks her, ignoring my question.

Why is he stirring shit?

Emily looks defiant. "I'm not embarrassed."

Matt smiles even wider. "Are you sure about that? What will your friends say if you turn up with us? It can't be good for your reputation?" He doesn't say it maliciously, but there's an edge to his voice—a challenge.

"I'm not embarrassed!"

"Matt!" Dallas warns in a sharp voice, subtly shaking her head.

Ignoring her, he leans in to tug a strand of Emily's blonde hair, rolling it around his finger. "Let's play a game, princess."

"Go on," she breathes out in a quiet voice.

Matt clucks his tongue, chuckling. "How about a bet?"

*Oh, no, no, no.* I look at Dallas in alarm.

"Matt? No," she blurts, staring at him wide-eyed. With his eyebrow raised, Matt wets his lips expectantly.

"What's the dare?" Emily asks carefully. She has every right to be cautious.

"Well," he grins, pushing off the couch and taking his pussy smell with him, "I dare you to take us to Jack's party and deceive him by leading him on. You will make him think he's about to get his cock wet, and then you're gonna tell him you need the bathroom." He walks back to the couch and leans his elbows on the back of it. His lips are mere inches from Emily's. "When he goes looking for you, he'll walk in on you with Ben and Dallas." Leaning in closer, his lips brush her ear as he whispers, "Fucking."

Silence descends on the room. I know we play some crazy fucking games, but he's asking her to commit social suicide.

Princess stands up, rounds the couch and walks over to him, her hips swaying. The hunter has become the hunted. I see it in her eyes when she trails them down Matt's body like she's seizing up prey.

She comes to a stop in front of him, slowly walking her fingers up his chest. "I will accept your bet on one condition."

Intrigued, he raises his eyebrows. "Yeah?"

Emily steps even closer, pressing her body against his. "I get to make a counter bet."

Nina snorts a laugh, Steph's eyes bug out, and Josh rubs his hands in anticipation.

Matt glances at us, then nods. "Let's hear it, princess."

It's about to get interesting. Princess likes our twisted games and gives as good as she gets.

"You're gonna suck Jack's dick. I'll only do my bit when you have the video evidence. How's that for a double dare?"

Matt's smile falls away. "Why would I do that?"

Emily laughs, and it's a soft, feminine sound with an undertone of something darker. She smooths down his T-shirt. "Baby, a queen doesn't keep her throne by allowing treason in her kingdom. And you, Matt, won't dethrone me anytime soon."

Her plan is ingenious. It would be stupid to throw her reputation out the window because of a bet, so she needs an insurance policy if Jack decides to talk after she makes a fool of him. This way, she'll have video evidence that Jack will not want to be made public.

"You should admit that you have a thing for watching people suck dick," Matt grumbles, grabbing a beer off the coffee table and making his way to the door. "What the fuck are you guys waiting for? Let's play some fucking games."

Nina jumps up. "I bet twenty bucks that Jack spunks within the first two minutes."

Steph pockets her phone and throws her arm over Dallas's shoulder. "Not a chance. He's as straight as they come. I bet you twenty he doesn't even go for it."

Sticking her tongue out, Nina follows Matt out the door. "You better hand over your money now, bitch!"

# CHAPTER
## *fifteen*

## EMILY

JACK LIVES in a contemporary colonial house, with matching statues at the gate, pillars, and a balcony stretching the entire upper floor. It's similar to the one I live in, but my parents decided against the statues. Apparently, they were too pretentious, but the rose bushes that our poor gardener spends hours on every week were not.

We walk up the busy drive. The lawn is littered with empty plastic cups, and music blares from inside the large house. A couple makes out against the side of the house, oblivious to us as we walk past.

We round the back of the property. The infinity pool is full of drunk teenagers, and girls dance nearby in tiny bikinis that make my black mini-dress look modest.

Steph grins. "I see Jack. He's over by the lounge seats."

"You don't have to do this," Dallas says to me, taking my hand in hers. "We can leave now or stay for a drink. No one is forcing you to do this dare."

"I want to." I wink at Matt. "If Matt can pull off his part of the dare."

Matt smirks. "Don't question my capabilities again, princess."

"Babe," April sings as she sidles up next to Matt, wrapping her arms around his midriff. "I can't believe you're about to join the cock-sucking club. My baby is growing up." Pretending to dab away tears, she continues, "I'm sure Josh will give you a pointer or two if you ask him."

Matt quirks a brow. "I don't know. Maybe I should ask you instead? You're quite the hoover."

She tuts, unfaced by his dig. "No, babe. Compliments won't get you anywhere. I remember when you said in the group chat that Josh is your favorite."

The man in question is staring longingly at a group of bikini-clad girls nearby.

"I think his brain cells have gone on holiday." Nina giggles, waving a hand in front of Josh's face.

"I knew the group chat was a bad idea," Matt grumbles, before looking over at Jack in thought. "I'll just wing it, but first, I need to plant the camera in the bathroom." He pats his pockets. "I've got my phone… It'll probably be the worst blowjob of his life."

"Or his best." Steph winks.

Matt rubs his face. "Let's just get this over with." He looks at me. "I'll forward the video to you later when it's done. I expect video evidence from you too."

"Fuck off!" Ben growls. "We'll film the door, but there's no fucking way I'm gonna let you see a video of Em like that."

Laughing heartily, Matt thumps Ben on the shoulder. "You mean like how you let me watch the video of her, Dallas and Rick?" He mimics a blow job and I glare at Dallas.

She raises her hands placatingly. "It's deleted! I couldn't keep it. Not after you chewed me out in the chemistry lab."

Before I have a chance to reply, Matt says, "You forget the time we watched her fuck Dallas in your living room. I've seen it all, Benny-boy." He enjoys getting a rise out of Ben.

"I don't fucking care!" Ben spits out. "We film the door to capture his reaction, or the bet is off. I'm already fucking angry that Jack will see her and Dell like that."

Tearing his gaze away from the bikini-clad girls, Josh shrugs. "You can always blind him."

Ben stares at him as if he's stupid. "That won't erase the memory from his brain, you dipshit."

They bicker back and forth until Matt says, "Film the fucking door if that makes you feel better. I'm going in." He turns on his heel, and we watch him disappear into the crowd of people. Jack is nowhere to be seen.

"What do we do now?" Steph asks, looking out of place as she scans the crowded backyard.

Josh rubs his hands together excitedly. "Now we get drunk. I spotted some provisions in the kitchen over there." He points to the big patio doors.

I feel a hand on my shoulder and I turn to see Hailey smiling at me. She pulls me into a bone-crushing hug.

She's drunk.

"Girl!" she hiccups. "I missed you! You didn't tell me you were coming here tonight, and look, you brought your friends." She lets me go before pulling Steph in for a hug, blowing her wild curls out of her face.

Steph stares at me wide-eyed while patting Hailey awkwardly on the back.

"I love your curls!" Hailey hiccups. "Em has told me so many things about you. Is it true that you fuck in front of each other?"

*Oh my god.* She has no filter.

Steph narrows her eyes on me, and I smile innocently.

"Girls talk, Steph."

Laughing under her breath, Dallas waves to Hailey. "I'm Dallas. It's nice to finally meet you."

Hailey flashes her professionally whitened teeth. "Wow, you're so pretty!"

Drunk Hailey is a very happy Hailey.

She turns to Ben, who backs up a step, looking alarmed.

"Why green?" She tugs his hair none too gently, forcing him to bend his head down to her level.

Ben looks terrified.

I slap my hand over my mouth, stifling the laughter that bubbles up inside me.

"You're so cute!" She squishes his cheeks together. "I just want to take you home with me and keep you forever and ever and ever!" She stiffens as if she realizes how her words can be construed, then looks at me. "Oh no, Em. I didn't mean it like that. This…us…" she gestures between her and Ben. "…completely platonic."

Shaking with laughter, I steer her over to an empty lounge chair. Thankfully she goes willingly, waving to Ben over her shoulder. She's going to be mortified tomorrow.

"Isn't he the cutest? I love the lip piercing," she whispers, but in truth, she's really fucking loud.

"Cute isn't the word I would use. But yes, Ben is nice."

More hiccups. More giggles. She lies back on the lounge chair and strands of her long hair slide off the edge, touching the decking. "Nice? Bitch, don't be humble. You *looove* his dick! You *waaant* his dic—"

Pressing a palm over her mouth, I smile awkwardly at a group of girls laughing nearby. "Do you mind saying that a little bit louder? The people over there on the other side of the yard didn't hear you."

Hailey mumbles behind my palm, and I hesitantly remove it.

"You're in love. Oh my god, Em. You're in love!"

"Jesus, quiet, Hailey!" I hiss, grateful that the others are too far away to overhear us. The scary thing is that she's right. I've come to the same realization too, but this isn't the right time and place for this conversation.

Hailey mimics zipping her lips. "I won't breathe a word."

Just then, Nina sidles up next to me, popping her gum. The grin on her face says it all. "Matt did it. I saw them enter the bathroom together."

"No way!" I didn't think he could pull it off. I worry my lip as I pace on the spot. It's too late to back out now, but I don't want to back out, do I? God, I can't make sense of the myriad of emotions inside me.

Nina gives the others the thumbs up—a signal to say that the game is underway.

"I'm missing something, aren't I?" Hailey observes from her upside-down position on the lounge chair. Before I can respond, she jumps up and throws herself in Jamie's arms. I didn't even notice him until now.

"Hey, Em," he says in his deep and gravelly voice before turning his attention to the giggling girl in his arms. "How much have you had to drink, babe?"

My phone vibrates in my purse, and my heart begins to pound like the thundering hooves of wild stallions. I swipe the screen with shaky hands. There's a new message in the group chat.

Matty: I rocked his world! *rock on emoji*

Matty: Break his heart, princess ;)

"Holy shit! I can't believe it worked," Nina laughs next to me
We move further away from the crowd.

"Did you watch it yet?" Dallas asks, looping her arm through mine as she and the others join us.

"No, we're about to now." I scan the area to make sure we are alone before pressing play on the phone and holding it out so everyone can see. Nina's face is close to mine, her bob tickling my cheek.

Matt and Jack enter the spacious bathroom with its twin sink and walk-in shower. The lavishness is lost on Matt. He goes in for the kill, kissing Jack hungrily before Jack barely has a chance to lock the door. They collide against it, fisting each other's shirts and growling into each other's mouths. Matt pulls Jack's belt through the loops with eager fingers, then drops to his knees, starting on the buttons.

Not that Jack seems to mind—quite the opposite. He grips

hold of the sink behind him and plants his feet, looking down at Matt. I never thought Jack would go for it, but judging by the blatant lust in his eyes, he's not as straight as he wants everyone to believe.

Matt lowers Jack's boxers, and his big cock springs free, bobbing against his stomach, precum beaded on the tip.

"God, he's hot, isn't he?" Nina groans next to me, her hair tickling my cheek.

Nodding in agreement, I smile when Ben's eyes narrow on me. "Don't be jealous, babe."

Jack's voice draws my attention back.

"Eyes on me when you suck me." He strokes his dick, grabbing a handful of Matt's blonde hair. "I've fantasized about this for a long time."

"What?!" April squeals opposite me and I meet her wide eyes.

"Oh, yeah?" Matt grins. "Today's your lucky day." With his eyes on Jack, he takes him in his mouth, stroking the long shaft.

Widening his stance, Jack groans through clenched teeth.

"This is so fucking hot!" April breathes out, and Nina nods eagerly next to me. I'm inclined to agree. Matt doesn't do anything by halves, and this is no different.

Matt stares up at Jack, moaning low in his throat before picking up speed and taking him deeper.

"Fuck!" Jack's eyes are glued to his cock in Matt's mouth. He grabs a handful of Matt's short blonde hair and begins thrusting his hips, setting a pace he likes.

"Matt is a natural," Josh chuckles, palming himself. "This is going straight in the spank bank for later."

I roll my eyes, but I'm also amused.

"What's happening now?" Steph asks.

We watch as Jack pulls Matt up by the hair, slamming their lips together and attacking his belt and jeans. He moves Matt's boxers down to his ankles, and Matt lifts his head, throwing a surreptitious look at the camera over Jack's shoulders.

His attention is soon back on Jack, though, when he begins stroking Matt's cock in long, firm pulls. "Fuck, that feels good!"

They watch each other, panting.

"You want more?" Jack breathes out and his lips curve as he grabs Matt by the hips. Spinning him around, he presses a firm hand to Matt's back, forcing him to lean over the twin sink.

"I'm not letting you fuck me!" Matt snarls, looking through the mirror at Jack behind him.

With a dark smile, Jack strokes himself while running his other hand over Matt's ass. "Maybe not tonight." He spits on his palm and wets his cock, placing it between Matt's ass cheeks.

*"Oh, fuck!"* Matt groans, pushing back against Jack, who smirks.

"You'll be begging for my cock soon enough."

Steph laughs. "We've let loose a monster."

Waving her hand frantically in the air, April shushes her. "It's about to get interesting."

I chuckle too. It's certainly heating up.

Jack leans over Matt, resting his palm on the sink. He begins to move, his eyes locked on Matt in the mirror. Reaching down and palming Matt's cock, he strokes it in time with his thrusts. "You'll beg me to fuck your ass one day, and when that day comes, I'll take you so fucking hard, you won't be able to sit for a week!"

"Never gonna happen!" Matt pants, his face screwed up in pleasure.

Jack chuckles, watching him in the mirror. "Keep telling yourself that, pretty boy." He picks up speed, thrusting hard and fast between Matt's cheeks.

Matt shakes and groans as he edges closer. Jack works Matt's cock faster and harder until he spills his seed in spurts over the sink cabinet. Before Matt has a chance to recover, Jack comes with a grunt, covering Matt's ass with cum.

"Jesus, fuck!" Jack curses, dropping his forehead to Matt's shoulder, breathing hard.

"You should leave first, so we're not seen together," Matt chokes out, still trembling.

Jack straightens and runs a hand through his cum on Matt's ass, smearing it. "I like you like this, freshly fucked and covered in my cum."

Pushing off the sink, Matt tucks himself back in. He winks as he buttons up his jeans and says, "You haven't fucked me yet."

Chuckling, Jack tightens his belt. "See you around, blondie."

The door clicks shut behind him, and Matt walks over to where the camera is hidden. Crouching down, he smirks. "Not bad for my first time. It's your turn, princess. Go crush his dreams."

The video ends.

"I don't think I could crush his heart even if I tried," I say, laughing weakly.

Nina scoffs. "He's into women. Don't worry."

"And men," I whisper, still staring at the phone in my hand. "You guys know what to do," I say to Ben and Dallas. They're to find us an empty bedroom upstairs while I flirt with Jack.

Maybe it's a cruel game, but I can't deny the thrill. Jack won't care. If he gets upset, it'll only be because of his bruised ego.

"I don't like this," Ben whispers in my ear, his hand on my hip.

I press a finger to his lips. "It's just a game, babe."

Unconvinced, he searches my eyes. "If he touches you Em—"

I hush him, smiling. "Don't worry so much. Let's have fun."

# CHAPTER
## sixteen

## EMILY

AFTER SEPARATING FROM THE OTHERS, I make my way straight to the spacious kitchen in need a drink to ease my nerves.

I'm pouring myself another shot when Jack finds me. Placing the bottle down, I smile to myself. I knew he would seek me out despite my earlier doubts, and here he is, leaning against the kitchen doorway, dressed in a black Henley and distressed light blue jeans.

"Fancy seeing you here, Em."

I don't reply.

His brown hair falls in his eyes and he drags a hand through it, messing it up further. "Are you having a good time?"

I take a sip, eyeing him over the rim. "Sure am."

Jack is attractive, and he knows it. I can tell by the way he carries himself. Even I feel drawn to him when he pins me in place with his jade eyes.

Pushing off the doorway, he invades my space, placing his hands on the island behind me.

I neck my shot and put the glass back down. I'm boxed in against the island with nowhere to go. Jack is so big, I can't see past him.

As I swipe my tongue over a drop of tequila on my bottom lip, Jack's eyes follow the movement, lingering on my mouth. It's confusing to me how he looks at me as if he wants to take me right here on the kitchen island, when he was all over Matt earlier. I can't make sense of him which is both intriguing and frustrating.

The Jack I know cares about what others think of him. His image is important. However, the Jack who let Matt seduce him in the bathroom is not the same guy looming over me now.

We're a lot alike, and I hate to admit that he intrigues me. I want to find out more.

"Dance with me." I take his hand, leading him into the crowded living room. The cream couches have been moved aside to create a temporary dance floor and the overhead lights muted.

Jack pulls me to him just as 'Somebody Else' by The 1975 starts playing. I bury my hands in the curls at the nape of his neck and press up against him as he begins moving us to the beat. He leans down and nips my neck playfully with his teeth.

Why does he have to smell so good? *Feel so good?*

Closing my eyes, I let myself enjoy his hard body against mine. I love how he commands my body to the beat with such ease. His touch is firm and confident.

In a different world, I could fall for Jack. We make sense together. Too much sense.

Turning me in his arms, he guides my hands behind his neck and bands his thick arms around my waist. His lips brush my ears. "You know how to move."

With a teasing smile, I grind my ass against his crotch. "You're not so bad yourself, big boy."

He chuckles, guiding me in his arms again until I'm staring into his jade eyes. His forehead comes down on mine and he moves us to the beat. It's just the two of us in this moment while everything else fades away. Even the bet is forgotten about as we move together.

My fingers tangle in his silky brown locks and I pull on the strands to bring his lips closer to mine.

I'm turned on, shamefully so.

"Close your eyes, Emily," he whispers.

I do, losing myself in the song. In his heat and breath on my tingling lips.

Cupping my jaw, he releases another trembling breath. "Em —" he whispers, but my head shakes no.

"Let's just dance, Jack."

I don't want to ruin this moment. Not yet.

We move together effortlessly. His heart beats rapidly beneath my touch as I run my hands down his hard chest and over his contracting abs.

My fingers hover inches away from his waistband when I feel eyes on me. There's only one person whose gaze can burn a path over my skin like that.

Jack turns me in his arm and buries his nose in my neck, wrapping his large hand around my throat. It's not a tight grip, but it's possessive. My eyes clash with Ben's across the room. His jaw is tense, and his stormy eyes flash with jealousy.

Brushing my hair off my shoulder, Jack skims his hot lips over the sensitive area below my ear. I know my physical reaction to his touch is evident in the parting of my lips. I can't stop it. Ben wasn't supposed to be here to see this.

Dallas drags Ben away by the elbow, and he throws me one final look over his shoulder before the crowd swallows him up.

I try not to feel guilty. This is part of the bet, so why is he getting jealous? I'm supposed to lead Jack on. It's what we agreed on. Ben knows it's not personal.

Jealousy has no place on this game board, so when Jack leans down and presses his lips to mine, I let him. A masculine sound rumbles in his chest. I turn in his arms and kiss him back, fisting his black Henley. The kiss goes from slow and sweet to explosive within seconds.

Jack groans into my mouth and grinds his hard cock against my stomach until I squirm with need. But while it's his tongue in my mouth and his hands on my body, it's the fire in Ben's stormy eyes that I see behind my closed eyelids. It's the memory of Ben's groans in my ears. And his big hands, commanding my body to his will.

These thoughts flitter through my mind as Jack deepens the kiss. I swallow his deep groans, clutching him to me.

Is he here with me, or is he somewhere else too? Perhaps in the arms of a certain blonde-haired boy with a killer smile and dimples? Is he using me as much as I'm using him?

I reluctantly break away. "Let's get a drink." Grabbing hold of his warm hand, I pull him along behind me through the crowds of people.

Matt and Josh watch us curiously as we walk past, and I swallow down the sense of unease swirling in my stomach.

*It's just a game.*

Pulling me to him, Jack drapes his arm over my shoulder as we re-enter the kitchen. The island is littered with discarded plastic cups and drink bottles. Swiping his arm over the surface, Jack sends the contents crashing to the floor. He lifts me up like I weigh nothing and deposits me on top. I pull him to me by his shirt, my legs wrapping around his waist.

"What are we doing, Jack?"

He smirks, toying with a strand of my hair, oblivious to the other people in the kitchen. "Wasting time, Em."

Intrigued, I cock my head. "Why do I get the feeling there's more to you than you let the world see?"

There are layers to Jack. Secrets. We are not so different after all. We both have darkness in us. I can see it in his eyes when he narrows them on me.

"Stop trying to figure me out." He pulls my hair a little too sharply, and the threat in his voice isn't lost on me. Instead of scaring me off, it entices me further. I'm drawn to him like a moth to a flame.

I skim my fingers along the smooth, warm skin where his T-shirt meets the waistband of his denim jeans. "Why Jack? Skeletons in your closet? Don't worry, mine come out to play at night too," I taunt, poking the beast hidden within the shadows that flicker in his eyes.

Wrapping his hand around my throat in warning, he whispers darkly but deliciously, "Careful, Em!"

I laugh loudly, surprising us both. "Oh, Jack. What a pleasant surprise you turned out to be."

He growls deep in his throat, pushing me down on the island. I go willingly. The sticky, hard surface is cold against my back, and broken glass crunch beneath his feet as he leans over me, bringing his face close to mine. Students watch us curiously, but my attention is solely on Jack. His intensity sparks something primal inside me—something as dark as she shadows in his eyes.

"There are some demons you don't wish to invite out to play," he whispers, tightening his grip on my throat.

Who is toying with who now? The lines are blurred.

I trap my lip between my teeth while I take in his rigid posture. There's so much restrained power. Jack is holding on by a thread, and when his carefully constructed tower of cards comes tumbling down, it'll be glorious.

Smiling, I show him the darkness that consumes my own soul. "You see me, don't you, Jack?" I glance around the room, nudging my head toward a group of cheerleaders nearby. "Not the version of me I allow others to see, but the real me."

I look back at Jack. "It turns you on, and that confuses you. Do you know why, Jack?" Leaning up on my elbows, my lips ghost his. "It turns you on because we share the same darkness, you and me. We're the same. It's why you feel alone and unseen amongst your friends. It doesn't matter how many girls suck your dick"—*or boys*— "or how popular you are at school. You hunger for something darker." Stroking my hand down his chest, where his heart thrums wildly, I smile. "Your darkness responds to mine. It calls to it." I palm his hard cock through his jeans, feeling it harden even more in my hand.

His control snaps and he slams his lips to mine. We both know this is purely physical. I give into him entirely as he ravages me on the kitchen island. His hands roam everywhere, tangling in my hair and palming my ass before exploring the planes of my taut stomach over my dress. I kiss him until my lungs burn. Biting his bottom lip, I lick away the coppery blood that rushes to the surface. I have him where I want him.

His hand disappears beneath my dress and he cups my pussy, rubbing his palm over my clit.

My panties are soaked.

I break away from his lips, breathing hard. It's time to move things along before I do something I regret later.

Jack moves in for another kiss, but I lean out of reach. "I need to use the bathroom upstairs."

"Don't be long." He reluctantly lets me go, his eyes following me as I leave the room. I walk past Matt and Josh, who had front-row seats to the show, but I don't look back.

The hallway upstairs is empty except for a drunk cheerleader who exits the bathroom and wobbles downstairs. My fingers tremble with nerves as I dig through my purse for my phone.

Dallas: Third bedroom on the left.

This is it. My nerves threaten to get the better of me as I turn the handle and step into the room. I make sure to leave it unlocked for Jack. I know he'll come and find me.

The room is dark except for a single lamp on one of the bedside tables. I look around the vast space. It's a big room with cream walls and a four-poster bed with sheer white curtains. Next to the bed is a moss-green recliner chair and a small bookshelf filled with paperbacks and an artificial plant. It's not the master room, but it's not an unused room either, judging by the book and drinking glass on the nightstand.

Sweeping my eyes past the bed, I spot Ben and Dallas by the window seat, watching me expectantly. The fire from earlier still burns in Ben's eyes.

My heart starts racing in my chest and I gulp, fidgeting on the spot. My hands are clammy with nerves. I've fantasized about this moment, but I'm not sure what to do now that it's happening.

"Come here," Ben smirks, quirking a finger.

I swallow thickly, my eyes moving between Ben and Dallas. It's only a matter of time until Jack comes looking for me, so I need to act, but I'm nervous. I have no experience with this. My heart thunders in my chest as I place one foot in front of the other.

Ben and Dallas box me in.

"You're nervous," Dallas says, running her soft fingers over my collarbone, and my pulse jumps at her touch. Ben towers behind me. Leaning down, he kisses and nibbles a path along my jaw. I arch my neck to give him better access when a moan slips from my lips.

"You smell of him," Ben growls, gripping my waist possessively and grinding his hard cock against my ass. I like this jealous side of him.

He skims his fingers up my bare thigh, lifting my skirt up in the process, and all thoughts evaporate when I feel his touch brush my damp panties. "Is this for him?" he whispers darkly, hooking his fingers in my panties and moving them aside.

I can't stop a whimper from dancing on my lips as he strokes his fingers through my wet slit and begins to circle my clit.

*God, yes...*

Dallas leans in, pressing her plump lips to mine. She tastes like watermelon lip balm and tequila. I moan into her mouth, burying my hands in her long, raven hair.

Kissing me hungrily, she palms my breasts, tweaking my hardened nipples through the fabric. I need my clothes off. They've never felt more restricting than they do now. Dallas grins knowingly against my lips.

"Answer me!" Ben snarls, plunging two fingers inside me savagely.

I moan into Dallas's mouth, and she swallows my sounds of pleasure with hungry kisses that leave me gasping for air. Jack turned me on earlier, but this… it's something else. It's too much and not enough at the same time.

"Oh god!" I whimper when she breaks away to kiss a path down my neck while Ben keeps up his assault on my pussy, pumping his fingers in and out until my legs shake. Dallas moves the straps off my shoulders, tugs down my dress and bares my aching breasts. I have fantasized about this moment so many times, but nothing could prepare me for the overwhelming sensations.

Leaning in, Dallas covers my nipple with her hot mouth. Looking up at me through black-rimmed eyes, she begins circling the hardened tip with her tongue. She wants me to watch—to see her plump lips wrapped around my peaked nipple.

She palms my other breast and digs her sharp nails in, causing me to cry out and clamp around Ben's fingers when she bites down on the flesh.

"You like that, baby?" Ben breathes in my ear. "Does it turn you on when we mark you?"

I moan in response, my head falling back on his shoulder. This feels so right and yet so forbidden.

Dallas strips me down until my dress lies in a pool around my feet. I step out from their arms and walk backward to the bed, unhooking my bra. I twirl it in the air with a playful smile. It feels good to change the power dynamics.

"Strip! I demand, throwing my bra at Ben. It smacks him on the chest and falls to the floor by his feet. "What's the matter, Ben? You look surprised." With a teasing smirk, I hold my lace panties up in the air. I look at Dallas. "Ready to catch?"

I miss my throw, and they land at her feet. She stares down at them in disbelief, then lifts her gaze. She's amused. I can tell by the expression on her face as she begins shedding her clothes. "It's like that, is it?"

Ben pulls his T-shirt over his head, causing his tousled green hair to become even messier. I squeal with laughter when he lifts me off the floor and throws me down on the big bed.

"I'm gonna fuck you so damn hard!" he growls, climbing on after me with his jeans and shoes still on. "You'll scream this fucking place down!

"Promises. Promises." My legs fall open and he comes after me like a lion stalking its prey.

Reaching down, I spread my glistening pussy lips. "Want a taste?"

Ben groans, looking tortured. Dallas joins us on the bed while Ben climbs on top of me, pressing me down into the soft mattress with his heavy body. I moan and writhe on the bed as Ben begins to grind himself against me. The rough fabric of his jeans rubs against my most sensitive parts. It's almost too much, but I buck against him and rub my pussy against his crotch. I want to feel him inside me. *I need it so fucking bad!*

Arching my back and pushing my naked breasts skyward, I reach for Ben's neck. Telling him without words what I need. He dives down, taking my aching nipple in his mouth, swirling his warm tongue over the hardened peak.

Dallas runs her hand over my other breast, tweaking the nipple. She leans down and smiles against my lips. "You're beautiful like this. Naked and at our mercy. Does it feel good, baby?" She pinches my nipple hard, making me gasp. "Do you want Ben's cock?"

*God, please.* Moaning loudly, I bury my hands in her raven hair. I love how thick it is and how she shivers when I pull and tug. I attack her mouth, kissing her deeply, before breaking away and looking from her to Ben. "Kiss each other."

Dallas doesn't hesitate. She pulls Ben to her by his neck and swipes her tongue along his bottom lip. He kisses her back just as fiercely, devouring her mouth. I'm reminded of all the times I watched them kiss before we met. I was curious back then. Longing to find what it's like to be a part of their group.

It's fucking arousing to lie naked on the bed with Ben's muscular body on top of me while they kiss. I'm so turned on by their display that I almost miss the sound of the door opening. I know who it is before I even turn my head.

Ben and Dallas are oblivious as they continue consuming each other.

Jack comes to a halt, staring in disbelief. It's almost funny. Well, it would be if my clit didn't pound so damn hard with its own heartbeat.

Dallas notices him and breaks away from the kiss with a gasp. Ben growls, covering me with his body to hide my nakedness from Jack's roaming eyes. Another shameless moan escapes my lips at the feel of his weight on top of me. I'm too aroused to care about my modesty or that we have an audience.

Ben silences me with a firm hand over my mouth. "Do you like what you see?" he sneers at Jack.

We wait for Jack to snap out of his shock and shout or storm out, but he smirks instead.

"In fact, I do." He looks down at me and winks. Dallas chuckles, but Ben stays silent, still glaring at Jack, who remains unfazed.

Jack swaggers over to the door and turns the lock.

*What is happening?*

He walks back over to us and takes a seat in the recliner next to the bed. "This is what you wanted, right?" He smirks down at me. "Is this why you set this up?"

Ben snarls deep in his throat like an animal. It must amuse Jack because he grins widely.

My heart is racing and I'm panting through my nostrils.

"You want me to watch them fuck you? Is that why you said you were going to the bathroom and then never came back? You wanted me to find you? Well, you got what you wanted, princess. It's what they call you, isn't it? Princess?" He throws his arms wide, grinning. "Well, here I am."

I whimper below Ben's palm, painfully aroused by Jack's intense eyes on me and Ben's hard body on top of me.

Dallas is watching me curiously.

Jack grins at Ben and says to me, "Your boy toy here won't

let me touch you, so why don't I stay," he leans back in the chair, removing lint from his jeans, "and watch them fuck you? I have a feeling you would like that very much." He stares down at me knowingly with a quirked brow and a barely restrained grin.

I nod beneath Ben's palm, far too aroused to feel any kind of inhibition because he's right. I do want him to watch.

Jack strokes a hand through his brown locks, then smiles and sweeps his hand out in front of him. "By all means, continue."

My clit pulsates painfully. I look at Ben and then Dallas, pleading with my eyes. I want it so much, it frightens me.

"Are you sure?" Dallas whispers, searching my eyes.

Ben doesn't remove his hand, and I can see that he's warring with himself. He narrows his eyes on Jack. "If you tell anyone about this, I will kill you!"

Jack chuckles. "You have my word. What happens in here stays in here. How about that?" He nudges his head toward me. "Touch your girl. She's dying for it!" Leaning forward, his elbows on his knees, he whispers darkly, "Or else I will."

Ben stiffens on top of me. "Over my fucking dead body!"

Jack shrugs. "That can be arranged. I wouldn't mind her warm, naked body in my bed every night while your cold corpse rots in a grave somewhere."

I squirm beneath Ben's heavy weight, ashamed to admit that the challenge in Jack's eyes turns me on, despite his cruel words.

Dallas breaks their stare off when she pushes Ben's hand off my mouth and trails kisses along my jaw, brushing her soft lips over mine. "We're gonna look after you, princess. Don't hold back, baby." Her fingers skim over my sensitive clit and I gasp, arching my back off the bed.

Ben throws one last glare at Jack, before climbing off the bed and pulling me down by my ankles. He maneuvers me, so my head hangs off the edge.

Palming my breasts, I stare up at him from my upside-down position, licking my lips in anticipation.

He smirks as he undoes his belt and unzips his jeans, yanking them down with his boxers far enough to free his hard dick.

My mouth waters. His green hair is a tousled mess, and his brown eyes shine with a sheen of possessiveness as he takes me in on the rumpled sheets, naked and at his mercy.

Dallas shifts on the bed, trailing a path up the inside of my thighs with her warm lips. She alternates between kissing and biting the sensitive skin on her way to where I ache for her touch.

I'm whimpering and gripping the bedsheet when she finally nuzzles my pussy with her nose. She breathes me in.

Rolling my head, I watch Jack through heavy eyelids. Does he want to join in, or is he happy being an observer?

His eyes meet mine, and he winks before sweeping his jade eyes down my body, lingering on my heaving chest.

"I want to see you."

His eyes collide with mine while Dallas swipes her warm and wet tongue over my slit. She then spreads my pussy lips with her fingers as she begins licking me in long, firm strokes.

Jack quirks a brow but doesn't object. Undoing his belt, he pulls it through the loops and throws it down on the floor. It clanks loudly. He starts on his buttons next, watching my every reaction while Dallas continues to eat me out.

Ben towers over me, stroking his rock-hard dick languidly. His eyes are hooded, and his lip is trapped between his teeth.

Jack frees himself. Palming his thick length, he swipes his thumb over the bead of precum. "Happy, princess?"

I fist the sheets as another whimper slips past my lips. The corded muscles in his forearm tense with every stroke. "Very."

Dallas slaps my pussy and I cry out in surprise. "Eyes on Ben, princess."

"I like this side of you, Dell." Ben chuckles.

Dallas looks up at Ben from between my trembling thighs, a sugary smile on her lips. "Just being helpful." Lowering herself back down, she fills me up with her tongue.

"Oh god!" I moan, bucking on the bed and clawing the sheets. I don't recognize my own voice.

Ben smirks down at me, rubbing the head of his cock along my lips. "Open wide, princess."

My tongue darts out and I taste the bead of precum on the swollen head. "You forgot the magic word," I tease, smiling up at him from my upside-down position.

Leaning down, he grips my chin roughly and pins me with his dark eyes. "Open. The. Fuck. Wide!" He drives home his point by slapping my face hard enough to make me gasp.

Surprised by the liquid desire I felt shooting down to my core, I chuckle darkly. "Do it again."

It's his turn to chuckle darkly. Massaging my reddening cheek, he slaps it again, not as hard this time but still with enough sting to make my clit pulsate.

"Fuck, Ben," I laugh. "Don't hold back, will you." I'm fucking delighted with this side of him.

"Trust me, princess. I don't plan to." His grin is deliciously dark as he pushes his dick past my lips. I try to take as much of him as possible, but he hits the back of my throat.

Dallas continues to fuck me with her tongue, moaning loudly between my legs. All of this is too much fucking sensation. I gag around Ben's cock, gripping his thighs. My sharp nails dig into his muscles.

He pulls back and thrusts back in, hitting the back of my throat again and again. "Swallow, baby!" he orders gruffly, not letting up.

I feel him down my throat as I swallow around his length.

Groaning, he grabs a handful of my hair. *"Fuck!* That's it! Good girl!"

Dallas sucks my clit painfully, and I convulse. It's too much stimulation. I'm in the sweetest hell and the most torturous heaven. I'm choking on Ben's cock, but it only makes me wetter.

Ben fucks my mouth with hard and fast thrusts. My face is

covered in tears, snort, and drool. Maybe I shouldn't like it as much as I do, but fuck it, I'm so fucking turned on.

Palming my bobbing tits, Ben pulls my nipples until they hurt, then soothes the pain with soft touches and praises while Dallas flicks my clit with her tongue. When she inserts three fingers and fucks me in time with Ben's thrusts, I whimper.

"Fuck, princess. Your hot mouth feels so fucking good!" Ben growls, palming my breast. He slaps it hard and I clamp around Dallas's fingers.

She laughs against my clit. "Slap her again, Ben."

"Yeah?" he chuckles, smacking my stinging breast.

Moaning, I squirm as tears soak my hair. If they keep this up, I'll come with Ben's cock down my sore throat.

"Let's move her," Dallas says, pinching my clit.

I feel like a ragdoll as they maneuver me on the bed until I'm lying close to the headboard.

Ben removes the rest of his clothing, then bites down on a condom wrapper that he plucked from the back pocket of his jeans. He tears it with his teeth and sheaths his impressive length. Stroking himself, he watches me on the bed. "You want my cock?"

God, I do! I want it so badly, I'm not opposed to begging at this point.

Dallas laughs loudly. "Stop torturing her, Ben." Climbing back on the bed, she positions herself over my face and grabs hold of the headboard. I pull her down by the hips and latch on to her throbbing clit, fucking eager to taste her.

She throws her head back with a moan. It only adds to the taboo knowing Jack is watching.

Ben bands his arm around my waist and lifts my ass off the bed. Reaching down between our bodies, he grabs his thick shaft and rubs his cock through my wet slit. I'm squirming in his grip, desperate to feel him inside of me.

Dallas holds onto the headboard with one hand and fists a handful of my hair with the other. "Fuck, it feels so good!" she moans, chasing her release with every roll of her hips. I love the sounds she makes.

*My name on her lips.*

Ben sinks into me and I break away from Dallas's dripping pussy. I cry out at the stretch. *Fuck!* I love that he doesn't wait for me to adjust to his size. He doesn't care if it hurts or not, as he pulls almost all the way out then slams back in. He's wild, rough, and out of control. The sound of slapping skin fills the room, and the smell of sex permeates the air like a cloud of cigar smoke at a poker party.

"I'm close, Dell," Ben warns, tweaking my sore nipples. "Fuck, fuck!"

Dallas comes with a drawn-out cry, clamping her thighs around my head and holding onto the headboard for dear life. She rides my face until I fight for air beneath her dripping cunt.

"Oh god!" she whimpers, trembling on top of me as she finally comes back to earth. "Jack, get over here." She climbs off and lies down beside me, toying with my too-sensitive clit, grinning like the devil. "Come on her."

Jack climbs on the bed while Ben pulls out of me, discarding the condom on the floor.

Leaning in, Dallas whispers in my ear, "Watch." She nudges her head to the boys kneeling on the bed, stroking themselves over me. "Do you like what you see?" She asks Jack.

His sweaty hair lies plastered to his forehead. Ben, who was jealous and possessive before, smirks at him.

I tweak my nipples and bounce my eyes between them, admiring the bunched muscles and masculine power on display.

"So fucking much!" Jack growls, stroking his cock faster. "I wish I could come in her mouth or inside that tight pussy of hers."

"Never gonna happen," Ben breathes between strokes. "She's ours, and you're lucky we even let you look at her."

Jack chuckles, then groans, his face scrunched up in pleasure. "Trust me, I get it."

Dallas thrums my clit and leans down to lap at my nipple. My muscles tingle and my insides warm as something fierce builds in my belly. It crashes over me like a powerful wave, and I come hard, throwing my head back on the pillow.

"Shit," Jack growls as I whimper and convulse. I feel his hot seed on my tits and look up in time to see Ben come too, shooting strings of cum on my pussy.

Dallas grins like the cat who got the cream. She runs her fingers through Jack's cum on my nipples before pushing her fingers past my kiss-swollen lips. I suck them clean, moaning at the taste on my tongue. She does the same with Ben's cum. Smearing it through my folds, she leans in close to my ear, slipping her wet fingers into my mouth. "That was fun, don't you think, baby?"

It was everything I craved and so much more.

Kissing me deeply, she hums when she tastes the guys on my tongue. "You never cease to surprise me."

The same can be said about her.

"Not a fucking word!" Ben warns Jack as they get dressed.

Jack tightens his belt. "My lips are sealed. Let's do this again sometime." He winks at me cheekily. "Thanks for letting me come on your tits."

I should feel embarrassed, but I don't.

Ben stiffens next to me. "Don't fucking look at her!"

Great, possessive Ben is back.

Chuckling, Jake waves him off. "Chill, man. I'm going." He gives me one last cheeky wink before leaving the room and closing the door behind him.

I wonder what he makes of the night. First, he had his dick sucked by a guy, and then he partook in whatever this was.

I put my dress back on.

"Are you okay?" Ben asks when I brush my fingers through my tangly hair.

"Don't worry about me."

The bed dips as he sits down next to me, threading his fingers through mine. "I would never willingly hurt you. Sometimes, our games get a bit out of hand, and I know we can take things too far. The last thing I want is to make you feel uncomfortable."

Dallas takes a seat on my other side and grabs my free hand. "We just want to make sure you're okay with what happened here. We took it further than we intended."

I squeeze their hands. "I promise, I am more than okay with what we did. You make me feel safe. I know we haven't spoken about what this is between us, but I need you to know that I care about you both." I clear my throat. "I'm *in love* with you both. Maybe it makes me greedy, but I can't help how I feel."

Ben's voice is thick with emotion. "Remember when I spoke to Rick and told him that I'm falling for you? I meant it, Em."

Dallas lifts my chin. "I'm in love with you too. It's fucking scary, to be honest with you. I've already lost everyone I love. The thought of losing you… It terrifies me, but I'm here, and I'm all in. Others may not understand our unusual relationship dynamic, but it works for us. And like Ben said, we sometimes take our games too far. You need to tell us if you feel uncomfortable."

"I promise to tell you if I feel uncomfortable, okay?"

Dallas presses her forehead to mine. "You're perfect."

My head shakes and I kiss her softly, smiling against her lips. "I'm not, but you like my darkness just like I like yours and Ben's. Let's never conform. It's us against the world."

Placing a soft kiss on my shoulder, Ben hums in agreement. "Where have you been all this time?"

My heart feels too big for my chest. We're from different worlds, an unlikely match, but we love each other despite our differences.

*Love…*

Wow, what a big word, but it feels so right.

"I wasn't gonna tell you yet," Ben says hesitantly, like he isn't sure of how I'll react. "Dallas told me what college you applied for, so I went to see the career advisor, and she helped me apply too."

My head pops up.

"You did?" I ask, afraid of his answer in case I misheard him. *Does this mean we will all be together next year?*

Ben smiles, palming my cheek. "Yes, princess. I'm not letting you go. I want this—us. And the dog. You can name it whatever ridiculous name you want."

My tears spill over. This moment feels too good to be true. "But how, Ben?" I ask, running my fingers over the stubble on his cheek.

He smiles. "I'm a smart cookie, princess. I qualified for a scholarship and was eligible for financial aid because of my circumstances. The career advisor pulled out all the stops for me."

I look at him as if for the first time. Why did I ever doubt him? Why did I judge him based on his clothes and the crowd he hangs out with? I've seen him hand in his homework on time and participate in the few classes we've shared. He always surprises me with his intelligence and quick thinking.

Returning his smile, I kiss him softly. A thought occurs to me, so I pull back and look at Dallas.

She drops her gaze. "I can't afford it, princess. I'll have to stay here." Her quiet voice cracks at the end.

*No…*

It's not true. She can't do this to us. We aren't complete without her. Until this very moment, I had come to accept that we wouldn't be together next year, but now…

I shake my head. I don't want to hear it. Whatever happens, we'll make it work. "You're coming with us. We're not leaving you behind." I turn to Ben, begging him with my eyes to back me up.

We're not leaving her behind in the same town as Greg. Not to mention, I'll never be able to hold her or kiss her. "Right?" I whisper shakily. "Tell her, Ben. We can't leave her here."

Ben swallows thickly and the sadness in his eyes feels like a dagger to my heart. "We discussed it, baby. Either we both stay here, or I go with you. We agreed."

"Wha…" I don't understand. "We agreed? What does that mean, Ben? What did you agree on?" I turn to Dallas, frantically searching her eyes for the truth. "Tell me, dammit! What did you agree on?"

"Princess," Ben whispers, but I cut him off, yelling, "No! Fuck you, Ben! You don't get to make decisions for me." I shoot to my feet. "I'll just stay here. It's not too late to apply for colleges nearby. My family has connections. I can even take a year out."

"Emily," Dallas says, taking my hand, but I step out of reach. "Please, Em. I don't want you to stay behind because of me. That's the last thing I want. Look, you applied to a great college with a fantastic art program. It's your dream come true, and I want you to go, okay? I *need* you to go." She rises from the bed, taking my hand in hers.

I try to pull away, but she won't let me. She forces me to listen. "I need you to take Ben with you. He's had a shit life, and he deserves a new start—with you. He deserves happiness. You love him. I know you will make him happy."

I meet her kohl-rimmed eyes. "I do love Ben, but I love you too. What about you, Dallas? What about *your* happiness?"

"Princess," she whispers softly.

It only angers me even more. "Don't call me that. I can't believe you made decisions without me!"

Dallas sighs and lets go of my hand, raising both of hers placatingly. "Okay, look. You already applied, right? Your plan was always to go."

The worst part is that she's right. I could have applied to a college closer to home. But I wanted to escape the expectations of my family and friends and go somewhere completely different— be someone new. I didn't give this thing between us much thought. I assumed we were simply having fun.

Why am I so upset when I always knew it would come to this?

"You know I'm right. You wanted this new future for yourself. It's a decision you made for yourself because it's *your* dream. I don't want to stand in the way of that. I can't think of anything worse. I don't want to hold you back, Em. Besides, it's not forever. I'll visit you as often as I can, and you can come to see me. We'll make it work, but please, Em. Do this for me."

How can she ask this of me? Yes, it's what I wanted when I applied, but that was before she confessed her feelings to me. I don't know what I want anymore. All I know is that I don't want to let her go, and it hurts that she can let us go easily without a fight.

"I thought you said you were all in? Are you really not gonna fight for us?" I ask disbelievingly, searching her eyes for any signs of regret. "You're just gonna let me go, Dallas?"

Her blue eyes fill with tears, and she swallows thickly. "Baby…" she holds her hands out helplessly. "This is me fighting for us. I'm setting you free. I'll only hold you back otherwise. Don't you see? Why are we fighting about this now? There's still time until we graduate, Em. Don't do this."

I scoff, wiping away tears. "Well, I'm sorry, okay? I'm sorry, I fucking care!"

She winces and Ben rises from the bed. The way he approaches me with his hand held out, palm up, reminds me of someone trying to calm a frightened animal. "Babe, listen to Dallas. Please. We didn't mean to hurt you."

My eyes narrow and I point a stern finger at him. "Don't you dare talk down to me, Ben!"

At this point, I don't know what makes me more angry. Them for making decisions behind my back or me for putting myself in this position in the first place. If I'd never applied to that stupid college, and if I hadn't let myself fall in love in the first place…

"I can't do this," I whisper. Panic is quickly rising inside of me. "I'm sorry."

Running from the room, I race downstairs, pushing my way through throngs of people. Matt and Josh shout for me to stop. I burst through the front door, almost tumbling down the steps.

I've been to Jack's house enough times to know of the worn

path through the forest at the edge of his yard. It's a long walk home, but I need the fresh air to clear my head.

I leave my car behind and use the flashlight on my phone to light up the forest floor ahead of me. How did the night turn so suddenly? We were playing a reckless dare. Now my heart feels like it's been torn from my chest.

I breathe a sigh of relief when I arrive home to a dark house. The last thing I need right now is my mom to see me like this and ask questions.

Unlocking the front door, I step inside as quietly as I can. When James, the cat, pads up for a fuss, I stroke him behind the ear and whisper, "Hi, sweetie."

I feed him and go upstairs, cringing every time the stairs creak under my feet. My phone is vibrating in my purse. It stops and then starts back up again.

After closing the bedroom door behind me, I sink back against it and slide down to the hard floor. Moonlight filters through the sheer curtains, bathing my room in a silvery glow. If I questioned my feelings before, I don't anymore. I'm in love with Ben and Dallas, and it changes everything. It's no longer just a bit of fun.

I sigh shakily and wipe away the wetness from my cheeks as I power off my phone.

"What am I gonna do?" I whisper, rubbing my hand over the ache in my chest.

# CHAPTER
## *seventeen*

**EMILY**

I'M MIXING colors and humming along to the music playing through my speakers. I fell asleep on the floor last night, which is a first. I think I'm all cried out. My phone is still switched off on my bedside table. I need space. The more I think about last night, the more of a clusterfuck it becomes. I'm angry and sad, but also scared. I'm going to lose what we have no matter what, so why are we allowing ourselves to fall even deeper? What's the point if it's only going to hurt even more further down the line?

When I'm happy with my selection of colors, I set to work on my painting. Abstract art, with its explosion of colors, seems like the best fit for me right now. It represents the multitude and complexity of the emotions fighting for space inside of me. There are too many colors and shades to pick apart and make sense of.

I nearly jump out of my skin when I feel a hand on my shoulder. Mom is watching me with a deep crease between her brows.

Reaching for the remote, I pause the music, smiling shakily. "Hi, mom."

She wipes away a streak of paint on my cheek before sliding her hand down my arm. "What's the matter, sweetheart?"

My eyes sting with unshed tears. Here I thought I had none left. Urgh! I shrug, blinking rapidly to stop them from falling. Why do parents have to be so perceptive? I don't know how to talk to her about this. How do I tell my mom that I have a new boyfriend *and* a new girlfriend? Let's not forget that I still haven't told her about my college application, and the longer I wait to bring it up, the harder it gets.

I feel alone.

"Sweetie, talk to me." She leads me by my elbow over to the bed. The floral notes of her perfume hang in the air. "I know your dad and I are busy a lot of the time, but I'm always here for you."

I scoff before I can stop myself and I immediately regret it. None of this is her fault.

"Where is this coming from, Emily?" she asks, taking my hand in hers.

I brush away a tear. "It's nothing, Mom." If I'm honest, I want her to leave me alone. I know she means well, but I feel pulled in so many directions. I can't make sense of my own emotions.

She looks hurt for a moment before she pulls herself together and says, "I get it. I received an interesting phone call from a college that I didn't know you had applied for."

My head shoots up.

Smiling softly, she squeezes my hand. "I put two and two together. I've been waiting for you to come to me."

Guilt slams into me hard, and my throat constricts with emotion.

She sweeps her eyes over the canvases and drawings on my walls. "You're really talented."

I don't know what to say, so I stay quiet.

"I regret not being more supportive." She wipes away tears from her eyes before shifting on the bed to face me. "When I spoke to the lady on admission, I realized I don't really know my own daughter. I assumed you would follow the same path as your dad and I… I should have taken the time to appreciate how talented you are. I never asked you about your dreams."

I stroke my hand down her arm. "Mom, don't cry. It's okay. It's not your fault. I never spoke up."

Mom shakes her head. "No, I should have asked you about what it is that *you* want to do. What your dreams are. I have pushed you down a path that would have made you miserable. I mean, look around you, sweetie." She gestures to the easel I worked on when she walked in.

"You express yourself through your art. I don't know what's going on in your life right now, but just by looking at your painting, I can see that you're in pain. You're confused. You put into art what you can't say in words. As your mom, I should have encouraged that side of you. I'm sorry it took me this long. I wish you felt like you could approach your dad and I about your college application. Trust me, sweetie. We will always support you."

Relief floods through me. "Thanks, Mom." I spent months worrying about her reaction, thinking she would be disappointed. It didn't cross my mind that she might be supportive.

She tucks my hair behind my ear and her touch lingers for a brief moment before she reaches for my hand. "The college rang because they were impressed with your work."

"What about Dad?"

She strokes my cheek. "You know what your dad is like. Give him time. He'll come around."

I throw my arms around her, feeling lighter than I have done in a long time. "Thanks, Mom."

"Don't forget us when you're having the time of your life in the sun," she says, rubbing my back, but her voice cracks at the end.

With my nose buried in her neck, I whisper. "Never, Mom."

A soft knock interrupts our moment. I sniffle, wiping my nose as we break apart.

Rick stands in the doorway, shuffling awkwardly. "Your dad let me in. I can come back if this is a bad time?" he says, jerking a thumb over his shoulder.

Mom smiles at me before rising from the bed. "It's okay. I think Emily can do with a friend right now." She squeezes his arm affectionately and leaves the room.

When the door is closed, Rick joins me on the bed. "I returned your car." He holds his spare key out and I place it down on my bedside table. Now that we're not dating anymore, there is no need for him to have a spare key if I lose mine. "Do you want to talk about what happened last night?"

I lean my head on his shoulder, breathing in his familiar and comforting smell. He wraps his arm around me.

"Just sit with me, please."

He kisses the top of my head. "I can do that."

Tracing the veins on his tanned hand, I thread my fingers through his. "Where will you be next year?"

He rests his chin on the top of my head, and for a moment, I don't think he'll answer me as we sit in silence. "Penn State is interested in me," he replies almost reluctantly.

I straighten. "But that's in Pennsylvania."

He doesn't reply. I feel the heat of his hand when he places it on my knee, squeezing it before shifting us onto the bed. We still don't talk.

I'm lying with my head on his chest, listening to his steady heartbeat. "Everything is changing," I whisper after a while when the silence becomes too much.

Rick hums deeply in his chest, stroking my arm absent-mindedly.

It's a strange realization that the friends I've known my whole life are going their separate ways. Even Rick, who I always assumed would stay close, is moving thousands of miles away.

I prop my chin on his chest, trailing my eyes over the planes of his face.

His smile is tender. "You're gonna be okay, Em."

My eyes fall closed, and I smile softly as he traces his fingers up my arm. Who knows what the future has in store for us all, but I refuse to worry about tomorrow. "You better remember me when you're a famous footballer." I rest my cheek back down his hard chest.

He chuckles. "Trust me, Em. I'll never forget you."

Something tells me this is one of the last times Rick and I will be alone together like this. Life is about to send us down different paths. Everything is about to change, but we'll be okay.

―――――

*DALLAS.*

"I checked everywhere," Matt says when he joins us behind the bleachers.

Nina hands him the joint while I scroll through my phone for the hundredth time. Why hasn't Emily replied to any of our messages?

"She'll come to us when she's ready," Steph says. "She's definitely at school. Nina saw her arrive with Rick this morning."

"Fucking Rick," Ben mutters, kicking at the dirt with his already scuffed Vans.

Josh rubs his face. "What are we gonna do?"

Matt passes me the joint. I take a big hit, holding it in my lungs. My eyes land on Ben. He rarely shows emotions, but he's on the verge of snapping right now.

I sigh, passing the joint to Josh next to me. "It's my fault."

"Don't Dallas," Ben starts, but I hold my hand up, silencing him.

"I hurt her, so it's me who should go talk to her. I need to sort this mess out."

Nina's eyes shine with sympathy. "You only did what you thought was best. Don't be so hard on yourself. Emily will come around. She just needs time."

I shrug. "Maybe, but she's not responding to my text messages, so I need to find her."

Ben paces like a caged animal, tugging his green hair.

Steph side-eyes me before crushing the joint beneath the heel of her shoe. "Let's go find our princess."

"It's okay. You don't need to help."

"You're my friend, Dallas. I'm here for you." She gestures to the others. "We're *all* here for you."

———

"Well, we found her," Matt says drily behind me when we enter the bustling cafeteria. "And who is sitting next to her? Jack, of course."

Josh nods, rocking back on his heels. "He's like a flea infestation."

Nina pulls a face. "Sometimes you're so fucking random. A flea infestation?"

"Matt, you get what I mean, don't you?" Josh asks, thumping him on the shoulder.

"No, not really."

Josh stares at him, then Nina. "Fleas are hard to get rid of. You have to blast them with a ton of chemicals, and even then, it's likely to fail." He points to Jack, who's leaning in close to Emily. "He's a flea!"

Jack's laughter travels across the cafeteria.

I suck on my teeth as annoyance flares up inside of me. "Or a disgusting tick on the underside of your boob that you don't find until it's big and juicy."

Ben stares at me. "What the actual fuck?"

I shrug. "It happened once."

Nina looks thoughtful. "I read somewhere that lemon repels ticks."

"Right," I reply, dragging the word out. "I'll make sure to rub my boobs with lemon from now on or keep a couple of slices stashed in my bra."

"It's an idea," she agrees.

I roll my eyes.

"Why are they so comfortable together?" Ben growls, his jaw ticking.

"Well," Josh says, scratching the back of his neck. "Probably because you let him bust a nut on her tits."

We all turn to stare at him.

He looks confused. "What? It's an ice breaker."

"An ice breaker?" laughs Ben incredulously. "It wasn't a fucking group interview."

Josh shrugs. "An ice breaker nonetheless. Is he or isn't he whispering in her ear right now, and is she, or isn't she laughing?"

"This conversation is stupid," I sigh, rubbing my face. "I'm going over there to talk to her."

Emily's easy smile falls away, and Rick looks over his shoulder as I approach their table with my heart in my throat.

"Hey." My voice trembles. I try to read her face, but it's a blank mask.

She sweeps her gaze from me to Ben and the others.

"Looking good," Jack purrs, resting his arm on the back of Emily's chair.

My cheeks flame. Images of our night together flash through my mind.

"Can we help you?" Jamie asks, looking at us in disgust. Raking his eyes over Nina's scuffed combat boots and leather skirt, he scoffs dismissively.

I fist my hands by my sides and bite back the retort on my tongue.

"Don't be a dick!" Hailey glares at him.

He glowers at her suspiciously.

"I'll see you guys later." Emily smiles at her friends, rising from her chair, but Jack pulls her down on his lap.

Ben stiffens next to me.

"Chill, man," Matt whispers under his breath.

"Looking a little green there, dude," Jack says to Ben. He skims his fingers underneath the hem of Emily's skirt and winks. She doesn't stop him. Jealousy pours off Ben in waves. He shifts tensely next to me as Jack leans in to whisper in Emily's ear.

She laughs, then stands back up, gesturing to the door. "You want to talk? Let's go."

———

We find an empty classroom further down the hallway. Ben walks in first with Emily close on his heels.

I close the door behind us.

Laughter filters in through the open window.

"I'm sorry I haven't responded to your messages. I needed time," Emily says, wrapping her arms around herself protectively, eyes trained on her heel scuffing against the floor.

Ben points at the door, his jaw tight. "What the fuck was that?! You like Jack now?"

"Calm down, Ben!" I look at him pointedly. Emotions are running high. I know how torn up he's been over the other night, but he'll push her away if he doesn't reel in his temper.

"You have nothing to worry about. Jack and I are just friends."

Scoffing, he shakes his head. "You sure looked cozy."

Emily laughs bitterly, but it soon dies. "I don't need this," she whispers in disbelief to herself, then pokes Ben in the chest. "You don't know me at all if you think I would tell you I love you and then go fuck someone else."

His teeth grind as he clenches his hands by his sides. "Careful, princess."

She narrows her eyes, but then the fire fizzles out and she looks down at the floor.

A heavy silence descends on the room. Her shoulders slump and she takes a step away from Ben. "I don't think I can do this. I feel too much! You said it yourselves that we can't all be together next year, so we shouldn't let ourselves fall any deeper than we already have."

My blood turns to ice. Ben stops breathing too.

She takes another step back, inching toward the door. "We should have known from the beginning that we wouldn't work.

We're too different," she whispers, her eyes glassy with unshed tears.

"Em…" My voice breaks. "What are you saying? I know you're upset, but Ben only reacted the way he did just now because he's terrified after you ran out on us. You don't answer your phone. You ignore us at school."

"You know what?" she spits, pointing at Ben while glaring at me. "I wish you wouldn't make excuses for him. He can talk for himself."

My mouth drops open. "I didn't mean—"

"Save it!" She walks over to the door and her eyes find mine over her shoulder. Then she's gone.

The door clicks shut.

My eyes burn with unshed tears. I've stopped breathing. My lungs don't function anymore. I used to be numb, now I feel as if my heart has been torn from my chest.

A loud crash startles me, and I tear my eyes away from the door.

Ben is breathing hard, eyes trained on the indent in the wall. By his feet, on the floor, lies an upturned chair.

"Please, calm down," I plead, clutching my aching chest, but he can't hear me. Lost in his own inner torment.

Bending at the waist, he picks up another chair and throws it with an anguished roar. I jump at the loud crash. Ben storms out, slamming the door shut. I stare after him, tasting tears on my trembling lips.

# CHAPTER
*eighteen*

## BEN

IT'S BEEN two weeks since Emily dropped the bomb on us in the classroom. I'm a shell of the person I used to be before she crashed into my life and blew it all to fucking pieces.

She hasn't responded to any of our countless texts or spoken to us at school. It's like we don't exist. Lunchtime is torture. I'm forced to watch Jack flirt with her, and the worst part is that she doesn't discourage him.

I don't understand how she can switch off her emotions so easily while I feel like my heart has been fucking ripped from my chest and stomped on. I hate that I let myself fall for someone so out of my league.

I put my uneaten sandwich down on the tray just as Jack throws his arm over Emily's shoulder. Ham and cheese. It used to be my favorite, but now it tastes like ash.

Smirking at me, he deliberately tries to rile me up by pulling her into his body.

It's working.

"Come on, man. Stop staring!" Matt pleads, as frustrated with my pussy-whipped behavior as I am.

"Are you gonna eat that?" Josh grabs my sandwich and takes a bite before I have a chance to respond.

"Screw this!" I tip my chin to Samantha, a brunette on the

track team. We fucked a couple of times before Princess ruined me for other women.

Never one to turn down a good time, she scoots her chair back and saunters over. My eyes sweep over her tight jeans and low-cut tank top.

*"You want to fuck right here? On the principal's desk?" She giggles, papers crinkling under her naked ass.*

*Shoving her pink panties in her mouth to shut her up, I pull down her tank top and wrap my lips around her peaked nipple. "Why the fuck not?"*

"Long time no see, Ben," she practically purrs, running her hand over my shoulder.

I pull her down on my lap.

Dallas slams her bottle of soda down on the table. "Are you for fucking real right now, Ben?"

Ignoring her little temper tantrum, I bury my hands in Samantha's dark curls as I loose myself in her kiss. If this little show doesn't get Princess's attention, then nothing will. I just want the fucking pain gone, and Samantha's tight pussy seems like the perfect escape.

Straddling my lap and snatching up my bottom lip between her teeth, she rolls her hips. I can feel the disapproving looks from my friends, but I don't care anymore. Let them look and judge. I'll fuck the whole town if it takes away the pain.

Samantha smiles against my lips, nips my jaw and dives in for another kiss, tugging the short strands of my hair.

It's no longer green. I dyed it a deep blue the night before to distract myself from my own destructive thoughts.

Breaking away from the kiss, Samantha leans in, brushing her lips over my ear. "I want you in my mouth."

My dick strains against my jeans. I squeeze her ass before lifting her off me, chancing a look at Princess across the room.

Big mistake.

Her blue eyes connect with mine for the first time in two

weeks, and it hits me like a fucking bullet to the chest. She doesn't try to mask the hurt in her eyes.

Fuck her! She did this to us. She hasn't spared me a glance in two weeks, so why should I feel guilty for being with someone else?

But I do.

Guilt weighs heavily on me.

Pushing back my chair, I ignore the disapproving looks of my friends. Dallas grabs my arm. "Think about this, Ben. You can't take it back."

I hiss, "What I do is my business. Not yours." Shrugging out of Dallas's grip, I throw my arm over Samantha's shoulder. Burying my nose in her vanilla-scented neck, I lead her outside to my car.

———

"Don't you want to close the car door at least?" I laugh when she grapples with my belt.

"No one is gonna see us." She grins, pulling my zipper down. "You've never worried about shit like that before." Palming my dick, she wets her lips.

"I'm not fucking worried." I buck my hips closer to her waiting mouth. She wraps her lips around the hard head and sinks down on my throbbing length until I hit the back of her throat. I like that she never bothers with teasing.

"Oh shit," I groan, burying my hands in her long hair. I close my eyes. I can't watch her suck me. Her dark hair looks and feels wrong in my hands. It's not blonde, and it doesn't smell like warm summer evenings of all things.

Despite how good she makes me feel, I can't shift the guilt that's pressing on my chest. It pisses me off more. Emily doesn't want me. Not the other way around. And why the fuck am I thinking about her right now?

I force myself back to the present moment and the hot mouth working me closer to the edge. Her head moves in my hands, and she hums when I tighten my grip on her hair. She sucks on the tip, circling it with her tongue while jerking my thick shaft with her hand. Faster and harder. Diving back down, she swallows around my cock, deepthroating me.

It feels so fucking good.

I'm close to coming when she suddenly shrieks, and my eyes fly open. Emily pulls her off me by the hair, throwing her against the side of the car. Meanwhile, I sit with my wet cock out, staring in shocked disbelief.

"You fucking whore!" Emily throws a punch. I hurriedly tuck my dick back in my pants before stepping out of the car and rounding the hood.

Emily looks feral as she throws another punch. "Don't you fucking touch him!" She's shrieking and pulling on Samantha's hair.

I snap out of it and drag her away.

"You're fucking unhinged!" Samantha shouts, blood pouring from a cut in her lip.

I'm pacing. When she leaves, I drop my hands from around my neck. "The fuck just happened?" I don't know who I'm asking. I'm so fucking confused right now.

"How could you?" Emily shrieks, a wild look on her face.

"What? I ask, bewildered. She's not yelling at me for trying to move on, is she?

"It's only been two weeks, and you let some skank suck you off in your car?"

I stare at her in disbelief for a moment before shaking my head and laughing bitterly.

*Unbelievable...*

She has some fucking nerve blaming this on me. "You haven't even looked at me for two weeks. I've had to sit and watch you flirt with Jack of all people, and you think you can shout at me for letting some girl blow me? Newsflash, princess—you left me! How do you think that makes me feel? I told you I love you!"

Her smile is mocking. "Yeah, some way of showing it."

Closing the small distance between us and pointedly ignoring how good she smells, I grit my teeth. Anger radiates from my every pore. "Don't! I haven't looked at another girl since I met you. Not once! You were the only one I saw and the only one I wanted to touch.

You discarded me like I meant nothing. I can't switch off my feelings like you. I'm not that cold, so forgive me for drowning this fucking pain, "I hit my chest, "in someone else."

Her cheeks are wet with tears and I feel a pang of regret before reminding myself that we're in this situation because of her. She won't reply to my texts, and she doesn't acknowledge me at school. What the fuck am I supposed to do?

"What do you want from me?" I ask, leaning down. She's forced to meet my gaze. "I get that you're scared. I'm scared too, but this? You're making us all lose. You're running away because it's the easy way out. So who's not fighting, Em? You! That's who!"

I walk away. I can't look at her or the tears trailing down her cheeks. How did it come to this? Why did I ever let myself fall for her?

———

*Emily.*

*"My mom is gonna kill me!"*

*Hailey giggles next to me. One of her piggy tails has come loose. "It's slime. It will fall down soon."*

*I look away from the yellow slime on my ceiling. "Or it will stay there forever."*

*Hailey tightens her piggy tail, but it's askew. One is much higher than the other. "Maybe your mom won't notice?"*

*I look at her skeptically. "You think?"*

Plop.

*We stare at the slime on the floor between our bare feet.*
*"Told you it would fall down."*

I stare at the stain on the ceiling, my stomach twisting uncomfortably. I don't recognize myself anymore. I thought I did the right thing by ending things with Ben and Dallas before we fall even deeper, but I'm not sure anymore? And that poor girl in the parking lot? I can't believe I beat her up because I was jealous. I don't like this version of myself.

Dragging my hands down my face, I sigh heavily. Why did I follow Ben and that girl to his car? I wish I could unsee his face scrunched up in pleasure. And the girl's lips, smeared with lipstick, wrapped around his dick.

Jealousy is slowly eating me up inside. I feel terrible for what I did to Samantha. I've never hurt anyone before, but my vision turned red when I saw her bob on his dick. Ben is correct, though. I have no right to feel betrayed. I made my bed on this uncomfortable mattress, and now I have to lie on the hard springs.

My phone pings on my nightstand.

I haven't left the group chat. I can't bring myself to do it, and they haven't removed me.

Josh: I've scored some good quality weed. The lake, anyone?

Steph: I'm with Dallas at the skatepark. Maybe in an hour?

Josh: Benny-boy? You in?

Matty: I'll be there.

Ben: *thumbs up emoji*

Nina: I can't. I'm giving private lessons to the chess-geek if you know what I mean ;)

Josh: April, are u coming? Nina, go easy on the poor fucker.

April: Josh, babe, when am I not in? I'll be there.

Matty: I'll bring the alcohol.

Josh: Cool. I'm out. See u fuckers soon.

I place my phone down on the nightstand. God, I miss them so much.. Why am I torturing myself like this?

Rolling over on my side, I reach for the photographs inside of the drawer. Ben left me another one today. It's one of us at the skatepark a couple of weeks back when the three of us went alone.

My first instinct when I discovered it was to find Ben and do what? I don't know. Throw myself at him and beg for forgiveness or slap him for being so fucking sweet? Maybe both.

I read the scrawled words on the back.

*"I miss your smell."*

He left me another photograph earlier in the week too. I found it on my desk when I arrived for my English lesson. It's a picture of me eating ice cream on a park bench in town. It was windy that day.

*His smile is blinding behind the camera. He reaches out, brushing away a piece of strand stuck to my lipgloss.*

*"There's no point," I laugh, lips tingling from his touch. "It's too windy."*

*Winking at me, he leans down and takes a big bite out of my ice cream, his eyes sparkling with mirth. "Fucking tasty!" he groans around a mouthful.*

*I lick the melting ice cream that's dripping down the cone. "Enjoy your brain freeze."*

*His eyes are trained on my mouth. "I can handle my ice cream, princess."*

*"Is that so?" I laugh when he scrunches his face up in pain.*

*"Jesus, fuck!"*
*I take a long lick, moaning exaggeratively. "So tasty!"*
His messy handwriting tugs at my heartstrings.

*"I miss the sound of your laughter."*

My heart twists. Why is he doing this? Why make it harder?
But I also don't want him to stop.

———

The days pass by in a blur. I focus on my exams, practice for a
cheer competition out of state, and paint.

I'm working on a new abstract painting in the art room after
school when Matt walks in with a sketch pad in his hand.

"Hey, princess," he says, smiling at the paint splatter on my
arms, then points to the easel in front of me. "It's good. Really
good!"

I'm relieved he isn't making this more awkward than it needs
to be. "Thank you. I'm not much for abstract art, but it seems to be
the only thing I can create lately." I shrug.

Smiling, he rubs the corner of his lip with his thumb. "I doubt
that. I've seen what you can do. You pull everything off."

I wave him off. "Come on, Matt. We both know that's not
true. I'm terrible at sketching." I gesture to the worn folder in his
hand.

He holds it up in the air. "Oh, this old thing? I think you can
pull it off."

Suppressing a smile, I suck my lips between my teeth.

"I have an idea." He grins widely. "I challenge you to create an
amazing sketch, and I will attempt abstract art."

I laugh, pressing a hand over my mouth. We both know Matt
is fantastic at what he does but abstract art? Not his forte. "Okay,
deal."

This should be fun.

Matt moves the easel as I go to sit at a desk across the room. This way, we can't peak at each other's work.

It's an understatement to say that I'm amused.

He studies the blank canvas with furrowed brows before his deep voice fills the room. "Okay, princess, what do I do now? Just chuck paint at it?"

I chuckle. "Now you have to feel the emotion you want to portray."

"Feel the emotion… Riiight… And then do I chuck paint at it?"

I shake my head with a smile. "Matt, at no point do you just throw paint at it. You have to create something real."

Doubt is written all over his face. "Create something real, you say?" He points to the easel I worked on before he interrupted me and continues, "No offense, princess, but that is paint splatter and nothing more."

Throwing my head back, I laugh. "Whatever. What do you want me to sketch?"

Matt rubs his chin in thought. "Why don't you draw me since I'm here and you can study my handsome face." He messes up his already tousled, blonde hair and strikes a pose, making me laugh. "Don't tell me you don't want some of this."

I chuckle to myself as I start the outline. "Your ego is so inflated, it's bound to explode one of these days."

He shrugs. "Maybe, but you can't deny that I'm a sexy fucker."

We both laugh as we set to work. Conversation flows easily between us, reminding me of why I always liked Matt. He's funny and knows how to make people feel comfortable.

An hour later, I eye the sketch in front of me with pursed lips. It could do with a bit more shading and a few more details, but it's not a bad attempt either.

"We're hanging out at the lake tonight. You should join us."

I look up from my drawing. "That's not a good idea, Matt."

"It's okay. I get it…" He rears back and flicks the paintbrush at the easel, causing specks of paint to fly everywhere.

We both laugh, exchanging a glance before he cocks his head, pretending to inspect his artwork with a critical eye.

I get up and join him, cocking my head too, lips pursed.

He elbows me playfully, his blue eyes twinkling with amusement. "What's the verdict, princess?

"It's good, Matt." I mean it, too. Matt's playful nature is portrayed in his work. Especially in this one. It's there in the patterns and the choice of colors.

My thoughts are interrupted when he strokes his warm hand down my cheek, lingering on my jaw. "We miss you."

I drop my gaze. My throat is thick with emotion. Walking over to the desk, I pick up my own sketch to show him. It's not complete yet, but it's not far off, either. Fidgeting with the drawing in my hands, I walk back over and hold it out for him.

He searches my eyes for a moment before taking the sketch, and while he looks at it, I study the way his blonde hair—curling at the ends—falls into his eyes. It has grown out a lot these last couple of weeks.

My eyes slide down to the muscles in his arms. The cut-out sleeves in his Metallica T-shirt reveal specks of freckles on his tanned shoulders. The chain attached to the wallet in his pocket clinks against his thigh when he turns to face me. "It's really good, Em. You shouldn't question yourself."

Unable to look away from his blue eyes, I swallow.

"Look," he starts, handing me the sketch and rubbing the back of his neck. The action draws my eyes to his bulging bicep before he drops his hand down by his side. "I don't know what you're running from, but we all miss you. Fuck, even April whines." He chuckles, and so do I. "Well, when we see her. She's been absent a lot lately... We're meeting at the lake tonight. You're welcome to join us, Em."

I swallow thickly.

He smiles at me, then dips his chin, eyes trained on his combat boots. "Just think about it, yeah?"

"Okay," I whisper so quietly that I don't think he can hear me, but his head snaps up.

He looks at me through his dark lashes.

"I'll be there."

His answering smile takes my breath away. Pulling me to him, he sways us side to side. I laugh and wrap my arms around him. I don't know how long we stand there in each other's arms, but we eventually break apart and begin to tidy up our supplies. When we're done, Matt walks over to the door, glancing over his shoulder. "See you later, princess."

My heart hammers wildly in my chest.

What will Ben and Dallas say if I show up? Is it even the right thing to do?

———

The school is empty this late in the afternoon except for a few teachers working late. My car is the only one left in the parking lot.

After I have strapped myself in, I flick down the visor and take in my tired face. I haven't slept well these last few weeks, and it shows in the dark circles under my eyes.

I'm in the middle of reapplying my lipstick when something on the windscreen catches my eye. Flicking the visor back in place, I step out of the car. Held in place by the windscreen wipers is a photograph that flickers in the afternoon breeze.

My heart begins to race as I lean over the hood and stare at the photograph of Ben and Dallas smiling faces. There's me, squished in the middle with an unbelievably big smile on my face.

*"Dallas," Steph shouts, waving her camera in the air. "Do you want in on this picture or not?"*

*Ben nips my neck with his teeth, causing me to giggle.*

*Dallas climbs back down the apple tree in Nina's garden, abandoning her mission to grab one of the ripe apples hanging just out of reach. "I'm sorry, princess," she says, handing me a much smaller apple.*

*Ben snatches it out of her hand, taking a large bite before I have a chance to reach for it. He winks, pulling me into his side.*

*Steph grins behind the lens. "You ready?"*

*Dallas snakes her arm around my waist.*

*"Say cheese, fuckers!"*

I carefully remove the picture. On the back, in Ben's scrawled handwriting, it reads: *"How about Dognald Trump or Queen Elizabark?"*

Laughter bubbles up inside me. I'm crying and laughing at the same time. I wipe away the wetness from my cheeks, but for the first time in weeks, they're happy tears. Ben remembers the day at the beach when we joked about silly dog names.

I get back in the car and place the photograph on the dash. Unlocking my phone, I scroll through Dallas's messages.

Dallas: This will be my last message. I hope you read it one day. I'm letting you go, Em. I can't fight anymore when I'm greeted by silence. I have so many good memories from our time together. I hope you'll look back one day with fondness and know that you changed something inside me. You gave me hope.

The message was sent over a week ago. I blink, seeing but unseeing, placing the phone down with trembling hands.

What have I done? I pushed away the people that I cared about the most.

Why?

Because I was scared.

I grip the steering wheel with both hands and press my forehead against it.

Why am I so fucking stupid?

Breathing deeply, I take a moment to compose myself, before starting the engine and driving the short journey home. The streets pass in a blur. My mind wanders. Will they ever forgive me? And after graduation, what then? I'll still be thousands of miles away, and Dallas will still be here. Alone.

My fingers drum a beat on the steering wheel.

At the very least, I have to save our friendship. Maybe we don't have a future together past graduation, but I don't want this to be Ben and Dallas's last memory of me.

———

The sun is setting over the horizon when I pull into my driveway. It's a quiet evening. The neighborhood children that usually play out in the street are nowhere to be seen.

As I put the car in park, the front door opens and Mom descends the front steps with a thick envelope in her hands. I gulp. She has my future in her hands. Literally.

Inhaling a steadying breath, I get out of the car and meet her halfway. Neither of us says a word while we stare down at the envelope in her hands.

My younger sister laughs loudly from somewhere inside the house.

"I'm scared, Mom," I whisper.

She places the envelope in my hands and smiles softly. "I know, sweetheart. Let's open it together, shall we?"

I nod, tearing the seal. It's a thick envelope, so I'm not surprised when I stare down at the acceptance letter in my hands. This is it. I'm officially leaving this town. I don't know how to feel. Excited? Terrified? A bit of both?

"You got in," my mom breathes next to me, pressing both of her hands to her mouth. Her eyes fill with tears that threaten to spill over like a dam. "Oh my god."

"Mom?" I whisper shakily, and she pulls me to her, crushing the letter between us.

"Ssshh, sweetie. I'm so proud of you!"

The setting sun casts an orange glow over the front lawn, high-lighting the fresh lawn stripes.

She leans back and cups my cheeks. "The world is yours, sweetie. Go grab it. I know you're scared. I am too. But don't let fear hold you back. If you fail, which you won't, then you can always come back home to us. This will always be your home to fall back on when life gets rough, but darling... You have so much fire in you. So much potential. You can do anything you set your mind to. This is a fantastic opportunity. You'll learn new things, meet new people and gain new experiences."

I blink through my tears. "Thanks, Mom."

The door opens, and Dad steps outside, looking at our tear-streaked faces with a deer-caught-in-the-headlights look.

I laugh and Mom soon joins in.

Dad looks from Mom, to me, to Mom. He clears his throat, his thumb hitched over his shoulder. "I can go back inside."

"No," Mom smiles, holding her hand out to him.

Dad walks toward us hesitantly, and when I hand him the acceptance letter, he takes it. His eyes scan over the text before he looks at me questioningly. "Art," he says, but it's not a question.

I nod. "Yes, Dad."

He glances at my mom for a moment then pins me with his eyes, not unlike my own. "I don't know what to say, pumpkin." Swallowing thickly, he shakes his head as if to clear it. He hands me the envelope and puts his hands on his hips. "Why didn't anyone tell me?"

"Please don't be mad, Dad. I didn't tell Mom either. I didn't want to disappoint you. I know you and Mom have different expectations of m—"

He holds his hand up. "Let me stop you right there, kid. Where is this coming from?" His eyes search mine. "I know I haven't always been the easiest on you. I have pressured you to perform well at school and in life in general, but it's never been my intention to make you feel as though you can't pursue your own dreams. Art school..." He shakes his head disbelievingly. "I didn't see it coming, but I'm not surprised either. The house has been covered in your drawings and paintings ever since you were old enough to hold a crayon in your hand. I'm not going to lie and say I necessarily think it's the best career path to pursue. But if it's what you want, I'll I support you, pumpkin."

He pulls me into one of his rare hugs that I love so much, and I breathe him in, fighting back the tears. "Kiddo, you have to stop putting so much pressure on yourself," he whispers. "No one expects you to be perfect all the time. Life requires you to make decisions for yourself that may not make everyone around you happy sometimes."

"Why is Emily sad, Mommy?" my little sister asks, and her cute pigtails bounce as she descends the steps.

Mom picks her up, kissing her chubby cheek. "She's not sad. She's happy."

My sister twists in her arms, reaching out for me. After settling on my hip, she squishes my cheeks together with her small hands. "Why are you crying if you're happy?"

I rub my nose against hers. Eskimo kisses are her favorite. "Sometimes we cry when we're happy. But they're good tears. Happy tears."

She giggles. Her innocence is refreshing. It's hard to imagine that I used to be equally as innocent back when Rick and I were young kids with scraped knees and mosquito bites who used to race our bikes and build dens.

"Come on," my dad says, lifting his chin toward the house. "Let's go inside and have dinner together."

# CHAPTER
## *nineteen*

## EMILY

I HOLD onto the car door as I pop my head back inside. "Thanks for the lift, Dad."

He waves me off. "Yeah. Yeah. I'm pretending you didn't ask me for a lift here so you can drink." Peering over my shoulder, he continues, "Who are you meeting anyway?"

I shrug. "Just some friends."

"Just some friends?"

"Yes, Dad. Friends."

He leans back in his seat and shakes his head. "I won't be held responsible for my actions if you return home pregnant."

"Oh my god," I squeal, much to his amusement. "You can trust me."

"Famous last words." He grins.

My eyes roll. "I'm going now." When the car door is shut, I wave goodbye and start walking toward the sound of laughter. The bonfire, visible beyond the tree line, flickers in the distance.

I don't remember the last time I was this nervous. What if they won't want me here?

I brush my clammy hands down the purple skater dress I picked out after much deliberation.

They all fall silent when I step through the trees. My heart beats a staccato rhythm as I wring my hands, eyes trained on my flats.

No one says a word.

I chance a look. They're all staring back at me in surprise. Matt is the only one who doesn't look shocked to see me. His lips curve.

April is the first to get up. Running over to me with a wide smile on her face, she throws her arms around me. "Shit, girl! We fucking missed you!"

I wrap my arms around her, surprised she's willing to forgive me so quickly.

"I'm sorry," I whisper sincerely. We sway for a moment before she drags me over to where the others sit around the small fire. I plop down, looking around. Unsure of what to do or say, I wave lamely.

Josh, who lies on the sandy grass, leaning on one elbow, laughs. "Good to have you back, princess."

Steph hands me a beer, and I take a long pull, drinking it down greedily. Liquid courage is a real thing, after all.

Scooting up next to me, Nina wraps her arm over my shoulder. Placing a kiss on my cheek, she hiccups drunkenly. "Don't run away again."

I smile fondly. "Am I late to the party?"

"Pfft," she laughs, tapping her bottle to mine. "I'm just getting started."

My eyes connect with Ben's across the flickering flames. I can't get a read on him. His face is blank and void of emotions, but I don't miss the way his throat bobs.

I sweep my eyes over to where Dallas sits next to him on his right. Her lips curve, much to my relief, and I smile back tentatively.

"Scoot over," Matt orders April before sitting down beside me, elbows on his knees. "You made it."

Winking, I nudge him with my elbow. "You convinced me."

He grins, then shifts us so that I'm seated between his legs. Cupping his mouth, he hollers, "What do you say, guys? Are we fucking happy that Princess is back or what?"

I laugh, but my smile falls away when I catch Ben looking at me. Shadows flicker on his face and his dark-blue hair looks black in the firelight.

He breaks eye contact and stares out over the lake. I turn my attention on the fire, watching the flames dance while the others chat and laugh around me as though I've never been gone.

Only Ben stays quiet and pensive.

"Did you hear? I'm dating the chess geek," Nina says, interrupting my thoughts.

"The lessons went well then, I take it?"

She wiggles her eyebrows, then tips the bottle back and takes a swig. "Em, he's like a trained puppy."

"Has anyone ever told you you're crazy?"

Nina pretends to think about it before tipping the bottleneck at Steph. "She likes to remind me once or twice a month."

Steph looks over at us questioningly. "Whatever she said about me is a lie."

I giggle, leaning back against Matt's solid chest, and he wraps an arm around me.

"Where is chess boy tonight anyway?" he asks Nina.

Hiccuping, she waves him off. "He's preparing for tomorrow's spelling bee."

"Fuck off," laughs Steph. "You're making this shit up."

Nina grins. "Am not."

"You're full of shit, Nina." Matt's deep chuckle vibrates against my back.

Looking affronted, she digs in her pockets for her phone. "Fine, you don't believe me, dickhead? Let's phone him."

Dallas giggles from across the fire draws my attention, and I get caught in her gaze. We share another smile.

"Hey babe, let me put you on speakerphone," Nina slurs, squinting at the screen.

"Give me that." Matt grumbles, pulling the phone from her hands when she tries and repeatedly fails to activate the speakerphone.

"Nina? What's going on?" Chess boy asks, and we all cheer in victory when we can finally hear him.

"Here you go," Matt says, handing the phone back to Nina.

"Hey babe, are you excited for the spelling bee tomorrow?"

We lean in closer to hear over the crackle of the fire and crickets in the tall grass behind us.

"Are you drunk?" Chess-boy asks.

With a giggle, Nina slaps a hand over her mouth. "He really doesn't like alcohol," she whispers, burying her face in April's neck, her shoulders shaking with muffled laughter.

"Nina?" Chess-boy questions again.

"He sounds irritated," Josh whispers.

"He really does," April agrees, throwing her empty bottle in the fire.

"I'm here," Nina replies, giggling behind her hand as she struggles to compose herself. "So, spelling bee? How's it going?"

He sighs deeply as if he's exasperated. "Yes, Nina. It's going well. I'm confident that we'll beat the competition tomorrow."

Shaking with silent laughter, Matt buries his face in my hair.

Nina beams with pride. "That's great, babe. Go you!" she cheers enthusiastically, fist-pumping the air.

I bite my lip hard to hold in my own laughter.

"Err, okay..." he replies awkwardly. "I'm gonna hang up now?" It comes out as a question.

Nina makes a series of kissy noises before disconnecting the call and looking over at us all expectantly. "See, I've landed myself a smart one. He can lick pussy like a pro, solve complicated mathematical problems and hold a debate about climate change."

"Wow, what a catch," Josh teases, before rolling on the sand to escape the large stick she chucks at him.

"You should talk to Ben and Dallas," Matt whispers in my ear.

I look at Ben. His stormy eyes are on Matt. "You think so?" I fidget with a rip in Matt's jeans. "Ben doesn't exactly look happy to see me."

Matt sighs and his hot breath falls across my neck. "He loves you, princess. He's just wary of getting dumped again. There's no nice way to put it. You hurt him."

Tears prick my eyes as I run my finger over the exposed skin through the rip in his jeans. Ben loves me, but it doesn't mean that he'll take me back.

"Okay," I whisper, getting to my feet. "I'm gonna talk to him."

Dallas smiles up at me encouragingly as I walk over.

I do another lame finger wave. "Hi, Dallas."

"Hey," she breathes out, patting the space next to her.

I debate if I should ask Ben to come to talk with me now or later since he seems less inclined to hear me out, if his lack of eye contact is anything to go by. In the end, I sink down beside Dallas in the sand.

Yes, I'm a coward.

"I read your last message," I say. There, straight to the point, like ripping off a band-aid.

She turns her body to face me fully, waiting for me to speak.

"I'm sorry," I whisper, my heart galloping in my chest. "I hurt you because of my own stupid insecurities. It wasn't fair on you to go cold like that." I pull at the hem of my dress and she puts her hand on mine to stop me from fidgeting.

I lift my eyes.

"Yes, you hurt me, but you haven't lost me." She tucks her hair behind her ear. "I can't hold grudges like that anymore, not after I lost my family. Life is too short. Let's promise to lean on each other when we get scared instead of running away. I want to be there for you. I'm here, even if it's only through the phone."

Her words are my undoing. I crush my lips to hers, swallowing her soft sound of surprise. She smells of bonfire and tastes of forgiveness and second chances. Her hands are in my hair, and mine clutch the lapels of her leather jacket. I don't ever want to let her go.

"I'm so sorry," I whisper between kisses. "I'm so, so sorry."

Palming my cheeks, she smiles against my lips and whispers, "It's already forgotten. Just kiss me."

I take her mouth greedily, swiping my tongue against hers, and moan when she pulls me closer. Her hands are back in my hair, tangling in the strands. I can lose myself in her forever, but my heart is only half-healed. There's a certain blue-haired boy I need to make things right with.

I break away, breathing heavily, lips tingling. Dallas leans back in, but I shake my head, eyeing the empty spot next to us.

"Where is he?" I question, scanning the tree line. He's nowhere to be seen.

"Shit," Dallas breathes out, clawing her hair. Her eyes skate over the clearing when Josh hooks his thumb toward the trees behind him.

"He went that way."

"Ben?" I shout as I get up and run toward the edge of the clearing, praying he's close by. The trees swallow me up. I duck beneath a branch, then pause to listen.

"Please talk to me," I plead, walking deeper into the woods.

Silence greets me.

The moonlight's silvery hue guides my steps over sticks and stones and past low-hanging branches, but the darkness is still pressing in.

Hugging my arms around me, I shiver. Not from the cold but from nerves. "I love the photographs, Ben. I look at them every night when I'm in bed. The one you gave me today made me laugh. Dognald Trump. Did you google it?"

Sticks crunch beneath my feet as I walk farther and farther into the dark night. "I've been thinking about it, Ben. We should get three dogs. That way, we can name one each."

What am I saying? Why can't I shut up or come up with something less juvenile? My cheeks are wet with tears as I continue talking to myself, hoping he's listening somewhere nearby.

"You were right, Ben. I ran like a coward. I hurt you. I know you probably won't believe me when I tell you this, but I'm done running. No more, Ben. I know you're scared. I'm fucking terrified too."

I chuckle miserably.

"Movies make love out to be this amazing, simple thing, but the reality of it is that I've never been more scared in my entire life. You do that to me, Ben. You terrify me. The thought of falling even deeper in love only to lose you scares me more than I can possibly put into words. It wasn't fair of me to hurt you because of it, but I thought I made the right decision." Throwing my arms out wide, I shout brokenly. "I thought I did the right thing, okay?"

It sounds lame even to my own ears, but it's the truth. My chest aches. I screwed everything up.

Leaves crunch behind me, and I swivel on the spot.

Ben shoves his hands in his jean pockets, a haunted look in his eyes. "I can't go through it again, Em," he whispers.

A sob breaks free at the deep timbre of his voice.

He averts his gaze. "I want to let you back in. I want it more than anything, but I don't trust you not to hurt me again."

Pain sears through my chest. He's right. The only assurance I can give him is my word, and it's not enough to heal the damage I've caused.

We watch each other in silence while the sound of laughter filters through the trees. I don't know how to mend this broken bridge between us.

"Ben, I—"

My phone pings, cutting through the silence. It's a new message from Jamie.

Jamie: You need to listen to the audio from the night they spray-painted my car.
     ((video attachment))

My phone pings with another text, this time from Hailey.

Hailey: Don't watch it! It doesn't matter anymore. It will only hurt you.

My fingers hover over the screen as I lift my gaze and look at Ben warily. Whatever is in the video will break my heart. I know it will. Why else would Jamie send it to me?

I consider Hailey's text. Does what's on the CCTV footage not matter? I want to know the truth. No matter how painful. If my friends know, then I need to know too.

With my mind made up, I open Jamie's video attachment before I have a chance to second guess my decision.

Dallas's voice filters into the quiet night.

*"How about we play a little game?"*

Ben's head snaps up, but I ignore him as I stare at the phone in my trembling hand. I'm barely breathing.

*"Emily is here."*

"Don't watch it, Em," Ben pleads, striding toward me, but I hold my hand up, stopping him in his tracks.

*"Emily? The cheerleader?"*

Ben starts pacing in front of me, eyes wild, hands fisted by his sides.

My mind screams at me to switch it off.

*"I'm gonna fuck her boyfriend, Rick."*

Ben curses and swipes for my phone, but I spring away.

"Don't you dare, Ben," I warn.

*"Not only that, but Emily is gonna watch me fuck him and love every moment of it."*

"No…" I whisper in disbelief, my throat thick with emotion.

*"You want to make a bet?"*

I gasp. It all makes sense now. Why have I been so blind? The warning signs were there all along. Why else did they welcome me so readily? I've been nothing but a game to them.

"Please, switch it off, Em," Ben pleads, eyes desperate as he tugs his hair and continues pacing in front of me.

*"I do. You want to play?"*

*"I want to play, but I want to make a bet of my own too."*

*"What's your counter bet?"*

"Fuck, just switch it off. I'm begging you!"

I ignore him.

*"I'll get her to agree to a threesome with us if you fuck her boyfriend and make her watch."*

"What?" I breathe out. My voice is barely audible above the buzzing in my head. Steph laughs in the background, telling him that I'll never fall for it.

*"You're right. It's why Emily won't be able to resist choking on my dick. I'll be the perfect escape from her boring little life."*

The video stops playing.

I continue staring at the phone in my hands, seeing but unseeing.

"Please say something," Ben whispers.

Still staring at the blank screen, I swallow thickly. Ben and Dallas's cruel words echo in my head. I'll fall apart any moment now, and I need to be far away from here when it happens.

My head shakes as the first tear falls. "I guess you both won, huh? She fucked my boyfriend, and I agreed to a threesome. I hope it was worth it."

I dig my sharp nails into my palms, welcoming the physical pain. It's preferable to the emotional pain that's slowly ripping me apart from the inside.

"It wasn't like that." He tries to reach for me, but I take a step back.

"Don't touch me!" I will fall to pieces if he does. They played me this whole time, laughing behind my back. Is it possible to die of heartbreak? It certainly feels like it right now. I'm struggling to draw a breath, my lungs burning.

"Please, Emily," Ben pleads desperately. "It wasn't like that. Yes, it started out as a stupid dare, but then we got to know you. It was real when we slept together for the first time."

I shake my head, my lip curled in disgust. "How much money did the others bet?"

Ben grabs my upper arms and leans down, forcing me to look at him. "It doesn't matter, Em. It was real between us. It *is* real!"

"How much?" I press, refusing to back down. "Are we talking in the tens? Hundreds?"

He squeezes his eyes shut as if it hurts to look at me right now. "I tried to stop it."

"What a saint you are," I spit. "I can't believe that I let you touch me. Trust me, I won't make that mistake again!"

Ben's eyes brim with tears. "Listen to me, Em. I never wanted to hurt you. It was just a fucking bet, and it meant nothing. I'm in love with you!"

With a scoff, I tear myself from his grip. "Don't touch me, Ben."

Grabbing the back of his neck, he begins pacing in front of me. "What can I do to get you to forgive me? Tell me what to do, and I'll do it."

"I want to let you back in, Ben. I want it more than anything else, but I don't trust you not to hurt me again," I sneer, throwing his own words back at him.

His hands fall from his neck.

"I guess we hurt each other too much."

Shaking his head in denial, he attempts to close the distance between us again. I jump out of his reach, barely managing to escape.

"Don't say that. We can fix this." His voice breaks.

Why is he doing this? Has he not hurt me enough already?

"Please, let me hold you," Ben pleads desperately, invading my space and trapping me in his arms. He's too strong for me. I push against his hard chest, kicking and screaming, desperate to escape—to be away from him. He's done nothing but hurt me. I've been a game to them all along.

"Calm the fuck down!" he roars, tightening his hold on me as I scratch his face. "I'm not letting you go. Not until you listen to me. You said you're tired of running."

Quickly losing strength, I sob. "Just let me go!"

His brow comes down on mine. "Never! I'm sorry! Is that what you want to hear? I'm so fucking sorry! I will never hurt you again. Just please… don't leave."

I screech in frustration, my fight quickly waning. I can't be here anymore.

"What the fuck is going on?" Matt asks, watching us warily. The others are close on his heel.

"Fuck off!" Ben sobs as his grip on me tightens even more. I kick his shins and try to slap his face, but he grabs my wrists, forcing them behind my back until I'm pressed up against him.

"What the hell?" Steph murmurs worriedly as Josh and Matt tear Ben off me.

He's sobbing and fighting against their grip.

With hurried steps, Dallas walks over to me, but I hold my hand up. "Don't! I know about the bet."

Her face pales.

"Oh shit," Steph whispers, her eyes shining with sympathy. "I know this looks bad. They love you, Emily. We *all* care for you."

I sneer. "Fuck you, Steph! I was a joke to you. Ben refused to tell me how much the money pot was worth in the end, so why don't you enlighten me since you say you care about me so much? How much money did you win when they got in my pants?"

Beside her, Dallas winces.

I look over at Nina and April. "How about you? Not willing to talk either, huh?"

My phone rings somewhere on the ground, where I lost it in my scuffle with Ben. I drop to my knees and frantically search for it amongst the wet leaves and pinecones.

"Hello?" My voice shakes when I press the phone to my ear.

"I saw the video. Are you okay?" Rick's concerned voice brings on a fresh wave of tears.

I choke on the pain in my chest. "No, I'm not okay."

He curses. "Okay, where are you? I'm coming to get you."

I get to my feet. They watch me like I'm a wild, frightened animal. Ben tries to break free, but Matt and Josh are too strong for him. The heartbreak in Dallas's eyes mirrors my own, but unlike Ben's loud scuffle, she doesn't attempt to approach me.

"The lake," I whisper, eyes still locked on Dallas.

The line goes dead.

Without another backward glance, I set off toward the dancing firelight at the edge of the trees. I've lost a fucking shoe.

"Please, let's talk about this," Dallas begs.

"What's there to talk about? You fucked Rick and won your part of the bet. I hope it was worth ruining my relationship for."

When we reach the clearing, she pulls me to a stop, stepping far too fucking close. "Don't do this."

"*You* did this!" I yell, pushing her away. "Don't you get it? If not for you and the bet, I would still be with Rick. I wouldn't leave my family behind for some stupid fucking dream that wasn't even there in the first place before you fucked up my life."

A small part of me hates myself for shouting these things because I know I don't mean any of it. Still, I can't stop the poison spewing from my lips. "I had everything before you and Ben decided to involve my relationship in your sick games. I can't believe that I let myself fall for you. How could I be so fucking blind? You're incapable of feelings. You toy with people like they mean nothing."

I sneer at the others. "And you're no better! I hope you got a good fucking laugh at my expense."

Ben breaks free and stalks up to me. "If you leave now, don't bother coming back. Do you hear me?"

My mouth falls open and I stare at him in disbelief. "Are you for real right now? Do you think I want anything to do with you after what I heard in that recording? Seriously? You're the biggest fucking mistake of my life, Ben!"

He rears back as if I slapped him.

"Emily," Matt warns, his tone sharp. "Careful before you say something you can't take back."

My eyes snap to his just as a car door opens, and Rick enters the clearing with Hailey, Jamie, and Jack. I'm wrapped up in a set of strong arms while Jack and Jamie force Ben back.

"Ssshh," Rick soothes, stroking my back. "I've got you now."

I didn't realize I was sobbing.

"Emily," Ben pleads, his voice breaking. "Please, look at me, Em."

I don't. I fist Rick's Henley tighter, creasing the tear-soaked fabric in my clenched fists. Rick is safe. I'm not a bet to him.

"Back off, man. You're done!" Jack says, stepping in front of Ben and forcing him back.

Rick's hold on me tightens as if he knows I need the anchor. He sneers at Ben, "You'll be drinking through a straw if I see you near her again. You've hurt her enough!" His threat hangs in the air.

Walking me back to his car, he straps me in the passenger seat and tucks my hair behind my ear. "You're gonna be okay, Em. I promise."

The car rocks when he shuts the door and rounds the hood. I lean my head against the window, willing this day to be over. The tires squeal as he drives us out of there. Rick reaches out, interlacing our fingers in my lap while we drive in silence. The illumination of the amber streetlights comes in waves.

I roll my head, watching his handsome profile. "I've been a fool, haven't I?"

His eyes meet mine before focusing back on the road. "No, you couldn't have known this would happen. You fell in love..."

Rick grinds his teeth, clenching the steering wheel until his knuckles turn white. "You did nothing wrong, Em. It's my fault. I should've known!" He hits the steering wheel, causing me to jump in my seat. "I should've stopped them from getting close to you."

I shake my head no. "None of this is your fault, Rick."

Glancing at me, he winces. "Sorry. I didn't mean to frighten you."

With a sigh, I lean my head back on the window, wiping away

tears. The adrenaline is wearing off and exhaustion is taking its place. How have I been so blind? Ben and Dallas don't know the meaning of love. How many nights did they spend planning on how to get close to me? How to make me fall for them so I would agree to the threesome? Was any of it real, or was it all staged to lure me in?

Ben said I wouldn't be able to resist choking on his dick. Does that mean the afternoon we spent at the lookout was part of their plan? I went down on him...

Did they laugh about it afterward?

The thought makes me sick. I dry heave, clamping a hand over my mouth. My throat burns with stomach acid. Rick looks at me, his eyes widening, before he curses and pulls over by the roadside.

Throwing open the door, I fall out of the car and proceed to spill my stomach's content all over the dried grass. Why did I let Ben and Dallas touch me? It sickens me that I was nothing more than an object in a game they played to cure their boredom.

Rick holds my hair back while my stomach continues to contract. I would still be with him if not for Ben and Dallas. Rick and I should be busy planning our future together. He's never hurt me and never will.

I hate myself for falling victim to Ben and Dallas and their sick games. Despite this, there's a small voice inside me reminding me that I wasn't happy before I met them, but I ignore it. It's easier to shift blame than to admit that Rick and I were never in love in the first place. He offered me stability. My heart was safe with him. Right now, I value that more than this fucking heartbreak.

"Ssshh, babe. Let's get you home." Rick's concerned voice brings me back to the here and now, and unfortunately, the disgusting taste of vomit in my mouth.

I let him lead me back to the car as more tears blur my vision.

I've screwed everything up.

# CHAPTER

*5 months later.*

## EMILY

CLOSING THE TRUNK, I bite down hard on my bottom lip to stop myself from squealing with excitement. The day is finally here. My bags are packed, and I'm ready to set off on the long drive to college. I'm anxious about what lies ahead and not seeing my friends and family every day, but I'm also excited. The last couple of months have been hard, and I'm more than ready for a fresh start.

Ben and Dallas left me alone after that night. It was hard to accept at first and I spent weeks working my way through a heap of complicated emotions. I wanted them to fight for me, but I also never wanted to talk to them again.

Despite the occasional lingering look in the hallway or cafeteria, they kept their distance. I'm grateful because it allowed me time to heal. The wound still hurts, but at least I'm no longer walking around like a zombie. Haunted by images of them laughing behind my back.

It was a huge relief the day I removed my cheer uniform for the last time, folding it up in a neat little pile. The old Emily, who placed such high expectations on herself until she felt like she was drowning, was laid to rest.

Hailey clears her throat behind me, startling me from my

thoughts. Her eyes are glassy with tears as she wraps me up in her arms. Leaving her behind will be the most challenging part of all of this. She's been by my side for as long as I can remember.

My best friend through thick and thin.

She's struggled lately, too. Hailey and Jamie decided to break up, knowing they wouldn't be able to do the whole long-distance thing. It was bittersweet.

Stroking her hair, I hold her to me while she cries softly against my shoulder. I always knew this day would be difficult, but nothing prepared me for this.

"I'm gonna miss you so much, Em," she whispers.

My eyes sting with tears. "I'll miss you too."

We sway side to side, neither of us wishing for this moment to end.

"Promise you'll visit."

I smile against the crook of her neck. "You know I will. You're my best friend, Hailey. Nothing will ever change that."

She nods, then takes a step back and grabs my hands. "And I will visit you as often as I can."

"Have you packed your things?" I ask, stroking my thumbs over the back of her hands. Rick has already left for college, and she's setting off tomorrow.

"All packed and ready. My parents insist on following me there in the car despite the thirteen-hour drive."

I squeeze her hands. "They love you. It must be hard to see their only child go to college that far away."

My mom clears her throat. "Don't I know it! It's not any easier because you have a sister."

Hailey pulls me in for one last hug. "Phone me every day."

"Morning and night."

Next up is my mom. She crushes me to her until I feel like my head might pop.

"You behave over there, young lady." Her voice is thick with emotion.

"I promise." I'm not too old to admit that I will miss her hugs. And her cooking.

"You need to phone us every day."

I laugh. "I will, Mom. You're squeezing me to death."

"Kiddo, come here," my dad says when Mom finally releases me. He holds me for a long moment. "You phone me if a boy hurts you, okay? I don't care about the distance. I will drive over there with my shotgun."

"You don't own a shotgun, Dad."

He chuckles. "Old man Grant down the road does. I'm sure he'll lend me his."

I look up at him with an affectionate smile. "He was asking for Elvis Presley in the grocery store last week. I doubt he remembers where he placed it."

My dad laughs before pressing a soft kiss to my forehead and lifting his chin toward my car. "Get going, kiddo. Before I change my mind."

After kissing his cheek, I turn to my little sister, tugging one of her pigtails. "Be good for Mommy and Daddy while I'm gone, okay?" I press her cute little button nose and make a beep sound, delighting in the sound of her giggles filling the morning air.

———

I settled in well at college. The first couple of weeks was a lot to take in. It's strange to attend such a large college compared to my small high school back home. The anonymity is a welcome change. No one knows who I am or has any preconceived notions about me. I can be anyone I want which is a breath of fresh air.

I share a room with Scarlett, a lovely flamboyant girl who took me under her wing right from the start. She has long brown hair that falls past her shoulders, and she likes to dress edgy, reminding me of a bohemian girl with flowers in her hair one day and of a singer in a rock band the next.

She studies political science, is obsessed with Battlestar Galactica, and owns a record player. We're each other's opposites which is partly why I'm drawn to her and appreciate our friendship so much.

At first, I feared running into Ben, but I didn't need to worry. This college has more students than the entire population of my small town back home, and the likelihood of us running into each other is slim. I find myself wondering at times how he settled in and if he is enjoying himself.

"You look deep in thought," Landon says, placing his laptop down on the table and taking a seat next to me.

I smile at him, tapping my pencil against my bottom lip in thought.

Landon and I met here in the library one afternoon after class. The other tables were occupied, so he asked if the chair next to me was free. This has been our regular meet-up spot since.

I sometimes feel his eyes on me when he thinks I'm not looking, and would lie if I said I don't like the attention. Landon is good-looking with his green eyes and chestnut hair which he keeps styled in a fade.

Still waiting for a reply, Landon smirks.

I tear my eyes away from the white T-shirt that hugs his chest, blushing fiercely, embarrassed to have been caught staring.

He smiles knowingly, his eyes falling to the open notepad in front of me. "What are you studying today?"

My cheeks heat as I avert my gaze, mumbling, "One of my friends back home challenged me to sketch more. I've been trying to improve."

Do I look as awkward as I feel?

Leaning in close to peruse the drawing, Landon traces his fingers over the sketch of me sitting on a cliff, staring out over a blanket of trees below.

His heady cologne teases my senses.

"That's you."

I swallow thickly, my eyes locked on his profile. His soft lips and straight nose.

"Who's that?" he asks, moving his fingers over the paper to the other figure sitting next to me.

My eyes drop to the sketch of Ben. I captured him perfectly. The way he looked at me that day, and his windswept hair. My fingers itch to get hold of color pencils so I can color in his hair the perfect shade of green. I clear my throat, fidgeting with the rubber in my lap. "It's an old friend of mine."

Landon glances at me before leaning back in his seat and starting up his laptop. "Boyfriend?"

I bristle. It's been six months, but the wound is still fresh. My head shakes. "No."

He watches me for a moment, his eyes flicking between mine while I fight the urge to tuck tail and run.

"He hurt you."

"He's not the only one," I reply before I can stop myself. Landon doesn't need to know about my unusual relationship dynamic with Ben and Dallas. I wave him off. "Ignore me. What are you studying today?"

He turns his laptop toward me and I laugh when I see his screen.

"Better you than me."

Landon studies computer science. I won't pretend I understand any of it.

"I have to write an essay on the benefits and drawbacks of artificial intelligence in modern society."

"Sounds fun."

Landon laughs, placing his arm over my shoulder.

"There you are," Scarlett says, interrupting our moment. She dumps her bag on the table and falls into the nearest chair with dramatic flair. "I'm convinced Mr. Hill is failing me on purpose. He's a dictator!"

"I've heard the horror stories," Landon replies, and Scarlett levels him with a glare.

"Bad day?" I ask.

She rolls her eyes dramatically. "Oh, Emily. You have no idea."

Landon's fingers trace patterns with his fingertips over my bare shoulder as Scarlett goes into details about her day. She hypes up the drama with big hand movements and wide eyes.

I'm too distracted by Landon's touch to pay her any attention. My heart is racing and I feel something akin to butterflies in my belly, but there's a sense of guilt and unease underneath it. Why do I feel like I'm betraying Ben and Dallas? I need to move on, so why does my heart fight me at every turn?

Landon's fingers on my shoulder pause their stroking, and he leans in close, whispering, "You're thinking again."

His hot breath on my ear and neck causes me to shiver. Leaning back, he unscrews the lid on his soda, then winks as he brings the bottle to his lips.

Scarlett's voice filters back into my consciousness. "It's so fucking unfair! Did no one give him a break as a kid? Is that the reason why he's made it his mission in life to torture students?" With a look of disgust in her eyes, she shakes her head. "I'll be right back. Megan is over there, and I need to discuss the assignment with her. Wait for me."

She walks off.

I watch her for a moment, nibbling on my lower lip then turn back to Landon and blurt, "Go out with me on Friday."

He chokes on his soda.

Feeling self-conscious, I blush at my own brazenness. But I'm determined to move on with my life. I can't continue feeling sorry for myself.

Landon wipes droplets of soda off his chin as he eyes me. "Yeah, sure. Where would you like to go?"

"I don't know this area very well."

That perks him up and he sits up straighter in his chair, placing the drink on the table. "It's lucky I happen to be born and raised in these parts."

I blow out a relieved breath and smile. "Pick me up at seven?"

Landon leans in close and his lips brush mine as he whispers, "I'll be there."

A heartbeat passes where it's just his breath and mine before he grins. And then he's gone, his chair scraping on the floor.

My heart thunders in my chest while I stare at his broad back as he walks out.

I'm aroused.

Looking back down at the sketch, I force down the rising feeling of unease. Landon is the perfect guy to help me move on.

And I'm attracted to him, so why do I feel like I'm making a mistake?

Grabbing my bag and crumpling up the sketch, I throw it in the nearest trash can on my way out.

———

"Jamie drunk called me and told me he loves me," Hailey says when she answers the phone, and I squeal with excitement.

The loud sound has Scarlett looking up from her book.

"No," Hailey whines. "It's not good news. I'm trying to move on over here. How am I supposed to do that when he's cute?"

I wouldn't describe drunk calling as cute, but I don't argue with her. "Why don't you give the long-distance thing a try at least?"

I can hear laughter in the background as she sighs tiredly.

"I want to, Em, but it's too hard. I'd worry all the time about girls flirting with him. I don't want to be the jealous girlfriend on the other end of the phone."

I don't blame her. It's not like Jamie is a saint by any means, but he changed when he started dating Hailey. He only had eyes for her, which is the equivalent of snow on Mars in the world of Jamie.

"How about you?" she asks.

My gaze lands on Scarlett. The book lies abandoned on the bed and she's now painting her toenails. "I'm going on a date this Friday with the guy I told you about."

Eyes still on her toes, Scarlett smirks.

Hailey squeals in my ear. "That's so exciting. Have you decided what to wear? Did you pack the gold sequin dress? You look smoking hot in that one."

"Hailey, he's taking me for a meal. I need to wear something more casual than a party dress," I laugh, but it feels forced.

"I wish you could see my eye roll right now."

"Oh no, not the infamous Hailey eye roll."

She laughs.

"Hailey?"

"Yeah?"

"You don't think..." I trail off, feeling unsure. "Is it too soon?" I keep my voice low, not wishing for Scarlett to overhear what suddenly feels like a very private conversation. I haven't told her about Ben and Dallas. It's not something I feel ready to share yet.

"Em," Hailey replies in a soft voice, "I think it's time. You're ready for this."

When I was at my lowest, she was there for me and kept me supplied with tissues, ice cream, and crappy movies. She understands my hesitancy.

I worry my bottom lip. "Then why don't I feel ready? And why the guilt?"

Hailey is quiet for a moment, weighing her words. "I understand it's hard. I can sympathize somewhat since I'm over here, pining over Jamie. I know it's not the same; the breakup was mutual, and he didn't break my heart. But I know it's hard. It'll feel strange the first time you kiss this guy, but it will get easier with time. You know the saying: the best way to get over someone is to get under someone else."

Her analogy makes me laugh.

Humming with approval, she continues, "You know logically that you have nothing to feel guilty about, but your heart needs time to catch up. Give it a go if you like this guy. What's the worst that could happen?"

"I could end up hurting him," I deadpan.

"Em, don't be afraid to love again. You can't let what happened with Ben and Dallas stop you from meeting someone."

I think she's trying to convince herself as much as me.

Loud voices ring out in the background, and Hailey sighs. "My roommate is suffering an existential crisis over here. Call me tomorrow?"

Smiling, I nod even though she can't see me. "Of course. I love you, Hailey."

"Love you too, Em."

"She's right, you know?"

I drop my phone down on the bed and look at Scarlett. "What do you mean?"

With a shrug, she dips the brush in the nail polish bottle before setting to work on her pinky toe. "I didn't hear what your friend said, but I got the gist. You have a date with Landon, and you worry that it's too soon for you to date again. I'm not blind. Anyone with eyes can see that you're fresh out of heartbreak."

My hackles rise. While I trust her, I'm not sure if I'm ready to share this part of me. I would never admit it aloud, but I kept the photographs Ben gifted me. I'm not proud of it, but I miss Ben and Dallas. Especially late at night when I'm alone with my thoughts.

"Don't give me that look. I haven't pried. It's none of my business... But I will say this—you can't let fear hold you back. Give Landon a chance. You deserve to at least try, and he might surprise you."

I blow out a breath. Scarlett is right. It's not as if Ben and Dallas are knocking on my door. We're over, and it's time to move on. Besides, I don't want to get back with them, do I?

I wiggle my toes. "Will you do mine?"

"Do I get to pick the color?"

"Go crazy."

———

"Wow…" Landon says, swallowing thickly. "You look great!"

Brushing my hands over my red dress, I smile. Hailey helped me pick it.

I leave him in the doorway and retrieve my purse from the end of my bed. After sliding on my favorite black heels, I quickly check my hair in the mirror, running my fingers through the curls. It's Friday, and Landon is here to pick me up for our date.

Surrounded by comic books, Scarlett winks at me from her spot on the bed. "Don't forget to use protection."

I studiously ignore her as I close the door behind me. Gesturing down the empty hallway, I smile at Landon. "Shall we?"

Scarlett's muffled laughter follows us to the stairs, and I make a mental note to strangle her later.

It's just a date, so why do I feel so nervous? And not in a good way. But I smile and say nothing because what other choice do I have? I can't mope about the past forever.

Landon holds open the door to the dorm building. It's a warm evening, but it's always warm here, unlike back home.

"Where are we going?"

Landon smiles. "There's this little Italian restaurant downtown that does a mean lasagna. Is that okay? I never thought to ask if you like Italian." He looks sheepish.

"I love Italian."

His fingers thread through mine and he flashes a relieved smile.

"How was your day?"

While he tells me about his day, I take the opportunity to study him as he runs his hand down the buttons on his navy blue shirt. His black dress pants fit just right.

He cleans up nicely.

*Very nicely.*

His lips curve in a knowing smirk. He's holding open the passenger door to his black Camaro. "Whenever you're ready."

"Oh." Blushing, I get in the car and strap myself in while he rounds the hood. It's the second time he's caught me checking him out.

His cologne fills the car as he starts the engine. It purrs to life. He keeps his car immaculate, and the only sign that it doesn't belong in a showroom is the pair of dice dangling from his rearview mirror.

Landon slides his hands down the steering wheel.

"She's your baby, huh?"

Looking both proud and sheepish, he grins. "Is it that obvious?"

"You should be proud. It's a nice car."

Diplomatic answer. Now isn't the time to point out that I've been around expensive cars my whole life.

Landon checks the mirrors. "So, tell me about yourself. What did you do in high school?"

*Please, any question but that.*

I tug down the hem of my dress to cover more of my bare thighs. "There's not a lot to tell. I have a little sister, as you already know. I've always loved to paint and was a cheerleader in high school."

Landon looks me over before focusing his attention back on the road, a smile hovering on his lips. "A cheerleader? I can see it. Let me guess, you dated the quarterback?" Glancing at me, he winces when I fail to reply. "You did…"

I cringe. "It's cliché, isn't it?"

Landon sucks his lips between his teeth to suppress a laugh. "Maybe a little. I'm no better, though. I played lacrosse in high school. We didn't have cheerleaders like the football team," he looks at me pointedly, "but I did date a lot."

"A lot?" I chuckle, and it soon turns into a full-on belly laugh when he cringes.

"That didn't come out right."

Amused, I pat him on the shoulder while he rubs the back of his neck. "It's okay. I don't judge."

"What made you apply for college over in this part of the country?"

*So many questions.*

The streetlights pass by in a blur. "I needed a change."

I feel his eyes on me, but he makes no further comment, and we soon pull into the parking lot. The restaurant looks quaint from the outside, with fairy lights lining the roof—reminding me of Christmas back home—and a beautiful view of the beach behind it.

Opening the door to the restaurant, Landon guides me through with a hand on my lower back. The mouthwatering smell of food hits me first. Pizza. Bolognese. Lasagna. It's a small restaurant with a homely feel to it, rather than lavish. I like it immediately.

As we weave between candlelit tables, my eyes dance over the scenic pictures of Italy on the walls. The air is alive with Italian music and the hum of muted conversation.

We find a table toward the back, situated next to a window overlooking the beach.

It's perfect.

Taking a seat, I watch the waves lap at the beach with a content smile on my lips.

"You like the view?" Landon asks, placing the menu back down.

"It's beautiful."

His eyes warm my skin, and I try not to fidget under the intensity of it.

His throat bobs before he reaches across the table and takes my hand in his big one. "You look stunning tonight."

My skin erupts in goosebumps when he begins tracing his fingers over my wrist. As I stare into his intense emerald eyes, I wonder what his hand would feel like touching other parts of my body.

Heat sinks to my clit at the thought.

"Welcome to Alfredos. Are you ready to order?"

My spine stiffens.

*That voice..*

I squeeze my eyes shut as my hand begins to tremble in Landon's warm palm.

"I'll have the lasagna and a coke," Landon says. "Oh, and can I have extra fries on the side as well?" He tightens his grip on my hand to get my attention.

*Fuck, why is this happening right now?*

Taking a deep, steadying breath to calm my racing heart, I open my eyes. Dallas is as breathtaking as always. Smiling politely, I say, "I'll have the same."

What is she doing here?

Her face is a blank mask while she juts down our order on the small notepad in her hands.

Hands I've had on my naked body.

She looks down at our interlaced fingers on the table and I tear my hand away, unable to shake the overwhelming feeling of guilt.

Landon looks at me questioningly.

"Your food won't be long."

Her curt voice makes my insides twist. After carefully placing the notepad in the pocket of her black apron, she leaves. Her ponytail sways as she makes her way over to the counter and pins our order up.

She works here? Since when? Did she follow Ben here?

"Are you okay?"

I reluctantly look away from her silky black hair and creamy neck. Shame hits me hard. I shouldn't be pining over Dallas when I'm here on a date. I shouldn't pine over her at all. We are over. "I'm fine. So you played lacrosse? What else did you do in high school?"

The change of subject works. Landon smirks, reaching for my hand again.

I fight the urge to rip it away.

"I was in a band for a while, and before you ask—we sucked."

Smiling distractedly, I scan my eyes over the restaurant. "What instrument did you play?"

"I didn't."

I look back at him, brows furrowed. "You didn't? Then what did you do?"

Scratching his jaw, he chuckles. "I provided the vocals."

A surprised laugh bursts free "You sing?"

He scoffs and reaches for his drink. "Didn't you hear the part where I said that we sucked?"

My fingers trace over the smatter of hairs on the top of his hand. I feel more at ease. "You'll have to sing for me later."

The incredulous look on his face is too much. Laughter climbs up my throat. "The look on your face," I choke out when I've composed myself enough to speak.

His answering laugh rings out in the restaurant. I love how he laughs with his whole body, eyes sparkling in the candlelight.

Just then, the hairs on the back of my neck stand on end, and I don't have to look to know that Dallas is watching us.

I seek her out like a moth to a flame.

Our eyes collide across the room, and my smile falters as my heart begins to race.

I break eye contact first.

Focusing my attention back on Landon, I resist the urge to look at her again.

I can't believe she's here… My chest aches with a longing I haven't allowed myself to feel for months, and I hate how easily it resurfaced just when I thought I was ready to move on.

She returns with our food, placing it down on the table. I feel her watching me, but I keep my eyes trained on the plate in front of me as Landon thanks her and goes back to telling me about a movie he went to see earlier in the week.

Dallas lingers for a moment too long before finally moving away.

Air rushes back into my lungs. Reaching for the fork, I stab a piece of pasta. Landon wolfs down his food like a starving man while I eat without tasting. All the while, Dallas takes orders, wipes down tables, and jokes with her colleagues, her laughter ringing out like chiming bells. I remember a time when it was me who made her laugh like that.

"Good, right?" Landon asks around a mouthful.

My stomach churns with unease as I hum in agreement, scanning my eyes across the room again. I'm distracted, but Landon doesn't seem to notice. He just keeps on talking.

"I need the toilet."

Landon points his fork toward the front of the restaurant. "It's through there."

"I'll be right back." Scooting my chair away from the table, I make my way through the busy little restaurant to the bathroom. Panic is quickly rising inside me, and I need a moment alone to get myself together. Seeing Dallas here is like having a curveball thrown at me.

Why is she here anyway? She told me she couldn't afford to come here. It's what kicked all of this off in the first place.

Closing the bathroom door behind me, I lean against it, taking deep breaths to calm my pounding heart. My reflection in the mirror above the sink tells me to get a grip on my emotions. If only it was that easy.

I'm in the process of banging my head against the door when there's a soft knock. The door handle rattles, so I move back even though my heart is screaming at me to barricade the door with an army of soldiers.

Before I can listen to its desperate call, Dallas steps inside and locks the door.

"What are you d…" I start but trail off. It's the first time we've been alone together since the breakup, and I'm suddenly very aware of how small the bathroom is.

Sliding her eyes down my body, Dallas swallows thickly. Wringing her hands, she asks in a quiet voice, "You moved on then?"

I bristle. Since I'm here on a date with Landon, it shouldn't be a surprise that she's jumped to conclusions.

"What are you doing here?" I ask instead, avoiding her question. I don't know why I don't tell her the truth. Maybe because it feels like I'm cheating on her by being here with someone else.

She worries her bottom lip. "Ben made some inquiries and managed to find me this job. I'm saving up for college." She shrugs, but it's no minor deal.

My chest swells with pride and I smile. "That's great!"

I'm glad things worked out after all. Despite everything, I'm proud of her.

"Em," she whispers and the longing in her voice is unmistakable.

There's no air in here. I can't breathe when she looks at me like she is now.

"I'm truly sorry for what we did to you. The bet. Everything."

My eyes sting with tears. I clear my throat, blinking rapidly. "How's Ben? Is he alright?"

At war with herself, she wrings her hands. "He misses you."

I avert my gaze, unwilling to go there with her now that I'm finally trying to move on.

"I'm sorry," she whispers, closing the distance between us and brushing her fingers against mine. I make a pained noise in my throat. The bathroom is too small, and she's too close. My walls are crumbling.

Dallas takes another step forward, forcing me back against the tiled wall. Her breath falls across my lips in short bursts, warm and inviting. She doesn't hide the raw emotion in her voice as she whispers, "I miss you, too."

It's too much. I'm not strong enough. My battered heart hurts.

"I can't do this." I pull my trembling hand away from her touch. "Landon is waiting for me."

She makes no move to stop me when I push past her, running from the bathroom.

· · ·

I sink down on the chair and Landon looks up from his phone, his eyes skating over my face. His plate is empty. I'm breathing heavily like I've been in a marathon and not in an enclosed space with Dallas.

"Can we go? I'm not feeling well." Maybe I'm rude, but I'm beyond caring at this point.

Landon looks at me but doesn't comment. He stands up, throwing money down on the table. "I'll take you back to the dorms."

I'm grateful for the arm he wraps around my waist as we make our way to the door. I need his strength right now.

Dallas watches us leave, our eyes meeting briefly before Landon guides me outside in the quiet evening.

The drive back is quiet. My mind spins with questions and my fingers still tingle from Dallas's touch. I can still feel her hot breath on my lips and smell her watermelon lip balm.

Looking over at me, Landon threads his fingers through mine. He stays silent as if he knows I need this time to work through my emotions.

I've been a crappy date.

"I don't know what happened tonight," Landon says when we're parked up outside of my dorm, "but I'm here if you want to talk."

I roll my head toward him, attempting a weak smile. "That means a lot to me, Landon."

Shifting in his seat to face me fully, he strokes the backs of his fingers down my cheek. "He's a lucky guy. Whatever he did to hurt you this much, I bet he regrets it every day. How could he not? You're great."

"There's no—" I begin, but he cuts me off when he shakes his head with a grim smile.

"Hear me out. I like you, okay? A fucking lot. But your heart belongs to someone else, and I don't want to be your rebound." Landon slides his hand down my arm. "Come find me when you're over him."

Dropping my chin to my chest, I nod. "I will."

"I'll still see you in the library, yeah?"

I smile weakly, wiping away a stray tear. "Of course… You know where to find me." Unbuckling my seatbelt, I lean in close until his lips are a hair's breadth away from mine. Maybe I'm selfish for doing this, but he doesn't stop me. I brush my lips against his once, then twice before applying pressure. I'm curious to find out if I feel anything at all for the boy in front of me. I can't leave this car until I know for sure.

His hot breath fans my lips, but he makes no move to deepen the kiss. Neither do I as I kiss him again—just a brush of lips.

Blinking my eyes open, I search his. "I'll see you around, Landon."

I step out of the car, watching his taillights fade into the distance. My tingling lips are a stark reminder that I haven't moved on at all. My heart still belongs elsewhere. The question is, can I forgive the past? Am I brave enough to let down my barriers again?

# CHAPTER
## twenty-one

**EMILY**

THE NEXT TWO months pass by in a blur. Hailey has been to visit, and I keep in regular contact with Rick. Landon and I have become close friends despite our butchered date. Scarlett is her usual crazy self, dragging me to parties and keeping me up watching movies until the early hours.

I haven't been back to the restaurant, but my thoughts keep straying to Dallas and her whispered words in the bathroom.

"You're thinking again. Spill!" Scarlett says, turning a page in her book.

I lean back against the headboard. We're in our dorm room. "I miss two people that I used to be close to, and I wonder if it was a mistake to let them go?"

Closing the book, she gives me her full attention. "Have you tried reaching out?"

My head shakes no. "It's complicated. They hurt me... and so much time has passed. I don't know if it's too late."

I chance a look at Scarlett.

She's watching me with a soft smile. "Babe, you won't know if it's too late unless you try."

Nodding in thought, I drop my eyes to the bedspread. Scarlett is right, but I don't even know where to start. I still remember Ben's last words to me—he told me not to come back.

"Do you believe in fate?" I ask, feeling a blush creep up my neck. The question feels so juvenile.

Scarlett purses her mouth in thought. "I think I do. If two people are meant to be together, then the universe will conspire to bring them together. Sounds cheesy, but yes, I do believe that."

"I hope you're right," I whisper quietly.

"Why don't you tell me what happened?"

"It's a long story, Scar. Besides, you'll think I'm weird."

She snorts a laugh, moving off her bed and joining me on mine. "Have you met me? If anyone here is weird, it's me. I would never judge you. I'm curious about these mystery people." She winks.

"Fine, I'll tell you," I chuckle, "but it's a long story."

She beams. "Great! But wait…" Her eyes scan the room. "Do we have snacks?" Jumping off the bed, she rummages through her bag. I watch on in amusement, biting back a smile.

"Bingo!" She throws a packet of Skittles in my lap. The bed dips as she sits back down and rips into her own packet. Throwing a handful of Skittles in her mouth, she chews loudly. "Right, where were we?" She clicks her fingers. "Mystery people. Drama."

I can't help but laugh. Scarlett always knows how to lighten the mood.

I tell her the whole story from beginning to end. It's nice to share this part of myself with her and it makes me wonder why I waited this long.

"You said you have pictures of them?"

"Yeah, in my bedside table," I reply, digging through my bag of Skittles for the red ones. My favorite.

Scarlett retrieves the photographs and sits back down, leafing through the pile. There aren't that many, only a handful.

Tracing her fingers over one, she murmurs, "You look so happy here."

My chest aches. "I was. Until I found about the bet."

"Don't you think it started out as a bet and then became real?"

I pick at the bedspread as I whisper, "I don't know. Maybe."

Scarlett places a photograph in my lap. It's one of Ben, kissing me on the cheek at the skatepark. "He's in love with you, or at least he was when this photograph was taken," she says, pointing to Ben.

"What makes you say that?"

Scarlett tuts. "Babe, are you blind? Can't you see how he looks at you?"

She hands me another photograph, and I squeeze my eyes shut. I can see it. So, why am I in denial?

It's simple. If Ben was in love with me, I ruined it all because of my own fear and inability to look past my own hurt feelings.

*No...* I refuse to downplay how much it hurt to find out about the bet. It broke me. I went through emotional hell in the first couple of weeks and months afterward.

"What do I do?"

Pointing to the pictures in my lap, Scarlett smirks. "Do you have more photographs?"

"Well, no," I start, but then a thought occurs to me. "I still have the pictures on my social media."

"Perfect! Print them out. You're gonna woo Ben the same way he wooed you."

I laugh in disbelief. "There's only one problem with that. I haven't seen Ben since I moved here. This place is huge."

Her face splits in a Cheshire smile. "Oh, sweetie. It's a good thing that I know where to find him."

My mouth drops open.

She collects the photographs, placing them back in my bedside drawer as if she didn't just drop a bomb on me.

"Wait a minute. What do you mean?"

"He's a business major. We take political science together."

I shake my head to clear my thoughts. "Wait, what? Why didn't you say anything?"

Scarlett barks a laugh. "Emily, this is the first time you've ever mentioned Ben to me. I didn't know you liked him, or I would have said something sooner."

I'm scared to ask, but my own curiosity gets the better of me. "What's he like now? Is he doing okay?"

Her demeanor changes and she looks away. "I don't know him that well. It's not like I talk to him or anything."

"What are you not telling me?"

"I don't know what he was like when you knew him, but he's a bit of a manwhore now." She cringes, looking apologetic.

Attempting a shaky smile, I fight to keep my emotions from showing on my face. What did I expect? That he would stay celibate?

"Oh, Emily…" she whispers softly. "Don't let it put you off. He doesn't know you're still in love with him."

"You're right. He doesn't." Why are we even having this conversation? Ben doesn't miss me. In fact, he's never sought me out or tried to contact me. The best thing would be to move on with my life and let him and Dallas do the same. I'll stop loving them eventually, right?

Scarlett swipes my phone off the bed. "I like this one," she mumbles, scrolling through my photographs. "Oh, this picture is cute. Why haven't I stalked you on social media before?"

"Maybe because you're the only person our age that doesn't use social media," I laugh.

"I don't feel the need for it," she replies with a shrug. "I'd rather meet people in real life."

I understand her point of view. Admire it even.

When she has finished printing out numerous photographs, she hands me a pen and orders me to write my emotions on the back.

I raise an eyebrow skeptically.

This feels too cheesy.

"Trust me on this, okay?"

I scoff but do as I'm told. I don't trust her for one minute, but what do I have to lose at this point? Nothing.

There are six photographs in total. Before I start, I take a moment to study each one before writing on the back.

*"I miss us."*

*"I miss your lips on my skin."*

*"I'll never hurt you again."*

*"I'm sorry."*

*"I'm waiting."*

*"I love you."*

When I'm done, Scarlett picks them up and scans her eyes over the written messages. She hums her approval. "Not bad. So here's the plan: I'll place a photograph on his desk before he arrives for class. Jane studies economics with him, so I'll get her on board too. Together we will break him down."

"You're quite scary when you want to be."

She winks, tapping the side of her nose. "Trust me, I live for this stuff. Anyways, you know where Dallas works. Just turn up and be yourself."

It sounds so simple.

As I sink back down on the bed, doubts creep in. "What if Ben doesn't want me back?"

Scarlett rolls her eyes. "Don't say that. Besides, he's a dick if he doesn't take you back. Don't you want to at least try? If it doesn't work out, then who knows, maybe you'll finally be able to give Landon a shot?"

I laugh. "It's not like that with us."

"Girl, don't. Landon is crazy about you. It's platonic in your head, but not in his. Let's just say he's playing the long game. So for your sake and his, give this a try so you can move on either way."

"You're right."

I need to move on either way, and this will be my final try.

———

Landon's arm is heavy on my shoulder. I stare at the fountain in front while he talks to his friends. The sound of the splashing and gurgling water drowns out their conversation. Looking up, I freeze when Landon pulls me into his body. Ben is walking across the grass near the front steps of the business building.

I can hardly breathe as emotions well up inside me like a burst dam. The whole world seems to simply stop. So does my heart when I spot the girl clinging to his arm. Ben smiles at her, and it hurts knowing it used to be me on the receiving end of that smile.

Gone is the brightly colored hair. It's now black, reminding me of Dallas's raven locks.

As if he can feel me watching him, he turns his head, and our eyes connect. It hits me right in the chest like an arrow to my heart.

The sound of Landon's deep laughter and the weight of his arm around my shoulder fades out. Ben falters in his step before sweeping his gaze past me to Landon. Looking away, he takes the steps to the building two at a time.

Shrugging off Landon's arm, I take chase. I don't think. I just run. Landon shouts after me, but I don't look back. Running up the steps to the building, I burst through the doors as if my clothes are on fire. I've never been inside this building before. Students crowd the main hallway that branches off in several directions. I push forward, sweeping my gaze down side corridors, praying I haven't missed him. I refuse to lose him this time.

"Ben!" I yell when I finally spot him outside one of the auditoriums further down the hallway.

He stiffens, turning slightly and looking at me over his shoulder. Students stare at me as I run to catch up to him.

I round him, deliberately blocking his path. "Hey…"

With his brows pulled down low, he stares at me, and my smile falters.

"I haven't seen you in a long time. How are you?" I search his brown eyes for any kind of sign that he still feels something for me, but his mask is iron-clad. He gives nothing away.

Turning my attention to the girl by his side, I muster up my last bit of courage. "Hi, it's nice to meet you. I'm Emily." I hope my smile looks friendly and not as forced as it feels.

She blinks, then turns her attention to Ben. "I'll see you inside, baby."

Okay, that was rude...

Wait, what? *Baby?*

My heart pounds painfully in my chest when she leans up on her tiptoes and grabs him by the back of his neck, kissing him —*with tongue.* All the while, his eyes stay locked on mine, and it's impossible to look away even though my heart cracks open and starts bleeding out on the ground by his feet.

*He's moved on.*

Swallowing past the thick lump in my throat, I wish I hadn't chased after him. Why am I pouring salt on an open wound? I wrap my arms around myself as the kiss goes on.

*Wow... I've been so stupid.*

The girl finally lets him go and saunters into the auditorium with a smug smirk on her lips.

"Em?" Landon asks behind me.

My eyes fall shut. The concern in Landon's deep voice is too much. I don't want to fall apart right now. Not here.

When I open my eyes again, Ben is watching me.

"I'm glad you're doing well, Ben."

"You okay?" Landon asks me, searching my face before extending his hand to Ben. "Hey man, I'm Landon."

"I'm Ben," Ben replies coolly, shaking Landon's offered hand. I don't miss the way he sizes him up, drawing conclusions.

Good. Let him think I'm fucking Landon. God, I'm so angry with myself for longing for the boy in front of me when he has a girl waiting for him behind that door.

Reaching for my hand, Landon nudges his head back toward the way we came. "We should get going, or we'll be late for class."

Ben's eyes fall to our joined hands, and I fight the urge to move away from Landon.

"It was nice to see you," I say with a shaky smile. Ben frowns, searching my eyes. He knows me too well.

Refusing to let him see how he affects me, I slam my mask in place. Landon leads me away, and we're just about to turn the corner when Ben's deep timbre rings out in the corridor, "See you around, princess."

Looking over my shoulder, I hold his intense gaze until he disappears from view.

Did I imagine my own emotions mirrored in his eyes? Did his throat bob, or is my mind playing tricks on me?

———

"What are you looking for?" Scarlett asks me after school when she finds me crawling underneath my bed.

"You haven't seen a skateboard lying around, have you? I could have sworn I put it under my bed."

I have a strong urge to go skating after my run-in with Ben. Crawling further underneath the bed until my calves stick out, I blow a dust bunny out of the way. "When was the last time we vacuumed under here?"

As I move a box filled with vacuum-packed clothing out of the way, I strike gold. There it is, right at the back, flush against the wall next to my abandoned roller skates.

Reaching for it and shuffling back out, I sit back on my haunches. I turn the skateboard over in my hands. So many fun memories.

Smiling, I trace my fingers over the drawing Matt did on the back of it with a black felt tip. I was like a newborn lamb on shaky legs back then, but I don't remember the last time I laughed so much.

It was the day I fell in love with them all. Not just Ben and Dallas but Matt, Josh, Nina, April, and Steph too. They welcomed me into their group and were there for me when I went through a really challenging time of self-discovery.

Now that my anger has simmered down enough for me to think more objectively, I can finally see that the bet brought us all together. We wouldn't have met otherwise, and they wouldn't have gone out of their way to befriend me.

"I'm going out. Do you want to come with me?" I ask, even though I already know the answer.

"As exciting as it sounds, no," she deadpans, flopping down on her bed. "I have like a million essays to write, and I've procrastinated long enough."

It's probably for the best as I need time alone to think. "I'll see you when I get back." I grab my things and wink at her as I open the door.

Scarlett bites into a pear, speaking around a mouthful. "Don't break any bones."

———

The air outside is mild. Autumn has arrived, and winter is around the corner, but the temperature never drops as low here as back home, where the air is crisp at this time of year.

Yellow and orange leaves crunch beneath my new black Chucks. Yes, I bought myself a pair. I also got myself jeans. Gone are the summer dresses.

Just then, my phone rings in my pocket. I fish it out and smile when I see the caller ID.

"Hi, Rick. What's up?"

"Just phoning to see how my favorite girl is doing?" he replies. I can hear the smile in his voice.

"Nothing has changed since yesterday," I reply with a soft laugh, but it dies in my throat. "Actually, I saw Ben today."

There's silence on the other end. I look at the screen to check the call is still connected. "Rick?"

He releases a breath. "I'm here... Are you okay?"

*He's worried.* I smile softly. "I'm fine... He was with another girl. It hurt to see, but I'm glad he's doing well."

Rick sighs heavily, running a hand down his face. I don't have to see it to know it. His mannerisms are second nature to me.

"Don't worry about me, I'll be fine. I'm already doing so much better."

"I know, Em, but you were in such a bad way. Be careful, okay? It fucking kills me to think of you getting hurt like that again and being so far away."

I make a noise in my throat. "Thank you for being a good friend, Rick."

"You would do the same for me."

"Guess what?" I say in a much lighter tone, changing the subject. "I'm on my way to the skatepark."

The entrance is up ahead.

Rick bursts out laughing, and my mouth drops open in mock offense. It's not *that* funny.

"Let me talk to her," I hear Jamie say in the background. They both ended up playing for the same team, which was no surprise.

"Em," Jamie's gravelly voice greets my ear, "you better be fucking careful because I can't deal with Rick if something happens to you. I swear he's more whipped now than when you were together."

Rick swears up a storm in the background.

"Don't let his girlfriend hear you say that," I laugh.

Jamie still pines after Hailey. The notorious playboy has been captured and reigned in. It's too bad for him that Hailey still insists on keeping their relationship platonic. For now.

"Give me that, you dick!" Rick curses before coming back on the line. "Sorry about that, Em."

Kicking a pile of leaves, I smile. "Jamie will be Jamie. I'm at the skatepark. Speak again soon?"

"You bet…" Hesitating, he clears his throat. "Promise me you'll be careful with Ben, alright? You know I support you no matter what. I just don't want to see you so broken again."

"You have my word." I scan the empty park. "I'll speak to you soon."

We hang up. I pocket my phone, taking a seat on the nearest bench.

It's not the biggest park, but it has a vert ramp. If I go on it, I'll probably break a leg or two. That won't stop me from trying.

When I'm done strapping on my protective pads, I stand up and put on the helmet. Reaching for the skateboard again, I place it down. Then I kick off with my foot, sticking to even ground for now. It doesn't take me long to get back into it.

I'm on a mission to master an Ollie, failing miserably when I spot someone watching me from the sidelines.

Removing the helmet, I wipe beads of sweat off my forehead.

Dallas is sitting on one of the benches.

My heart lurches in my chest while I take her in. Her raven hair moves in the wind and gets stuck in her lipgloss, but she makes no move to brush it from her face. Her skateboard lies forgotten by her feet; she must have had the same idea as me.

Abandoning my skateboard, I make my way over to her.

Dallas flashes a small, tentative smile as she removes her hands from her pockets. She leans forward, gripping the edge of the bench, peering up at me from beneath long, wispy lashes.

Swallowing thickly, my eyes dance over her beautiful face. Did Ben tell her that I chased him down in the hallway earlier today?

"Tell me a secret," she whispers, low and smooth, taking me off guard.

*Is this a test?*

I worry my bottom lip, searching her blue eyes as I take a moment to gather my thoughts. Dallas waits patiently for me to speak, a faint smile playing on her lips.

"I put on a brave face, pretending to have moved on. The truth is, I'm still in love with you and Ben."

Dallas ducks her head, hiding her expression. Toeing the tarmac with her sneaker, she asks in a quiet but hopeful voice, "Do you mean it?"

"Yes. I mean it." My eyes brim with unshed tears as I fidget with the sleeves of my thick jumper. "Tell me a happy memory." My voice is barely above a whisper.

She brushes away tears of her own, staring at something in the distance.

I hold my breath while waiting.

"I fell in love with a girl once… When we used to watch movies together, she would lie with her head in my lap. I remember stroking my fingers through her blonde hair, wondering how I got so lucky."

She looks down at her hands as if she can physically remember the feel of my hair between her fingers. "I remember thinking it was too good to last. Turns out, I was right."

"No," my head shakes softly, "you're wrong."

Searching my face, she sweeps her eyes over my shoulder, swallowing hard. Tears glisten on her pale cheeks. "That day at my work… You were with that guy…" she trails off.

My heart squeezes painfully in my chest. "He's my friend. We went on one date, but I wasn't over you and Ben."

"And now?" she asks softly, her eyes clashing with mine.

"What do you mean?"

"When I asked you to tell me a secret, you said that you're still in love with Ben and me. Did you mean it? You're not over us?"

Standing up, she comes to a stop in front of me. Her eyes lock on mine briefly before she strokes her thumb over my bottom lip.

My breath hitches, and she moves even closer, her lips inches from mine.

Time is standing still.

Her eyes flick up, searching mine for permission before she drops her gaze back down to my mouth.

Pushing up on my tiptoes, I press my lips to hers while snaking my hands around the back of her neck. My fingers tangle in her silky hair as I sigh into her mouth.

She's trembling now. Her hands are on my hips, pulling me to her.

"Dallas," I whisper.

"Fuck, I've missed you," she says between kisses, brushing her thumbs through the wet tears on my cheeks. Leaning back, she runs her blue eyes over my face. Then her mouth is back on mine, stealing another tender kiss. "I'm sorry. I never meant to hurt you."

We share a smile.

"Stop apologizing and take me somewhere. I need you."

"My car is parked over by the entrance." Her lips curve in a smile and she takes my hand in hers, leading us back toward the entrance and the parking lot just beyond.

We fall into the backseat of her car, laughing and breathing hard. I pull her on top of me, and her smile slowly fades. She watches me for a long moment, her eyes flicking between mine. Shifting, she presses a thigh to my core, and I gasp. The pressure hits me in all the right places.

Gazing down at my parted lips, she trails a finger down the column of my throat as she whispers, "You're so beautiful."

Her raven hair falls around us like a curtain, shielding us from the outside world. "I'm gonna make you feel so good."

My clit throbs like a pulsating heartbeat when she moves her hand down my body and begins to unbutton my jeans.

Eyes locked on hers, I make a sound in my throat.

She lowers my zipper and dips her hand below my waistband.

"Are you wet, baby?" she whispers against my lips, her fingers sliding over my damp panties.

Arching my back off the seat, I moan. *God, her touch…*

"You are." She smiles approvingly, then dips down to suck on the sensitive skin below my ear.

I whisper her name on a breathy whimper as I buck my hips, seeking her touch. I can't believe she's here with me, touching me again after all this time.

Her fingers hook in the damp fabric and she moves my panties aside, trailing her digits through my wet slit.

Digging my nails into her back, a soundless cry falls from my lips. Dallas takes her time, keeping me on a razor's edge by teasing me and driving me slowly insane but never applying enough pressure to get me off. It's both torture and bliss at the same time.

Pushing up on an elbow, I pull her to me by the neck and slam her lips to mine. I kiss her deeply, our tongues clashing and rubbing.

Dallas groans, plunging two fingers inside me. *Yes... Oh my god, yes!*

I cry out, moaning into her mouth, and she swallows my sounds of pleasure, pumping her fingers until I see stars.

So many fucking stars...

"I've missed you," she breathes out, smiling into the kiss while flicking my clit with her thumb. "You feel so good wrapped around my fingers, princess."

Rocking my hips, I meet her thrust for thrust, chasing my release. This moment is everything.

I need to touch her, so I reach down between us to undo the buttons on her jeans, frantically pulling at the fabric. "I need to feel you."

My tingling lips miss hers when she sits up and removes her jeans and panties. After tossing them in the footwell, she helps me out of the rest of my clothing.

As I lie naked in the backseat, my nipples harden in the cool air. Dallas still wears her top, but I don't care. I'm too fucking eager to feel her. Pulling her back down on top of me, I lock my thighs around her waist, kissing her with seven months of pent-up longing.

She removes my hand from her hair and guides it down between our bodies. "Touch me."

Braced on my elbow, I memorize her face while slowly stroking my fingers through her wet folds before bringing them up to my mouth and sucking them clean.

Her blue eyes darken with lust when I moan. She lies back down on top of me and dips her fingers inside my wet heat, pumping with more force this time.

I lose myself in the sensation of being taken by her as she moves on top of me. She alternates by stealing my breath with hungry kisses and sucking on my sensitive nipples.

I don't want to fall off the edge without her, so I stroke her clit in fast, firm circles while holding her to me with a hand twisted in her sweaty hair.

"Baby," she moans against the crook of my neck.

I love hearing the pleasure in her voice as I watch her creep closer to the edge. I love that it's me making her feel this way and no one else.

"I love you," I whisper, pushing my fingers inside her tight heat.

Her head snaps up, our eyes colliding. For a breathtaking moment, she's all I see and feel.

When I grind the heel of my palm over her clit, her pussy clenches. She's close.

I make love to her with my every touch and whispered word.

"I'll never hurt you again." I sink a third finger inside her, meeting no resistance. She's so beautiful, watching me through hooded lids and parted lips, a bead of sweat trailing down her temple. I don't want anyone to see her like this but me.

Moving together, we moan each other's names.

Panting breaths and rough touches.

Soft whimpers, heavy eyes, and biting kisses.

"I love you too!" Dallas chokes out before gasping, coming hard on my fingers. It tips me over the edge, and we hold each other, shaking and trembling as we fall apart.

"I didn't mean for our first time together again to be in my car," she says when we've both caught our breath.

My chest constricts painfully as I think back to when I was alone with Ben in his car at the lookout. It was the first time we touched.

"I'm sorry," she whispers regretfully when she realizes where my mind has gone. Sliding a strand of damp hair from my cheek, she presses her soft lips on mine.

"Don't be."

She kisses a path down my naked body, over the bite mark she left on my breast and past my rosy nipple, but not before snatching it up between her teeth. Dipping her tongue in my belly button, she looks up at me. "I'll talk to him."

My head shakes. "Please, don't. Not yet. I need to try and handle this on my own"

I caress her cheek and skim my finger down the bridge of her nose. "I'm so happy you're here with me."

"Me too."

"What happens now?"

She circles my dusky nipple with her finger.

It hardens again.

Leaning down, she sucks it into her mouth before releasing it, causing a cry of protest to climb up my throat. It amuses her.

"I'm not letting you go again. I don't care if Ben comes around or not. I'm in love with you and I want to be with you."

"I'm not letting you go either," I reply, fingering a tendril of her hair.

Dallas rests her cheek on my bare stomach. The sun is setting. We're lucky not to have been discovered yet.

"I miss him," I admit quietly, convinced she won't hear, but she lifts her head and peers up at me through her thick lashes.

"He misses you too. He's just…" She worries her bottom lip, weighing her words. "He struggled after that night."

"It's okay. You don't have to explain."

There's nothing more to say. We hurt each other, and only time will tell if we can move past this or not.

Dallas's hot lips descend on my skin, trailing lower and lower until all thoughts of the past evaporate like morning mist.

# CHAPTER
## twenty-two

**EMILY**

SCARLET PLOPS DOWN in the chair next to mine with her usual dramatic flair before glancing at Landon, who lifts an eyebrow. She holds her phone out to me. "It's done. I placed the first photograph on Ben's desk this morning and filmed his reaction for you. It's obviously not the best quality since I had to be discreet about it."

I freeze and my heart jumps to my throat as Scarlett's words sink in. "Which one?"

Smiling, she leans in close, her flowery perfume invading my senses. "I figured the best one to start with was the *'I'm sorry.'* Nice and simple. And it's a cute photo of you on Ben's shoulders."

My knee is bouncing beneath the table. I inhale a steadying breath, staring at the phone in my hand. What if Ben hated the gesture? Or even worse, what if he didn't care at all and threw the photograph away? I don't think I could handle it if he did.

Reading my thoughts, Scarlett places a hand on my arm. "It's okay. Trust me."

I want to trust her, but it's hard.

*"If you leave now, don't bother coming back."*

Her eyes soften, and she flicks her gaze down to the phone cradled in my hands. "Watch it."

"Okay..."

I'm still hesitating and my fingers are trembling, so she helps me unlock the screen before pressing play.

I hold my breath.

Ben appears on the screen and drops his backpack down on the floor by his chair. Black jeans mold to his nice behind, and a gray T-shirt hugs his chest.

My heart thunders in my chest when he spots the picture on his desk. It's just visible from this angle.

"I made sure it faced upwards so he could see it straight away," Scarlett whispers next to me, a mischievous smile on her lips.

Ben stiffens, staring down at the photograph for a long minute before reaching out to pick it up. He's just about to touch it when he pauses, and his fingers—only inches away—hover midair.

*What is he thinking?*

He looks over his shoulder as if he expects to see me there. Eyes pricking with tears, I clamp a hand over my mouth. He gingerly picks it up and studies the photograph for a moment, then flips it over and reads my handwriting on the back.

*'I'm sorry.'*

Ben rubs the back of his neck, drops the picture on the desk, and stares out of the window, lost in thought.

The girl from the previous day comes up behind him, stroking her manicured nails over his back.

Nails I want to rip off with tweezers.

Snatching up the photograph from the desk, Ben puts it in his back pocket. The girl's private smile tells me all I need to know as she rounds him, pushing her tits against his chest.

Next to me, Scarlett whispers my name, her arm wrapping around my shoulders in a rare display of affection as if she knows my heart is breaking.

They take a seat. I know Ben too well to miss the tension in his shoulders. Rubbing his palms over his face, he drops them down on his spread thighs. His eyes scan the room, searching each face.

The camera stops filming.

"He tore out of there like a bat out of hell after class. Even I could tell the picture affected him."

"I'm not getting my hopes up yet, but it's worth a try, isn't it?" I smile weakly.

"Girl," Scarlett squeezes me, "it's definitely worth a try, and he's a fool if he doesn't take you back."

Landon clears his throat. "Scarlett and Jane told me the other day."

I snap my head to Scarlett, burning her to a crisp with my glare. "Jesus, Scar. How many people know?"

She opens her mouth to reply, but Landon beats her to it. "No one else. I promise. You have nothing to worry about. I was curious, so Scarlett showed me the photographs."

I go to protest, but he waves my concern away. "I won't tell a soul. You have my word. I would like to help."

My brows hit my hairline. He can't be serious? "Why?"

Amused by my incredulity, he chuckles. "I like you, Em, and want to see you happy."

Scarlett snorts next to me.

Breaking eye contact with Landon, I look at Scarlett questioningly.

"Aren't you the gentleman?" Her voice drips with sarcasm.

Landon, used to her attitude, ignores her. "I did some digging and found out about a house party that he's going to this weekend. I would invite you to tag along, but you're going away to visit Hailey."

He's right. The tickets are booked, and I'm due to fly out on Friday afternoon to stay the weekend. It can't come soon enough.

"I can hide a photograph for him to find. He'll never see it coming."

I snort a laugh. "How are you gonna manage that at a party? But sure, it would be great if you could do that."

Landon nods as if that settles things, then puts his laptop back in his bag. He stands up, but I rise from my seat and pull him in for a hug before he can make his escape.

"Thank you."

"He's a lucky guy," Landon replies, his nose buried in my hair.

———

That Friday, I leave a teary Dallas behind as I board the plane to go and spend a couple of days with Hailey. If all goes to plan, Ben will find the second photograph this weekend.

I agonized for hours over which one to give to Landon, and in the end, I settled for one that Steph took of me and Ben at the skatepark when we weren't looking.

*"I love it when you look disheveled like this," Ben whispers in my ear as he comes up behind me when I remove my helmet to wipe the sweat off my forehead.*

*I grin, dropping the helmet to the ground before turning to face him.*

*"You like me sweaty, Ben?"*

*Biting down on his bottom lip in a move that's sinfully sexy, he lifts me off the ground, making me giggle as I wrap my thighs around him. "I especially like you sweaty." He nips my jaw. "And naked."*

*Smiling against his lips, I bury my fingers in the green hair at the nape of his neck and bring our bodies flush. "Kiss me, Ben."*

I step through the arrival gates, pulling my heavy suitcase behind me while scanning the crowds for my best friend.

When she spots me, Hailey immediately pulls me in for a bone-crunching hug. We squeal like twelve-year-old girls at a boyband concert, drawing looks from strangers.

"Oh my god, your hair." I finger a tendril of her much shorter haircut. "It suits you."

"Nevermind my hair. Look at your tan."

Linking arms, we make our way past reuniting families and bored children running in circles around a baggage cart.

"I have so many things planned for us this weekend. But first, ice cream!"

I laugh. "I trust you have scouted out all of the local ice cream parlors by now?"

Hailey winks as we step outside. "I know the best place in town."

————

"How many flavors did you get?" I laugh, tears streaming down my face.

Hailey looks at me like she's seen a flying pig. The poor waitress keeps bringing more bowls to our table until every inch is covered.

"Trust me, you'll never want vanilla again after trying every flavor in here."

My smirk is slow to form. I pick up my spoon and scoop up a spoonful of Unicorn flavored ice cream. "You know I don't do vanilla."

Snorting a laugh, she follows suit but instead of Unicorn flavor, she picks the Stardust.

"Who thought of these weird flavors?" I ask. "What does the Unicorn actually taste like?" It's not strawberry or any kind of berry flavor, but definitely fruity.

"Who knows. This Stardust flavor reminds me of a mixture between bubblegum and Sweethearts."

I moan around a mouthful of Sunshine flavor. "Okay, this one is definitely tropical."

Hailey digs in the bowl of good old chocolate ice cream. "How are things going with you and Dallas?"

A blush warms my cheeks despite the ice cream cooling my insides. "Really good."

"Really good?" laughs Hailey. "Is that all I'm getting?"

Grinning, I shrug. "I mean, yeah… We've seen each other every day since we got back together."

Now I'm definitely blushing.

"And Ben?"

My smile falls. I reach for the bowl of chocolate ice cream. "He's fucking some girl."

"Want me to fly back with you and pull out her hair extensions?"

Laughter bubbles up from my chest. "I missed you, Hailey."

Her smile softens. "I missed you too. It's not the same, is it?"

My head shakes, and I lick the last bit of chocolate ice cream off my spoon. "No."

I point my spoon at her. "Enough of that. When are you getting back with Jamie?"

Hailey's cheeks warm. "We've talked about this, Em. It's not happening."

"He's like a fucking puppy, wagging his tail at the mention of your name."

Reaching across the table for a bowl of purple ice cream, Hailey laughs. "He behaves like one too. Just last night, he phoned to serenade me at three in the morning. It's not like I need sleep or anything."

I choke on my ice cream. "He didn't?!"

"Oh, he did! I've never heard a worse rendition of 'I Just Called To Say I Love You' in my life."

"Oh my god!" I blurt out, snorting with laughter. "I would pay money to hear that."

Raising an eyebrow, Hailey smiles. "Trust me, you don't want to."

She takes another mouthful of chocolate ice cream, scrunching her face up. "Shit! Brain freeze."

I wait until she has finished banging her fist on the table. "Admit it, Hailey. You secretly like that he's still chasing you."

Dropping the brave act, she looks defeated for a moment. "Being in love fucking sucks."

I snort. "Tell me about it. It's fucking shit."

Our eyes meet for a brief second before we burst out laughing, clutching our midriff.

———

My phone pings on the nightstand. It's too fucking early in the morning. I groan, burying my face deeper into the pillow. My mouth tastes sour and my head bangs thanks to Hailey plying me with shots the night before.

She's snoring next to me as I reach for my phone, knocking over her alarm clock.

"Shit," I curse, picking it up from the floor before lying back down and unlocking my phone.

Landon: ((video attachment))

I blink, and suddenly I'm wide awake, shooting up in bed. I nudge Hailey next to me. There's no way I can watch the video alone without the support of my best friend.

"Hailey!" I shake her shoulder again.

She groans. "It's too fucking early, Em."

Normally I would laugh, but my stomach is twisting with nerves.

"Landon messaged me a video from last night."

That gets her attention. She throws back the quilt, scoots up in bed and attempts to tame the birds' nest on her head. "Don't keep us in suspense. Press play."

My thumb hovers over the play button. "I'm scared… Landon didn't type a message. It could mean anything."

Hailey rubs her face. Her smile is soft when she looks at me and threads her fingers through mine. "I'm here, Em."

Holding my breath, I press play.

Tinny music begins to play, and the phone camera shakes for a moment before Ben comes into view, laughing with a friend. The photograph sticks out from underneath one of the cups on the beer pong table behind him.

Hailey gasps next to me. "Landon is a genius!"

I want to laugh, but I'm too nervous. I settle for a shaky smile instead.

Rounding the table, Ben's friend throws the ping pong ball in the air and catches it with a grin. Ben stops dead in his tracks, staring incredulously at the photograph.

"Are we playing or what?" his friend asks, throwing the ping pong ball in the air again, eyes flicking to Landon. He winks, amused to be in on the trick.

Reaching for the picture, Ben scans the room as if expecting to find me hiding behind a plant or something.

"He thought you were there," Hailey comments next to me, echoing my thoughts.

Ben reads my handwriting on the back of the photo.

*"I miss your lips on my skin."*

His eyes flit back up and land on Landon.

A gasp falls from my lips, and Hailey squeaks next to me.

"He's coming over."

We share a nervous glance when Landon lowers the phone down by his side.

"No!" Hailey and I groan in unison.

"Hey, man." Ben's low and gravelly voice has me scrambling to hold the phone up higher so that we can hear better.

"You're the guy from the other week, right? In the business building?" Landon asks.

"Err, yeah. Is Emily around?"

"Oh god…" My voice trembles.

Hailey hushes me.

"She's out of town, visiting her friend this weekend."

Hailey and I share a look.

"I can message her if you want."

"No, it's alright. Are you…?" Ben hesitates, clearing his throat.

"Are you like a thing or?"

Landon doesn't skip a beat. "We're keeping it casual."

My eyes bug out as Hailey laughs next to me.

"Casual?" I whisper hiss.

Hailey winks. "Strategy, Em. Make him feel threatened."

I roll my eyes.

"She's hung up on an ex who sounds like a dick if you ask me."

This time we both laugh.

"Hey, Ben," the guy over by the beer pong table calls out. "Are we playing or what?"

Ben clears his throat again. "I better get going." Hesitating, he adds, "Good luck with the girl."

The video ends.

Wiping my wet cheeks, I release a heavy breath. "I tried, right?"

I attempt a shaky smile, but Hailey sees right through my brave façade.

"This doesn't mean anything," she says, taking my hand. I want to believe her, but I heard Ben when he wished Landon good luck with me. He's moved on.

"This is a good thing," I whisper, nodding as if to convince myself. "I can move on. I got Dallas back, at least."

Hailey lifts my chin with one finger. "You still have a few photographs left. Don't give up after two. Don't forget, Ben asked if you and Landon are dating. Why would he do that if he doesn't have feelings for you?"

Why is hope such a fragile thing?

"Maybe," I reply, tasting tears on my lips. "I'll hand out the rest of the photographs, but I'm also gonna use this opportunity to find closure. I can't keep doing this. It's time to move on, Hailey."

I don't know when I fell in love with Ben and Dallas. But I gave them my heart somewhere along the road, and this is the price you pay for love.

Hailey squeezes my arm, and I nudge her with my shoulder. She has her own complicated love life. We're such a miserable pair. It's almost funny.

"It's our last day together. Let's not sit here and cry over boys," Hailey says, taking my phone off me and placing it down on the bedside table.

I agree. Boy-trouble can wait. "What do you have in mind?"

She yawns, stretching her arms overhead. "Let's go paintballing."

My eyes bug out. Is this the same Hailey that I had to console for over an hour when she got a streak of mud on her brand-new heels last year? Or who squealed bloody murder when one of the boys in class pulled the nib of a pen and threw the shaft across the room, splatting ink on her dress.

Amused by my reaction, she giggles. "You should see the look on your face."

I laugh too.

"You're not the only one who's changed."

"I like this new you. Let's do it!" I throw the quilt off, reaching for my clothes on the floor. I'm hopping on one foot, fighting with my sock. "There's a first time for everything, right?" Just don't cry like a baby when I win."

Hailey throws her hairbrush at me, and I duck just in time. "The only tears will be tears of joy after I beat your ass!"

# CHAPTER
## twenty-three

### EMILY

DALLAS TRAILS her fingers over my pebbled nipple.

Scarlett is staying out late with a couple of friends, so we're making the most of this rare time alone in my dorm room by exploring each other's bodies.

I tuck her wild black hair behind her ear. On the radio, a woman sings about her broken heart. It wasn't all that long ago I could relate to the lyrics.

Leaning down, Dallas skims her soft lips over my jaw. I crane my neck to give her better access, her breath falling in heated waves over my sensitive skin.

My hand slides over her hip and I squeeze gently, marveling at how soft her skin is. As I dip my hand between her thighs, I release a groan. She's still wet from our earlier lovemaking, and my fingers glide through her slick folds with ease. "God, Dallas…"

She drops her head to the crook of my neck and moans softly when I begin circling her still-too-sensitive clit. Slowly at first and then faster.

"Again? You're insatiable." She chuckles against my skin.

Nipping her bare shoulder with my teeth, I lay back down on the pillow, tracing my fingers over the mark left behind on her snowy skin. "I love you."

"Em…" Dallas trails her eyes over my halo of blonde hair on the pillow. "How did I get this lucky?"

My eyes roll, but secretly I love her compliment. "Don't go soft on me, baby."

Laughter climbs up her throat and she rolls off me. Staring up at the ceiling, she sighs contentedly. "Tell me a secret."

The sharp angle of her nose and her plump, kiss-swollen lips, smeared with my pink lipstick, draw my gaze. "I'm glad you made that bet with Ben."

She rolls her head, searching my face. "I hurt you."

Shifting onto my side and trailing my fingers over her collarbone, I watch her creamy skin erupt in goosebumps. There's no point in lying. "Yes, you did, but it's a price worth paying to be with you now."

Shifting closer, I taste myself on her bottom lip when I snatch it up between my teeth. "If not for the bet," I put my hand over her racing heart, "this wouldn't belong to me."

Then I reach for her hand, placing it over mine. "And my heart wouldn't belong to you."

"Fuck, Em… What are you doing to me?" she asks, pulling me on top of her. I cover her mouth with mine, pouring my emotions into the kiss as my tongue slides against hers. She pulls back on a soft moan, watching me through hooded eyelids. Desire burns in her blue depths while I trail my eyes over her naked body beneath me. She's so beautiful with her snowy skin and full breasts. I palm one and squeeze it. Just because I can. Palming the other one, I squeeze that one too. A soft groan slips from my lips. "I can't get enough of you."

Braced on my elbow, I press my lips against the sensitive skin below her ear while kneading her breast. My clit is throbbing now like the pulse in her neck.

She shivers. "I caught Ben looking through the photographs last night."

My lips pause on her neck. We usually shy away from talking

about Ben. I'm surprised that she's broaching the subject now. Placing a final soft kiss on her jaw, I pull back and search her eyes.

She runs her fingers along my jaw, her eyes following the movement while she weighs up her words. "I walked past his bedroom and saw him lying on his bed, leafing through the photographs."

Tracing her fingertips over my tingling bottom lip, she continues in a quiet voice, "He was smiling…" Her eyes meet mine. "I haven't seen him smile like that since you left."

I hold my breath. Those few words carry so much meaning, and I don't dare to get my hopes up.

Her gaze flicks back down to my lips. "Don't give up."

"Will you help me?" I ask, blushing. "I have a few more photographs. Jane is planting one tomorrow during class. Maybe you could put one on his pillow?"

Her hand falls away. "He will know it was me."

Rolling off her, I shift onto my side, watching her naked chest rise and fall with every breath. She's watching me too, a vulnerable look in her eyes.

I trace my fingers between the valley of her full breasts. She's so beautiful, it's hard to look at her sometimes. Shifting on the bed, I trail kisses over her left rib, all the way to her flat belly. My tongue darts out, tasting her skin, and her legs fall open.

"Does it matter?" I don't recognize my own voice. It's huskier.

When I reach the apex of her thighs, she shudders, watching me nuzzle her wet slit. With a quick shake of her head, she wets her lips. "No, it doesn't."

"Good girl." I reward her with a long stroke of my tongue, and she moans, arching her back.

I take my time with her, lapping at her throbbing clit until she's right at the edge.

Her legs spread wider and she lifts her head. Braced on her elbows, she watches me lick her pussy, her breaths coming thick and fast.

Working my fingers inside her tight heat, I suck her clit into my mouth, teasing the pulsating nub with my teeth.

"Aaah! Emily… Oh god," she mewls, falling back on the bed and fisting the sheet by her sides.

I look up from between her parted thighs, taking in the view of her heaving chest and hard nipples. She's biting her bottom lip and squirming on the bed. I want to see her lose control completely.

Lowering my head back down, I flick my tongue faster and harder while inserting another finger. Her hand lands in my hair, tangling with the blonde strands.

I bite the soft flesh of her thigh and lean back to admire my teeth marks on her skin before diving back in, latching on to her pulsating clit. She cries out in pleasure, tightening her grip on my hair.

My face is smeared with her slick arousal. "Are you watching, Dallas?"

I make a show of licking her in long, languid strokes before wrapping my lips around her hard little nub.

"Yes, yes, yes!" she cries, trapping her lip between her teeth and rocking against me.

Reaching up, I force my wet fingers past her plump lips, and she moans as she sucks them clean. I love how fucking filthy it is.

"Please. I need to come," she begs, throwing her head back on the pillow and bucking her hips.

"Well, when you ask so nicely."

I suck her clit into my mouth hard enough to make her hiss, then flick my tongue over it. Faster and faster.

Tightening around my fingers, her hot pussy squeezing them in a vice, she moans my name. I'll do anything for it to be the only name she ever moans out loud like that again.

After placing one last kiss on her clit, I crawl up her body, admiring her flushed cheeks and heaving breaths as she comes down from her high.

Wrapping me up in her arms, she nuzzles my neck. "We'll get Ben back. I promise."

My eyes fall closed.

I hope she's right.

―――

Jane plays her part by placing the photograph that says *'I will never hurt you again'* on the desk for Ben to find. It's the one that Dallas took at the beach on the day we joked about dog names. I'm seated between Ben's spreads legs, leaning back on his chest while he looks out over the water with a content smile on his face.

*"Would you stop wiggling your toes," laughs Dallas, placing her phone back down. She scoops up more sand in her attempt to wrangle my rebellious toes into submission.*

*I grin, straining my head back to look at Ben. He's peering out over the water. "Deep in thought there, big boy?"*

*He tears his gaze away and looks down at me with an affectionate smile on his lips. Lifting my damp bra from my skin, he peers at my nipple beneath the fabric.*

*Laughing, I swat his hand away. "This is a public beach. There are children here."*

*Ben sweeps his gaze over the beach. "I don't see any kids."*

*Amused by our banter, Dallas shakes her head.*

*"Beside the point," I say. "There could be children here."*

*"But there aren't," he says, wiggling his eyebrows and attempting another peek, but I swat him away like an annoying gnat.*

*Dallas laughs, giving up on my wiggling toe. "You're as bad as each other."*

*Ben lifts an eyebrow. "Don't tell me you don't want a peek. I know you better than that, Dell."*

*Shrugging, she bites her lip to suppress a smile. "I'm saying nothing."*

I also gave a photograph to Dallas, and she promised to put it on his bed before she starts work tonight. I'm not sure what else I can do. I'm at the end of the road. This is my last shot, and if it doesn't work, I'll step back and let him get on with his life.

At least I tried. That's what I'm telling myself.

"Are you nervous about his reaction?"

Looking up from my sketch, I smile at Scarlett as she sits down next to me. "I was, but not anymore." I shrug. "I think I'm too late."

Scarlett purses her lips. "You're lying. You're still nervous."

I laugh, waving her off. "You're too perceptive. I'm nervous, but I meant it when I said it's too late. Ben would have found me by now if he was still in love with me."

She eyes me for a moment before releasing a resigned breath. "Yeah. Maybe. But you can't give up yet."

Peering at a group of students at a nearby table, I tap my pen on the desk. Is it a mistake to chase Ben like this?

One of the guys looks up from the tablet in his hands and our eyes connect. He wears a cap turned backward, and wisps of blonde hair peek out from beneath it. He's cute.

I look away first.

Scarlett sniggers next to me. "So, do you want us to ignore the fact that he eye-fucked you?"

Scooting my chair back, I curse my blazing cheeks as I pack up my things. "It won't happen, Scar. I'm with Dallas. What we have is not an all-you-can-eat buffet. It'll just be us if Ben doesn't forgive me."

"But what about the sausage?" she shouts after me, laughing like a hyena when I run for the door.

———

*Ben.*

. . .

Closing the bedroom door behind me, I throw my backpack down on the floor. The photograph I found on my desk earlier is burning a hole through my back pocket.

I stare at the floor, my shoulders hunched, for a long moment before sliding the picture out and unfolding it. I remember this photograph. Dallas took it on the beach when we skipped school.

My chest hurts. Why is she doing this to me? It hits me like fucking wrecking ball every time I find one of these pictures. When we first met, it'd seemed like a cute idea at the time to gift her photographs as a part of our stalker joke. But now it's just a fucking painful reminder.

Seven months have passed since we broke up, and I can't make sense of the emotions that threaten to overwhelm me. I'm not over her. I know that much. But I had reached a point where I could fuck other women without picturing her in their place. I was making progress, and now I'm back at square one, as if she came along and flicked me back with her finger and thumb. What the fuck does she want from me?

I flip the photograph over in my hand and read her handwriting on the back.

*"I will never hurt you again."*

Yeah, right! My hand trembles. I drop the photograph like it's on fire, watching it flutter to the ground. Her smile taunts me, so I squeeze my eyes shut. Balling my fists, I take a moment to calm myself down.

*"Lie down, Ben." Emily pushes me down on the sand with her hand on my chest. "Dallas, let's bury him up to his neck in sand like they do in the movies."*

*"Do I get a say in this?" I chuckle, pulling her down on top of me, admiring the view of her full breasts squashed against my chest. If only she weren't wearing a bra.*

*Her lips brush against my ear as she leans down. "I'll suck your dick if you let us do this without complaint."*

*A deep chuckle rumbles in my chest. I place my arm behind my head. "You have yourself a deal."*

*Reaching for my arm, she forces it down by my side. "Your arms have to be down by your sides for this to work."*

*I play with a tendril of her damp hair, feeling grains of sand scratch my fingers. "Two blowjobs. One today and one at school tomorrow."*

*She pretends to think about it while Dallas begins pouring sand on my feet and legs.*

*"I'll do you one better. One blowjob today, and I'll let you fuck me at school tomorrow."*

*My dick twitches. "A blowjob today. Then a blowjob and a fuck at school. One tomorrow and the other on a day of my choosing."*

*Scooping up a handful of sand, she pours it over my chest. "You drive a hard bargain, Ben."*

*I squeeze her thighs on either side of my waist. "I'm only hard for you."*

*Amused, she laughs, pouring more sand on my chest. "Deal. Now lie very, very still."*

As I blink my eyes open, my newest tattoo catches my attention. It's a small crown on the inside of my wrist. *A princess needs a crown.*

My head shakes and I chuckle in bitter disbelief at how fucking pathetic I am. As I kick a stray notebook on the floor, it hits the wall with a satisfying thud. It's miles better to kick the shit out of random objects in my room than to deal with the raging emotions inside me. I don't want to fucking feel. I'm done with this fucking pain.

I pause as something out of the corner of my eye catches my attention.

On the bed is another photograph.

My heart stops beating in my chest, and I stare at it as if it's a venomous snake poised to strike.

No fucking way… There's only one person who could've put it there.

"Dallas!" I yell at the top of my lungs, grinding my teeth. I fist my hands and stalk over to the door without taking my eyes off the offending item.

Nothing.

Silence.

Thick, heavy, suffocating silence.

I search my pockets for my phone, my hands trembling as I shoot off a quick text to Dallas.

Me: You're in big fucking trouble! Keep her the fuck away from me.

Pocketing the phone, I grip the back of my neck. I'm pacing the room like a caged animal.

The other night, in a moment of weakness, I leafed through our old photographs, and for a moment, the old memories didn't hurt so much. But no amount of happy memories can wrangle the fear that's consuming me right now. There's no chance I will let her hurt me like that again. She left us twice already, so what would stop her from doing it again at the first sign of trouble?

The night she found out about the bet was the worst day of my life. I've never felt fear like it before. The thought of losing her…

I knew then that I could do nothing to get her back, so I left her alone. I never expected her to change her mind. Not now when I'm finally moving on. It's fucking cruel to be pushed back into the past at the click of her fingers. And to be reminded that when it comes to her, I'm still just as powerless.

I can almost hear her peals of laughter in the quiet room.

I eye the photograph on the bed.

Dragging my palm over my clenching jaw, I take a tentative step toward the bed. It's just a goddamn photograph, so why am I behaving like this? But it's not just a photograph. It has the power to tear down the walls I've erected over the last seven months.

My shins hit the edge of the bed.

She's smiling up at me with that sparkle in her blue eyes that I love so much.

*"Can I stay at yours tonight?" Emily whispers beside me, watching the flames dance and flicker.*

*I bury my nose in her hair, breathing in the smell of bonfire and her coconut shampoo. "What about your parents?"*

*She props her chin on my shoulder, peering up at my face. "They think I'm staying at Hailey's."*

*April's loud laughter interrupts our moment. I peck Emily's nose. "You can stay at mine anytime you want, but my bed is small, and it'll be cramped with the three of us in it."*

*Dallas, who's been laughing with Nina, looks over at us. "You staying over tonight, princess?"*

*Emily, sandwiched between us, dips her chin, her face shielded by her blonde hair. "Is that okay?"*

*Dallas lifts their joined hands, placing a soft kiss on the back of Emily's. "It's more than okay."*

*I look over at Steph and catch her grinning. Lowering her camera, she mouths, "Threesome."*

*I shake my head, my brows furrowed. I've tried to make her and the others fucking understand that the bet is off, but they keep raising the stakes.*

*Princess leans up and nips my jaw, drawing my attention back to her. "Let's skinny dip."*

*She stands up and pulls off her dress.*

*It lands in my lap.*

*My eyes bug out as she goes to remove her bra. "What are you doing?" I ask, ignoring Josh's wolf-whistle across the fire.*

*Princess shimmies out of her panties, and Dallas joins her, stripping out of her clothes. She then takes Emily's hand as they run toward the water, leaving me to stare after them with my mouth hanging open.*

*"The fuck are you waiting for?" Matt laughs, throwing a sticky marshmallow at me. "There's literally not a man out there who wouldn't be naked and in the water by now."*

I swallow around the thick lump in my throat, tears pricking my eyes as I reach for the photograph on the bed. She's just a girl, for fuck's sake, so why does she have this hold on me?

My heart is thundering in my chest. Dreading the words I know will shred me to pieces, I turn the photograph over.

*"I love you."*

I suck in a sharp breath, rereading the words. My hand is shaking now. I have to hold the photograph with both hands, or I'll drop it. I stare down at her handwriting, seeing but unseeing. She loves me? After everything, she still loves me?

My phone vibrates in my pocket.

I drop the picture and it flutters to the ground, landing face up.

Dallas: I'm not sorry. She needs you, Ben.

Releasing a heavy breath, I ball the hand that isn't holding the phone. This can't go on. Any more photographs and I'll fall to pieces. I need to find Emily and put an end to this once and for all.

I stalk out of the bedroom and take the steps two at a time, my heavy footsteps thundering on the stairs. Bursting through the front door, I hurry to the car with no idea of how to find her. All I know is that she lives on campus, which isn't helpful since it's a fucking big campus.

I unlock my phone and shoot off another text to Dallas before strapping on my seatbelt. My hands are so shaky that I fail several times.

Me: Where is she?

Dallas may not have told me outright that they're dating again, but I'm not stupid. I can smell Emily's scent on her, like soft summer evenings. I don't probe, and she doesn't tell me any details. It's an unspoken agreement we have.

My phone vibrates as I turn on the ignition.

Dallas: Promise you won't hurt her.

I chuck the phone down on the passenger seat next to me before lashing out on the steering wheel, hitting it once and then twice, causing the horn to sound. There's so much pent-up frustration and hurt inside me, I have no idea how to channel it. I love her, dammit. Why the fuck do I still love her?

As I hit the steering wheel for the third time, I feel something let go inside me.

Something I've fought against for too long.

The first tear escapes, trailing a path through the stubble on my cheek. I wipe it off. Fuck, I'm not letting her see me cry over her again.

Her smile flashes behind my eyelids. The way she bites her bottom lip to suppress it. The way she tucks her blonde hair behind her ear when she blushes. Or how her eyes light up when she laughs.

A gut-wrenching sob breaks free. I hit the steering wheel again, accidentally triggering the wipers. Up until now, I've dealt with the pain the only way I know how—balls deep in women I can't remember the names of, but I can't keep these emotions locked up inside of me any longer. Not even if I try.

Sam, the girl Emily saw me with, is the first girl I've allowed into my bed more than once. I'm not in love with her, but she's safe. She's easy-going and good in bed. Most importantly, she can't hurt me because I don't feel that way about her. Unlike Emily…

I recall the moment when Emily shouted my name in the hallway that day. The instant ache in my chest. How I froze up. It floored me to see her again until that guy, Landon, wrapped her up in his arms.

My insides twist.

*"Are you like a thing or?"*

*"We're keeping it casual."*

The thought of his hands all over her naked body and her moans in his ear makes me feel sick. Urgh, why the fuck am I crying in my car like a fucking baby while some other guy is fucking my girl?

Dallas has no problem putting the past behind her, so why do I struggle to do the same?

*Wait… My girl?* Shit, after all this time, I still think of her as 'my girl.'

Groaning, I rub my palms over my face. Enough is enough. I need to find Emily and sort this mess out one way or another.

I can't do this anymore.

# CHAPTER
## twenty-four

## EMILY

CERTAIN MOMENTS TAKE your breath away, and the sight of Ben leaning against his car across the road is one of those.

Scarlett bumps into my back, nearly dropping her takeaway coffee. "Are you okay?"

When I don't move, she rounds me and scans her eyes over my face, then follows my line of sight. "Oh, shit."

Ben's black hair is mussed up as if he's dragged his hands through it repeatedly. I drink him in while he watches me with an intensity I feel all the way down to my core.

His tattooed arms stretch the material of his black Guns N' Roses T-shirt and his jeans are ripped at the knees.

*Is he here for me?* My aching lungs scream for air. When did I stop breathing?

Pushing off the car, he looks left and right before crossing the road. I stand frozen while my heart beats like a wild animal trying to escape its confines.

"Okay…" Scarlett says, dragging the word out, "I'm gonna go now. Good luck." With a quick squeeze of my arm, she leaves.

I force air into my lungs, inhaling deep, steadying breaths. Now is not the time to pass out from oxygen deprivation.

Ben is in front of me now. He scans the street before pinning me to the spot with his brown eyes. Mine dance over the planes of his face. He's breathtaking. I don't know where to look first. The tattoo snaking up from beneath the collar of his T-shirt or the dark stubble on his cheeks? His sharp jawline? The curve of his lips?

His tongue darts his tongue out, and he toys with the circular barbell at the corner of his bottom lip. I can't look away. My hands twitch by my sides as I fight the urge to touch him.

He swallows thickly. Neither of us has said a word yet.

"Hey," I whisper, scared to break this spell we're under.

Clearing his throat, he grabs the back of his neck.

*He's nervous.*

"Can we go somewhere and talk?"

I nod, my heart fluttering in my chest. "Sure."

What does this mean? I want to smile, but I can't read him as he walks toward his car without a backward glance. I guess this means he wants me to follow him? Crossing the street and tightening my grip on my coffee, I hurry to catch up.

Ben watches me over the car roof, tapping it twice with his knuckles before opening the driver's door.

I get in, placing the coffee down in the drinks holder. It's weird to be back in Ben's car again. Everything is the way I remember it.

My eyes fall closed, and I breathe in the smell of him. God, I've missed him so much…

I keep stealing glances while we drive in silence. His posture is rigid and he wrings the steering wheel so tight, I worry it might snap. He's warring with himself.

Nothing about his body language reassures me. He looks angry, and I hate that I can't read him. Wishing for him to say something, I stay silent, worrying my bottom lip.

He soon pulls over by the roadside and cuts the engine. We're in the middle of the countryside, or as my mother would say: in the middle of nowhere.

"Ben?" I ask hesitantly while he stares out of his window at the maize field beyond. He stiffens at the sound of my voice but doesn't turn to look at me.

"Please…" My voice is barely above a whisper.

When he finally looks over at me, my heart aches. His brown

eyes brim with tears as he drops his head. He swipes at his face before unfastening his seatbelt and bucking his hips. Digging out my photographs from his back pocket, he throws them in my lap.

I tear my gaze away from his stormy eyes, and my vision blurs with stinging tears while I stare down at the pictures.

The car rocks as he exits the vehicle and slams the door shut behind him.

I stare after him with a lump in my throat before throwing open the passenger door and chasing after him, tripping over the uneven ground.

"Ben!" I shout.

He whirls on me. "Why?"

The pain in his voice stops me in my tracks and he laughs bitterly, throwing his arms wide. "Why can't you let me go? I was finally getting over you, but then you started this shit!"

He points to the photographs in my hands. "And now I'm back at square one. I want you, and I fucking hate myself for being so weak!"

He might as well have speared me with a sword. Tears run unhindered down my cheeks. Before he can spew any more poison, I throw the photographs at him. Our memories flutter to the ground like confetti.

"Don't worry, Ben. I won't fucking bother you again!" I spit out.

Shaking his head, he laughs darkly. "See, there you go running again. It's what you do. At the first sign of trouble or things not going your way, you run away. It's why I can't let myself get pulled back in."

"I was hurt, Ben. You hurt me! What did you expect would happen?"

Closing the distance between us, he forces me to take a step back or topple backward. "I expected you to fucking stay and fight, but no, you ran back into Rick's arms the first chance you got."

"I'm here now."

"Are you?" he asks and dips his head, forcing me to meet his unrelenting gaze. "Or were you about to run off again because I told you it makes me fucking angry that I still want you?"

I don't answer.

He scoffs, a cruel smile playing on his lips. "The truth hurts, doesn't it? It's fucking ugly, princess."

Shoving his hands in his pockets, he stares down at his scuffed Vans. The cruel smile from before is gone. He looks defeated. "I thought I had moved on. It still hurts at times, but at least I wasn't thinking about you all the fucking time. And then I saw you again... I knew it would happen sooner or later, but nothing could've prepared me for it. It felt like a fucking gunshot to the chest. I hate that I still want you. I can't let you have the power to hurt me again."

I release a shaky breath, swiping at my cheeks. "I won't hurt you this time, Ben. I know I'm asking you to trust me again, but..." I trail off, my shoulders slumping. I drag in a slow, shuddering breath. I've already lost him. I can see it in his eyes and hear it in his words.

"I want to, but I don't know how to get past this anger," he whispers, slapping a hand to his chest.

Nothing I say will change his mind or make him trust me. We're past words.

Taking a chance with my heart, I move the straps off my shoulders, slowly pulling them down the tops of my arms until my dress pools around my feet. My bare skin prickles from the chill in the autumn air. I stand before him in my lace panties, surrounded by yellow corn, fighting the urge to hug my arms around my naked chest. *What am I doing?*

"What are you doing?" he asks carefully, echoing my thoughts. The fear in his voice squeezes my heart in a vice. I hate that I put it there.

"Let's not talk anymore." Tracing my fingers over the curve of my breast, I circle my peaked nipple as heat pools between my thighs.

He gulps, balling his hands by his sides.

"Touch me, Ben," I whisper, trailing my fingertips over my collarbone, along my jaw, and over my sensitive lips. My heartbeat is pounding in my ears.

Breaking out of his stupor, he grabs me. His mouth comes down on mine, and he groans deep in his chest as he clutches me to him. It's not gentle.

I gasp and he takes it as an invitation to deepen the kiss, plunging his tongue against mine. His warm hands are on my ass now, and he lifts me off the ground and carefully lowers me down until I'm lying surrounded by our photographs. I stroke my hands through his silky hair and moan into his mouth as he continues kissing me like a man lost in the desert who stumbled upon a pool of cool water. His warm hands roam everywhere, exploring and squeezing.

"Fuck," he breathes out, diving down for another kiss. "I missed you so much. God, Emily. You're everything!"

My heart soars. I snatch up his bottom lip between my teeth and let go. "I need you, Ben."

His hooded gaze drops to my mouth. I'm stroking the thick bulge in his jeans, and one of his hands is palming my naked breast.

He pushes up on his knees and makes quick work of his belt. Freeing his dick, he strokes the hard shaft before swirling his thumb over a bead of precum glistening on the engorged head.

I pull him down on top of me. "I'm on birth control. I need to feel you."

Groaning deep in his chest, he shivers, his lips hovering over mine. He darts his tongue out, licking a hot path along my bottom lip. "This time will be hard and fast, okay? I'll take my time with you later."

Our lips clash in a violent kiss.

"Please, Ben," I beg, bucking my hips and guiding him to where I ache for him.

"Don't hurt me again," he whispers, his voice thick with

emotion. Hooking his fingers in my panties, he moves them aside. My lips part as he presses forward, stretching me with his wide girth. I struggle to take all of him. He's big, and it burns. My nails dig into his back as I whimper. It hurts so good.

When he bottoms out, he grunts and pauses for a moment to let me adjust to his size.

My eyes flutter shut. *God, he feels so good.* No other man can compare to how he makes me feel. I'm complete with lips on my skin and his weight on top of me, pinning me down.

*"Fuck,"* he groans, "I need to move." His arms by my head shake as he holds himself back.

I lift my head, whispering against his lips, "Fuck me."

With his tattooed hand wrapped around my throat, he pulls almost all the way out before slamming into me hard. My tits bob, and my lips part on a soundless cry.

"You're so fucking tight," Ben groans, slamming into me again. He grabs the underside of my knee and forces my leg wider. He fucks me hard and fast with months of pent-up frustration. It's like he can't slam into me hard enough or squeeze my throat tight enough. He's pounding into me with savage brutality. The nip in the air fades in comparison to the heat building low in my stomach.

Leaning down, he kisses me as fiercely as he fucks me, thrusting his tongue into my mouth in time with every punishing slam of his hips.

As he buries his face in my neck, I stare up at the cloudless blue sky overhead. This moment is better than anything I could have ever imagined. Feeling him inside me again, his hands on my body…

"Fuck me harder," I pant, coaxing another tortured groan from his lips.

My breasts bounce in the frigid autumn air. Ben latches on to my dusky nipple and sucks hard, swirling his tongue over the sensitive peak before doing the same to my other nipple. He stiffens when he comes. With his face buried in the crook of my neck, he releases a deep grunt. My arms are wrapped around his sweaty back beneath his T-shirt, and my lips are pressed against his neck. His dick throbs inside me, and I soon fall off the edge with him, milking his cock and moaning his name until we lay spent in each other's arms.

Ben rolls off me, and we stare up at the blue sky. Neither of us speaks a word, content to lie out here in the field. He shifts, scanning his eyes over my face. "You're cold, princess. We need to get you inside and warmed up."

Rising to his feet, he hands me my ruined dress, and his warm cum leaks out of me as I quickly put it back on.

Smiling, he nudges his head toward the way we came. "Let's go back to the car, and I'll turn the heating on full blast. We can drive to mine if you want. Dallas will be home soon."

My eyes sting with happy tears. He has no idea what this moment means to me. I never thought I would hear those words from him again.

Pulling me into his arms, he whispers, "It's okay, baby. We're together again, and I'm not letting you go this time."

———

The journey to his place is far more relaxed.

Ben threads his fingers through mine. "What are you thinking about?"

"I'm happy."

He grins. "Yeah?"

Stroking my thumb over the back of his tattooed hand, I hum in agreement.

"I'm happy too."

My heart feels too big for my chest but in the best way possible. But one thought won't leave my mind. "What about the girl I saw you with?"

He brings his attention back on the road. "She's no one."

A muscle jumps in his jaw as he wrings the steering wheel. "What about that Landon guy? You sure looked cozy."

*"Casual?" I whisper hiss.*

*Hailey winks. "Strategy, Em. Make him feel threatened."*

I smile at the memory. "Are you jealous?"

When I lean forward to nip his earlobe, he chuckles. The deep, husky sound does rude things to my body.

"Damn right, I'm fucking jealous. I'm not sharing you with another man."

"He's no one," I say with a teasing smile, echoing his words.

Amused, he looks over at me with a sparkle in his brown eyes. "Alright then, princess. I'm glad that's settled."

———

My eyes sweep over the small house. The front lawn is overdue a trim, and the rose bushes at the front have long since died, but besides that, it's a cozy little house.

"Dallas told me you live off-campus."

Ben unlocks the door and looks at me over his shoulder. "I lived on campus at first but moved here with Dallas. It's nothing special, but it's ours for now. Dallas is safe here. I couldn't leave her behind for long in the same town as that man. I don't trust him not to go after her again."

"You should have reported him to the police."

Holding the door open for me, Ben scoffs. "It would've been her word against his. No one was gonna believe her, and Greg or her uncle would have hurt her even more for snitching. It's better this way. At least we taught him a fucking lesson."

I know he's right, but it doesn't feel right knowing a man like Greg is free to do the same things to other girls even if he'll spend the rest of his life in a wheelchair.

The narrow corridor is lined with coats and shoes, most of which belong to Dallas. On my left is a small living room and on my right is the kitchen. Straight ahead is a set of stairs leading to the bedrooms.

Stepping into the living room, I turn in a circle. The walls are painted a deep purple, and on the floor is a black furry rug. The fireplace is lined with framed photographs. One, in particular, catches my attention.

*"I'll be late for class," I laugh as Nina pulls me down off the boulder.*

*"I don't care," Steph grins, positioning the camera on top of it so we all fit into the picture. "I want a photograph."*

*Dallas pulls me into her side, and Ben crushes the joint beneath his heel before joining us. He shoulders Matt out of the way.*

*"What do we say today?" April asks, wrapping her arms around the waists of Steph and Josh.*

*"Gubbins?" Josh grins.*

*Dallas laughs. "Gubbins, Josh? Really?"*

*"Seven seconds and counting, guys," Steph says, a fake smile plastered on her face in preparation for the flash.*

*"Fucking fine! Lollygag."*

*Matt groans while the rest of us laughs.*

*Josh looks between us. "It literally means you're messing around or wasting time. Isn't that we're doing?"*

*"Five seconds."*

*Ben groans next to me and concedes, "Fine! Lollygag it is."*

*"Two seconds. You better have your best fucking smiles on," Steph says through her teeth. Her perfect smile is still intact.*

*As one, we all shout, "LOLLYGAG!"*

"I love that picture," Ben breathes out in my ear as he wraps his arms around my midriff.

I lean back against his chest. "We were so silly back then."

He presses a kiss to my bare shoulder, and I take his big hand in mine, leading him over to the couch. He doesn't resist when I push him down and straddle his lap. Stroking my fingers over the scratchy stubble on his cheek, my eyes flick between his as I whisper, "This moment is everything."

His lips descend on my jaw, and he nips the sensitive skin with his teeth before trailing kisses down my neck. I shiver, holding on to his shoulders.

"Your skin is so smooth," he whispers, squeezing my bare thighs beneath my skirt, his thumbs teasing the edge of my panties.

I raise my hands in the air, showing him what I want without words, and he lifts my dress off, then unclips my bra. It joins my dress on the floor. Leaning in, he takes my aching nipple in his warm mouth, teasing it with his teeth.

His lips leave my skin and he pulls the back of his T-shirt over his head before palming my breasts and squeezing the flesh with his big hands.

"Ben," I whisper, my lips brushing the stubble on his jaw.

His hands leave my breasts and he grips my waist. His touch is rough, and his dick grows hard between my thighs. Lifting me off him, he gets up and removes the rest of his clothes. Then he drops to his knees in front of me, sliding my panties down my legs. "It's been too long since I tasted this cunt."

As he throws my panties over his shoulder, his dark eyes meet mine briefly before he opens my legs with his big hands. Cool air hits my pussy, and I gasp at the sensation. His gaze slides down my naked body, and a rumble sounds deep in his chest. My breaths are coming thick and fast, and his big hands are squeezing my thighs. He spreads them wider, then dives down, covering my glistening pussy with his hot and hungry mouth.

"Oh, fuck!" I moan, eyes rolling to the back of my head.

"Watch me eat your needy little pussy," he whispers, before licking the length of my wet slit with a long, firm stroke of his tongue. I'm held captive by the intensity of his dark gaze while he laps at me before pulling me further down the couch until my ass hangs off. He thrusts his tongue inside me, and I cry out in pleasure, squirming beneath his skillful mouth. Faster and harder he goes, licking and nibbling until my eyes roll to the back of my head and the world spins out of control.

Just when I think I can't take it anymore, he flips me over, pushing inside me until his cock is buried to the hilt. I squirm at the invasion of his thick length as I clench around him, moaning his name.

Grabbing the back of my neck, he forces my front down on the couch until my back is arched and my ass is high in the air. He eases back and slams into me before I have a chance to adjust to his size.

Rough Ben has come out to play.

I moan into the couch and hiss at the sting of being filled by him. Ben always knows what I need, and right now, I need him to give me his worst.

"You're so fucking tight!" he groans, wrapping his hand around my throat. He angles my head backward and sinks his teeth into my shoulder.

I hiss.

His fingers dig into my throat as he slams into me. Again and again. He smiles against the sore skin. "Have you missed me, baby?"

*He has no fucking idea…*

His hand is back on my neck, and my cheek is squished against the couch. He pulls out, fists his cock, and rubs the hard tip over my puckered hole.

Squirming, I gasp, but his hand on the back of my neck holds me in place. He presses forward just enough to make me hiss when I feel him crown my ass.

Ben strokes his fingers through my wetness, then pulls out and smears it over his cock and my puckered hole. "Has anyone fucked your ass before?"

I'm so turned on, I can't think straight. The answer to his question is no, but I want it all with him.

He inserts a finger slowly until he's knuckle-deep in my ass. I push back against him, loving how forbidden and filthy it feels to be at his mercy like this.

"You want me to fuck your ass, princess?" he whispers in my

ear as he inserts another finger, causing me to cry out in pleasure or pain. I don't fucking know which.

"Aah! Please!" I whimper, despite the burn, and he inserts a third finger. It feels all kinds of wrong, but fuck, it turns me on.

"Relax, baby." His lust-filled, gravelly voice has my pussy clenching.

The pain soon turns to pleasure as I grind against his fingers and silently plead for more.

Ben removes his fingers, runs them through my dripping juices, and uses it to lube his cock. "Try to relax, baby."

He presses forward, slowly, until his cock is buried to the hilt in my ass. The grip on my neck tightens, and his sweaty brow comes down on my shoulder.

"Move," I manage to choke out as I arch against him.

Chuckling, he brushes my hair away from my face before gripping hold of the back of my neck again. "Careful what you wish for, princess."

He pulls all the way out and slams into me, my head connecting with the back of the couch. His grip tightens on my neck and he takes me again, and again. My nipples chafe on the rough fabric as he fucks my ass hard.

"You feel so fucking good. Do you like my cock in your ass, princess?" he grunts, slapping my ass cheek.

His filthy words and the sharp sting cause a scream to rip from my lips. Yes, I like it a fucking lot. I love his raw strength and being dominated by him. I love the effect I have on him, too. I love knowing he'll think of this moment tomorrow in class when he's bored.

With one last grunt, he flips me over onto my back, slaps my pussy, and sinks back into my ass, riding it hard.

"Ahhh! Ben…" I moan, pushing up on my elbows so I can watch him take me.

"Fuck, you're so turned on," Ben groans, dragging his fingers through the juices dripping from my pussy before sinking two fingers inside me, watching them slide in and out.

Fuck, it's too much sensation.

"Harder, Ben," I order, grinding against his fingers and cock.

"Feels good, huh?" With a grin, he removes his fingers, pushing them past my lips. "Suck!"

I do.

God, I do.

I suck and lick. Tasting myself on him.

"Touch yourself," he instructs, shoving his fingers down my throat until I choke. His other hand wraps around my throat. "You love it. I can feel your ass squeeze my cock."

Releasing me, he grabs hold of my legs and pushes my knees up high until my ass is in the air. I reach down and rub my clit while he runs his eyes over my body, watching my tits bob with every slam of his hips. Everything about this is filthy, and it calls to those dark parts of me that only seem to come out to play in his presence. Dallas is more of a gentle lover, unlike Ben, who always fucks filthy. I'm sore for days after Ben.

"Fuck," he curses.

Dropping one of my legs, he grabs me in a chokehold again. "Look at me when I fuck you!"

I meet his gaze, gasping for air while rubbing my clit until I'm teetering on edge.

"Come on my cock," he orders, squeezing my throat and pressing me back against the couch.

I explode around him, thrashing and screaming his name as the most powerful orgasm I've ever experienced washes over me.

Releasing my throat, Ben clamps his hand over my mouth to stifle my moans. He pulls out, grabs my hand and wraps it around his cock. I stroke his silky length greedily until he comes all over my chest and neck, his warm cum coating my nipples.

His chest heaves, and his black hair—damp with sweat—sticks to his forehead as his hand falls away from my mouth. I ache everywhere in the best way possible.

"Stay there." He grabs his jeans from the floor and roots through his pockets until he finds his phone, holding it up.

"Are you recording me?"

He smirks. "Smear my cum over your tits, baby."

With a quirked brow, I drag my fingers through his cum and make a show of pinching my nipples before sucking my fingers clean, moaning at the taste.

Placing the phone down on the coffee table, he wipes me down with his T-shirt. When he's done, he throws it aside and takes my lips in a searing kiss, whispering, "I love you."

It doesn't take a genius to know that he punished and claimed me with his caveman act tonight, and I won't deny the fact that it turned me on.

———

We sit cuddled up on the couch, a movie playing on the TV when Dallas returns home from work.

"Ben?" her voice carries down the hallway before she steps into the living room, dropping her bag on the floor.

She blinks.

"Hi." I wave, then giggle when Ben nips my neck with his teeth.

"Oh my god," she whispers.

A huge smile spreads across her face before she runs over and throws herself on top of us. "I can't believe this. I thought for a moment there that you wouldn't take her back, Ben."

He scoffs, winking at me as Dallas takes a seat. "As if I ever stood a chance against her."

Blushing, I nudge him with my shoulder. "You did put up quite the fight."

Dallas pulls me in for a kiss.

"I had to make you work for it." Ben teases with a grin.

Dallas breaks away, laughing. "You're such a dick."

Pulling her back in for a kiss, I swipe my tongue along her bottom lip. Her clothes and hair smell of Italian food.

Ben presses a kiss to the top of my head, then stands up. He gestures to the kitchen. "I'm getting a drink. Do you girls want anything?"

"I'll have a beer," Dallas says, leaning her head on my shoulder

I shake my head no.

Reaching for my hand, Dallas threads her fingers through mine. We sit in silence.

"Are you okay?" I ask, my nose buried in her hair.

"Yes, everything is perfect now."

I smile. "Nothing is ever coming between us again."

"Never again." Ben smiles at us from the doorway.

Dallas pats the seat on my other side. "Sit down."

After handing her the beer that she asked for, Ben sits down beside me, resting his arm on the back of the couch.

"What are we watching?" Dallas asks, turning up the volume.

I wink. "Cruel Intentions."

Amused, she quirks an eyebrow. "It's a 90's movie about a bet to seduce an innocent virgin."

"Fitting, don't you think?"

Dallas bursts out laughing. "You have a twisted sense of humor."

I shrug. "We have to learn to laugh about it sooner or later."

Twirling a strand of my hair around his finger, Ben hums. "Ryan Phillippe's character dies in the end, doesn't he?"

I treat him to one of my rare glares, elbowing him hard. "I said there was a resemblance to our story. A *resemblance*, Ben."

His eyes sparkle with mirth.

When the credits play, I reach for the remote and turn the TV off. Standing up, I stretch my arms overhead. I bend down and kiss Ben, then Dallas. I kiss them slow and unhurriedly, pouring all of my intentions into it.

My hopes.

My dreams.

Leaving a trail of clothing on the floor like breadcrumbs, I abandon Ben and Dallas on the couch. With my hand on the doorframe, I glance over my shoulder, catching them with their mouths hanging open. I twirl my lace panties in the air. "What are you waiting for?"

Before they have a chance to respond, I sprint naked up the stairs and the sound of our laughter embeds itself in the walls as they take chase, their footsteps thundering behind me.

# EPILOGUE

*7 years later.*

## EMILY

"OH MY GOD," I breathe shakily, cupping my mouth as tears stream down my cheeks, but they are of the happy kind. I swipe at my cheeks and laugh in disbelief, staring down at the pregnancy test in my lap. Two clear lines tell me my life is about to change. Again.

Phoebe Ruffay whimpers next to me, and I pull her onto my lap, burying my nose in her scruff. She's a Boston Terrier we adopted three years earlier. Yes, I got to pick her name without too much of a fight.

"It's okay, sweets. Mommy's pregnant," I whisper, smiling against her fur. "How am I gonna tell daddy, huh?"

Phoebe whines and licks my face. I kiss her head just as the front door opens. The pitter-patter of claws on the hardwood floor grow closer before Snickers joins us, wagging his tail happily. He's a labrador and a gentle giant."

"Princess, are you home?" Ben's voice echoes through the beach house.

Rising from the toilet seat, I put Phoebe Ruffay back down on the floor, scratching her behind the ear. I wipe away my tears. There's nothing to be done about my red-rimmed eyes, unfortunately.

When I step out from the bathroom with Phoebe and Snickers close on my heels, Ben looks up from the mail on the counter and furrows his brows. He drops the letters. "You've been crying."

"Sweetie, remember, no shoes in the house," Dallas's voice rings out from the hallway. I break eye contact with Ben when Noah comes running down the hall and throws himself at me.

"Hey, my little soldier. Have you been good for Mama Dell?"

Noah was a surprise, much like this baby. He's a six-year-old bundle of joy with far too much energy, and he has kept me on my toes since the moment I found I was expecting. He has his daddy's dark hair and brown eyes, but I can see myself in his smile.

"You've been a superstar, haven't you, Noah?" Dallas says, ruffling his hair as she joins us in the open-plan kitchen and living room.

"We put fresh flowers on uncle Aaron's grave. They were so pretty, Mommy."

Dallas goes to use the bathroom, and Ben rounds the island. He's still dressed in his slacks, dress shirt, and tie from work. His business major paid off, and he now works as a project manager. Gone are the crazy hairstyles, but he kept his lip piercing—ever the rebel even in his late twenties.

Crouching down in front of Noah, he chucks him on the chin with a soft smile. "Remember, you promised to watch a movie with Daddy today. Why don't you pick one from the bookshelf in the den?"

Noah's eyes light up, and he runs off. I open my mouth to tell Ben the truth, but Dallas walks out of the bathroom with her palm pressed over her mouth and my pregnancy test in her other hand.

Rising to his feet, Ben swallows thickly. "Princess, are you…?"

I worry my bottom lip. "Yes…"

Dallas is the first one to react. She hurries over and pulls me into her arms. "Oh my god… How are you feeling?"

I search her face. "Are you happy?"

She must see my worry because her eyes soften. "Oh, Em. I couldn't be happier."

Ben pulls me from her arms and steals a kiss. "You make me the happiest man on earth."

"My turn, you big oaf. Let me kiss the woman," Dallas says, squeezing between us. Her lips taste of her strawberry lip balm. I can't get enough of them both, even after all this time. Our relationship raises eyebrows, but we are a family.

We haven't done too badly for ourselves. I co-own an art gallery downtown with Matt. Dallas saved up enough money to attend a good college. She now works as a social worker, helping children and teenagers in situations similar to the one she was in when we first met.

We have Noah, the dogs, and even the beach house that we envisioned for ourselves.

I remain close friends with Hailey, who lives nearby, and Rick enjoys a successful football career. He has a little girl who is my goddaughter. Life has blessed me in many ways with both love and friendships.

"What did you pick, buddy?" Ben asks Noah when he returns with a DVD in his small hands.

"Toy Story, Daddy," he grins, bouncing on the spot. "Can we have popcorn too?"

"Anything for you." Dallas winks.

"Mommy, come sit with me," he says, pulling me along behind him while Ben puts on the movie and Dallas goes to get the popcorn.

Noah gets himself settled on my lap. I place a soft kiss on his forehead.

"I challenge you to a double dare," Ben says, taking a seat next to us.

I roll my eyes.

Ben winks as Noah climbs on his lap instead. Phoebe wags her tail by my feet, demanding a fuss, so I scratch her behind her ear and make kissy noises, talking in my best baby voice. "Your

Daddy is so silly. Always challenging Mommy. We don't like it. Do we, sweetie? Bad Daddy!"

Noah giggles next to me.

I smile at him. "What do you say, buddy. Should Mommy listen to Daddy?"

Noah nods, looking very serious.

Sucking my lips between my teeth, I suppress a laugh. "Let's hear it then." I smile at Ben. "What's the bet?"

"Another dare? What's it this time?" Dallas asks through a mouthful of popcorn when she joins us on the couch.

Ben, sitting sideways, his elbow on the back of the couch, rubs his lips. "I dare you not to cry during the movie."

Dallas bursts out laughing and chokes on a kernel. "Ben, anything but that. Everything on TV makes her cry. Last night she cried to that cat food commercial, remember? She's hormonal right now, so it's an unfair advantage."

Agreeing with everything Dallas just said, I raise an eyebrow.

He waves us off, smirking. "Okay. I promise to reward her thoroughly tonight if she can sit through this movie without a single tear." He winks.

I groan. "That's just cruel. You know there's no way I won't cry."

Looking far too pleased with himself, he shrugs. "Good incentive, though."

Dallas chuckles, patting me on the shoulder.

"Mommy, you have to dare Daddy back," Noah grins.

I glare at Ben over Noah's head. "Look at the influence you have on our son."

Laughing, he throws his hands up defensively. "You heard the boy. What's my dare?"

I give it some thought as I ruffle Noah's hair. "If I manage to get through the movie without crying, I dare you to take up couple's yoga with Dallas."

His eyes bug out while Dallas laughs next to me, clutching her midriff.

"Why did I have to get pulled into this?" She gestures between us both. "Don't involve me in your games."

"Baby, we're in this together, remember. Besides, I get a free pass over the next couple of months," I say with a sugary smile that melts butter.

Amused, she scoffs. "You'll try to get away with anything."

She's not wrong.

Flashing a smile, I turn my pearly whites on Ben. "What do you say, babe. Do we have a deal?"

He does a poor job of suppressing his smile as he leans in close to Noah and stage whispers, "Mommy is crazy."

Straightening back up, he smirks. "It's a deal. Let's play some games."


The End.

# BONUS SCENE

## BEN

"HOW MUCH LONGER ARE WE gonna have to wait?" Matt groans, kicking a rock.

April practices a swing with her bat. "We only just arrived, dickhead. Give her a chance."

I look around the corner, through the window. Nina is leaning over Greg's table, squishing her boobs together. "She's working her magic."

We're standing in the alley behind the building next to the pub Greg likes to frequent.

As I lean around the corner again, my lips curve. "Here they come."

Walking further into the alley, we take cover in the shadows.

Nina's giggles filter through the night as an empty can roll across the ground. I kick it out of the way before planting my feet and placing the bat on my shoulder.

Now we wait.

April reaches up to brush a strand of blonde hair stuck in her blood-red lipgloss, and our eyes connect. Winking, she pops her gum.

"You're looking very handsome tonight," Nina purrs up ahead, her heels clicking loudly on the tarmac.

Greg is drunk but not too drunk to grab her ass as they step into the alleyway. They can't see us yet.

"Tired of boys, eh? Want a real man to fuck you?" he slurs, pushing Nina up against the brick wall, his hand disappearing beneath her skirt.

Batting his hand away, Nina laughs. "Oh, Greg."

He palms her tits with one hand, pressing his other hand on the wall to balance. He can barely stand straight. How he'll get it up is anyone's guess, but he seems fucking willing to try.

"What color are your nipples? Brown? Rosy?" He hiccups, nearly losing balance, but rights himself.

"I bet they're pink." His grin reveals smoke-stained teeth.

Popping her gum, April looks up at me with a quirked brow. I lift my chin and step out from the shadows with April, Josh, and Matt at my back.

Nina is pushing Greg's hands away. He still thinks he's about to get lucky. His hand disappears beneath her skirt again.

I clear my throat. "I wouldn't do that if I were you."

Greg sways. It takes a moment to register, but he eventually lifts his head and looks over at us, squinting his eyes. "Who the fuck are you?"

Pushing past Greg, Nina walks over to us, and April hands her a bat.

I flip the baseball bat end to end while Matt and Josh spread out. Greg hasn't realized it yet, but his only escape route is now blocked off. "I'm inclined to say that I'm your worst nightmare, but that would be a lie." My cruel smile grows as April steps out from behind me, popping her pink bubblegum. "She is."

Greg snorts a laugh, turning in a circle. "Is this a fucking joke?"

He's articulate for such a drunk man.

April taps him on the shoulder, and he wobbles as he turns around. She cocks her head, her eyebrows pulled down low. "Was it a joke when you raped my friend today?"

"I didn't fucking rape anyone?" he slurs, spit flying everywhere.

"Oh," April says, faux surprised. She laughs, and it's a cold, calculated laugh. "I didn't realize we were getting technical. "So, if my friend Josh here," she points her bat at Josh, "holds a knife to your throat and forces you to jerk his dick, it's not rape?" She taps her chin with a finger. "Interesting."

Greg attempts to wobble his way to the exit, but Josh and Matt step in his way.

"I don't think so, old man. You're not going anywhere." Matt grins, bat on his shoulder.

"You're all crazy. Fucking dipshit crazy!"

I like this part. Greg is catching on, and his fear is palpable in the air.

Giggling, Nina slides a hand over his shoulders. "Greg. Greg. Greg. What are we gonna do with you? What do *you* think is a suitable punishment for hurting my friend?"

I'm circling Greg and the girls.

"Josh," Nina lifts her chin, "a helping hand, please."

The sound of Greg struggling is music to my ears as Josh grabs him in a chokehold from behind.

Stepping up beside Nina, April points her bat at Greg's legs. "Pick a knee. I'm fine with either."

"No, no, no, no, no," Greg chokes out, struggling even more in Josh's grip, but the old man is too drunk and uncoordinated to stand a chance.

"Sshhh," Josh hushes him, grinning against his cheek. "This will be over so much quicker if you don't fight. Did you say that to Dallas when you forced yourself on her? Or did you just beat her into submission?"

My teeth grind. *Fucking asshole!* I can't think about what he did to her. It makes me want to kill the fucker. I swing my bat at a nearby trash can, causing garbage to fly everywhere. The blow didn't touch my anger whatsoever, but at least Greg is crying like a baby now.

April throws her head back, laughing. "Did that frighten you?" She pouts. "Poor baby."

Nina brushes his scruffy jaw with her bat. "Pick a knee, old man."

He shakes his head desperately. "Don't do this."

"You know," April says, doing up his shirt buttons, "you could get a job if you buttoned your shirts properly and stopped drinking so much."

She looks up, meeting his gaze, her eyes wide. "Oh, I forgot. You won't be able to walk after this." With a shrug, she leans down to pick up her bat again. "Oh, well…"

"Pick a knee," Nina yells in his face, then laughs when he begins to cry again. She looks at April. "That was fun. You should try it."

April pops her gum. "I'll leave the yelling to you."

Nina simply shrugs and turns back to Greg again. "I'm growing bored. Last chance. Pick a knee."

"No, no. Please, don't. Let's talk about this."

"Let's talk about this?" Nina scoffs incredulously. She looks at him for one long minute and then screams, "LET'S TALK ABOUT THIS?" The bat comes down on his foot, and Nina steps back, breathing heavily, her bob tousled, strands of hair stuck to her purple lipgloss. "Yeah, you scream, motherfucker!"

The guy is wearing shoes, but the crunching sound was disturbingly loud in the alleyway. I'm laughing. I can't fucking help it. Greg is so fucking pathetic, it's unbelievable.

"Stop wailing, man," Matt taunts from his spot near the exit. "She tapped your foot, big deal."

Even Josh is laughing. "You know that feeling when you stub your shoe on something? I bet that was like that times a billion. His foot is probably pulverized."

Patting her hair down, Nina rolls her shoulders.

"How the fuck do you make it look so easy?" April asks me as she tries to flip her bat end to end. She drops it. "Shit."

"Practice," I reply with a shrug, then wink at Greg.

"But it's heavy," Nina says, attempting to twirl it like they do in the movies.

Matt leans against the wall and crosses his arms. He's amused by the girl's banter.

Greg must have some fight in him left because he spits on the ground and says, "What a fucking bunch of pussies you are, getting the girls to do your dirty work. Can't you fight like fucking men?"

Raising my eyebrows, I saunter up to him. He reeks of beer and failure. "I'll be thinking about your screams when I jerk off tonight." I nod my head to April next to me before I walk over to Matt.

The satisfying crunch of his knee cap breaking is nothing compared to his pained screams.

# AFTERWORD

If you got this far, thank you for reading my book. I hope you enjoyed it and if you did, please leave a review on Amazon and Goodreads and connect with me over on Instagram.

# ACKNOWLEDGMENTS

I want to thank my best friend, Paula. It goes without saying that this book wouldn't have happened if it wasn't for her. She's supported my writing for years, and the poor woman has read every piece I've written since we met, whether it's a short poem or something much longer. She's tried to convince me to write a book for god only knows how long, and she challenged me to write one this year because she knows I can't back down from a challenge. So that brings us to now. I want to thank my partner for putting up with me locking myself away in the bedroom to write for hours on end without complaining. I want to thank everyone who has supported me this year. It has spurred me on when I felt like this project would never get finished. A big thank you to Chris for kindly offering to lend his editing skills. And lastly, I want to thank you, the reader, for giving this book a chance. I don't think you can imagine what that means to me. I hope you enjoyed it and if you did, please leave a review. It would mean the world to me.

Much love,
 Harleigh.

# ABOUT THE AUTHOR

Harleigh Beck lives in a small town in the northeast of England. When she's not writing, you'll find her head down in a book. She mainly reads dark romance, but she also likes the occasional horror. She has more books planned, so be sure to connect with on her social media for updates.

# ALSO BY HARLEIGH BECK

*Counter Bet series:*

Counter Bet

Devil's Bargain

*The Rivals' Duet*

The Rivals' Touch

Fadeaway

*Standalones:*

Kitty Hamilton

Sweet Taste of Betrayal

.

Made in United States
Troutdale, OR
12/28/2023

16518838R00189